The Orchid Hunter's Daughter

Friendship, love and dangerous orchids

Innerpeffray. The Scottish Library Series
Book 1

Jane Anderson

HOWE STREET
PUBLISHING

For Mark
My writing exists because of his support

Also by Jane Anderson

The Girl Who Fled the Picture

The Paintress

Chapter One

There had been no piano music in this house since Mama died; Papa and I had been unable to bear it. Still, I swallowed hard as her upright was carried out over the manse threshold. Two years since we lost her, but the raw pain hadn't receded.

The piano was heavy and awkward, and it took four men to manoeuvre it onto the cart. Their efforts to push it to the back resulted in an unmusical clatter amongst the strings. A discordant jangle echoed down the hill towards the village of Fowlis Wester, which must have caused my father's parishioners to look up in confusion. Once the men had tied it in place with good, strong ropes, I was confident the instrument would survive the journey. Most likely we wouldn't waste any money on a piano tuner. Neither Papa nor I had even lifted the piano lid in the last two years. Sadness engulfed me as I closed the garden gate and turned to go back inside. The piano had come to the manse when Mama arrived as a happy newlywed. Its departure marked one more step in my family's unravelling. This was Papa's last day as a minister and within

1

hours we would be evicted from the only home I'd known in my sixteen years.

A shiny black brougham carriage pulled in behind the cart, signalling the arrival of our church elder. Papa must have been expecting him because he appeared on the front step before the gentleman emerged from his coach.

'Good day to you, Mr Bruce.'

'I wish that were so,' he replied. 'In truth, this is a day I prayed I would never see.'

Papa inclined his head in silent agreement. The droop of his shoulders lanced my heart. He had aged ten years in the two since she died, weighed down by sadness and worry.

'Please come in, Mr Bruce,' Papa said.

Both men wore the same black tail coats. Not mourning garb in particular, the Church of Scotland favoured sombre colours. Mr Bruce's broad shoulders caused a strain across the cloth, whilst my father's weight loss was evident in the way his shoulder seams crept down his arms. My own dress was charcoal grey. I'd stopped wearing black this year, but any hint of colour today would have been an affront. Even the light reflecting on the grey pearlised buttons was jarring.

Papa paused in the hallway. 'Iris, would you bring a pot of tea to my study?' He turned to Mr Bruce and extended his arm towards the small room overlooking the back garden.

I'd little confidence I could fulfil my father's wish, since I thought all kitchen items were already in boxes, but my mother's good china on the kitchen bunker stopped me in my tracks. I lifted a cup. It was light as a feather. Imagining her touch, I ran my thumb over the hand-painted pink rosebuds. The delicate porcelain was reserved for visits from only the most prestigious guests, and I'd hardly seen it since Mama's death. Father had lost interest in entertaining, but he clearly hadn't forgotten her insistence on good manners. She would have been mortified if we'd served our chief elder tea in ordinary cups.

The silver teapot with its sugar bowl and milk jug made the tray heavy. I rested it on the hall table, then lifted my skirts off the floor to further silence my approach, hoping to eavesdrop.

Mr Bruce's voice sounded pleading. 'Are you sure you won't reconsider, Andrew? I hate to see you and Iris turned from your home.'

I pressed my ear to the door to hear my father's reply.

'Your patience with me over these months is a testimony to your Christian values, Daniel. But my conscience prevents me from standing in front of my congregation for even one more day. How can I offer them pulpit guidance or hope of the hereafter, when I have no such faith myself?'

'Can't you give it longer?' Mr Bruce said. 'Pray on it some more. The Lord will find a way to bring you back to His fold.'

'I cannot find the words to pray anymore,' my father muttered, his voice so anguished, my eyes pricked with tears.

I was shocked by Papa's words. I'd realised months ago that his deep sadness was linked to more than the loss of my mother, but I wished I could unhear his confession.

'I can see your mind is made up, Andrew, so we are forced to accept your resignation.' The elder's reply in his deep, sonorous voice had a sad air of finality. 'I wish you God's blessing. You have been a faithful servant to Him, and I'm certain He will continue to look over you both.'

I took a deep breath, picked up the tray, entered and laid the tray on Father's desk.

'Thank you, Iris. You can leave me to pour.'

As I turned to leave, Mr Bruce smiled at me. There was pity and compassion in his eyes but surely also the conviction that Papa was bound for hell.

. . .

After Daniel Bruce left, my father went into the garden, where he stood with his face turned up towards the sky, his hand resting on the old apple tree trunk. Mama often sat beside the roses in the shade of this tree. If Papa had lost his faith in heaven, he must have also lost belief in their eventual reunion. No wonder he was broken.

In the kitchen I washed and dried each piece of precious porcelain, wrapped them in newspaper and placed them in the last open crate. I'd meant to help Mrs Munro pack the kitchen items this morning, but couldn't cope with our housekeeper's constant weeping. Mama persuaded the church to take her on when I was a baby and they'd been close. Mrs Munro had to stay to serve whichever Church of Scotland minister would inherit Papa's position. Money would be scarce in our new life, so I planned to keep house for my father. I could do nothing for his soul, but prayed daughterly loving care would keep his body safe until his faith returned.

While I was seeking the foreman to nail the crate shut, Aunt Leonora came barrelling down our front path.

'Good afternoon, Iris. You look terrible. Your mother would wish you to be strong for your father today. That long face must surely make him even more miserable.'

My mother's sister was well-meaning, but Papa found her stridency wearing. It was the last thing he needed now. She meant to rush past me, but I stood my ground. 'Papa has had the most difficult morning. Is your business something I can help with? We could call into Drummond Castle before we go to Culdees.'

I received the full force of Aunt Leonora's most disapproving glare. She had been the driving force behind securing a new position for Papa. Mr Speir of Culdees Castle had employed him to manage the creation of his garden. My father's horticultural hobby would be his new profession. A drop in status, and our new cottage was small compared to

4

the manse, but the appointment had been an immense relief. It allowed Papa to resign from the church without making us destitute or homeless. Aunt Leonora likely thought me ungrateful.

'Stand aside, Iris. I've come because my good news will change your plans.'

I backed up against the bannisters as she swept past me. Like my mama I consider myself tall enough at five foot four, but I have always found her sister's extra three inches intimidating. The smell of roses was unexpected. Aunt Leonora rarely wore scent, and the aroma of Mama's favourite flower triggered bittersweet memories. I hurried after her.

'Good news, Andrew,' Leonora shouted as she marched into the garden. Stopping directly in front of him, she pushed back her shoulders and planted her umbrella into the grass with double-handed determination.

Papa greeted her with a forced smile.

'It's all agreed, but the plans must be brought forward. There's a ship leaving Liverpool docks next week and your passage is secured. You must proceed to Liverpool immediately. The acquisition of clothes and supplies for your journey to South America requires urgent attention.'

I gasped. 'South America?'

The expression on my father's face flickered through joy, excitement and now finally guilt as he turned to face me. 'I planned to tell you soon, but I wasn't sure if Robert Speir would agree to the expense. I proposed a trip to Ecuador to search for new species for the gardens and hothouses. Culdees Castle gardens will be raised in prestige to rival the best in the land.'

'So, are we to travel together?'

Papa grimaced and wrung his hands. Despair flooded through me like an icy wave as he shook his head.

My eyes brimmed with tears. He meant to leave me.

'Dearest Iris. We've read of the great plant hunter adventures together. I'll travel into the Andes and it will be a most arduous journey. I need to know you are safe here.'

'Great plant hunters like Mr Douglas who came to a grisly end.' I couldn't keep the anger from my voice. He was abandoning me and risking his life.

'Mr Douglas was unusually unlucky and I shall take great care not to fall into any wild animal traps.' He smiled, although he must surely know it wasn't funny.

'If it's a safe pursuit, let me come with you.'

Papa looked towards Aunt Leonora.

'Don't be difficult, Iris. Your life is about to take an exciting turn, too,' my aunt said. 'The Baroness has agreed you may move into my quarters in Drummond Castle. It's time for you to begin your education as a lady. I will ensure you meet the right people.'

My father clasped his hands together. 'This is the best news. Thank you, Leonora. I don't know how I can ever repay you for your kindness towards us.' I ignored my father's glance, he clearly expected me to voice gratitude, too.

'It is the least I can do for my dear sister,' Leonora replied. 'All my efforts are in honour of her. Iris shall have the advantages she never had.'

'My mother was happy,' I whispered under my breath.

Papa sensed my mutinous mood and his expression turned to panic.

I'd no wish to live as a charity case in Drummond Castle, and Aunt Leonora's plans filled me with dread. Father abandoning me was a betrayal that felt like a physical blow.

'Please, Papa, don't go.' I tried to modulate the childish pleading in my voice to a more adult whisper. 'I cannot lose you, too.'

Papa had never been able to refuse me. 'Well, perhaps... I mean, I don't know... Might the journey be delayed?'

Aunt Leonora dislodged her umbrella point from the grass. 'Don't be ridiculous, Andrew. This is a once in a lifetime chance. If you back out, Speir will send someone else.' She turned to me. 'And as for you, young lady, I never considered you the selfish type. You are sixteen, not six, Iris.' She set off towards her carriage, passing me in a cloud of rose scent and flinging her last remark over her shoulder. 'Mr Speir has arranged storage for your furniture, Andrew. Bring your personal belongings to Drummond Castle. Iris will move in tonight, and you can stay with her before your departure tomorrow.'

I glared at Papa, but his beseeching expression cut though my rage. 'Please, Iris,' he said quietly. 'Do this for me. If I succeed in this adventure and make a name for myself in the horticultural community, I might feel like a man of worth again.'

My heart folded up inside me. This was the only compelling argument. I doubted he would go if I insisted he must stay, but I would do anything to see his health restored. Despair choked my voice, but I managed a nod.

Chapter Two

The worn stone tread of the spiral staircase up to Innerpeffray Library was as familiar under my boots as the manse front doorstep. Aunt Leonora did not approve of my attachment to this precious place, but once a month during the last eighteen she had indulged me. I'd learned that her brusque manner hid genuine affection. I couldn't complain that she was unkind and my living quarters were grand beyond description. However the pain of missing Papa was worsened by deep loneliness. Books were my companions, a source of escape and solace.

Papa and I often used to visit here together. Knowing that I'd never return to my childhood home intensified the sense of belonging in the library and released a surge of happiness. In my haste, I stood on the hem of my dress and had to steady myself against the walls. Entering the library from the dark stairwell, the light flooding through the huge arched window momentarily dazzled me.

'Good afternoon, Miss Finlay,' said Mrs Birnie, the librarian.

I glanced around, surprised to realise we were not alone.

Two strangers were bent over a desk in front of the window. Identical manes of dark curls framing their faces, two sets of dark brown eyes looked back at me.

'We have company today, Iris. Two of my former pupils, Miss Annie Cooper and her brother Struan. Annie shares your interest in the plant world.'

The girl of around my age smiled shyly and nodded a greeting. Her hair had every quality I missed in mine, which was fair and stubbornly straight. When she shifted the hand resting on the magazine in front of her, I noticed her broken fingernails and red raw skin. The magazine was the copy of *Curtis's Botanical Magazine* I'd come to borrow. Perhaps my expression revealed my feelings, because the boy immediately got to his feet.

'Come along, Annie. This lady wants the magazine. We willnae** keep her waiting.'

The boy's words were polite, but his tone was gruff, and his expression grumpy.

'Did you want to borrow it first?' I asked.

The boy pulled on his flat cap. His eyes went to his boots, and he touched his cap peak. 'Nae matter, Miss Finlay. I've work tae be getting back tae.'

I recognised the boy now he had his hat on, and I felt a flush of annoyance at his initial grumpiness.

The girl lowered her head. 'Thank you for letting me see the new magazine, Mrs Birnie. I really appreciate it. Send me word when you have it again and I'll try tae get back,' the girl said.

I frowned at my stupidity. My clothes, and especially my gloves, gave me the look of a lady. Eighteen months in Drummond Castle had apparently infected me with a sense of enti-

---

* Many Scots words have recognisable English equivalents, there is a glossary of distinct dialect words at the back.

9

tlement. I'd driven this girl away. 'Wait. No. We could look through it together if you stay.' Annie looked hopefully towards the boy, who, from the strong resemblance, was surely her twin.

His dark brows furrowed, and he shook his head. 'I cannae be hanging aboot. We'll come back another time.'

Annie used both hands on the table to push herself up. She tied on her bonnet, smiled at me, and bobbed a small curtsey. 'Thank you for your kind offer, Miss Finlay. Dinnae rush wi' the magazine. There's nae hurry.' She picked up the walking stick hanging on the back of her chair. As she emerged from behind the desk, I saw that she was short, perhaps two inches smaller than me, and walked with a heavy limping. The boy's sour demeanour transformed as he offered her his arm. When they reached the head of the narrow stairs, he turned to walk down backwards. His arms hovered in the air, ready to catch her. The tender look they exchanged took my breath away.

Annie braced one hand against the wall. 'Dinnae fuss, Struan. I'll manage fine.' Leaning on her stick, she began her descent, tackling one step at a time with both feet.

They disappeared from view and I wished I could have persuaded her to stay. 'Might I have met the Coopers before?' I asked Mrs Birnie. 'I feel I recognise the boy?'

'He works in the gardens at Drummond Castle. Annie is his twin sister. They were here in the school together for many years. Their father's recent death left them both orphaned. Annie comes to the library, but only occasionally. She's unable to walk here and Struan works long hours.'

Mrs Birnie picked up the magazine and handed it to me.

'I'll try not to keep it too long. When will you be here again?' I asked.

'I'll be here as usual on Thursday, or you can hand it in at the schoolhouse when you're done. I'll come up to let Annie look at it when Struan can get away. She has few enough things to cheer her life.'

'I feel terrible for depriving her of it. Perhaps I could take it directly to her house?'

'You did nothing wrong. Annie prefers to come to the library to view things. You might get it back to me before Sunday? Struan has that afternoon off, so I can open up the library for her.'

I thanked her and made for my favourite desk, which faced towards the elegant triple window, with a view through the central glass arch to the green pastures beyond the River Earn. The smaller side windows framed trees in the church-yard outside. I gazed around the shelves of old books and inhaled the scent, trying to summon the calm this space usually gave me.

When Mrs Birnie went next door to the room housing their newly donated books, I allowed my brave face to slip. The overwhelming loneliness threatened tears. But when I brought my hands to my face, I realised there was something on my gloves. My fingertips were covered in white dust. Residue from the whitewashed walls left from my careless stumble in the stairwell. I brushed my hands together, trying to clean off the marks. Surely Annie and her brother had noticed and were now laughing at my ladylike pretence? A sob escaped and I heard Mrs Birnie's footsteps.

'Oh, Iris. Has it been a difficult week?' She put a comforting hand on my shoulder and gave it a squeeze.

I met her eyes, embarrassed about being such a baby. 'Not really. My aunt is away in Lincolnshire, so I'm left to my own devices. I should be grateful, but I find life at the castle dull.'

Her smile was sympathetic. 'Was there any word from your father recently?'

'Nothing, but letters take so long to get here. I'll likely hear when the next shipment of plants arrives.'

Mrs Birnie patted my arm. 'Read your magazine now. There are plant illustrations from Brazil and Ecuador to cheer you up.'

She went back to her cataloguing, and I flicked through the magazine pages. The beautiful image of a bloom with a profusion of bright yellow corolla caught my eye. It was apparently named *Mr Anderson-Henry's Calceolaria*. The magazine described how Professor Jameson of Quito University had discovered the Slipper Flower in the Andes and named it after this lucky gentleman from Edinburgh. This was what Mr Speir was hoping for. That my father would discover some new specimen to send back for his hothouse, and that it would bear Mr Speir's name. I hoped Papa would discover two specimens and the second plant would be named after him. *Orchidae finlayhii* perhaps. He would come home with his ambitions happily fulfilled. My father was living his dream after the nightmare of the last four years. My current loneliness would be worth it when he returned with his spirits restored.

Chapter Three

May 1869 – Muthill, Perthshire, Scotland

Struan was about to set off for Drummond Castle when Jock his fellow gardener turned up.

'Since you missed the pub again this week, I thought we might share this.' Jock grinned and held up a flagon of ale.

'You must be flush,' Struan said.

'Got it fae my brother, Alistair. I went tae visit him at Culdees on his day off, and since it's oor day off too, surely I can treat you?'

'That's a grand idea, but I cannae tarry long, I promised tae pick up Annie.'

Jock tutted and pushed past him into the gloomy cottage. 'Och, Struan, you behave like a married man. That lassie has you wrapped around her wee finger. Where is she?'

'Innerpeffray Library.'

Jock let out a laugh. 'In deadly danger in a library! Struan, where could she be safer? Jock picked up the two small wooden stools by their legs. 'I'll take oor chairs outside, you bring some tankards.'

Struan picked up the two tankards from the shelf. He

used to share a flagon with his pa, in the old days, but the habit had gone with his passing. Just Annie and him now and she didn't care for beer. Jock had set the stools in a patch of sunshine. He gave Jock his tankard and cradled his pa's while Jock poured the golden liquid. Struan took a deep draught of ale and felt his work-weary shoulder muscles relax. 'How is yer brother?'

'You know what Al's like. Aywis moaning aboot something, but he's basically fine.' Jock went on to describe the adventures of the Drummond Castle gardeners on their Friday night bar outing. 'Calum brought his fiddle and we had a sing song. I persuaded the barmaid tae dance. Honestly, Struan, you should've come.'

Struan shrugged, it was an old argument he'd no wish to revisit.

Jock stretched to fill up Struan's tankard and leaned his hands on his knees. 'You know yer sister's no a wee lassie anymair? How are you going tae ever have yer ain wife tae nag you if you never go oot?'

Struan simply shook his head and smiled. Jock thought he was an expert on fatherless sisters since his own was in the same position, but Elma was ten years older than Jock and lived with their uncle, it didn't compare at all. Annie never complained, but if Struan wasn't there after work she'd no choice but sit through the evening alone. He wished she had a friend nearby but there was no one. The other girls at school used to laugh about her limp behind her back, sometimes even called her names to her face. Struan struggled not to slap them. Annie was more placid tempered but he also knew she was easily hurt.

Jock's conversation turned to poaching, The estates in the area often rang out to the sound of gunshot, but Jock never persuaded Struan to join in that either. Annie wouldn't have stolen rabbits in the house and Struan couldn't risk the gamekeeper's wrath. They'd little money for a rabbit dinner so even less for a fine, and what would happen to Annie if he was imprisoned or deported? The church clock struck the half hour bell. 'Is that the time? I'm late, Jock. I'll have tae go.'

'Are you fetching the cart? I'll walk up tae Drummond Castle wi' you.'

'I cannae walk wi' you. I need tae run.'

Struan took off at a run towards the woods. He heard Jock laughing behind him. By the time he reached Drummond Castle stable yard he was out of breath, hot, and already ten minutes late. He swore at himself under his breath. Struan had enjoyed a drink with his pal, a rare moment of leisure, but Mistress Birnie would have locked up the library long ago and there wasn't even a bench for Annie to rest on outside the library.

Struan shook the reins to urge on the old carthorse, too elderly to be useful in Drummond Castle stables but fine for occasional errands. The horse moved from an amble to a slow trot. It was ten years since the horse's last canter and there was no point in forcing him beyond his elderly capabilities. Struan owned no timepiece but he knew he was very late. The thought of Annie standing alone leaning heavily on her stick, made his heart constrict.

Chapter Four

May 1869

My pony's dark mane fluttered in the breeze. Her spritely trot along the Crieff road suggested she was enjoying the outing as much as I was. I loved this little trap. She had taken to pulling the two-wheeled gig like second nature. The long whip was superfluous. Daisy needed no more encouragement than a shake of the reins. A lovely little bay Shetland, Daisy was my birthday gift the year before my mother died. One of the few connections to my life in a family. The head groom in Drummond Castle had turned a blind eye to me hitching her to my aunt's trap earlier today. What could be more respectable than a journey to church? I told no one that I was going to Fowlis Wester alone, nor that I wasn't coming straight home.

Soon we bowled down the long lane leading up to Innerpeffray Library. I was delighted to spot Mrs Birnie walking ahead, even more so, when I realised the person leaning on her arm was Annie Cooper. No sign of her grumpy brother. I stopped beside them.

'I was on my way to see you, Mrs Birnie. Can I offer you

both a ride?' They smiled up at me, but Annie looked embarrassed.

'Thank you, but we are very nearly there,' she said.

Mrs Birnie patted Annie's hand where it rested in the crook of her elbow. 'Struan usually helps Annie with the step up into the cart, but if you hold your horse very still, I think I can manage.'

'Of course. How silly of me. Give me your hand, Miss Cooper. Daisy is steady as a rock.'

Annie's grip was firm and with Mrs Birnie's help, she clambered up and settled herself on the seat next to me. We all three laughed as we set off again.

'What a lovely wee horse. Is she yours?' Annie asked.

'Thank you. I think so too. Daisy was a gift from my parents. She's too small for me to ride now, but she loves to pull the trap.'

We arrived at the library within a few minutes. I jumped down and Mrs Birnie and I helped Annie climb out. I tied Daisy to the schoolhouse rail and gave her a carrot.

Inside the library, I handed the magazine to Annie. 'It's full of fascinating articles this time. Do you have a particular area of interest?'

'I'm nae scholar,' she replied. 'But my ma had an interest in healing herbs and my pa was a gardener at Drummond Castle. You might say it's in my blood.'

'An inherited interest, just like me! My father is a keen horticulturist, and he's presently on a plant hunting mission in the South Americas.'

'How exciting,' she replied.

We grinned at each other. Might Annie Cooper long for a like-minded friend as much as I did?

Mrs Birnie held out a sketchbook. 'Why don't you show Miss Finlay your drawings, Annie?'

'Och, I'm sure Miss Finlay has better things tae do.'

'I'd love to see if you'd permit it. And please call me Iris. Truly, I'm no grand lady. I live in a castle under my aunt's care, but my father and I will move to the gardener's lodge at Culdees Castle estate when he returns from his expedition. Papa is managing the planning of their new garden.'

Mrs Birnie put the book in front of us. I gasped when I turned the pages. The sketchbook was full of gorgeous botanical drawings, some pencil, some in ink, and some painted in the most beautiful colours. The last drawing was an image I recognised from *Curtis's Magazine*. A glorious, yellow trumpet-shaped bloom. 'Oh Annie, *Allamanda nobilis*! Isn't it magnificent?' In my excitement, I grabbed her hand. 'A species from South America, where Papa is travelling. Just imagine coming across this beauty in the forest. I wish I could be with him and see such a flower.'

Annie gazed down at the sketch. 'I'm sure it would be thrilling. You must miss him terribly, being so far away.'

I nodded. 'Very much.' I'd forgotten I had her hand until she turned her fingers over inside my palm and grasped my hand tight. The kindness of her voice and the warm contact of another human touched me to my core. I turned to blink away my tears.

'My pa died last year. I miss him so much too,' she whispered.

'I'm so sorry. How awful for you,' I replied. Only one year, and Annie had lost her mother too. I must be less pathetic. I took several deep breaths and returned to the sketchbook. 'You are really talented. I so wish I could draw.'

'I wasnae much good when I started out, but the magazine drawings are so good, they're great tae copy.'

Annie took her sketchbook and flicked the pages back to the beginning. 'These first ones are gey rough.'

'I know these plants too. They're from *A Family Herbal*. Your drawings are not rough at all. So much better than the ones in the book. I recognise this, it's woody nightshade.' I pointed to the drawing of a dark green plant with purple flowers.

Annie coloured a little. 'This is just my selfish wee pastime now, but I started drawing wi' a purpose. My ma couldnae read, so Miss Christie, I mean Mrs Birnie as she is now, let me copy out the picture and description of plants I thought would interest Ma, then I'd read it to her at home. Later, I started turning my drawings intae something mair detailed.'

I studied Annie's sketchbook while she read the magazine. 'Look,' she said, pointing at the page. 'An iris.'

'One of my parents' favourite plants. That's why I was given the name.'

'Then I'll choose this one tae copy out today.' She replicated the drawing in her book.

'Will you paint in the colours? The yellow streak at its centre is such a lovely contrast to the purple.'

Annie shook her head. 'I never bring my paints intae the library, of course, but I sometimes paint my sketches up later. I keep what paints I have in Mrs Birnie's schoolroom.' She ran her finger over the Brazilian iris illustration. 'I cannae dae this one, though. I havnae the right paints tae mix up such a bonny shade ae lilac.'

Mrs Birnie came back, tying on her bonnet. 'I need to get on with Mr Birnie's tea now, girls.'

'Aye, Struan will be along for me soon,' Annie added.

Mrs Birnie locked up the library, and we walked together through the churchyard and under the ancient yew trees. Mrs Birnie left us outside the schoolhouse.

'When are you coming again?' I asked Annie.

She shrugged. 'It depends on when Struan is free and can borrow the cart.'

We stared up the long track leading away from Inner-peffray.

'Don't wait for me,' Annie said. 'Struan's maybe been held up, but he willnae forget me.'

'Why don't I take you down to the main road? Save Struan some time.'

'I'd love a spin wi' Daisy again,' she replied.

'Should I move Daisy to the mounting block?' I asked, embarrassed I'd forgotten her disability again.

'People underestimate us girls. You have a grand grip. Give me your hand. I can push off my good foot.'

I gave Daisy her carrot and unhitched the reins. Annie handed me her stick. With my help, she was up in a trice.

'Trot on, Daisy. Nice and steady, lass.' I smiled to have Annie beside me and we sped along the track. The air was fresh and the hedges full of the sound of chittering sparrows. High above, a skylark sang. Soon we were on the last long stretch heading for the main Crieff road.

'If I can borrow the trap again, I might pick you up and bring you here?'

Annie made no answer, so I turned to look at her.

Suddenly, a pheasant burst through the hedge directly in front of us. A flurry of wings and bright feathers in Daisy's face. My poor frightened pony reared up in her traces, then took off at a gallop. Annie screamed. Daisy veered into a ditch and we were both almost flung out of the gig. A terrific grinding noise confirmed a problem with one wheel, but Daisy bumped us out and charged onwards down the track. I hauled at the reins with all my strength, but she paid no heed. We clung on for dear life, heading straight for the main road.

When a cart turned into the lane, I was certain we would hit it. Struan jumped down and held up his arms, Daisy slowed a little. Just when we were about to collide, she veered to one side, and he grabbed her halter.

The trap skidded to halt but my racing heart was much slower to settle. I was tortured with the certain knowledge that we might all have been killed, at the very least I might have brought more injury and pain to my new friend. I closed my eyes and whispered 'thank you dear Lord.'

I turned towards our rescuer. 'Thank you so much. Daisy is usually steady but was spooked by a—' I stopped midsentence. Struan was white with fury.

'You stupid lassie! Why are you out wi' no groom? You might both have been killed.' He held his arms up to Annie, who allowed herself to be lifted down.

She looked back up at me. 'Forgive my brother's words.' Annie turned to Struan. 'You are too harsh. Any horse would be spooked by a big bird flying straight intae it. And we came tae nae harm.'

Struan dipped his head. 'Any groom would have had the strength tae hold the pony back,' he muttered under his breath.

'Struan,' she hissed.

'I apologise for my hasty words, Miss Finlay.' He lifted Annie into his cart, then turned to me. He lowered his voice, but anger still simmered in the words. 'There was harm done. Your trap wheel is damaged and your pony is lame. I'll go tae the castle and send someone tae fetch you.'

I jumped down, my heart in my mouth. Sure enough, the wheel was bent and poor Daisy had one foot lifted, barely touching the ground. If Daisy had broken a bone, they'd surely shoot her. I felt along her leg, but I couldn't tell. Daisy was still breathing fast and her eyes were wide. Was she in pain? Had the shouting added to her panic? Struan's cart was already on the road, heading back to Drummond Castle. Annie held up her hand and waved. Daisy nudged me with her nose, as if to say sorry. I laid my head against her warm neck and struggled to hold back my tears.

Chapter Five

May 1869 – Drummond Castle

I exited the castle into the courtyard, then walked to the steps overlooking the grounds. The view from here never failed to make me pause. Drummond Castle's extraordinary gardens were laid out in terraces leading down to a French-style formal parterre, with the geometric pattern of the beds focused on a central sundial.

I sped down the first few steps, settling into a more dignified walk through the shrubberies of the first terrace, then down into the garden level, without looking back. The grand reception rooms and chief bedrooms overlooked the garden, so it was likely I was being observed. I was acutely aware of my interloper status when Aunt Leonora was away. Nobody had ever been unkind, but my stay had dragged on longer than the Drummond family had been told to expect. Getting to Ecuador had taken months, and there was still no firm date for Papa's return.

I followed the gravelled path towards the sundial, then took a sharp right. Entering the west side of the garden took me away from the direct line of sight from the family quarters, allowing me to relax. This section was laid out in box hedge to create the pattern of the Drummond crest. Such an extremely regimented style was not to my taste. Clipping nature to mimic something manmade seemed vain and fool-ish. I took a different route each time I visited the gardens, challenging myself with the Latin plant names. 'Larkspur, *Consolida ajacis,* Petunia. *Violacea,*' I whispered. My father and I had laboured hard over this aspect of my education and I didn't want to get rusty. I glanced towards the hothouses and potting sheds. Mr MacDonald's gardening team were often found working there, and part of my anxiety in the garden was not wishing to come across Struan Cooper. I frowned at an ornamental yew tree with an unusual yellow hue at the edges of the spiny leaves. What was the name of this variety? I pinched off a shoot with the plan of cross-referencing it with Papa's plant directory.

'Did you lose something, Miss Finlay?'

I knew the voice before I straightened and turned, caught red-handed with the shoot grasped between my finger and thumb. Heat flooded my cheeks.

'Was it a cutting you were wanting for Mr Speir's garden? I could ask Mr MacDonald. That wee bit leaf willnae take. You need a piece ae the stem beneath the bud.'

I let the shoot fall onto the neat path, where it looked even more conspicuous.

'No, I mean, I didn't want it for planting. I...' Why was I explaining myself to this boy? 'I was merely trying to recall the Latin name. I have it now, *Taxus baccata fastigiata aurea.* Of course. Good day, Mr Cooper.' I forced myself into a digni-fied walk to the iron gate in the high garden wall.

As I turned the handle, I discovered the gate was locked. I heard the dreaded noise of the wheelbarrow trundling up behind me and sure enough, Struan appeared at my side, wielding a large iron key. The dark brown curls spilling out from under his cap were exactly the same shade as his sister's, but while everything about Annie pleased me, this boy was infuriating.

'Naebdae's been out this way today. We keep this gate locked at night.' I caught a mocking look in his dark brown eyes. 'Tae keep out thieves, like.'

'Thank you, Mr Cooper. Could you leave it open so I can come back through here?'

'You'll be going tae see that poor wee pony, then?'

It wasn't a question that required a reply, so I ignored him. I was convinced he only mentioned Daisy to shame me. I walked in a fury up the hill to the stable block. The narrow trail of trodden earth was rarely used by the castle inhabitants and ill-suited for long dresses. Thankfully, this year's crinoline style was narrower. I held my skirts up out of the dewy grass. Nevertheless, the back tier of green silk was soon wet through. In the stable courtyard, I headed straight for Daisy's stall. Mr Buchan, the head groom, had declared her leg wasn't broken but warned me it didn't mean she was out of danger. She was confined to her stall to allow the leg to heal and such inactivity could easily lead to colic. He'd bandaged up both her legs, explaining that tendon damage in one leg could cause an imbalance in the other. I looked over the stable door. All four of Daisy's hooves were on the ground and she whinnied a greeting. The irritation I'd carried up from the garden was replaced by joy when she walked towards me without limping. Daisy pushed her nose into my shoulder, snuffling in her search for the wizened apple I had in my jacket pocket.

I held my hand with the fingers outstretched to offer the apple from my palm. Daisy nodded her head up and down while she chewed, as if giving a thank you. 'I think you're on the mend, Daisy. I might ask if I can lead you out for a short walk tomorrow.'

The sound of wheels in the cobbled yard signalled the

arrival of a carriage. Mr Buchan strode towards me, pulling off his leather gloves. He handed his whip to one of the stable boys. 'Daisy's looking better today, Miss Finlay. I think she's going to pull through.'

'You've no idea how happy I am to hear that, Mr Buchan.'

'You know she'll not be fit to draw a trap for a long time? Not that it's in working order right now.'

'I know. I'm just grateful she's able to walk.' I tried to make my next question sound casual. 'Will the gig be back from the carpenter before my aunt returns?'

'Too late for that,' he said with a rueful expression. 'I'm just back from the station. I dropped the mistress at the castle.'

'Oh,' I replied.

'I told her,' he said, reading my mind. 'She was bound to hear, and it's better it came from me. I was able to reassure her that John Taylor will fix it good as new.'

I nodded. 'I'd better get back to the castle. Thank you for looking after Daisy so well. I really appreciate it.'

'I was happy to. She's a lovely old lass.'

I turned to head back down to the castle.

'Good luck,' he called after me.

Looking over at the castle's remarkable outline on the horizon, I was struck again at the unlikelihood of me living in such a place. Despite my discomfort in feeling I didn't belong here, I didn't take my good fortune for granted. The ancient keep that dominated the foreground had been there for centuries. Aunt Leonora and I occupied a tucked away corner of the newer section. This pretty crow-stepped gabled building, with the round fairy-tale turret set beside it, reminded me of a cruet set from this angle. The Drummond-Burrell Willoughby family had all those rooms with garden views, while we looked over the beech-lined drive at the back. Aunt Leonora's husband, who had been dead for ten years, was a distant cousin of Lady Clementina, and they'd taken Leonora in when her husband's death left her without a home. Their kindness to her had temporarily been extended to me.

I entered the castle and made my way through the rambling corridors to Aunt Leonora's room. Taking a deep breath, I knocked and went in.

'Welcome back, Aunt Leanora,' I said. 'I hope you had a good journey.'

My aunt was sitting in her usual armchair, drinking tea. 'There you are,' she said. I caught a chilly tone in her voice. 'The journey was bearable. Our train was a little late, but being able to come all the way from Edinburgh without using a carriage is a blessing.' She gestured toward the teapot. 'Help yourself.'

After pouring my tea, I sat opposite her, gripping both the cup and the saucer firmly. I wouldn't have my nerves betrayed by crockery.

'Did you enjoy your stay in Grimsthorpe Castle?' I asked. The family had the luxury of two castles to choose from, and they spent a lot of time at their Lincolnshire retreat.

She nodded her head from side-to-side, signalling ambivalence. 'Lady Clementina likes to check on her brother and it's a property better sealed against the weather, but I always feel more at home here.'

I got straight to the point. 'Mr Buchan will have told you about the damage to your trap. I'm very sorry.'

My aunt laid down her cup and saucer with a sigh. 'He assures me it can be repaired, but what on all earth were you doing so far from home on your own?'

'I wanted to attend the service in Fowlis Wester church, then I called in at Innerpeffray to borrow an item.'

Aunt Leonora frowned. 'I cannot understand your attachment to Innerpeffray Library. The family has been so gracious in granting you access to their library and it dwarfs the Innerpeffray collection.'

'The Keeper, Mr Birnie, takes a subscription to a horticultural magazine we do not have here. Father and I used to look at it together every month.'

She picked up her teacup and peered at me over its rim. 'Your recklessness has consequences, Iris. Repairing the gig is not an expense I budgeted for this month.'

'I'm most sorry to be a further burden on your finances,' I whispered. I'd no money to offer to pay.

'So no more gadding about, and really, Iris, you must come to the Episcopalian service with me from now on. It's a mark of respect to our hosts. I moved from Church of Scotland when I married and it isn't so very different.'

I needed to compromise. 'The new Fowlis Wester minister, Mr Cowan, studied with my father, and Papa likes to hear of the sermons in my letters. However, he would expect me to comply with your reasonable advice.'

I had to risk asking. I dreaded being unable to meet Annie. 'But may I visit the library occasionally? It was such a happy part of my routine with Papa.' I withheld the chief reason, Aunt Leonora might not approve of my new friend.

'I expect we can organise to take you from time-to-time.' Her gaze softened. 'And of course I understand you miss your father, so I hope the letter that arrived for you today will cheer you up. A delivery of seeds came to Culdees Castle yesterday, and they forwarded it on.' She gestured towards the letter sat on top of the mantelpiece.

I jumped up, snatched it and held it to my breast. It would be rude to rush out, but I so wanted to read it alone.

Aunt Leonora smiled. 'On you go. You can tell me about it later.'

It was too dark to read the letter walking down the spiral

staircase to my room. I flung open my bedroom door and took the letter to the deep stone windowsill for better light.

February 1869
Quito, Ecuador

Dearest Iris,
How are you, my darling girl? Your papa misses you so much and thinks of you every day.

I came down from the mountains this week to send some seeds to Mr Speir. I shall include this letter with his parcel. Unfortunately, I can tell from your most recent letter that I haven't received some of your correspondence and that you haven't received all my replies. I suppose, given my distance from home and my nomadic existence, it's a wonder that any letters do get through. Nevertheless, I suggest from now on that you write to me care of Quito University, at the enclosed address.

Professor Jameson, the elderly Scottish/Ecuadorian academic who, as I mentioned in previous letters, has been so very helpful, is actually travelling home to Edinburgh soon. In his absence, he assures me his colleagues at the university will be happy to hold my correspondence. I'm afraid I can't promise more frequent letters. I don't suppose I'll be back in Quito for a few months. You will be excited to hear that I carried down some small cacti with me this time and I'm sure they are unknown at home. Professor Jameson has kindly agreed to keep them for me here in Quito until we are ready to ship the rarer live plants. I had better admit to you now that I've decided not to sail home this year. I'm afraid I need one more autumn and spring season to complete our collection. Most likely I will begin the journey back with our last cargo of specimens around this time next year.

. . .

I laid the letter aside. How was I going to manage without Papa for another whole year? I sank into the little armchair, my only furniture apart from a single bed. Then, drew my handkerchief out of my sleeve to stifle my groan. Aunt Leonora was directly above me and I didn't want her to hear. Finally, after a few minutes, curiosity about the remaining paragraphs, and especially the plant drawing which I'd seen at the end of his letter made me sniff back my tears and pick up the letter up again.

Finally, dear Iris, I have a request. Can you get yourself back to Innerpeffray Library? Could you look for a specimen of orchid which I think featured in Curtis's last year? I believe its common name was the Amethyst-tipped Orchid. I've heard people talk of a mountain specimen found here in Ecuador that makes that huge orchid look as common and ordinary as a Bellis perennis daisy. This is the elusive plant I hope to find on my expedition. If the rumours are true, such a specimen would assure my place amongst horticultural experts. When you track the Curtis's entry, please copy down all its features, including size, petal and leaf details. I know you don't enjoy drawing but if you can describe all its features, I'm sure your skill with words will evoke an image in my head.

I so love to hear your stories from home. You reported that your life is dull, but I have to disagree. Your lyrical descriptions of the snow-covered fields in January, of the sight of a bullfinch in the black-thorn, then the appearance of the February snowdrops, are like a description of heaven to me when I am so very far away. You will guess that I suffer from homesickness, but I'm also loving my Ecuador adventure and am so glad I came. You would be pleased to see the transformation in my spirits. I wholly understand that living under Leonora's guardianship is a strange thing for you, but I hope it cheers you to know how much her help in getting me here was exactly what I needed. This month, when I woke to another glorious sunrise across the mountains, the certainty that I was witnessing God's glory drove me to my knees. So for the first time in much too long, I can finish with the assurance that you are in my prayers.

With very best wishes from your papa

Papa had included a drawing of a plant on a separate page, with a brief description below.

Excuse my draughtsmanship. Your mother could draw, so I fear your deficiency of skill was inherited from me. This is the Lupinus mutabilis, which is a common plant here and I thought you would like to see it because its appearance is not dissimilar to the Scottish lupins so loved by your mother, but this one doesn't share the reputation of having poisonous seeds. In fact, the Andean specimen has a white edible bean which is commonly used by locals in soups and stews. I loved it especially because of the colour which is a blueish purple with a yellow centre, just like your namesake Iris.

His description of the purple-coloured lupin made me feel nearer to him, and the marvellous news about his faith tempered my sadness with joy. I knelt beside my bed to add my prayers to his own.

Chapter Six

May 1869

Annie and Struan argued after the cart accident, their first since their father died. For days she refused to speak to him until he could bear it no longer.

'What's wrang, Annie. You could cut the air in this cottage wi' a pruning knife.'

'You know what's wrang, Struan. You embarrassed me in front of Iris. How would you feel if I shouted at one of your friends?'

'I see, Iris is it now? Has that fancy lady who lives in Drummond Castle been telling you that's she's yer friend? You don't think you might be kidding yersel', Annie?'

Annie stamped her stick on the ground. 'You aywis under-estimate me, Struan, I'm certain she enjoys my company and she asked me to call her Iris. I think she's as lonely as I am.'

Struan sighed, he hated to argue with her. 'I admire naebdae more than you, Annie, but counting on Miss Finlay as a companion will get you hurt when she finds someone of her ain class tae talk tae.' Struan reached out to touch Annie's arm but she shook his hand off.

'Miss Finlay,' Annie mimicked his voice, tugged at her imaginary cap and cringed into mock submission. 'It's you who has spent too much time grovelling tae Drummond Castle ladies, Struan.'

That riled him. 'I saw your friend Iris in the gardens this week and she spoke to me like a mongrel dog,' he shouted.

Annie sunk awkwardly onto a stool and rubbed her eyes. 'Let's no fight, Struan. It wears me out. I'll see Iris at church on Sunday. You'll see that she likes my company.'

Struan's work week was difficult. The weather was unusually warm and today he'd been tasked with preparing the hothouse flowers for the Drummond Castle housekeeper's weekly visit. He found the lily scent cloying and the woman was overbearing. Her arrival was announced by the jangle of keys at her waist.

'The mistress has requested yellow lilies this week and I'll need some long stem roses.'

Struan looked beyond the bucket of pink rose lilies the woman had ordered, towards the yellow lilies which were already overblown in the heat. 'Those golden lilies willnae last more than a few days. What aboot some tiger lilies?'

'Do you think me a fool, boy? Tiger lily flowers are orange. Did I ask for orange?'

'No, Mistress, but I know you can work wonders wi' your arrangements and I'll gie you some wi' lots ae buds which are yellow on the outside and I've some grand yellow roses.'

'The colour of jealousy, yellow roses aren't suitable at all.'

'Mr MacDonald says Her Majesty has them in the Balmoral rose garden.'

He saw consternation flicker across the housekeeper's face. Struan had made the Balmoral story up but Lady de

Eresby had admired the yellow roses on her walk the day before. 'I have some nice white roses if you prefer?'

'Oh no, definitely not white. We'll try the yellow.'

'I can easy change them oot if you dinnae like them.'

'I'll send down the parlour maid at nine. Don't keep her waiting.'

'No, Mistress.'

Struan picked up a trug and his rose shears, and escaped gratefully into the breezy garden. Some of the other gardeners scoffed at his interest in roses but it was MacDonald the chief gardener's passion too, so they daren't laugh openly. He was walking back with his pile of roses when Mr MacDonald appeared. His eyes travelled over the cut flowers, he said nothing but nodded his approval. 'Struan I'm sorry but there's no cart on Sunday. The laird has promised it tae the factor's daughter tae help her move hoose on Saturday and they'll keep it 'til Monday morning.'

'Don't worry, Mr MacDonald.'

'Will Annie manage the walk tae church? I hate tae disappoint the lassie.'

'If the weather's fine she can manage.' Struan's heart sank. He dreaded telling Annie because Mistress Birnie could take her to the library but he'd no way of getting her home.

On Saturday he went home via the Drummond Castle stables. Might the Finlay girl have access to a carriage? Had he the nerve to ask Mr Buchan the head groom? Struan discovered the small gig was still missing. He'd shouted at Annie's friend so of course he couldn't now suggest Annie ask her for a favour. He trudged home feeling useless, surely his pa could have solved it for Annie. Pa had been best friends with Mr Buchan. His long service made him easy amongst all the Drummond Castle staff. Struan knew everyone thought him still a laddie and that was reflected in his wages. He and

Annie barely brought in enough to feed and clothe them both, fancy journeys to libraries were just too difficult.

Struan broke the news after Saturday supper. Annie's reaction was much harder to bear than her previous anger. 'I see. Never mind. I'm lucky you get access tae the cart at all. I dinnae take it for granted.'

Struan saw the disappointment in her eyes.

The next morning brought blue skies and the Muthill church bells rang out their summons to the service. Struan put on a clean shirt and polished his shoes. When Annie emerged from behind the curtain that segregated her sleeping area, she was still in her nightgown. 'It's dry, Annie, will you no take a walk tae the kirk?'

She shook her head. 'My legs might manage but my mind isnae fit for honest prayer today. You go, Struan. Ask the Lord tae give me a steadier character. I'm ashamed ae my selfishness.' Annie limped back to her bed.

He put a pot of tea on the table and headed out towards the woods. He wasn't fit for honest prayer either. Struan hated that he couldn't fill the gap left by his father. He'd be sure to get the cart next week and he'd look for any small opportunity to make Annie happier.

Chapter Seven

May 1869

I t was disappointing to give up worshiping in Fowlis Wester church, but I didn't believe God cared which roof I worshipped under. Perhaps I should have done, because this choice between the Church of Scotland and Episcopalian faiths had split families and fuelled violence. I saw God's work most clearly in the internal structure of a flower, or the marvel of an ancient oak. Unsurprising that Papa had found his faith again in a mountain view, but I hoped my small prayers had helped. The following Sunday, Aunt Leonora and I attended the Episcopalian Church service in Muthill. I'd hoped to meet Mrs Birnie and her husband, but there was no sign of them.

I tried to borrow a carriage to get to Innerpeffray Library's Thursday afternoon open session, but they were all busy. I longed to begin my search for Papa's orchid and being unable to get anywhere independently was infuriating. Papa had taken me with him on most of his outings, so I'd never felt trapped as a girl. Now, I faced another full year of being entirely dependent on Aunt Leonora. She, in turn, depended on the whims of the Willoughby de Eresby family.

When the next Sunday came around, I made a determined effort to push these ungrateful thoughts out of my mind as I walked into church. My cage was a gilded one, and most of the young women in the congregation faced much more serious difficulties than lack of a carriage. My prayer for God's forgiveness soared heavenwards as I walked down the central aisle, passing the Birnies in their pew. Could this be a prayer answered. Aunt Leonora had promised that if Mrs Birnie could admit me, she would take a detour to drop me at the library before going home. Mrs Birnie smiled as we walked past. We took our seats in the third row, behind the Drummond family's regular pew. Lord and Lady Willoughby de Eresby entered the building a few minutes later, and the minister came up to give them a personal welcome.

'Good morning, Lord and Lady Aveland, how wonderful to see you on this particularly fine day.'

Now in her late fifties, Clementina Drummond was part of one of Scotland's most ancient families and her father, Peter Burrell, had been Baron de Willoughby. Clementina also became Lady Aveland, on marrying her husband Gilbert.

At the end of the service, the congregation waited to allow the Drummond family to leave the church first. I had no right to such an honour, but was glad of the opportunity it gave me to catch Mrs Birnie. I spotted Annie Cooper near the back of the church. I'd not seen her since the accident last month and her smile of greeting cheered me enormously. Thankfully, her brother Struan kept his gaze averted.

Mrs Birnie came out with her arm hooked through Annie's. 'Donald and I are taking Annie back to the library. Are you able to come with us, Iris?'

'Is there room in your gig?' Annie asked. 'I can easily ask Struan to take me in the cart.'

'Donald is driving and we can have the hood down on

such a fine day. You are both such slim girls, I'm sure we'll manage. Can someone come for you at around four?'

'I'll ask Struan tae take us both home,' Annie said. 'We go past Drummond Castle on the way home, anyway.'

'No need,' I interjected. 'I've already arranged it with Aunt Leonora. I'll just go and give Mr Buchan a time.'

'Och, what was I thinking?' Annie said. 'Of course you'll not want tae come in an auld cart in such a fine frock.'

I'd managed to sound over-privileged again. 'It's not that. I just don't want to put your brother to any trouble.' I could hardly tell Annie that the thought of close proximity with her brother brought me out in a cold sweat, but the misunderstanding made me squirm.

Innerpeffray Library was situated four miles south of Crieff on a bend in the River Earn. On our journey there, I recounted the story of my father's request for the orchid description.

'From what I remember, there were several orchids featured last year,' Annie said.

'I think so, too. Let's start in December and work our way back.'

'It will take us nae time, if we work together,' Annie replied. 'Would you like me tae make a copy ae the illustration when we find it?'

'Would you? I was going to ask. My father will get a much better idea of the look of the flower if there's an accompanying drawing.'

'I'd love tae help,' she said.

Soon, we were sitting at the library desk where I'd first seen Annie with Struan. The light from the window behind us illuminated the magazines. We worked through the illustrations together, taking a magazine each. The number of orchids featured last year was surely a symptom of the current fashion for exotic hothouse plants. We found several orchids from Ecuador, including one in the May edition, which had been discovered thirty years before by Papa's friend, Professor Jameson. I pointed it out to Annie, and she leaned over to read it with me. She was close enough for me to feel her the warmth of her shoulder against mine and hear her breathing. The friendly collaboration was joyous. I couldn't believe my luck in finding a fellow enthusiast, when I knew so few girls my own age.

'This is the right colours, could it be the one?' Annie asked.

The illustration of *Oncidium cucullatum* showed a plant with a spray of yellow centred, purple and white flowers on a long stem. I turned the page and ran my finger down the Latin description.

'You can read Latin?' Annie said.

'Yes, although there's a description in English here, too.'

'I think the flower is too small,' Annie said.

'I'm afraid you are right.' I stood up to fetch the January and February magazines.

Annie was still looking at the orchid illustration. 'Vincent Brooks,' she read. 'Is that the man who drew the sketch?'

'No, that's the name of the printer. This is the artist.' I pointed to the inscription on the bottom left. 'W. Fitch *del et lith*. The Latin means Fitch drew the original and painted it from a lithograph print. Walter Hood Fitch is *Curtis's* regular illustrator. A man from Glasgow, I believe.'

'Imagine being able tae earn your living drawing flowers. What a lucky man. I'm envious ae your Latin too. How did you come tae learn?'

'My father taught me. I'm trying not to forget it in his absence.'

'I used tae love Mrs Birnie's classes, but I left when Ma died. Struan went tae work full time and I dae housemaid's duties for a village family in the mornings.'

I was embarrassed to be caught glancing at her hands.

Annie shrugged. 'The soda I use tae scrub their tiles is awfy hard on your hands.' She turned her fingers over, revealing painful looking cracks. 'I should have been able tae work my way up tae being parlour maid by now, but naebdae is going tae give such a job tae a cripple.'

'Oh, Annie. Don't say that. Why ever not?'

'Can you imagine the disaster of me bringing their tea in on a tray? There'd be tea slopped everywhere.' Annie laughed, but it sounded bitter.

I took her hand and squeezed it, raising her smile.

'Really, I'm lucky. Struan looks aifter me fine. And Mrs Birnie lets me in here, even when it's not the normal day. She's been doing that since before she married. And now I've got your company too.'

The Innerpeffray librarian had the marvellous and ancient title, Keeper of the Books. Donald Birnie's main job was schoolmaster, as well as maintaining the library and its collection. Christian aided her husband in both duties, and she had also done so for her brother, who was the previous Keeper.

'We are both lucky. I so enjoy my time with you.' I put my arm around her thin back and hugged her. 'But we better get on with our task. Only these two magazines left. I do hope we haven't missed it.'

It was Annie who found the orchid. 'This is it! The very first entry in January. Goodness, Iris, it's a shame we didnae start at the beginning ae the year.'

I leaned into her to look at the picture, which was exactly as Papa had described it. Relief that we'd finally found his orchid was tinged with the knowledge that I'd happily have scoured all the previous year's magazines, if it meant spending more time with Annie. This very large white and purple spotted orchid, had a dark purple centre. *Cattleya amethystoglossa.* Mr Hooker, the editor, described the Kew specimen as being native to Brazil. 'If Papa finds something similar in Ecuador, plant collectors will certainly be eager to get hold of a new orchid with four-inch-wide flowers.'

'The artist has really captured the unusual crinkly texture of the flower. This will be a challenge to copy,' Annie said.

Mrs Birnie came in. 'It's gone four now, girls,' she said.

'I expect Struan is waiting for me,' Annie replied. 'Can I come back after church next week to sketch it?'

'Of course,' she replied.

'And I'll come to make a copy of the words,' I added.

Annie frowned. 'I'll remember tae bring the sketch of the iris I did for you. But I'm going tae face the same problem wi' lack of the right paint. It would be much better for your father if he knew the precise colour.'

'The new plant he seeks won't necessarily be the same colour, but let me see if I can find a way to get you some more paints,' I replied.

I stood in the shadows at the bottom of the library stairs, while Annie made her way towards Struan in the cart. She kissed him tenderly on the cheek before he lifted her into her seat. Envy was a sin and I was ashamed of such a base reaction when Annie had so little. I found Struan insufferable but the depth of their loving bond was very clear.

Chapter Eight

June 1869

I had a special parcel in my arms as I exited Muthill church after the service. Annie and Mrs Birnie were waiting for me.

'I'm going to Crieff and will return at four, Iris. Don't keep me waiting,' Aunt Leonora said.

Mr Buchan helped Aunt Leonora into the newly repaired trap. 'Enjoy your painting session, Iris,' she called over, as the black mare set off at a trot.

'Have you taken up painting?' Annie asked.

'That is what my aunt believes, and you might allow me a couple of brushstrokes to ease my conscience,' I replied, and handed Annie the large, brown paper-wrapped box. 'Open it.'

Annie stripped off the paper to reveal a large mahogany box with brass corners and embossed with the name *Alexander Hill, Princes Street, Edinburgh.*

'Aunt Leonora and my mother were both amateur painters in their youth and this was the box of watercolours they shared. Take a look inside.'

Annie turned the brass key and opened the lid. Inside was a wooden tray filled with watercolour blocks and paint-

41

brushes of different sizes. 'Look at all the colours! I've never seen such a bonny thing.'

Her obvious joy made my heart sing. 'Some of the paint blocks are well-used, the red and the yellow in particular, but I believe most boxes have only a dozen colours, so eighteen is very generous.'

'Aye, well, vermillion and yellow ochre are the most commonly used colours, but there's a wee bit left.' Annie picked up the ceramic colour mixing tray. 'They looked after it well. This doesnae have even the tiniest chip.'

'Aunt Leonora says it was their father's gift and a most prized possession. She hasn't painted for years but always kept it safe.'

'And she'll allow us tae use it tae paint the orchid for your pa? I think this violet is very close tae the shade I need.' Annie's eyes shone with excitement.

'She gave me the box. It's ours now.'

Annie looked shocked. 'Ours? But this must surely mind you ae your mother. I'll help you colour up the orchid illustration, then you must take the box home and keep it safe.'

'It is a beautiful object, but it's made to be used. I'll copy the magazine description while you colour in your illustration.'

'Would it be possible tae work in the schoolroom today?' Annie asked Mrs Birnie.

'Of course, I can check the magazine out to you, so you can work in there together.'

The Innerpeffray school was a fine stone building, tucked beyond the walled cemetery surrounding Innerpeffray Library and chapel. Inside were rows of wooden lidded desks. Annie headed straight to the one I assumed was her habitual place.

'Why don't you sit at my desk, girls? There's room for

you to work side-by-side,' Mrs Birnie said. Soon, we were working in companionable silence. Annie had two versions of the illustration in front of her. 'I wanted a copy for my sketchbook and I can use it tae practise before I dae the one for your pa.' She turned the illustrations upside down and began with the stems of the plant. 'This is the easiest part, tae get my hand in, but I dinnae want tae smudge the drawing ae the orchid,' she explained, while she mixed up several shades of dark green. Next, Annie blended yellow ochre into cadmium white for the petals of the creamy orchid. I copied out the description of the amethyst-tipped orchid. It took me ages because I was very distracted by watching Annie work. Finally, she began to mix the shades of violet, ending up with six different puddles of paint, from pale lilac to a dark purple. 'This dark one is for the crinkly lower petals ae the flower,' she explained. Annie pushed Papa's illustration towards me. 'Why don't you dae the one for your pa? Then you can tell him we did it together.'

I picked up a small brush and held my breath as I applied the paint. The way the paper seemed to suck the colour from my brush scared me, so I was glad to finish and lay the brush down. 'I'll leave you to do the spots. The very thought of making a mistake when we're so nearly finished makes my hand shake.'

We washed and dried all the items and replaced them in the box. Aunt Leonora's gig pulled up outside.

'Mrs Birnie has a high shelf in the cupboard where we can let your pa's painting dry,' Annie said.

'I'll take the box out to the trap,' I said. 'Back in a minute.'

I stowed the box under the seat.

'Successful painting afternoon?' Aunt Leonora asked.

'Very,' I replied. 'Annie, who was one of Mrs Birnie's

pupils, is a talented artist, and it is she who has the skill to do the flower drawings.'

'How interesting. May I see?'

'We planned to leave the sketch here to dry, since we're going on to Culdees Castle, but I can bring it out to show you.'

I raced back to the schoolroom, where I met Annie on her way out with her opened sketchbook in her hand. 'I'm taking it to show Struan,' she explained.

'Excellent. Can I show Aunt Leanora the orchid from your sketchbook, too? Come. Let me introduce you.'

'Oh, no, I dinnae think…'

'Don't be shy, she doesn't bite. Here, lean on my arm and give me your book.' I held the sketchbook, leaving Annie a free hand for her stick. I could see curiosity in my aunt's eyes as we approached the gig.

'Aunt Leonora, this is Annie Cooper. I'm so very lucky to find such a talented artist to help me with Papa's request.' I handed over the sketchbook, open at the last entry.

'So this is the orchid your father is excited about. What's so special about it?'

'The large size and rarity,' I replied.

Aunt Leonora glanced up. 'Iris is right, you have a remarkable talent, young lady. Shouldn't we take the drawing to Culdees, Iris? I expect Mr Speir would be highly interested.'

'I believe Papa might prefer to keep his quest secret until he finds the plant he seeks,' I replied.

'Of course,' Aunt Leonora said. 'Well, Speir is bound to be in a state of high excitement. His message said that his hothouse extension is finished.'

Struan's cart appeared in the lane. Annie bobbed a curtsey. 'My brother is here tae take me home now. It was a pleasure tae meet you, Ma'am.'

An idea struck me. 'Am I right that you live in Muthill?' I asked.

Annie nodded.

'Might we take Annie with us, Aunt? I'd love her to show her how my father's garden at Culdees Castle is coming together. Surely it would be no trouble to drop her in the village on our way home?'

'I don't see why not,' Aunt Leonora replied.

Annie frowned. 'I'd have tae see what my brother says.'

'Please tell him we can have you home before dark. The garden has some lovely plants already. I'm sure you'd find a subject to sketch.'

Aunt Leonora looked pensive as she watched Annie limp over to the cart. 'I recognise that boy. Is Annie related to old Mr Cooper, the Drummond Castle gardener?'

'His daughter. She is an orphan now.'

My aunt sighed. 'He was an excellent gardener and Annie seems like a nice girl, but I'm not sure they are really the kind of people you should be mixing with, Iris.'

I clenched my fists. 'She shares my interest in plants and I like her a great deal. Who are the people you would prefer me to mix with? I'm hardly inundated with invitations.'

'There is no need for such a tone, Iris. It seems you have entirely forgotten your manners. I fear the need to find you some society acquaintances is urgent,' my aunt replied with a glare, then rearranged her face to give Annie a welcoming smile.

'Sorry, Aunt Leonora,' I muttered. Struan's thunderous expression told me that my aunt was not the only one who objected to my friendship with Annie.

We came through the avenue of yews leading up to Culdees Castle. Mr Speir was standing in the sunken parterre garden with an extraordinarily handsome man by his side. This person was dressed entirely in black. His dark hair was oiled back off his face and his hands rested on an ebony cane, revealing that he was missing the smallest finger on his right hand. He smiled at us, exposing a white flash of teeth against his bronzed skin.

Mr Speir held out his hand to help my aunt descend from the gig. 'Lady Walker, Iris, welcome. It's my pleasure to introduce you to Mr Rafael de Rias. Señor Rias has brought a delivery of orchids from London. Just look at this new design of Wardian case.'

I was sure that Mr Speir would not usually introduce his delivery men, but this foreigner's direct gaze and straight back implied he was a gentleman. The wooden Wardian case at his feet had louvred wooden slats across the glass windows. This innovation would obviously protect the glass and also provide shade. An ingenious idea. The disadvantage was no clear view of the plants inside, so my curiosity was heightened by a tantalising glimpse of brightly coloured orchids.

'How exciting,' Aunt Leanora replied. 'Iris has brought her young friend, Annie, to see the gardens, Mr Speir.'

The foreign gentleman made an extravagant bow, before offering Annie and me his hand to help us descend. I could have sworn that he applied more gentle pressure to my fingers than was strictly necessary.

Chapter Nine

June 1869

We stood at the edge of the garden looking back at the Culdees Castle. The renovations Mr Speir had commissioned in recent years included a large extension and the addition of round turrets with spires. Papa had told me that this investment and the garden plans had been spurred on by Mr Speir's marriage the year before.

'I'd like to show you some new trees we've put in, ladies,' Mr Speir said. 'Follow me.' Mr Speir was physically unremarkable compared to the foreign visitor. A bearded young man whose brown hair was already receding, however his enthusiasm for his garden energised his appearance and I was so grateful he'd offered my papa a fresh start.

The foreign gentleman walked beside us, carrying the awkwardly large wooden box in front of him as if it contained the crown jewels.

Annie looked up at the high pink-hued sandstone walls. 'Such a bonny castle,' she murmured.

I offered her my arm to lean on and let the others walk ahead. I sensed she was nervous, trying to minimise her limp.

'We should try to get a look at Señor de Rias's orchids,' I whispered. 'It would be useful for my father to know which specimens Mr Speir has bought, so he can focus on acquiring something different.'

Annie nodded.

Mr Speir walked round the far end of the house and stopped beside a grove of coniferous saplings. 'These little trees are giant sequoia from America,' he said. 'Apparently, they live even longer than our yews and grow to huge size.'

I stepped forward to feel the frondy foliage between my fingers, quite unlike the needles of our native conifers. '*Wellingtonia gigantea*. I've seen an illustration of this enormous tree in the back copies of *Curtis's*. Will it really grow here in Scotland?'

Mr Speir smiled. 'Iris is the daughter of Mr Finlay, my plant hunter,' he explained to the visitor. 'I'm assured it will,' he said to me. 'Perhaps you and Annie will live to see them get close to the two or three hundred feet I'm told they can attain.'

'I'm very impressed by your botanical knowledge, *Señorita*.' Señor de Rias's voice was deep and seemed to drip with honey.

Aunt Leonora must have noticed the gleam in his eye, because she moved to stand between us. 'I can hear from your accent you are not from our shores, sir,' she said.

I had to cough to stifle a snort. Everything about this exotic man screamed, 'Not British.'

'My family is in Spain,' he replied.

'Rafael's father is a Spanish viscount, Lady Walker,' Mr Speir interjected.

'So we should address you as Viscount de Rias?'

'I am the third son and not in line for the title. Also, my passion for plants took me away from my family many years ago, Lady Walker.' He gave Aunt Leonora the same intense gaze and blinked slowly, perhaps to draw attention to his long eyelashes.

Aunt Leonora raised her eyebrows. 'May we see the new orchids?'

I could have hugged her for asking, but Señor de Rias shook his head. 'Only what you can see through the glass, unfortunately. The sealed container maintains the special conditions. However, I do hope you will visit when all the plants are in. I will stay to assist the planting.' He extended his hand to include Annie and me, and Annie blushed under the intensity of his languorous gaze.

'Will you take some tea, Lady Walker?' Mr Speir asked.

'Thank you,' my aunt replied.

'May I take Annie to see the hothouses? She shares my interest in plants,' I asked.

'Of course,' Mr Speir gave me a warm smile.

'I will accompany you. I need to do a survey of progress today.'

A flicker of annoyance passed over Aunt Leonora's face, no doubt at the Spanish gentleman's forwardness.

'Could I borrow Mr Buchan to take us to the glasshouses, Aunt Leonora?' The walled kitchen garden and hothouses were only ten minutes from the castle, but I guessed the walk might be too much for Annie.

Aunt Leonora agreed and she and Mr Speir went inside. Señor de Rias held out his hand to help first Annie, and then me, into the trap. When he climbed in and sat beside me, Buchan turned around. His expression told me he doubted my aunt would approve. My cheeks burned. I was sure she would not, while my heart quickened at the warm pressure of his thigh against mine.

'Mr de Rias has brought some orchids from London,' I told Buchan. 'Can we drive slowly? The plants are very precious.'

49

Buchan glanced down at the large box, which was now wedged in front of our feet. He set the mare off at walking pace. A few minutes later, we pulled up in front of the walled garden to the right of the ornate and crenelated stable block and our companion helped us to alight.

'We'll not stay long, Mr Buchan. Lady Walker wants to leave within the half hour.' He nodded and led the horse and trap into the stable courtyard.

The Spanish gentleman led us towards an open doorway in the high garden wall. I glanced over my shoulder at the gardener's lodge. This should have been my home for the last two years. A happy life with my father seemed no closer.

The glasshouses against the back wall of the kitchen garden were almost as large as those at Drummond Castle. The main glass entrance was flanked by two long sections, both with another small hothouse jutting out at their ends.

'Each section will house species requiring a different temperature,' the Spaniard explained. 'The delicate orchids will be in the warmest room beyond the wall.'

He led us through the main entrance. Several workmen were on their hands and knees assembling the heating pipework. We entered the doorway set into the wall, emerging into another glasshouse. It was empty apart from a row of staked climbers leaning in one corner. 'Bougainvilleas to bring the colour of my homeland,' the Spaniard said.

I reached out to touch the bright pink flower and was surprised by its papery texture. 'Will you train them against the castle, Mr de Rias?' I asked. I leaned in to sniff the bloom, but there was no discernible scent.

'Please call me Rafael, *señorita*, no need for formality. We'll plant the bougainvillea in the hothouse first,' he answered. 'They can grow in England but Scotland's weather is too cold. I bring a climbing rose and a honeysuckle which are being planted beside the new pergola, if you looking for a scented plant. If we go back up to the castle garden I will show you.'

We walked back between the neatly laid out beds. There were all sorts of vegetables for the castle kitchens, as well as flowers to supply the housekeeper with blooms for both the big house and its chapel.

Back at the castle, Rafael led us into the garden. Culdees Castle was smaller than Drummond, but its sunken parterre garden was similarly laid out to give the best view from the family quarters. The pergola was a new addition and a junior gardener was busy training plants around its iron arches.

'How beautiful,' Annie murmured, when we stopped beside the pergola. She immediately got out her sketchbook. 'Do you mind?' she asked, looking at Rafael. 'This rose is so perfect, I want tae try and capture it.'

I gazed up in awe. 'I believe my father would love to have a drawing of the pergola. He told me it was in the plan.'

'Climbing rose on one side and honeysuckle on the other. Those were the instructions we were given,' Rafael added.

'*Lonicera caprifolium,*' I murmured, reaching up towards a red and pink honeysuckle bloom.

Rafael cupped the flower between his fingers. '*Exacte-mente.* Your expert knowledge and the Latin names tell me you are truly your father's daughter.'

As I turned to answer him, his fingers brushed against my cheek. Surely not an accident and shockingly I didn't care.

'We had this species in the manse garden,' I muttered towards my feet, not trusting myself to catch Annie's eye.

'What is this word, manz?' he asked.

'The Scottish term for the house associated with the

church. My father was a minister before he joined Mr Speir's team.'

'So you don't live in this church house now?'

'I live with Aunt Leonora in Drummond Castle, until my father returns.'

'Then I might see you when I visit. Mr Speir promise to take me to Drummond Castle to see their hothouses.'

'It's not very likely. Like here, the glasshouses are some distance from the house.'

'But you might meet my brother, Struan. He's a gardener there,' Annie said.

'I'll look out for him,' Rafael replied.

Annie sat down on a nearby bench to rest her sketchbook on her knees. I took the place beside her and the Spaniard looked over her shoulder.

'Bravo, *señorita*, you have talent.'

Annie shrugged without looking up. 'It's just a sketch. I'll make a better copy tae send tae Mr Finlay later.'

'May I see?' Rafael took the book from Annie's grasp without waiting for an answer. He flicked through the pages. 'You are a botanical illustrator,' he said in a surprised tone.

'I copy botanical illustrations,' she replied, 'although I'd love tae learn tae make my own sketches.'

'I am happy to help.' He handed Annie her book back. 'Let us walk round rest of the garden and you can tell me if there is a plant you to want try.'

We walked in silence until I saw Aunt Leonora waving at us from the first floor loggia. 'I believe my aunt is ready to leave.'

'I hope you will visit again soon. I expect to be here for many weeks,' Rafael said.

'I hope to visit the orchid house when it's ready. I'd like to be able to describe it to my father.'

'I will ask Mr Speir to send word.' He plucked two rose

buds from a nearby bush, then bowed and gave them to Annie and me in turn. 'It has been a great pleasure to meet you both,' he said in his purring accent. He locked eyes with me, as if trying to impart some secret message. A shiver scuttled down my back.

'What do you think of Señor de Rias?' I asked Annie as we walked to the gig.

'He's very handsome and certainly has a lot ae confidence.'

'Maybe the one is a consequence of the other, or perhaps because of his aristocratic background?'

'I've always found most gardeners tae be quiet men. My father, his colleagues, and Struan too.'

'My father can be talkative when he gets on a subject he is passionate about.'

'I have a feeling Struan wouldnae take tae this man.'

The thought of dour and grumpy Struan meeting this articulate gentleman made me smile. 'I think you're right.'

Aunt Leonora frowned as we approached. 'I hope you haven't been picking flowers in Mr Speir's garden,' she said.

'Mr de Rias gave them to us.'

My aunt pursed her lips. 'Be careful with that man. He is the sort who takes liberties,' she replied.

I resolved not to tell her he had volunteered to help us. Nor that I found the idea of close cooperation with the glamorous Spaniard quite thrilling.

'I don't think my aunt is a fan either,' I whispered to Annie, as I helped her up into the gig.

Chapter Ten

June 1869

Struan watched Annie climb into Lady Walker's trap and be driven off by Mr Buchan. No doubt his sister thought this proved him wrong about Miss Finlay's genuine friendship. He'd heard their exchange of words and it sounded true enough. It wasn't that he thought this girl malicious, but he feared the friendship wouldn't last.

Annie arrived home with her eyes sparkling with happiness. She sat outside their cottage in the fading light of the evening and expanded on her sketches.

Struan looked over her shoulder. 'Those are good, Annie. Honeysuckle and a climbing rose.'

'It's a new pergola at Culdees. Iris's father designed the plan and she wants tae send him a drawing.' She closed her sketchbook and went inside. Annie moved the lamb stew she'd started this morning back onto the range. They tried to have a wee bit of meat on a Sunday, then she'd mix in today's leftover potatoes and some oats with onions to make it into stovies the next night. Struan set their bowls and spoons on the table. In the middle was a single pink rose in one of their ma's egg cups.

'Mr Spier is going for roses then? That's no a climber.'

'He is, there's a whole section for rose bushes. It's going to be lovely when they all bloom.' Annie leaned over to smell the rosebud, something in her eyes made Struan uncomfortable. 'Speir gave you the rosebud?'

'No, one of his new workers.'

An evasive answer. Struan was quite certain no ordinary gardener would be authorised to go plucking his master's roses for a lassie. He was reluctant to ask which gardener. He'd seen a stranger visiting Drummond Castle gardens with Mr Speir. The man dressed like a toff. He and Jock had laughed when Mr MacDonald told them the man claimed to be a gardener up from London. A gardener who wore a top hat and carried a cane was maybe just the kind of man to take liberties with the stock. Things between him and Annie had been so open, had his anger over Iris Finlay driven them apart? Was she mixing with strangers from London now too? Annie remained distracted throughout the evening.

'Do you think I might go tae Innerpeffray this week?' Annie said as she prepared for bed. 'Iris has got hold ae of some paints and I want tae colour up the sketch tae send tae her father.'

He watched her back as she brushed her hair. There was a determined straightness, something in her thoughts beyond this moment. If he could gain her trust again would she tell him?

'I'll ask Mr MacDonald.'

It wasn't difficult. Mr MacDonald sought him out the very next day. 'I've a rose I want tae show you, Struan. Yer pa would have been excited, I'm hoping you will feel the same.' In a quiet corner of one of the greenhouses, Roderick MacDonald kept the bank of both pink and white Scottish roses that formed his obsession. He parted the multiple stems of one of the white bushes, to reveal a single rose well hidden in the centre of the plant, the same colour as the others but the white petals were all tinged with pink. 'Oh, it's bonny.' Struan knelt beside the plant to examine it more closely. He thought it one of the loveliest flowers he'd ever seen.

'It's so hidden I missed it budding. Only one flower isnae enough but it proves the thing possible. I've a reason tae ask if you'd like tae help me, Struan.' MacDonald held his hand out in front of him. There was an almost imperceptible tremor, Struan had noticed it of late but would never had said. 'Fertilising such a small rose takes patience and a steady hand. If we work together we might have a reliable new rose we could show the laird next year.'

'It would be an honour, Mr MacDonald.'

'Good. Come in early tomorrow and I'll show you how it's done.'

Struan nodded. He might have rushed home to tell Annie but her thoughts were elsewhere. He'd wait tae see if his new duties might improve their money situation.

'How is yer sister?' Mr MacDonald seemed to read his thoughts.

'She has a new art project, drawing flewers for Miss Finaly's pa. She's hoping tae get tae Innerpeffray tae paint them up during the week.'

'I'm sorry I cannae give you the cart every weekend. But take it after work this week. I'd love tae see her drawings when she's done. Is Mr Finlay still away in Ecuador finding plants for Culdees?

'Aye. Annie's been tae visit the new garden and she's drawing it tae send tae him.'

'Lord de Eresby is most interested in the mission. I think he maybe put some money intae the project.' They left the greenhouse, closing the door behind them. 'Seems odd tae me, when we've such wondrous plants here at home.'

Struan rose half an hour earlier every day, to get free time with Mr MacDonald. His sister got dressed and left early too.

'I'm sorry if I woke you, Annie.'

'I wanted tae be up. It's good tae make the maist ae the light mornings for work, then I've got the long evenings for drawing.'

'I'm awfy busy too but Mr MacDonald says I can take you tae Innerpeffray this week.' Struan was rewarded with a broad smile.

'That's kind ae him.'

'I'll call past in the aifternoon for an early bite tae eat and take you there. Will Mrs Birnie let you hang on a bit longer? I'll return tae work and might no be back when the library session is over.'

'It'll be fine. I'm doing the painting in the schoolroom anyway. A library's no the place for paints.'

Struan was content that he'd kept Annie happy, so was in good spirits all day Friday. When it rained in torrents during the afternoon, Mr Macdonald let the whole team go home at five. Struan had no good excuse for not joining everyone in The Drummond's public bar for ale and some laughter. Calum's fiddling was grand and he joined in the singing of 'The Bonnie Lass o Fyvie'. It was only just gone half past six when he left, but being unused to drinking, he was aware his progress home to Muthill was slower than it should have been. He was surprised to find Annie at the table drawing.

'Sorry I'm late, I went for a drink wi' the lads.'

'Is it late? I'd lost track of time.' Annie jumped up. 'I've got us a wee bit of haddock. I'll put on the tatties, the fish will take no time.'

'Would you like me tae peel?'

Annie screwed up her nose and pushed him towards his chair. 'You stink ae beer and tobacco, I'm no trusting you wi' a knife.' It was said in a laughing way, so her good mood had held.

'What are you drawing? I thought the pergola painting was finished yesterday? He picked up her sketchpad from their wee table, it featured the inside of a honeysuckle flower.

'If I'm to sketch botany properly I need tae practise drawing the insides ae the flower too. It's a shame it's too wet tae draw outside today.'

'How was work?'

'Just the same. Tomorrow will be hard though, with everyone trailing their feet through all this rain.'

'I wish you didnae have tae dae such back-breaking work.'

'Your work is worse and the hours are longer,' she replied.

Struan laid his wages on the table. 'A bit short this week. I had a couple ae ales. Sorry.'

'Och, Struan, it's fine.'

After dinner he fell asleep in his chair and woke up in the dark. Annie was already in bed. He had a terrible drooth and the ale tasted stale in his mouth. He had enjoyed the singing but he'd likely regret the drink when he was up at dawn in the morning.

Chapter Eleven

June 1869

The following Sunday, the Drummond Castle inhabitants were all away in Edinburgh, so I slipped into the church pew beside Mr and Mrs Birnie. 'The new edition of *Curtis's* is finally in,' she whispered.

'Can I take it down to Annie in the schoolroom? She's been working on a drawing of Mr Speir's pergola and is ready to add some colour.'

Mrs Birnie smiled and nodded.

The minister began his sermon. Mr Speir and his young wife sat near the front of the church, I hadn't a clear view of her face but admired her bonnet embellished with small, blue silk flowers. Her hair pulled at the nape of her neck, revealed her to be fair like me. There was no sign of Rafael, but I guessed the Spaniard was most likely Catholic. Church of Scotland people disapprove of Episcopalians, describing their practices as too Popish, but Aunt Leonora's congregation deplore the Catholics too. The godly folk in Scotland had a talent for division.

Annie and Struan walked ahead of us out of the church. Struan was already driving off in his cart when we got outside and Annie and I climbed into the Birnies' gig, Annie handed me her sketchbook. I opened it to a pretty pencil sketch of the pergola. I was surprised to see transected views of both the rose and honeysuckle flowers in the bottom corners.

'How did you manage that?'

Annie screwed up her face. 'It was the strangest thing. Mr de Rias left them wi' a note at my workplace. The house-keeper, Mrs Nichol, said he'd turned up asking for me the previous afternoon. She wasnae best pleased.'

'How did he know where you worked? Did Struan tell him?'

'I'm quite sure he didnae. I asked Struan if a foreign gentleman had visited Drummond Castle Gardens, and he said, aye. Said that man was the maist unlikely looking gardener he'd ever seen.'

'What did he say about the flowers?'

'I didnae tell Struan. It would only rile him. The other maids were awfy curious, having seen the man. They thought I had a secret admirer. I showed them the cut up flower buds tae silence them, and they all laughed their heads off. Said if that was the Spanish idea ae sending flowers tae a lassie, then they'd stick wi' Scottish lads.'

Mrs Birnie and I both laughed.

'What's funnier is I was mair pleased wi' the gift than if it had been a whole bunch ae flowers. I really want tae practise drawing like a proper illustrator.'

In the schoolroom, Annie opened up the paintbox and set about applying colour to her sketch. *Curtis's* magazine lay unopened on the desk in front of me. I'd looked forward to being here all week and now I was tetchy and discontented. I pushed back my chair and went to the window.

The crops in the fields beyond the River Earn swayed in the breeze. A large magpie strutted across the grass in front of the window, his iridescent feathers shining in the sunshine.

This handsome bird had a bad reputation. A murderous thief who eats baby chicks. Revolting but a scientific view would recognise the success of that strategy.

My inner turmoil needed honest analysis. Rafael had sought out Annie instead of me, and it left a bitter taste in my mouth. This was an unreasonable and ridiculous reaction. He'd brought her something to help her in her work, when I'd no need of his help. I hated the notion of sharing Annie, too, but that was selfish. She was talented and deserved every opportunity.

When I turned back from the window, Annie was an image of concentration. Her straw bonnet hanging on the back of Mrs Birnie's chair, she was bent over the desk with her face hidden making light brush strokes with one hand, while her other hand was thrust into her dark curls, causing her hair to escape from its pins. She looked up and smiled as at me.

I smiled back, sat beside her, and opened *Curtis's*. 'I'll look for another image for you to practise on.'

'Are there any orchids? I want tae be ready for the challenge ae copying the precious plants in Mr de Rias's glass box.'

'There's this one from Costa Rica. *Ondontoglossum krameri*.'

We looked together at the cream coloured orchid. Its many flowers had violet-red centres and large over-arching leaves.

'Oh, that's so bonny. It'll take me ages tae draw and colour, but I'll have a go.' Annie squeezed my hand.

'Why not take the magazine home with you? There's still plenty of daylight in the evenings. Take the paintbox too.'

Annie smiled sadly and shook her head. 'Not in our poor wee house. It's mair ae a lean-to really, wi' tiny windows and in the constant shadow ae the houses around it, I cannae draw there.' She screwed up her face and went back to her painting.

I was a complete dolt. 'I'm sorry, Annie. You must imagine my life to be very grand living in a castle, but my room is tiny.'

Annie gave me a sceptical look.

'But I do realise my good fortune,' I muttered.

'Ours was a house full tae the brim wi' love when my parents were alive, and at least Struan and I have been able tae keep staying there. It has happy memories. Anyway, you are right about the light evenings. I'll try tae get back here during the week.'

A few days later, I was reading in Aunt Leonora's room. She encouraged me to use the extra space when she was away. I jumped to my feet when Lady Willoughby de Eresby rapped on the door and came in.

'Welcome home, Your Ladyship,' I said.

'Leonora's not here?'

'I believed she was in Edinburgh with you?'

'Of course,' Lady Willoughby's fingers went to her forehead. 'This is her week for going to meet her friend. I forgot.'

I had no idea what she was talking about, so I made no reply.

'Could you ask her to come to see me when she returns? I'm choosing new drapes and I want her opinion.'

I nodded and curtseyed. When she left, I laid down my book and paced the room, puzzling over Aunt Leonora's whereabouts. I was sure she had given me the impression that she was with the Willoughby de Eresby family. Why the secrecy? Was it possible that her friend was a man?

Searching for clues I picked up a blue glass bottle with a white label from her dressing table. *Acqua Distilllata Alle Rose tonico rinfrescate*. A skin tonic. One sniff of the almost empty bottle confirmed this as the source of Aunt Leonora's signature rose scent. Was it unusual for an aging lady to use a skin tonic? I'd never given any thought to my aunt's single status. She was an attractive woman in her late forties. It wasn't beyond the realm of possibility that she might marry again. Would that leave me homeless?

The clench in my stomach was surely an overreaction. My aunt cared for me but might some new man put pressure on her? Lack of financial independence made me vulnerable. Could I support myself? Mr MacDonald had some women in his team of Drummond Castle gardeners, but they probably earned even less than Struan. In any case, although I had lots of horticultural knowledge, I wasn't skilled as a gardener. I had some fluency in Latin and French. Could I use that? Perhaps as a governess? I knew Aunt Leonora hoped she might find a way to introduce me to a promising husband but it didn't seem likely. I never met any bachelors at all, never mind one who would want an awkward girl with no money. I'd have to hope I was safe here until my father returned.

Aunt Leonora arrived back the next afternoon. I went up when I heard her footsteps in the room above. She was looking in the overmantel mirror with her hat in her hand.

Taking the hairpin from her mouth, she met my eyes in the reflection. 'Buchan tells me that Clementina returned yesterday.'

'Yes. She asked if you would go to see her on your return. Was your friend well?' I might as well get it out in the open.

Aunt Leonora held my gaze. 'She was.' She pinned back a stray lock of hair.

At least I could stop worrying about her getting married. Aunt Leonora's next remark confounded me again.

'In fact, you will meet George next month.' She smiled broadly, perhaps at my shocked expression. 'Georgina is going to visit me in Drummond Castle. She is on the Queen's staff and will meet Her Majesty off the train in Perth later this month. Such details are a secret, of course, so please don't repeat them outside this room. George is coming ahead to ensure Balmoral is ready, so she'll squeeze in a visit to me.'

'Your friend works for Her Majesty? How very exciting.'

'She does, although I'm not sure that she would describe it as exciting. I on the other hand, am very excited. George and I have been friends since girlhood and meeting twice in so many weeks is cause for celebration. The Queen keeps her very busy.'

'Does Lady Willoughby de Eresby know about the royal visit? She mentioned choosing new drapes.'

'If we were to have a royal visit, we would need more than just new drapes. They built a whole tented pavilion when the Queen and Prince Albert came here twenty-five years ago. Unfortunately, although the Queen spends many months in Scotland, she ceased all house visits after Prince Albert's death. Georgina's life might be less dull if they got out more.'

'Did you speak to the Queen when she visited the castle? I would love to meet her.'

'I was present at the banquet, but I wasn't introduced.'

'But still, you saw her. Even to see her from afar would be a story to tell my papa. I fear my letters are very dull.'

Aunt Leonora looked thoughtful. 'I will ask Lady de Eresby if I might be spared overnight and perhaps arrange for us to meet Georgina in Perth. I imagine she might be able to arrange for you to witness Her Majesty's arrival.'

'Thank you. I would love to meet your friend too. Did Mama know her?'

'No, but they met at Archibald's funeral.'

Leonora came over and put her hands on my shoulders. 'I

promised your father to introduce you to society, and I have failed utterly. I'll take you to Perth and look for a way to get you out more. Eighteen is an age for parties and soirees, something more fun than church and a tiny library.'

I smiled. 'I'm not eighteen until September.' The truth was that I was never happier than in Innerpeffray Library with Annie at my side.

Chapter Twelve

June 1869

At the end of the month, Mr Speir sent word that his hothouses were functioning and invited us to view his new specimens. On the morning of the planned visit Aunt Leonora was confined to bed with stomach pains.

I sat on the edge of her bed. 'I'll send Mr Buchan to Culdees Castle with our apologies.'

She tried to push up onto her elbows, but winced and fell back. 'You go without me. I know how much you've been looking forward to it. Mr Speir expects you and Mr Buchan will see you safely there and back.'

'Thank you. Is there anything I can get you before I go? You've had no breakfast.'

'Perhaps a tisane with honey. I've no appetite.'

Once in the trap, I asked Mr Buchan to stop in Muthill village. I'd told Annie to meet us, but was relieved not to have to ask Aunt Leonora. We arrived to find Annie waiting on a bench beside the village green. I jumped down to help her up into the gig.

'Aunt Leonora is indisposed this morning. We could easily have come up to your house to collect you and save you the walk. We'll drop you there on the way back.'

'There really is nae need. It's only just round the corner, but the lane is narrow and awkward tae get up, even in this wee gig.'

There was nobody outside when we reached Culdees Castle. I was about to climb down and ring the bell when the two men came around the side of the house, deep in conversation, and Mr Speir was laughing. 'There you are,' Mr Speir said. 'I'd begun to think you weren't coming.'

'Lady Walker sends her regrets, Mr Speir. She is a little under the weather.'

'I'm sorry to hear that. Please tell her to call in when she feels better. I'll leave Rafael to show you his precious hothouses, I've already done my turn around them today.'

Rafael got into our gig. This time, Buchan's relaxed shoulders indicated he had accepted the Spaniard's right to be there. We alighted at the walled garden and Rafael held out his elbows to take our arms. This was unnecessarily familiar, but he did take care to walk slowly for Annie's benefit. We entered the hothouse entrance on the far left. I breathed in the scent of exotic plants when he closed the glasshouse door behind us. A metal grate above a drain ran through the floor along the length of the greenhouse. The path and the channel beneath it were lined with fine gravel. Our shoes caused a scrunch to echo off the glass. It seemed a shame to have disturbed such a tranquil place.

Rafael gestured around. 'The climate in each section of

the greenhouses simulates nature. This is the coolest and driest room, suitable for those plants from high mountainous regions. You might like this variety of *Saxifraga*. It is new to this country. We may try it outside once the weather improves.'

We admired the specimens from Southern Europe and the Americas in the second glasshouse, before entering through the door in the wall into the final section. Here the air was very humid, and the musky warmth had a very particular smell. In the furthest corner beside the wall, there was a profusion of orchid plants.

'Oh, my,' Annie murmured.

'Mr Speir had some plants sent from a nursery in Edinburgh. The more unusual specimens I brought up from London are on the right.'

The orchids were pretty, but none of them had flowers bigger than two inches, nothing even close to the giant species my father sought. As we stood in front of Rafael's orchids, one of them shed a tiny flower. It was a beautiful plant with a hanging stem loaded with over twenty flowers. He picked up the pale yellow bloom between his thumb and forefinger.

'*Angræcum citratum* has given you a gift, Miss Annie. If you would like to draw the plant I can dissect the flower for you.'

Annie nodded, then got out her sketchbook immediately and started to draw.

'I'll prepare the flower before it starts to fade. You'll find me in the gardener's lodge.'

'The lodge?' I asked, but Rafael had already closed the greenhouse door behind him.

Annie looked up from her drawing. 'Isnae that the house Mr Speir promised tae you?'

I struggled to reply. 'Yes. But I suppose it makes no sense

to leave it empty when this gentleman needs somewhere to stay.' That was the reasonable answer. Envy and self-pity twisted in my stomach to a physical pain.

When Annie had captured the orchid's graceful curves, we made our way to the gardener's lodge, a single-storey dwelling in the same rose-coloured sandstone. The tiny garden was overgrown with shrubs and threaded with large, heavy-headed roses. A heavily-scented Queen of Denmark rose climbed up a trellis, and framed the door. The sight of this cottage conjured thoughts of all the challenges I'd faced in the last two years. A longing for Papa brought a lump to my throat. I stopped on the doorstep, unable to face going in. I was searching for some excuse to leave when Rafael opened the door.

'Welcome to my home,' he said, ushering us in with his arm.

I'd only been inside the lodge once, the week before we'd left the manse and when I had imagined myself about to become mistress of this house.

'Excuse the mean dimensions of this simple place,' he said.

I sensed Annie's glance at me, but didn't turn. The lodge consisted of a sitting room, two small bedrooms, and a scullery. The son of a viscount might find it mean, but I'd hoped to call it my home and I guessed it was many times larger than Annie's home.

Rafael led us into the front room. He'd set a desk and chair in the window. The orchid flower lay neatly divided on a blotting pad. Two freshly sharpened pencils were lined up beside it.

'You can take the flower with you to match the colour, but

the form will fade quickly now it's cut. You might want to sketch it now,' he said.

'You've gone tae so much trouble. Thank you,' Annie replied in a quiet voice.

'It's my pleasure to encourage your talent. You are welcome to come here as often as you can get away. You might work through the orchids one-by-one. I will collect any fallen flowers and leave the table set up and the cottage unlocked.'

Annie blushed to the roots of her hair. 'I dinnae know what tae say. You are too kind.'

Rafael turned to me. 'You might be interested in these magazines. It's a Belgian publication.'

I sat down on the threadbare couch and picked up the one of the magazines. The *Journal d'Horticulture Practique de Belgique* professed itself to be a guide for amateurs and gardeners.

Rafael squeezed in beside me, then leaned over to turn the pages to the first colour illustration. 'This *helianthemum* is pretty.'

He flicked through the illustrations one by one. I couldn't concentrate because my mind was engulfed by other senses. His thigh's warmth next to mine and the most delicious smell. My father never wore cologne, plain soap considered sufficient for a man of the cloth, but this man wore a heady perfume. Top notes of lemons most definitely, oranges too, with underlying scents of rosemary and something woody. I struggled to resist the urge to move even closer. When I looked up at him, he raised one eyebrow and smiled.

Annie shifted in her chair, breaking the spell. I took the magazine from his hands and went to sit alone on the window seat. My aunt had told me he was not the kind of man to trust. All my instincts were telling me I didn't care. I flicked through the pages, willing my heartrate to slow. The colour illustrations were not as fine as *Curtis's,* but the magazine set me thinking. Might there be a market for an English magazine for amateur gardeners? I didn't have Annie's drawing skill, but I loved writing. *Curtis's* was academic and serious. Wouldn't something more descriptive appeal to a wide range of readers? Could this be the source of income we needed?

Chapter Thirteen

June 1869

The next morning, I was surprised when one of the maids brought up a note to my bedroom. I never received any post. My father's letters always came via Mr Speir. The paper was folded but unsealed. Miss Iris Finlay, was written in bold and flowing handwriting. The maid hovered, her wide-eyes betraying her curiosity. I guessed she had witnessed the sender deliver the note. The distinctive scent betrayed his identity.

'Were you asked to wait for a reply, Jenny?'

'No, Miss.' She sighed, but took the hint.

I waited for the door to close behind her before I unfolded the paper.

Dear Miss Finlay

Mr Speir has asked me to advise Mr MacDonald on the care of the orchid he has donated to the Drummond Castle collection. You will find me in the glasshouses if you are free to come down. I have another magazine I believe might interest you.

Yours,

Rafael de Rias

. . .

I glanced over at my mother's brass carriage clock. This wedding gift was the sole ornament on my tiny mantelpiece. I'd breakfasted with Aunt Leonora and my time was my own for the next hour. I snatched my bonnet and pinned it in place. There was no opportunity to change my green dress, since Aunt Leonora had already seen it, and in any case, I didn't think my grey dress was more flattering. In the mirror, my eyes sparkled with excitement, and my complexion had lost its usual pallor. I pinched my cheeks, grabbed my parasol and fled down the stairs and into the courtyard, taking the right-hand path to skirt the empty parterre garden out of sight from the family's windows. A glance back at the house revealed no sign of life. I passed through a gate, and down steps to the orchard and hothouses. There, I stopped and tried to steady myself. It wouldn't do to arrive out of breath. I didn't go directly to the glasshouses, not wishing to reveal I'd been summoned. Not to Mr MacDonald and most especially not to Struan Cooper, who might be nearby. I put up my parasol. There was little strength to the sun this early in the morning, but my cheeks felt flushed. Perhaps a post breakfast stroll was a feasible cover story.

I came around the corner of the potting shed adjoined to the hothouses. Struan stood in the open doorway with his arms crossed, his dark eyebrows scrunched over his eyes in that now familiar scowl.

'You'll find the Spanish gentleman wi' Mr MacDonald beside the orchids,' he said.

I gritted my teeth, annoyed both at his assumption that I was looking for Rafael and the futility of denying it. I nodded my acknowledgement, holding my head high until I turned the corner. There was no time to regather my wits. Rafael and

Mr MacDonald emerged from a door further down the path, and the Spaniard raised his cane to wave a greeting.

'Miss Finlay,' Mr MacDonald said with a touch to his cap peak.

'What a lovely walking morning it is,' I replied, refurling my parasol and waving it towards the meadows beyond the orchard. It was a ridiculous pretence that I'd come to this working part of the garden as part of a normal stroll.

Rafael smiled at me. 'How lucky to see you, Miss Finlay. I have another edition of the Belgian magazine you admired.'

I took the magazine Rafael held out to me. 'Thank you.'

'I show you the orchid we give to Lord de Willoughby.' He offered me his elbow without waiting for my answer. I glanced towards Mr MacDonald, but he dropped his gaze. 'Good day, Miss Finlay,' he said, before walking away.

I allowed Rafael to guide me into the glasshouse. To be here at his side and alone was most definitely what I'd hoped for, but I was uncomfortable. Perspiration gathered on the back of my neck. It was much too hot in here on such a sunny day and also something in his words struck a raw nerve. He'd used the word 'we', as if he were a trusted member of Mr Speir's team, almost as if they were equals. But what about my father?

I decided to broach the subject. 'I believe the Willoughby de Eresby family suggested the appointment of my father as the most suitable manager for Mr Speir's garden project. Papa was doubly delighted when this led to the opportunity to seek prize specimens overseas.'

Rafael appeared oblivious to the deliberate barb regarding my father's position. Instead, he looked into my eyes. He placed his hand over mine, where it rested on my parasol handle. 'You must miss him.'

Those gentle words in his velvet voice struck straight to the heart of my loneliness. To my horror, tears blurred my vision. Rafael placed his arm around my shoulder and steered me to the bench in the corner. He sat sideways, facing towards me, so our knees touched. I inched back in my seat and wiped away the tears with my gloved fingers. In my haste, I'd left my room without a handkerchief. Rafael's dark brown eyes were full of sympathy. As if he read my mind, he handed me his own handkerchief.

'Tell me about your father. This make you feel better.'

'He is a very good man. He was a minster, you know,' I said.

'You told me.' Rafael smiled.

'Papa was bereft when Mama died. I couldn't imagine how he would ever get over it, but this expedition had been so all-consuming. I can tell from his letters that his spirits have improved.'

'Your father must be a very brave man. The jungles and mountains of Ecuador have amazing plants but also much danger.'

I looked at him in surprise. 'You've been to Ecuador?'

'Sorry. I do not wish to frighten you. I'm sure your father is safe but a man needs to be brave to cope with extreme weather. I have done some plant hunting in the southern Andes.'

'I'm sure Ecuador has a challenging climate, however, my father's letters describe it as extraordinarily beautiful too.'

'Spectacular. I expect he tells you of many undiscovered species.'

He was leaning towards me. The delicious smell of his cologne worked its spell. His expression said I was the most important and interesting person in the world. Somehow, our knees were touching again. The urge to lean towards him almost overwhelmed me. A drop of perspiration slithered between my breasts inside my dress.

I stood up. 'You were going to show me an orchid, Señor de Rias.'

He displayed not one hint of embarrassment. 'Of course. Just here.'

Three steps took us to the plant. 'Shall we ask it for a gift for your little friend?'

He grasped my wrist lightly, and in one swift movement, pulled my glove off from the fingertips. He shook the plant stem and sure enough, a single bloom fell off onto my palm.

'It's *Angræcum citratum*. Annie sketched this one already.'

'You are right. Then this flower is for you.' He released my wrist, then placed his other hand beneath mine, to cup my fingers over the orchid flower.

As he raised my hand towards his face, I realised he was going to kiss it at the exact moment I remembered I was inside walls of glass. I snatched my hand away. Beyond the glass, Struan thrust his spade into the ground. Heat, confusion, embarrassment and an unfamiliar sensation I had to admit was desire, collided with disappointment.

'I must get back, Señor de Rias. My aunt is expecting me.'

'That is a pity. But please, beautiful Iris, call me Rafael.'

'Thank you for the magazine, Rafael. I shall return it.'

'You know where to find me. I will expect you.' His expression of longing, was more imploring than a simple invitation. Doffing his hat, he gave a slight bow, before leaving the glasshouse and striding up the path heading towards the stables. My mouth was dry and my heart pounded. Perhaps I might have raced after Rafael, but Struan, his broad shoulders bent over his spade, stood between me and the stables path.

Reluctantly, I turned back to the castle. At the top of the steps into the parterre level, I saw Aunt Leonora coming towards me and I pulled my glove back on before we met beside the central sundial.

She put her hand over her eyes and peered towards the hill leading to the stables. 'Is that Señor de Rias?' she asked.

'Yes. He came to talk to Mr MacDonald about an orchid gift from Mr Spier.'

She narrowed her eyes. 'What have you in your hand?'

'It's a plant catalogue from Belgium.' I hoped she might assume I'd borrowed it from Mr MacDonald.

'A gift from the Spaniard?' she asked.

'A loan,' I admitted. 'I shall return it.'

'No need. I plan to visit Mr Speir after we've been to Perth. Now hurry up to your room. Buchan is coming to take us into Crieff and you need to change your gloves.'

Looking down at my glove, I saw a yellow stain on the palm. Back in my room, I stifled a cry of distress as I peeled off the glove and the crushed orchid flower fell to the floor. Rafael de Rias set my head in a spin. I feared he was trying to insert himself into Mr Speir's inner circle, which must surely threaten my father's position. On the other hand, his nearness filled me with elation, and I craved his touch. I must find a way to visit him.

Chapter Fourteen

July 1869

Struan hadn't been able to find time for the roses this morning. A long dry spell had left the garden parched. For the third day in a row, the whole team were out watering from six in the morning to get through as much as possible in the cooler part of the day. There was a system of pipes bringing water down from the house, but still, the many beds had to be done by watering can. It was back-breaking work. As it got hotter, Struan poured water over his cap and put it back on his head to cool down. The main part of his day was set aside for the summer trim of the topiary bushes. He needed step ladders to reach the conifers and had to get on his hands and knees for the box hedges and balls. Tough work in sunshine, but a job he enjoyed. Drummond Castle Gardens were famous for the topiary and they had some excellent specimens. He worked alone with his shears in hand. The sense of satisfaction when he looked out at the order he'd achieved, made him smile. On the way home he called into Jimmy the blacksmith's. He had a stone he used to sharpen his small shears but Jimmy had a grand wheel for honing the long ones.

'I'll pick them up before work,' he said.

'No need. I'll get straight to it and call past wi' them on my way home.'

Jimmy was a gossip and always looking for an excuse for a chat. 'Well, you'd be welcome. I've no ale in but I'm sure Annie will make you a cup ae tea.'

'That'd be grand, Struan. I saw the lass this aifternoon. It's great she can manage a walk in this nice weather.'

'It is,' Struan replied, although he wondered where Annie was going. She rarely ventured out after she got back from her maid's work in the early afternoon.

Annie gave him a big smile and offered him tea when he got home. Her good mood had lasted but he noticed shadows under her eyes. 'You'd better fill the kettle full, Jimmy is bringing in my shears soon.' Annie turned her back to swing the kettle onto the range. 'He said he'd seen you oot,' Struan said.

'Aye, I walked past him yesterday.'

'He said he saw you today. What's taking ye oot in the aifternoons?'

'Just drawing.'

She brought him his tea. He covered her hand with his. 'Watch you dinnae overdo it, Annie.'

Struan worried all night but managed not to nag Annie. He knew she hated it. Iris Finlay must surely have taken Annie to and from the library to allow her out to paint two days running. Annie would never confess to frailty but her condition meant her chest was weak. She'd once caught a feverous lung infection in childhood and the doctor had warned they might lose her. Their mother had been strict about not letting her overdo it. Annie was old enough to make her own choices now and insisted she was stronger than he imagined. Struan wished they could afford for her to give up maid's work but his wages weren't enough to cover all their bills.

The following week their neighbour Mrs Lamont told Struan she'd seen Annie walking into the village. Why in God's name did Annie not ask Iris Finlay to drop her at their door? He knew the likely answer to that. Theirs was not the kind of dwelling where you invited in ladies who lived in Drummond Castle. He held his tongue and quietly fumed. Annie looked more tired by the day and he thought her limp was getting worse too.

Struan was working in the flower bed nearest Drummond Castle terrace when he saw the Culdees Castle gig pull up, scattering gravel when the pony was reined to an abrupt halt. He was unsurprised to see the foreigner driving, his brother had ranted about the offence the Spaniard had caused in the Culdees stables. Alistair was the second groom and frequently drove the gig for Mr Speir, while the chief groom was furious that this man had acquired the little carriage for his personal use but not trusted his staff to drive for him. Struan would tell Alistair how the poor pony had shaken the bridle in his mouth, no doubt in pain after the rough treatment.

'Boy.'

Struan heard the voice but didn't immediately realise the Spaniard was addressing him.

'Are you deaf, boy?' The Spaniard prodded him with his cane as he walked down the steps into the parterre garden. 'I have an appointment with Mr MacDonald. See to the trap. I'll pick it up from the stables later.'

Struan stared after him. This was not the Spaniard's first visit to the castle so he knew how to drive to the stables.

Since he was reputedly a gardening man he also knew the difference between stable duties and groom work. Nevertheless, the Culdees pony was tossing his head and pawing the ground, left there untethered he might bolt at any minute. Struan had no choice.

He went to the beast and stroked his nose. 'It's all right, lad, I'm sorry he hurt you. Let's go and see if Mr Buchan can find you some oats.'

He got into the gig and although he took the reins he used the gentlest twitch to get the pony to turn, then murmured encouraging words all the way to the stables. Mr Buchan was out, but he found a stable lad and made sure the pony was safely uncoupled from the trap and put in a quiet stall with some breakfast oats. Struan didn't return to his task but followed the trail to the glasshouses. A man who mistreated a horse was not to be trusted, he wanted to see what he was up to. Spying him in the orchid house with Mr MacDonald he withdrew to the potting shed. Miss Finlay appearing at that corner was a surprise, he had never seen her in this working part of the garden, he guessed she was seeking the Spaniard.

'You'll find the Spanish gentleman wi' Mr MacDonald beside the orchids,' he said.

She didn't bother to deny it. When she joined the group and Mr MacDonald walked away, Struan moved closer. Miss Finlay had entered the glasshouse on her own with the Spaniard, this was so irregular that they must both know it a terrible idea. He sunk his spade into the ground in a place he could observe them and also be seen, this feckless girl needed a chaperone. He hoped Mr MacDonald wouldn't return and question him being so far from his assigned task. When they sat on a bench he couldn't see properly but he could tell from the tops of their heads they were much too close. Annie's friend wasn't his responsibility but his sister's description revealed that they thought him a good man and Struan was afraid they'd misjudged him. Miss Finlay stood up suddenly and the Spaniard emerged from the greenhouse. He treated Struan to an oily, self-satisfied smirk as he walked past. Miss Finlay emerged from the other door, as she walked towards the castle he saw one hand was gloveless. Her naked hand looked so small and vulnerable. He was angry with her for overworking his sister but his distrust of the Spaniard made him fearful for her safety. He observed her rejoin her aunt with the glove restored. He might have warned Lady Walker but that would be overstepping his place.

Struan spent the rest of the day weeding. His troubled mind wasn't capable of any difficult task.

Chapter Fifteen

July 1869

Aunt Leonora and I travelled by train from Crieff to Perth, arriving mid-afternoon. My aunt had recovered from her stomach ailment and looked particularly elegant in a tailored mauve dress with a small bustle which flattered her tall, erect frame. Her hair, swept up under a matching mauve hat showed some streaks of grey but I noticed she drew admiring glances. We'd arranged to meet Georgina for afternoon tea in the hotel dining room. Aunt Leonora's wide smile alerted me to her friend's entrance.

'Perfect timing, Georgina. I've just ordered fresh water for the teapot.' Leonora extended her arm towards me. 'This is my niece, Iris. She is very excited to get a glimpse of the Queen tomorrow. Iris, this is my dear friend, Lady Georgina Bradley.'

I stood and curtseyed.

'I can certainly promise you a glimpse, but I'm afraid Her Majesty is unlikely to be in good humour tomorrow. She is sleeping on the train tonight, so I doubt she will be well rested.'

Georgina squeezed Leonora's hand as she sat down. 'It's so lovely to see you again so soon. How are your rooms?'

'I haven't viewed Iris's. The top floor is too much for my legs, but I have a room on the first floor, with a view towards the river.'

'I'm on the first floor too, and it sounds like we have the same view. I'm in thirty-four.'

'Then we are neighbours. I hope for your sake that the walls are thick because I'm told I snore,' Leonora replied with a wry smile.

Who had told Aunt Leonora that she was a snorer? Sleeping below her in Drummond Castle, I knew it to be true, but would never have broached the subject.

'You look tired, George,' my aunt said.

'A little weary from the journey north, but really, I'm fine. In fact, I thought we might venture out tonight. There's to be a concert in City Hall. I've asked the hotel to secure us three tickets.'

My aunt nodded her approval. 'Good idea. I promised Iris's father that I further her education and I've been failing in that regard.'

'Thank you so much, Lady Bradley,' I said. 'I've never been to a professional concert.'

'Perhaps being a clergyman, your papa would not approve? I never thought,' Lady Bradley said. She looked so perplexed, I worried she might change her mind.

'He will be pleased to hear I have been granted this opportunity. He often talked about how he and Mama saw Jenny Lind perform in Perth the year they got married. Sadly, my mother's health was delicate. They rarely ventured far from Fowlis Wester after I was born.'

'And now I hear he has gone to Ecuador. Quite a change of circumstances.'

'Iris shares her father's horticultural interest,' Aunt Leonora explained.

'How fascinating, do tell me more,' Georgina said.

I glanced at Aunt Leonora for her approval, anxious not to appear rude by talking too much. She nodded, so I recounted all the different species my father had described, including an orchid he didn't think had been seen in this country before. Aunt Leonora scrunched up her linen napkin. 'I need a nap if we are to go out this evening. What time is the concert, George?'

'Seven.'

'It's such a lovely day, I might take a stroll to the park,' I said.

'Then I shall meet you in the lobby at six thirty,' my aunt replied.

'I'll come up with you. I want to show you my new gown,' Lady Georgina said.

The two friends left the dining room arm in arm. When I picked up my shawl, I noticed Aunt Leonora had left her gloves on the table. I slipped them into my pocket. She wouldn't need them until this evening.

It was a perfect afternoon. Neither too hot nor too cold. I let my shawl fall from my shoulders into the crooks of my elbows, as I walked along the path beside the River Tay. The park was busy, and being amongst so many people buoyed my spirits. I'd loved sleepy Fowlis Wester, but now I craved more stir, more variety of company. The wide, tree-lined path flanking the inside edge of the North Inch thronged with families and the air was full of childish shouts and laughter. An avenue of very smart townhouses overlooked the park, and several had carriages waiting outside. Some of the inhabitants would likely be in the concert hall this evening. After a circuit of the park, I walked back towards Smeaton's Bridge, admiring the substantial pink sandstone structure. I paused in the middle to look over the stone balustrade into the water.

Confusing feelings about Rafael de Rias crept into my quiet moments like these. I relived for the umpteenth time the sensation of his fingers on my skin, his alluring scent, the anticipation of his lips on my fingers. Certainly, I was longing for something dangerous. Aunt Leonora would have been horrified.

Today was Thursday and I wondered if Annie was sitting in Innerpeffray Library or schoolroom. The gentle gurgle of the River Earn was the constant background sound in Innerpeffray, a sharp contrast to this fast-flowing and turbulent river. Nevertheless, the small fish that had darted through the shallows of the Earn might pass this very spot, since the Earn merged with the Tay a few miles upstream. Thinking of Annie made me reflect on how much more relaxed Aunt Leonora seemed when she was around her friend. Leonora had met Georgina before she'd married. I so hoped I could retain Annie's friendship into my later years. The obvious difference in our circumstances as friends was the common background shared by my aunt and her friend. Aunt Leonora had gained her title through marriage, while Georgina Bradley's father had been a lord. Now, neither was wealthy, but they moved in the same aristocratic circles. It was so unfair that a woman's destiny was governed by her father or whom she married. I had to find a way to a new future for me and hopefully for Annie, too. I stared into the swirling river current, pondering whether my idea of an illustrated magazine was practical.

. . .

Back at the hotel, I climbed the stairs towards my bedroom. I hesitated on the first landing. If Aunt Leonora missed her gloves, she might mount a pointless search down to the dining room. I stood listening outside her door at the end of the corridor. Might she still be sleeping? Then came the muffled sound of her voice, which was immediately followed by a reply in soothing tones.

'Shush now, I'm sure there is no need to worry. We'll manage, Leo. We have always managed.'

I was sure I could hear Aunt Leonora crying as she replied. 'But what if he doesn't come back in time? I can't bear the thought of her being alone.'

Lady Georgina had called her Leo. My aunt had always seemed brave as a lion to me. Hearing her sound sad and vulnerable was a shock. My heavy room key fell from my fingers, hitting the wooden floor with a clatter. All sound from Leonora's room stopped. Cursing my clumsiness, I snatched up the key and fled upstairs. My heart was pounding when I reached my bedroom. Was Aunt Leonora talking about Papa and me? Back in time for what? Was Aunt Leonora planning to go somewhere?

I waited in the lobby at six thirty. It was unlike my aunt to be late but it was almost six forty-five when Lady Georgina came downstairs alone.

'Is my aunt unwell?' I asked.

'Nothing to worry about,' she replied, 'but she decided not to come to the concert. Let's go. We don't want to miss the beginning.'

The earlier breeze had disappeared and our brisk walk to the concert hall meant I was already warm when we took our seats. Lady Bradley had brought her fan and I was glad of the movement in the air, wafting the smell of roses towards me.

The concert was the music of Mendelson and I found it rather sombre for a summer evening. Georgina nodded off, her chin drooping towards her chest. Everyone got to their feet quickly when the interval arrived, anxious to get out of the stifling room. The temperature had risen even further during the concert. Not a state of affairs Scottish audiences faced very often.

Lady Bradley leaned in to whisper in my ear. 'Would you mind terribly if we went back to the hotel? I don't find the musicians accomplished enough to make it worth enduring the heat any longer.'

I smiled and nodded. 'I recognise your rose scent. Isn't it the same as Aunt Leonora's?'

'Ah, you have a botanist's nose. I must remember to give her a new bottle. It has to be imported from Florence. Luckily, they send it to the Queen every year and she always passes the gift on to me.'

We emerged back into the crowded street. Quite a number of the audience had the same idea.

'I suppose you are used to a higher musical standard in London theatres,' I said.

'Sadly, I rarely venture out in London. We used to attend all sorts of events when the Queen first married. Prince Albert was a keen patron of the arts. Now, Her Majesty cannot tolerate music, or even less the sight of people enjoying themselves. It reminds her of what she has lost.'

'The poor lady. After seven years of such deep mourning, it's a tragedy she is still so affected.'

'It really is very sad and particularly difficult for her younger children who are robbed of all gaiety,' Lady Georgina replied. 'Still, we will be in Balmoral soon. It is the place where she finds at least a measure of contentment.'

'I heard Her Majesty has published a book about her time in Scotland.'

'She has and is extremely proud of it.'

'Perhaps Mr Birnie should get a copy for Innerpeffray Library? I believe local people would be interested in reading about Her Majesty's life.'

'Leonora told me about your love of this library.'

'I adore it,' I said. 'I always went with Papa, and reading the botanical magazines makes me feel part of his adventure. My friend Annie has been helping me copy the illustrations, to send Papa details of the plants he's interested in.'

'I'm glad you have a friend. Tell me about her.'

As we walked, I tried to explain why Annie was so special, describing her endless cheerfulness despite her disability and her amazing talent in botanical drawings.

'She sounds like a splendid person,' Lady Georgina said.

'She is, but I'm not sure my aunt approves of the friendship. Annie is from a very ordinary background. Her brother is a gardener at Drummond Castle.'

'Gardening is a noble pursuit,' she said.

'Of course. My own father has taken to the horticultural life. However, Struan is as far from being a gentleman gardener as you can imagine. The family is very poor.'

Lady Georgina was a good listener and didn't seem at all judgemental. I confided my dreams of finding some income for Annie and me from botanical magazines.

'It sounds like an interesting project,' she said.

Something in her tone made me uncomfortable. It had to be more than a project if it were to bring income.

At the hotel entrance, I looked for the words to voice my fears, pausing in the doorway. 'I feel so guilty that I remain a burden to Aunt Leonora. She agreed to take me in, but I've been at Drummond Castle much longer than was planned. I doubt my father is contributing towards my upkeep. I wish I could make some money of my own. Enough to live independently.'

'You mustn't worry. I'm certain Leonora doesn't think of you as a burden.'

'But it's not just the money. Being responsible for me is a tie. It obliges her to be in Drummond Castle.'

Lady Georgina gave me a questioning look. I didn't want her to know I'd listened at the door.

'My aunt is such an independent woman, and she hardly gets any time on her own now.' I flushed. Was I making it worse?

Georgina took both my hands.

'I've known Leonora for thirty years and I've never seen her fonder of anyone. It's good for her to have company. Especially now that the Queen is so demanding and I can get away so rarely.'

'Surely not fonder than her husband?'

Georgina laughed. 'Most certainly. Archibald was a difficult man. It wasn't much of a love match.'

'Then I'm most glad she has a good friend.'

'She has, and I'm very delighted she now has another. It's good for us old ladies to mix with the younger generation.' She dropped my hands and smiled.

We went inside the hotel. 'Goodnight, Lady Bradley.'

'Goodnight, Iris, and you must call me Georgina. I'm very glad to have made your acquaintance.'

The next morning, I was up early and almost dressed when there was a tap on my door.

'You aunt is awake and feeling much better,' Lady Georgina said. 'She suggests you join her for breakfast in her room. I must check all the preparations and be on the platform when the Queen arrives. I'll try to get you inside the station to see the royal train, and I hope to see you later, before we head north.'

. . .

I joined my aunt for breakfast. Her face betrayed no sign of yesterday's sadness. We ate quickly before donning our gloves and hats and leaving the hotel. My heart sank at the sight of the crowd outside Perth General Station, but Lady Bradley waved from the entrance. A policeman walked over, to usher us down the side of the crowd.

'I've arranged with the manager of the John Menzies bookstall that you can stand there,' Georgina said before rushing off. Aunt Leonora and I walked along the platform in the direction of the clock, coming to a halt beside the bookstall. A middle-aged man tipped his hat. A young man beside him snatched his cap off and turned a deeper shade of red. The elder man, who introduced himself as Mr Brown, the manager, sported a bushy moustache and eyebrows, which bristled with self-importance. Both men wore dark suits and ties.

'My assistant, Mr Crawford,' the manager added with a perfunctory wave in the young man's direction.

Mr Crawford replaced his cap and blinked at us nervously. His high colour had now reached his sticking-out ears.

'My assistant is so excited he can barely speak,' the manager said, rolling his eyes.

I smiled at the boy and hoped I was doing better at hiding my own excitement.

At that moment, the train came through the tunnel and the canopy above the platform filled with steam.

We watched as Georgina boarded the royal coach. A few minutes later, the Queen was helped off by the stationmaster. The Queen, who was dressed completely in black, including a black hat with a feather, was rounder and smaller than I had expected, no more than five feet tall. She walked off at such a rate, Lady Bradley had to hurry to keep up with her. Georgina shot us a rueful look. I feared that her anticipation of the Queen's mood had been accurate.

'She didnae even gie us a look,' said young Mr Crawford, crestfallen.

'Why did you imagine Her Royal Highness would be interested in you, laddie?' said Mr Brown.

'You mustae thocht she'd be interested since we spent three solid days cleaning,' he replied.

It was true. The shiny gold lettering on the John Menzies sign above the stall gleamed and the whole construction showed evidence of very careful polishing.

'Less ae your cheek,' Mr Brown replied.

'My friend who works with Her Majesty explained she has endured a long journey overnight to get here. She feared it might overtire her,' Aunt Leonora said and smiled sympathetically at the man. 'Your bookstall is a huge credit to you both. I've never seen a neater one.'

'Thank you, Your Ladyship. I'm most proud of it and appreciate you saying so.'

Both men managed a smile when we walked away. Aunt Leonora was gruff sometimes, but she could be sensitive too.

'We might give the bookstall some trade when we pass on the way home,' I suggested.

'Good idea. I'll buy us both a journal,' Aunt Leonora replied.

We exited the station in time to see the royal carriage depart. The people in the crowd looked bewildered. The Queen was obviously not in a mood to meet her subjects.

Back at the hotel, we packed our bags and followed the porter down to reception. The dining room was closed to the public, but when a waiter came out, Georgina spotted us through the open door and came rushing into the lobby.

'I'm glad I caught you. Can you delay your departure for a few minutes? I was describing your library to Her Majesty, and she wants to donate a copy of her book. She has sent a valet to fetch one from the train.'

'Mr and Mrs Birnie will be delighted,' I said.

Let's wait here for his return,' Aunt Leonora said, sitting in one of the reception's armchairs.

'The notion that local people would like to borrow the book has really lifted her mood and will make the rest of the journey more tolerable for everyone.'

'So her journey here wasn't good?' Aunt Leonora asked.

'Honestly, it's no wonder,' Lady Georgina replied. 'The new royal carriage is fitted entirely in bright blue silk. The drapes, the upholstery, every single thing. It is a very glaring colour and not at all calming.'

'It must be intolerably hot too,' Aunt Leonora said.

'Especially since poor Beatrice must be at her side at all times. The Princess looks worn out.'

'Will the rest of the family come, or only Princess Beatrice?'

'They will all be expected to put in an appearance. I believe Princess Louise will be with us next week. I hear her sculptor friend is coming, too. The Queen has commissioned him.'

Aunt Leonora raised her eyebrows. 'That will be interesting.'

Lady Georgina laughed. 'Princess Louise always livens things up.'

The valet came in through the side entrance with empty hands.

'That's not good. Wait here,' Lady Georgina said, then followed him in. She emerged a few minutes later. 'The valet couldn't locate a book for you. Nevertheless, the Queen is determined to get a copy to Innerpeffray. She doesn't feel well enough to visit the library herself, but has asked you to visit Balmoral, Iris. Her Majesty will give you a copy to take back to the library.'

'Oh, Iris, what an honour,' Aunt Leonora said.

Lady Georgina grinned and slipped her arm around my aunt's waist. 'And of course, Iris needs a chaperone, so, my dear Leonora, you are invited, too.'

My heart went into a gallop. A personal invitation to the Balmoral court from the Queen. What an adventure.

'Now you must excuse me,' Lady Georgina said.

'But I will see you very soon, George.'

'You shall,' she replied. 'I'll write to both you and Lady Willoughby de Eresby with a date.'

'She will be delighted to spare me to fulfil the Queen's wishes.'

Lady Bradley embraced me and then Aunt Leonora. When they parted, Aunt Leonora's eyes glistened.

'What an extraordinary day,' she said.

I certainly had a story to tell my father now.

Chapter Sixteen

July 1869

I was desperate to tell Annie about my invitation to Balmoral, so was disappointed she wasn't in church on the Sunday. Mrs Birnie said if Struan didn't manage to get to church, he occasionally brought Annie to the library later. Aunt Leonora agreed I could travel with the Birnies and Mr Buchan would pick me up at four o'clock. The warm summer weather had made the River Earn so shallow it was possible for the Birnies to drive through it and get to and from Muthill church. The long trip by road via Crieff could take over half an hour when the river was in full flow, but the distance as the crow flies was under three miles. On our shortened journey to the library, I recounted my exciting news.

Mr Birnie looked astonished. 'Her Majesty wishes to donate us her book? How marvellous! Well done, Iris. Our readers will be squabbling over who can borrow it first.'

Mr Birnie was a man of few words, and his obvious pleasure made me very proud.

Mrs Birnie patted my hand. 'You've had quite an adventure, Iris, and now you are to meet the Queen. I'm so pleased for you.'

'I do hope Annie comes today. I can't wait to tell her.'

'She came in to paint up some sketches yesterday, but I was very occupied in the library, so I didn't chat to her. Annie must be busy too. She didn't even take time to look at the new edition of *Curtis's*.'

In the library, I placed myself facing the window, so I would see Annie arriving. The ferryman didn't work on a Sunday, so only barefoot boys were able to cross on foot, along with a number of gigs and carts. There was an extra attraction to lure people across to Muthill this year. Mr Speir had taken up stained glass as a hobby and had recently installed his beautiful new creations in Muthill church. The flow of vehicles slowed to a trickle, and I turned my attention to the magazine. The very first illustration, *Dendrobium densiflorum*, was a white orchid with a yellow centre with a profusion of small flowers hanging on a central stem. Annie would surely want to sketch it. In the meantime, I copied out the description. Once I'd finished, I went to the back room to return the magazine. I hesitated in the open doorway. Mrs Birnie had her head in her hands. When she looked up, it was obvious she had been crying.

'I'm so sorry. I didn't mean to intrude.'

Mrs Birnie smiled and wiped her eyes. 'It's all right, Iris. I feel melancholy at times.'

My expression was most likely gormless and she had to explain further. 'Mr Birnie and I have been married for over four years. We had hoped to have a family.'

'I'm sorry,' I said, lost for any more useful words.

She stood to take the magazine. 'I'm luckier than many. Mr Birnie doesn't blame me and I get joy from the children in my classes.'

I was shocked by the notion that any man might blame his wife for not having children.

'And I have my work,' she added. Her desk was strewn with old books.

'What are you working on?'

'The history of Innerpeffray and the surrounding area. It is a passion of mine. I hope to write a book about it one day.'

'You're a writer? I've been wondering if Annie and I could collaborate on some sort of magazine. Annie's paintings should have an audience. I love writing, but perhaps it's vanity to imagine people might pay to read my words?'

'I think that's an excellent idea, Iris. I'd be happy to help you if I can.'

'Thank you. I'm turning around some ideas in my mind. I'll have a stab at an article and you might tell me what you think?'

'I'd be pleased to.'

We embraced when I took my leave, sad not to have seen Annie.

'I believe Annie left her sketchbook in the schoolroom,' Mrs Birnie said.

'I might have a look. I'd love to know what she's been working on.'

I found Annie's sketchbook on the usual shelf in Mrs Birnie's cupboard. The drawing of a bright pink orchid was beautiful, and it contained the detail of the reproductive parts, as was required in a proper botanical illustration. Annie was learning fast. I flicked through the pages and the evidence of her hard work was clear. Orchid after orchid, six in all. Annie must have visited Culdees very often to have completed so many illustrations. This set my imagination on a treacherous path. Annie had surely spent a lot of time with Rafael. I swallowed to quell the jealousy. My vulnerable heart had only just learned the sensation of sweet longing. Apparently, bitter jealousy was as easily etched, but there was nothing welcome about this new feeling.

The schoolroom windows were open, and I heard the sound of loud splashing coming from the river. Looking through the window, I saw a large carthorse was crossing the ford, and the rider was obviously in a great hurry. Struan Cooper. My heart sank to see his furious expression. What now?

I went outside. Struan cantered up the hill and leapt down, not even taking the time to tether the carthorse.

'Tell Annie I've come tae take her hame. She's poorly wi' all this gallivanting. I telt her already she must stop.'

'Annie isn't here.' My brain was spinning. If Annie was missing, I had a very good idea where she was. Struan looked up towards the library. 'I've just come from the library and she's not there,' I said.

He scowled at me, thrust his hands into his pockets and made towards the library door.

'You may take my word for it, Annie isn't here.' I had to find Annie, and I didn't want Struan to question Mrs Birnie about how much time she'd been spending here. 'Annie must have been here recently. Her sketchbook is inside. Perhaps she's gone home via Crieff?' Nothing I'd said was untrue, but I was trying to mislead him.

Struan looked up towards the Crieff road. 'I hope you're right and I'll find her at hame. I dinnae ken what you two are up tae, but you should know that your selfish obsession is bad for Annie's health. She tells me she's fine, but I can tell she's lying tae me. Her limp is much worse and I ken my sister. The doctor has told her that her chest is weak. She has that glazed look in her eye I've seen before. If she succumbs tae the fever again, she might no get through it.' Struan's voice cracked with emotion. 'I have tae warn you, Miss Finlay, that I cannae bear the thocht ae losing Annie, and I'd never forgive you.'

His distress cut right through me, and the warning sent cold fear through my veins. 'I would never deliberately do anything that would hurt Annie, Mr Cooper,' I said quietly.

He turned and remounted his horse, facing the beast towards the Crieff road. 'Whether deliberate or not, you've got Annie doing mair than she's able for, and I'm truly fearful for her.' With that, he cantered off.

Dread caught itself up into a hard lump at my breastbone. I didn't doubt Struan's love for Annie. He was quite right that I had put her in harm's way, but it might be even worse than he feared. Mr Buchan was approaching. I ran inside and swept up Annie's sketchbook. I knew she'd not want to be without it for long.

'Can we go home though the river and via Culdees Castle, Mr Buchan?'

My mind was in turmoil. I didn't want Annie to have been with Rafael. I ached to believe that the promise in his eyes was only for me. But there was no other explanation for the sketches. He'd given Annie the dissected flowers. I would surely find her at the gardener's lodge. What was I about to walk into?

Twenty minutes later, we passed through Culdees's yew avenue.

'Take me directly to the walled garden, please.' I made for the garden entrance, but when Buchan led the trap into the stable yard, I doubled back towards the cottage. It wasn't proper to be observed entering a gentleman's house on my own, even when I was certain he had company.

I tapped on the door, and Rafael opened it. 'Is Annie here?' I asked.

He wore no jacket or tie, and his white shirt was open at the neck. His black hair was less severely oiled than usual and one lock fell over his forehead. The shirt seemed particularly white against his bronzed skin. The scent of his cologne was divine.

'How lovely to see you, Iris.' The man's demeanour was guiltless.

Annie stood in the living room doorway and her face was full of it.

'I've brought your sketchbook. The new illustration is dry.'

Her expression softened. 'That's great news for I have another orchid ready tae draw.' I followed her into the living room. Struan was right. Her limp was more pronounced. I pulled a chair up to her drawing table and looked into Annie's eyes. They had a feverish sheen.

Rafael picked up his hat and jacket. 'I'll leave you ladies to catch up. I have some plants to check in the glasshouse. Close the door behind you, Annie. See you tomorrow.'

The informality of his words caused a gut-wrenching stab of jealousy.

'Look at this,' Annie said, gesturing towards an orchid stem in a vase on the table. It was covered in at least twenty deep purple blooms. One flower lay on the blotting pad, its frilly centred petals dissected open to reveal its reproductive parts.

'A beautiful specimen,' I said. 'What's it called?'

Annie opened her sketchbook and pointed to the name *Epidendrum jamesoni*, written beneath her draft sketch in Rafael's handwriting.

'Then it was surely discovered by my father's colleague,

Professor Jameson. But why do you need the full stem? Could you not sketch its form in the hothouse?'

Annie shrugged. 'Apparently one of the gardener's broke this stem by accident, so Rafael brought it in for me.'

I registered her use of his first name, and the clean cut of a knife visible on the plant's stem through the glass vase. Someone had deliberately removed it.

Annie began embellishing her sketch. Her pencil swept the plant stem and began creating blooms. The speed of her work and concentration in her expression seemed feverish. I touched her forehead, but it felt cool. She glanced up at me, shot me a smile, but went straight back to her work.

'Annie, are you sure you are quite well?'

She didn't look up. 'You sound like Struan. I'm fine. I'm just eaten up by the urge tae learn. Tae make the most ae this chance tae better myself.'

'Struan is worried you are working too hard.'

'I am and it's so frustrating tae be constricted by this useless body. I willnae be held back. Rafael has given me a tincture that he finds gives him energy.' She nodded towards a teacup on the table.

I picked up the cup and sniffed the puddle of murky liquid lying in the bottom. The smell was not a herb I recognised. Was this the cause of her glazed eyes? What was he feeding her?

'Annie, stop.' I laid my hand on her fingers and gently took the pencil from her hand.

Finally, she met my gaze and blinked.

'Struan came to Innerpeffray Library looking for you. He thinks you've been spending all this time with me.'

Her guilty look returned. 'Sorry. I had tae tell him something. I've come every day since we were here together. Rafael has taught me so much.' She took my hands. 'He's like nae man I've ever met. Doesn't treat me like a cripple. He understands why I'm driven tae better myself. I've never felt so alive.'

My heart lurched, twisted by jealousy and now anxiety. The protective instincts were genuine, but envy curdled that well-meaning instinct. I squeezed her fingers. 'I understand that. But Struan is worried about you and now I am, too. I don't think you should be drinking this, and you are definitely limping more than usual.'

Annie sighed and sat back in her seat. 'I cannae have anyone see me in the gig wi' Rafael. I have him drop me on the edge ae Muthill when he takes me home, and when I go tae the schoolroom, he waits out ae sight. It means I'm walking more than usual.'

'You need to take more care, Annie. Struan could be on his way here at this very minute. He knows you were not with me and I'm quite sure someone in the village will have seen you with Mr de Rias in the gig.'

'You're right. I wear my hood up tae disguise my face, but I saw our neighbour, Mrs Lamont, on the edge ae Muthill twice this week.'

'Let me take you home. If Struan comes here, there will be a huge scene, and he is the one who will be blamed if there are angry words. I fear your brother might even strike Rafael if he imagines he has compromised your reputation.' There. I'd used his first name. Was I confessing to Annie that I'd felt attracted to him, too?

Annie's cheeks flushed. 'We havnae done anything wrong.'

'I am sure you haven't, but others will judge and you are bound to get caught out. Please don't come here alone again.'

Words of a true friend or a jealous rival? Could I be both?

'I cannae bear tae give this up, Iris,' Annie said quietly.

Was I being honest with myself? She'd spent many hours in Rafael's company. Aunt Leonora's vigilance would never allow that for me.

'Let me take you home now. Struan took the road through Crieff. We might still get there before him if we hurry.'

'I havnae finished my sketch.' Her dejected expression was pitiful.

'Look, I can't come tomorrow, but Aunt Leonora is going out with Lady Willoughby de Eresby on Tuesday. I'll go to the library to collect the paints, then I'll bring you here. Your new sketches are amazing, but you need to get some rest. This one can wait an extra day.'

I helped Annie into the gig. We had barely reached the end of Mr Speir's drive before she fell asleep with her head on my shoulder.

'Do you know where the Coopers live?' I asked Mr Buchan when we came into Muthill.

He nodded and took us up a narrow lane at the back of the village. He pulled up outside a ramshackle building that looked like an outhouse. Annie's home was even more modest than I'd imagined.

I shook my friend awake. 'We're here, Annie, and we're in luck. I don't think Struan is home yet.'

'You didnae need tae bring me all the way tae the door,' she said, as Mr Buchan gave her a hand down.

'You are walking too much. We'll pick you up from here at three o'clock on Tuesday.'

'Thank you. You are a good friend tae me, Iris,' she replied.

Remembering the contents of the teacup and also Rafael's manner towards to me, I was genuinely worried about Annie's reputation and Rafael's intentions. Simultaneously, I longed to be in his company and to have his attention all to myself.

'I'm not sure I've been good enough,' I murmured to myself.

Chapter Seventeen

July 1869

Struan had pleaded with Annie to rest but he knew from her wearied state in the evenings that she persisted. She worked every single day including Sunday and said he didn't need to pick her up from Innerpeffray. Annie was pushing him away but he didn't know why.

The following Sunday it was the same story. He knew it was a bad idea to interfere but he could bear it no longer, he had to talk to Iris Finlay. Annie was good at hiding her exhaustion and would be telling her friend she was fine. It wasn't just her clear tiredness, there was a glassiness in her eyes that surely predicted an imminent collapse. He'd risk Annie's ire and the scorn of her fancy friend but he had to prevent this disaster. He went to Drummond Castle stables and Mr Buchan confirmed he was leaving to pick up Lady Walker's niece. Struan didn't want to miss her so he persuaded the old carthorse into a trot overland towards the Innerpeffray ford. Mr Buchan would take the Crieff road since the water was too high for a pony but this carthorse would manage the depth easily.

Miss Finlay appeared outside the library as he reached the

edge of the river and he urged the horse across to get there before Mr Buchan arrived. He flung down the reins and marched up to her.

'Tell Annie I've come tae take her hame. She's poorly wi' all this gallivanting. I telt her already she must stop.'

'Annie isn't here,' she claimed.

She had to be here. Struan had given away his anger, so perhaps the Finlay girl was protecting Annie, he'd just go up and find her.

'I've just come from the library and she's not there,' the girl said.

He'd check for himself. Struan walked on.

'You may take my word for it, Annie isn't here, but she must have been here recently, since her sketchbook is inside. Perhaps she's gone home via Crieff?'

Buchan wasn't here yet. How was Annie getting home? Was some other person ferrying her about? That was a new thing to worry about, but since he was here, he'd say his piece and put an end to this nonsense.

'I dinnae ken what you two are up tae, but you should know that your selfish obsession is bad for Annie's health. She tells me she's fine, but I can tell she's lying tae me. Her limp is much worse and I ken my sister. The doctor has told her that her chest is weak. She has that glazed look in her eye I've seen afore. If she succumbs tae the fever again, she might no get through it.'

Iris Finlay looked shocked and the thought brought him embarrassingly close to breaking down, he wouldn't have this feckless girl see that.

'I have tae warn you, Miss Finlay, that I cannae bear the thocht ae losing Annie, and I'd never forgive you.'

Chapter Eighteen

July 1869

Aunt Leonora woke me early on Monday morning. 'I heard from Georgina last night and we are to be in Balmoral next week. We both need new dresses and you need a hat. Given the urgency, I've decided we must leave today. Two nights in Edinburgh should be enough to get everything. Clementina has kindly agreed to delay her plans until Thursday.'

I gasped. 'I've promised to meet Annie tomorrow.'

Leonora gave a deep sigh. 'If Baroness de Eresby sees fit to change her plans around the Queen's wishes, then I trust your young friend will understand.'

After a hurried pack we set off for the railway station to catch the ten o'clock train.

Aunt Leonora frowned at me as we bowled down Drummond Castle's beech-lined drive. 'You could try to look a little more excited, Iris. Two nights in Edinburgh and the prospect of a new outfit is surely not such a terrible hardship?'

'I'm sorry. It's only that Annie isn't very well and I'm

worried she won't receive my note of explanation in time.' I planned to post it from the station.

My aunt addressed Buchan. 'Mr Buchan, would you find time to deliver Iris's note after you drop us off?'

'Of course, Your Ladyship.'

Still, I worried that Annie wouldn't want to wait until Thursday to return to her drawings. I had no real evidence that Rafael was a bad influence and the improvement in her technique was clear. Was I being overprotective like Struan? Or was I jealous?

'Is there anything you would like to do when we're in the capital, Iris?'

'Might there be time to visit the Botanic Gardens?'

'What an excellent idea. I haven't been in years. We shall go directly to my seamstress this afternoon. If you choose your style today and if we find a hat easily, then we might have some free time tomorrow. I'm looking forward to this journey. The line finished last year will take us via Perth and then straight through Fife. I expect some pretty views.'

We changed to a smart new train in Perth. My aunt leaned forward when the line split south of Perth, sending us towards Fife. We passed through a dramatic section, where the line hugged a cliff.

As we approached a loch, my aunt exclaimed, 'Oh, that's Lindores House, Lady Maitland's home. I've visited by carriage with the Baroness.'

I saw a three-storey mansion nestled in trees beyond the loch. 'What a lovely view it has.'

'Both beautiful and tranquil.' My aunt replied. 'I wonder what Her Ladyship thinks about being able to see steam from the train, now. Her late husband, Admiral Frederick Maitland, was a hero of the Napoleonic Wars. He brought Napoleon to England in his ship, after he surrendered to him.'

My aunt sat back. 'The pace of change these days is dizzying. A railway across a whole county constructed so quickly. Who knows what miracles you will witness in your lifetime, Iris?'

Independence was the miracle I dreamt of, but I kept the thought to myself.

At Burntisland we boarded the steamer ferry, then from Granton Harbour we took the train to Canal Street, in the centre of Edinburgh.

Aunt Leonora chose a particular hotel in Edinburgh's Princes Street, both for its proximity to the railway station and its temperance leanings. The vista of the castle had always been part of the hotel's attraction but another landmark now dominated the view from the hotel windows. The enormous Scott Monument towered two hundred feet above Princes Street Gardens on the opposite side of the road. I was an ardent admirer of Sir Walter. Father's reading taste had not included novels, but Lady Clementina was a fan. Working my way through all Sir Walter Scott's books had been a labour of love for me over my long and lonely months living in Drummond Castle.

'Are you ready, Iris? We shall go next door to look at the material in Kennington & Jenner, before we go to the seamstress. They also have a selection of hats.'

The store windows were full of all manner of colourful things to persuade pedestrians to stop and admire. Luckily, Aunt Leonora was not the type for idle window gazing because visiting the Botanic Gardens depended on us completing most things today. We entered the huge shop and headed straight to the fabric department. Queen Victoria still wore mourning dress, so my aunt advised me to choose sombre tones. I settled on a dark blue damask. We found a small hat with a feather and were assured the plume could be dyed to match the dress fabric. We then walked to visit Mrs Graham, the seamstress, who lived and worked on the top floor above Gray's haberdashery at the west end of George Street. I carried my bolt of fabric under my arm, so that Mrs Graham could begin work on my dress immediately.

The seamstress was a woman of few words. She nodded approval of my fabric, rolling it out on a large table near the window.

'How many yards did you get?' she asked my aunt.

'Seven.'

'I shall need all of that. There is a pattern match in the damask to consider. Please stand on this stool and I'll double check your measurements.'

'Are you sure I need a bustle?' I asked. 'How will I sit down?'

'It sits above your *derriere* and won't interfere with sitting. Without a wide crinoline, this gives the balance to the dress shape. I guarantee you'll see it amongst the ladies at court.'

'It's important not to look too much like a clergyman's daughter, Iris.'

I spun round to protest, but caught the twinkle in my aunt's eye, then she laughed. Aunt Leonora was teasing me.

'You wish me to hide my true self?'

'You were born a clergyman's daughter, Iris, but who knows what you may become? Clothes are like armour. Believe me, you will feel more at ease wearing the right gown.'

Mrs Graham shook out her tape measure. 'What about your dress, Lady Walker?'

'I didn't find fabric I liked in Kennington & Jenner, but I promise to get it to you tomorrow. 'How much fabric will I need?'

'If you choose a plain fabric, you may need only six yards, but I recommend a contrast silk for the trims and bows. Let's say another two feet.'

I sighed at the prospect of the entire next day being spent in fabric shops.

'You may go to the Botanic Gardens in the morning, Iris. I'll enjoy a morning in my usual fabric haunts, then join you for a stroll in the afternoon.' My aunt checked her hat in the mirror, then handed me my gloves. 'When shall we return, Mrs Graham?'

'I have your measurements, Lady Walker. If you can both be here for a final fit on Wednesday morning, I'll have everything tacked.'

'And when might we expect delivery? I am sorry to be in such a hurry.'

'I'm thrilled to think my work will be seen in Balmoral. Both dresses will be on the train on Saturday.'

'You won't forget K&J are sending Iris's new hat to you.'

'I shan't forget, Your Ladyship.' Mrs Graham bobbed a curtsey and immediately picked up her tailor's chalk to get to work.

Aunt Leonora and I made our way down Castle Street to walk back through Princes Street Gardens. Emerging from the gardens beside the National Gallery, I spotted Alexander Hill's artist supplies shop on the opposite pavement. 'My paintbox needs two replacement colours. Might we go into the shop?'

'Oh, yes. This was a favourite of your mother's.'

The shop was stocked to the ceiling with every imaginable thing a painter might need. I vowed one day that I'd bring Annie here. I asked the assistant for blocks of vermillion and yellow ochre. He got a ladder to reach a drawer halfway up the wall. In the meantime, my attention was drawn to the watercolour paper. The pad I picked up was perhaps a third bigger than Annie's sketchbook.

'Are you short on paper?' Aunt Leonora asked.

'We haven't any in this larger size.'

'Then we'll get this, too. It can be your apology to your artist friend for deserting her.'

The next morning, Aunt Leonora had the carriage driver drop me at the gates of the Botanic Gardens, which lay in the Inverleith area, north of the city centre. 'Enjoy your morning, Iris. I'll meet you inside these gates at thirty minutes after two.'

I walked up the hill to get a feel of my surroundings. The view was incredible. The ordered pattern of newly built grand houses in Edinburgh's New Town lay below me. Above them, the craggy outline of the ancient castle reigned over the town as it had done for hundreds of years. Beyond there were rolling hills. I wished I had Annie's talent to sketch so I could share the experience with her. Edinburgh really was the most impressive city. I headed towards the hothouses situated near the northern wall. Curiosity drew me to the impressive Palm House first. A very grand design, with a curved roof, much like an ornamental Wardian case, but on the scale of a house. A smaller octagonal glasshouse stood to one side. My leisurely stroll amongst the huge palms and water lilies made me feel near to my papa. Surely he must have walked amongst such equatorial beauties.

I spent time studying all the exotic specimens on display before going to the orchid house, which was filled with plants of every size and colour. I opened my new journal from John

Menzies in Perth to record some names, then sat in a corner to write up the descriptions.

A young couple came in. The very tall man was talking about his botanical studies to a small auburn-haired lady whom I took to be his wife. I stopped writing because their conversation was of great interest.

'You are so lucky, Alexander, to have access to this collection on our doorstep and to have found such an expert teacher,' the young lady said.

'That's true. Mr Balfour has unleashed so many avid botanists into the world, and how could I not be inspired by this?' The gentleman swept his hand through the air.

The lady pulled her collar away from her neck and flicked open her fan. 'I love the orchid house, but today it's too warm. Could we go outside? The orchid is a plant best studied in winter.'

'Of course, how thoughtless of me. Professor Jameson says orchids are not restricted to warm climates. He has found several species growing high in the cool mountains.'

They turned to leave, but the mention of that name had already brought me to my feet.

'Excuse me, I couldn't help overhear. Is the professor you mentioned visiting from Ecuador?'

'Indeed he is. A close friend of my professor, Mr Hutton Balfour,' said the man.

'Is he still in Edinburgh? I would love to meet him.'

The couple looked at me curiously. I realised my interruption was probably quite rude.

'Excuse me for delaying you. My name is Iris Finlay, and my ears pricked up to hear the name. My father is a plant hunter currently in Ecuador and he has often mentioned Professor Jameson.'

'A plant hunter. How very fascinating.' The gentleman

extended his hand. 'I am Alexander Donaldson and this is my wife, Elspeth. I'm studying medicine at the University of Edinburgh but I confess botanical studies are my favourite.'

The lady gave me a warm smile. 'I know Alexander is going to ask you a million questions about your father's work. Would you walk with us, Miss Finlay? I find it rather too warm in here.'

'I would love to,' I said, following the couple outside.

'I saw Professor Jameson walking in the Gardens with Mr Balfour yesterday,' Mr Donaldson said. 'I'm sure Balfour could put you in touch with him.'

'Unfortunately, I don't live in Edinburgh and I'm going back to Perthshire tomorrow.'

'That's a shame. Why don't you leave your card with me to pass onto Mr Balfour? I will explain the connection to your father.'

It was hugely frustrating that I'd missed the chance to meet someone who had become father's friend. 'I don't have a card, but if I leave you a note with my address, do you think Mr Balfour might pass it on to Professor Jameson?' I sat down on a bench and tore a leaf out of my journal. My slide pencil was not the most appropriate tool for addressing an eminent academic, but it was all I had to hand.

Dear Professor Jameson,

My name is Iris Finlay, and I am Andrew Finlay's daughter. I am in the Botanic Gardens today, enjoying this beautiful place and admiring their many species. Imagine my surprise to learn from Mr and Mrs Donaldson that if I had been here one day earlier, I might have had the honour of meeting you.

Unfortunately, I have to return to Perthshire today.
However, might you send me your address? I would very much like to
make your acquaintance if I come back to the capital before you
return to Ecuador.
You can reach me care of Lady Leonora Walker, Drummond Castle,
Crieff, Perthshire.
Best wishes,
Miss Iris Finlay

I folded the note, addressed it, and handed it to Alexander Donaldson.

'I'm sorry to use pencil.'

'It's the most beautiful and useful thing,' Elspeth said.

'I agree. I am most lucky to have it.'

'May I see?'

I handed the small pencil to her. Made of silver, it had a highly decorated shaft and an orange agate stone on the filial. 'It is my most prized possession.'

She cradled it in her palm. 'So the lead slides inside when not in use? Such a practical solution for working outside. Do they make them for gentlemen too?'

'I believe so.'

'Probably beyond my budget, but I wonder if I could persuade Papa that it would be a suitable gift for your birthday, Alexander?'

'Mine was a gift from my aunt.'

'So, are you a botanist too?' she asked.

'I haven't studied formally, but I learned from my father.'

'How interesting,' Alexander Donaldson said. 'I envy his Ecuador visit. I'm told it's a place brimming with new species.'

For the next hour, we walked the paths of the Botanic Gardens. I described my father's adventures and we stopped often to discuss the various plants and trees we passed. Mr Donaldson was a particular expert on rhododendrons.

I left the Donaldsons when it came time for me to go and meet my aunt. We exchanged addresses, and I promised to visit them the next time I was in Edinburgh. Aunt Leonora listened attentively to my description of my encounter. The rest of the visit continued in the same harmonious high spirits. We enjoyed a fish dinner together in the hotel, where Aunt Leonora described the fabric she had found and her pleasure in walking and browsing in Edinburgh.

The next morning, we rose early to pack. We had less than two hours to complete the final fittings and catch our train home. Aunt Leonora took down the pad of watercolour paper from the top of her wardrobe.

'Will this fit at the bottom of your valise, Iris? It would be a shame to crush it.'

I placed the pad carefully at the bottom of my bag and layered my clothes on top to protect it. 'I have an idea to help Annie get her illustrations published, and she needs larger paper for the purpose. I will provide the words for the article. Elspeth Donaldson, the young lady I met yesterday, has a father in publishing. She promised to look into it for me.' I glanced at Aunt Leonora to see her reaction.

'Well, you are good with words, Iris. Do they accept submissions from ladies?'

'Many horticultural magazines certainly accept illustrations. Perhaps they will accept my words if they are good enough?'

'I believe there is a Miss Kirby who writes books on botany, and Lady Dalhousie was a famous expert. As I said before, who knows what you will become, Iris.'

For a few seconds, I basked in the glow of the compliment before she added, 'Of course it will depend on what your future husband might think.'

Chapter Nineteen

July 1869

I'd written to Annie, suggesting that I take her to Culdees on Thursday morning. Her note of reply, which was waiting for me when I got home, said she would meet me there. I feared she'd ignored my advice and gone there in my absence.

Mr Buchan helped me into the gig outside Drummond Castle. 'Good morning, Mr Buchan, thank you for being here early. And I see you've already been to Innerpeffray.'

'Mistress Birnie is an early riser, even when the school is out.'

I laid my hand on my mother's mahogany box. I hoped I might persuade Annie to paint up her illustrations whilst I was with her at Culdees. If only I could get there frequently enough to dissuade her from going on her own.

I arrived to find the front door of the gardener's lodge open. I hesitated on the doorstep.

'Hello?' I called.

'I'm in here.' I knew from Annie's voice something was very wrong.

The living room was almost entirely empty. All the books and personal items were missing. Annie sat in the desk chair. Her eyes were swollen from crying. Her stick lay on the other side of the room.

'He's gone,' she said. This was an Annie I didn't recognise. She had a hard life but was always cheerful. Such despair was terrible to witness. Simultaneously, I experienced a nauseating sense of abandonment. Something inside me was torn in two, but the look on Annie's face helped me stifle the urge to break down. Rafael was entrancing but hurting Annie was unforgivable.

'Where has he gone?'

'Nae idea. I sat there wi' him just the day before yesterday.' She pointed to the sofa. 'Three blissful hours. He took me through my sketchbook page by page and he encouraged me wi' kind suggestions. I dared tae hope it might be a tenderness we'd share forever.'

Annie's sketchbook was face down at her feet. I put down the paintbox, picked up the book, smoothed the crumpled pages and laid it on the desk at her elbow.

'Oh, Annie,' I put my hand on her shoulder. How could I scold her for coming alone when she was so upset?

'He kissed me.'

Those words, which should have been full of joy, were said in a hopeless tone.

I helped her to the sofa, sat down beside her, and drew her into a hug. 'He didn't tell you he was leaving? Was there some family emergency?'

'Maybe. Or more likely he came tae his senses. He'd let his emotions run away wi' him, as had I.' Her eyes blazed with anger. 'I'm sure he realised the madness ae saddling himself wi' a cripple.' She glared at her discarded stick. 'So he ran.'

'What decent man would behave like that, Annie? There must be another explanation.' I was struck by a terrible thought. 'Only a kiss, Annie? He didn't...'

She shook her head.

Mr Speir's voice came from outside. 'Miss Finlay?'

Annie looked at me in a panic. I picked up her stick and gave it to her. 'Stay here. I'll try to keep him outside.'

I went to the doorstep. 'Mr Speir, how lovely to see you. I've been in Edinburgh for a few days. I came here hoping to speak to Señor de Rias about some plants I saw in the Botanic Gardens.'

'I saw your trap coming up the drive, I have good news. Rafael has gone to take some new style Wardian cases to your father in Ecuador. Imagine how much more quickly your papa might return with the help of another.' He beamed at me, clearly certain I'd be pleased.

My disquiet on discovering Rafael's flight ratcheted up to a shiver of fear. I wanted him nowhere near my father. He'd never mentioned any interest in going to Ecuador. Why the sudden departure?

'Naturally, I'll be delighted if Señor de Rias's help brings my father home earlier,' I lied. 'Is Papa expecting his arrival?'

'I've written to him with the good news. Rafael was very persuasive in explaining the benefit of better quality Wardian cases. And of course his fluency in Spanish will be invaluable in transporting the specimens back.'

'Of course,' I replied. I didn't feel reassured at all. My father reported he'd made huge progress in his Spanish and he was a proud man. If Rafael meant to barge in and take charge, Papa would not be pleased.

Mr Speir gestured around. 'You and your friend are welcome to continue to use the gardener's lodge and the glasshouses for your studies. Feel free to pick up the lodge key anytime.'

'Thank you.'

'Rafael reports your friend is a beautiful artist.'

'She is,' I replied. Did he mean Annie was beautiful or her drawings? Would Rafael have boasted about their intimacy? Surely not. It didn't reflect well on his character.

'He plans to come back here on his return from Ecuador.' Mr Speir then raised his hand. 'I'll take my leave of you now. Give my regards to your aunt.' Mr Speir seemed unperturbed about how I might take that piece of news. Surely Papa and I would live in the lodge on his return? There was no room for another.

Annie was still sitting on the sofa where I left her, looking as forlorn as before. 'I'm sorry,' she said.

'For what?'

'For forcing you tae cover for my lack ae discretion.'

'I told no lies,' I answered.

'So, he's gone tae Ecuador. Dae you think that was always his intention?' Annie gave me a searching look.

'I don't know. Such an expedition surely takes time to arrange. How do you feel about knowing he will return here?'

Annie looked down at the damp handkerchief she still held in her hand. She shook her head and stuffed it back up her sleeve. 'Right now all I feel is pain. He didnae even leave me a note, Iris.' She looked up, close to tears again.

'Perhaps he couldn't find the right words? Try not to dwell on it.' I held out my hand to help her up. 'Shall I take you home? You look exhausted.'

'Thank you. You can tell me all about your Edinburgh adventures on the journey. Were the Botanic Gardens pretty?'

'More beautiful than you can imagine. I've made notes to share with you. I saw hundreds of new plants.'

As we walked to the gig, I described my adventures of the last few days. Annie leaned heavily on my arm. She had evaded damage to her reputation, but her heart and her health were compromised.

In the trap, she slumped beside me. I talked to distract her, telling her about the Donaldsons and my idea for us to try submitting articles.

'Dae you have a subject in mind?' she asked.

'I know you've spent a long time studying orchids, but how would you feel about tackling plants that don't grow in hothouses? Perhaps this would have more general public interest'

'Why not?' Annie replied, then grimaced. 'I've gone right off orchids.'

We were almost in Muthill before I remembered the pad of paper I'd tucked under the seat.

'I nearly forgot. This is a gift from Aunt Leonora.'

Annie took the pad out of its brown paper wrapping. 'How very kind ae her.' Her face clouded over again. 'There's another problem. Rafael took his scalpel wi' him and he didnae show me how tae prepare a flower.'

'Why not ask Struan if anyone in Drummond Castle can do it? Gardeners carry a sharp knife to take cuttings or graft a stem.'

'I'll ask him,' she agreed.

Annie and I spent Sunday afternoon working together at Innerpeffray. I'd asked her to do me some sketches to take to Balmoral. Unfortunately, we had the first rain in weeks. I leafed through a batch of *Curtis's* magazines for inspiration. I'd always been drawn to the exotic illustrations; plants drawn in Kew Gardens or other specialist collections. Today, for the first time, I pondered the advertisements in the opening pages. Seedsmen and plant nurseries were touting their catalogues. William Bull of Chelsea boasted of their selections of pelargonium seeds. Henry Cannell offered descriptions of their hybrid fuchsia plants. These were lists with no illustrations. Surely buying seeds or seedlings without knowing the colours was like working in the dark? Of course, there was the matter of cost. Engraving and hand colouring was surely expensive. Papa might have had Curtis's delivered to our home had the cost of nearly four shillings not been beyond his means. Could I appeal to those enthusiasts without bottomless purses? I had to do more research.

At the end of the afternoon, we went outside. Mr Buchan was already here and Struan was fording the Earn with his cart. This time at a normal pace.

'I'll put the paintbox back in the schoolroom,' I said.

'When do you travel to Balmoral?' Annie asked.

'The visit was postponed until Thursday.'

'If we get a dry day tomorrow, I'll come and draw the outside view,' Annie replied.

'I'll try to borrow the trap tomorrow and bring you back here.' I hugged my friend. 'Are you alright?' We hadn't mentioned Rafael today, but I knew he lurked in both our thoughts.

She sighed. 'I'm sleeping better. You and Struan were both right. I was overdoing it. But do I feel better? Not really.'

I grimaced. 'He treated you badly.'

'I miss the excitement.' She sighed again. 'I miss him.'

Her words caused a spasm in my own heart. It felt like a betrayal. I couldn't admit I'd harboured the same feelings.

'It will take time to get over.'

'That's what people say. At least it was only my heart that was lost.' She shrugged and limped towards Struan's cart.

I went into the schoolroom to deposit the box. I was

surprised to find Struan Cooper waiting for me when I came out. I could see Annie already seated in the cart.

'She willnae tell me what happened.'

I blinked, but said nothing. I would never betray Annie's confidences.

He looked down at his boots. 'I think I was wrong. She wasnae wi' you.'

Still, I made no reply. What could I possibly say?

His expression was so anguished I couldn't help but feel sorry for him.

'I'm sorry for my angry words, but I worry about her.'

'I know. I think she'll be all right,' I replied.

He nodded. 'Maybe I can help you both now. Mr MacDonald told me I'm tae have a promotion. I've asked tae join the nursery team, tae learn about the breeding and planting side. Now, I'll be able tae get stuff for Annie tae draw. I think it'll cheer her up, like.'

'That's good news.'

He nodded and walked towards the cart.

'Congratulations,' I called after him.

He turned, and for the first time ever, he smiled at me.

Chapter Twenty

July 1869 – Aberdeenshire, Scotland

D*ear Papa,*

Today, I shall be introduced to Queen Victoria.

If you didn't receive my last letter, I can imagine your astonishment. The honour is so extraordinary and unexpected that I'm resolved to record every detail of these days.

Are you nervous for me? Perhaps you think me too young to deal with such a responsibility? I'm determined I shall not disgrace you, and I can tell Aunt Leonora believes me up to the task. You will find me quite grown up when you come home. I had a growth spurt through last year and Aunt Leonora tells me that I've exceeded Mama's height. How strange you will find it to look me in the eye.

I hope you will find me grown in maturity too. I've prepared carefully for the meeting today. The Queen has expressed a specific interest in Innerpeffray Library, which is the reason for my invitation. I have spent several hours with Mrs Birnie, learning about the library's history and I've written it up in my most careful hand. My friend Annie has done drawings of the building. My plan is to use the document as an aide-mémoire if I'm given a chance to describe my precious library. I'll leave the notes along with Annie's drawings for Her Majesty to read at her leisure. Aunt Leonora's friend Lady

Georgina assures me that the Queen is most genuine in her love of Scotland and in hearing stories about its past.

Aunt Leonora and I travelled here by train yesterday, arriving at Ballater Station in the evening. We spent the night in a guest house overlooking Ballater's green, just a short walk from the station.

Now I set my pen aside. I will imagine you walking alongside me to give me strength to make you proud.

Your loving daughter,
Iris

We expected transport to take us to Balmoral. In my naivety, I'd imagined a shiny coach with white horses. The open gig which arrived, drawn by a Highland pony and driven by a be-whiskered man, were decidedly ordinary. Then, I saw the lady in the back was Lady Georgina.

'George!' Aunt Leonora's exclamation told me a golden coach could not have made her happier.

'I asked Her Majesty if I might collect you,' Lady Georgina said as we climbed aboard.

'Iris has prepared some notes to give the Queen. If she feels disinclined to meet us in person, Iris could leave them for her,' Aunt Leonora said.

My heart sank. To have come all this way and not to meet the Queen would be so disappointing.

'No, no. I'm certain you will be admitted,' Lady Georgina replied. 'The Queen signed the book this morning and remembers you are coming. She is looking forward to meeting you.'

As the gig set off along the road, I showed her the drawings and the two pages of notes I'd prepared.

'Why Iris, this is charming. Are the drawings the work of the friend you talked about?'

'Yes. Annie is so talented. Really, it is she who should be meeting the Queen.'

Lady Georgina was quiet for a moment while she read, then looked up, smiling. 'You're wrong, Iris. You are talented too. This is a fascinating story and is just the kind of thing to capture Her Majesty's interest. Bravo.'

I coloured at the compliment.

'We are most grateful for the invitation,' Aunt Leonora said.

Lady Georgina squeezed her hand. 'In fact, everyone is looking forward to your visit. Life at Balmoral can be tedious for the princesses. Your presence will be a welcome break in the routine.'

The driver harrumphed. Lady Georgina's next words were directed at his back. 'You can attest to Her Majesty's genuine interest in all Scottish matters, Mr Brown. This library for ordinary people is exactly the kind of thing to capture her interest.'

'Her Majesty loves Scotland, as did Prince Albert. Her children need tae appreciate the importance ae her happiness.'

Luckily, the man faced away from us, for I fear my mouth fell open. Was it possible that this servant with the broad Scots accent had just criticised the royal children? Lady Georgina met my gaze and raised her eyebrows. I was surprised to learn that our journey to the castle would take fifty minutes.

'There were plans to extend the railway line nearer to Balmoral, but the Queen decided against it. Prince Albert was keen to preserve the wild nature of the area and Her Majesty tries to honour his wishes,' Lady Georgina said. 'But it's such a lovely day, and the route is scenic. I don't think you will be bored.'

Sure enough, a few miles outside Ballater, we reached an

elevation that gave us a beautiful view. The River Dee wound through the green valley below us, sparkling in the sunlight. I looked up at the sound of a distinctive cry. A pair of buzzards circled in the skies above us.

Lady Georgina followed my gaze. 'If you are lucky, we might see a golden eagle.'

The mountains beyond the river were tinted with a hint of pink. 'The hills must look glorious when the heather is fully out.'

Lady Georgina nodded. 'One of the reasons the royal family makes sure to be here when it's at its best in August. For the deer stalking too.'

The gig drove past a wooded area, and I peered into the gloom, searching for movement. 'It seems a shame to shoot such a lovely animal.'

'Balmoral estate is overrun with deer and the venison serves to feed both the royal larder and the local population,' Lady Georgina said.

The road edged closer to the river and soon we turned left. In the distance, I could see some buildings.

'Is that the gatehouse?' Aunt Leonora asked.

'Yes, we will be at Balmoral in a few minutes. Please pause on the bridge, Mr Brown, so the ladies can appreciate the river.'

The driver halted on what turned out to be a bridge made of iron.

'A good sturdy looking structure,' Aunt Leonora said.

'It is. Prince Albert commissioned it from Mr Kingdom Brunel,' Lady Georgina said. 'The Prince greatly admired his engineering prowess.'

The river below ran clean and clear past riverbanks edged with large, pale stone boulders. A little white-breasted dipper bobbed on its mid river perch and sang his heart out. 'My father would love to cast a fishing line here.'

The gig entered the palace gates and through an avenue of trees, Scots pines and many young imported species lining the drive. Cedars as well as Norway and Sitka Spruce. I caught sight of a Wellingtonia, like those Mr Speir had recently planted. The deep green, fresh smell was intoxicating.

The carriage emerged from the trees onto a sweeping drive. Balmoral was suddenly in front of us. A beautiful, turreted castle, perhaps an inspiration for Mr Speir's renovations. However, instead of pink sandstone, this building was pale grey and sparkled in the sunlight.

'Welcome tae Balmoral, ladies. The bonniest castle in all the land,' the ghillie announced, quite as if he were the proprietor.

'The castle is made from granite, Lady Georgina told us. 'The local stone. When the sun occasionally shines, it looks very impressive.'

We drove past a stone carriage portico that appeared to be the main entrance.

'We'll enter through the staff entrance on the other side of the castle. I've arranged a room for you to freshen up,' Lady Georgina said. Passing a large square tower with four turrets, we halted on the east side of the castle.

Mr Brown jumped down and took the pony's bridle

'Thank you, Mr Brown,' Lady Georgina said. 'Her Majesty has requested that you come back for Lady Walker and her niece at three o'clock.'

He touched his cap.

'Who is that terrible man?' Aunt Leonora whispered as we walked away.

'Mr Brown was Prince Albert's ghillie, and is now Her Majesty's most trusted servant,' Lady Georgina whispered. 'I would urge you to take great care around him. He has the Queen's ear and complete trust.'

'A ghillie! How extraordinary,' Aunt Leonora replied.

. . .

We entered Balmoral via a large door in the grey wall into a courtyard. The clattering noise and the number of maids rushing in and out of the rooms opposite carrying pans and platters suggested we were near the kitchen. Lady Georgina led us down a narrow corridor which first veered off to the left, then right, and left again, until I was entirely disorientated, although the paintings on the wallpapered walls indicated we had left the servants quarters and entered the living area.

'Her Majesty keeps some rooms for visitors to wait in,' Lady Georgina said, showing us into a room with easy chairs and a washstand. 'I will go ahead to tell them you are here.' She hugged me. 'Be brave, young Iris. I'm sure you will charm them all.'

I washed my hands and smoothed my hair, then replaced my white gloves. Despite my profession of bravery to my father, I was gripped by the sudden fear I might be sick.

Aunt Leonora smiled. 'Deep breaths, Iris. You'll be fine.'

After ten minutes, Lady Georgina returned. 'Her Majesty is ready for you.'

Lady Georgina led us round another turn in the corridor. When we entered the drawing room, which was filled with people, the assault of colour took me aback. I gazed around the large room with a white marble fireplace and an overmantel mirror which reflected the light from the west-facing bay window opposite. All the furnishings were in a pale wood, quite unlike the mahogany found in Drummond Castle. However, the strongest impression came from the profusion of tartan. The carpet, the drapes and all the many sofas and chairs were in various versions of a striking red and grey tartan. There were many more people in the room than I'd expected, but the small, black-clad figure sat on one end of the couch facing us dominated them all.

I sank into a deep curtsey, as did Aunt Leonora beside me. When I straightened, I saw the tall, kilted man standing at the Queen's shoulder was the ghillie, Mr Brown. A statue of a similarly kilted soldier held up every one of the many candelabras in the room. This entire space was a tribute to the Highlands.

'Your Majesty, allow me to present my friend, Lady Leonora Walker and her niece, Miss Iris Finlay,' Lady Georgina said.

'How delightful. Please be seated, ladies,' the Queen said. 'Lady Bradley informs me that you reside in Drummond Castle.'

'We both have that pleasure,' my aunt replied.

'Please give Lady Willoughby de Eresby my kind regards,' the Queen said. 'I have very happy memories of my visit to Drummond Castle with my dear husband. The gardens are magnificent.'

A maid arrived with a tray. She served tea to the Queen first, then all the other guests. Mr Brown stood stock still, as if on guard. He didn't take tea, but he nodded at the maid, to dismiss her.

The Queen turned her bright-eyed gaze towards me. 'Young lady, I have a gift for you.' She held up a green, leather-bound book that had been in her lap. 'But first I want to hear all about this library. Remind me of the name?'

'Innerpeffray Library, Your Majesty.' My voiced sounded scratchy. I coughed to clear my throat. 'If you don't mind, I'll read from my notes, so as not to forget anything.'

'I do like a well-organised girl. A sign of a tidy mind.' The Queen gave a meaningful glance towards the young woman on the adjacent couch, while the girl by her side smirked.

I took a deep breath and began. *Innerpeffray library was*

founded by David Drummond, the third Lord Madertie, in 1680. It is situated near Crieff and was Scotland's first lending library, continuing to serve the local community to this day. The library has always attracted readers from the clerical community, and my own father, who was a Church of Scotland Minister, is one of the many generations of religious scholars to use their excellent collection to further his studies. The library also caters for ordinary readers. It contains many volumes on natural history, farming, and my particular interest, which is botany and horticulture.'

I glanced up. The Queen seemed attentive, but the gentleman with an exuberant moustache covered his mouth to hide a yawn. This wasn't going well. I put my notes in my lap.

'I'm sorry I'm not capturing the magical atmosphere of Innerpeffray at all well. It's the feel of the place that makes it so special, but even then, that's not all.' I closed my eyes momentarily to summon my words, then leaned forward in my seat. 'Every sense feels sated there. The library is so beautiful, and infused with that special smell belonging to old books. The building is double-storeyed and white-washed, tucked in beside the graveyard of the old family chapel. It has very pleasing lines. I've brought you some sketches to help you visualise it.' I picked up Annie's drawings.

'I would like to see them,' said the Queen.

'I'll get them for you, Mama,' said the girl who sat beside her.

'I'll do it, Beatrice,' the other young lady interjected. She rose from her seat and took the drawings from my hand. 'Why these are excellent,' she said, glancing at them before handing them to the Queen, who smiled at her and said, 'Thank you, Louise.'

These young ladies must be Princesses Beatrice and Louise.

'Are you the artist?' Princess Louise asked.

'I am not. The talented artist is my friend, Annie Cooper. She was a pupil at Innerpeffray School and Mrs Birnie, the Keeper's wife, has taken great care to encourage her continued education.'

'Keeper as in gamekeeper?' Princess Louise asked.

'No. The Keeper of the Books, it is the traditional title for the Innerpeffray schoolmaster and librarian.'

'How charming,' she replied.

'Indeed. Mr and Mrs Birnie are as important to the library's good influence as all their books. Mrs Birnie helps her husband in both the lessons and administering the library and has done for many years. Her brother was the previous Keeper.'

'Good, honest and hardworking Scottish people. It is a story I hear time and again and one of the many things that calls me here so often.' Queen Victoria perused Annie's sketches. 'It is indeed a handsome building, and the library appears to be well-stocked.'

'The setting is very picturesque too, on the riverbank of the River Earn. It sits in a fertile area teeming with nature, surrounded by woodland and fields. Mrs Birnie has traced the Innerpeffray Estate back to the twelfth century and the area had historic significance many centuries before that. The Romans had a large encampment nearby. I've written more on that in my notes, which I could leave for you, if you are interested.'

'Thank you, I am most interested. I have already inscribed my book to the library and I would be grateful if you would take it to them.' The Queen proffered the book towards Princess Louise, who rose from her seat again, to bring me the book and take my notes to the Queen. The Princess rested her hand on the shoulder of the moustached gentleman as she took her seat. He smiled at her, then turned when the Queen addressed him.

'Mr Boehm, I feel quite invigorated by this description of Scotland and its marvellous people. I might sit for you this afternoon.'

'We had a tuition session planned, Mama,' Princess Louise said.

'You can delay it. Lady Bradley, please give our guests a tour of the grounds before they leave.'

We all rose when the Queen stood up. I followed Aunt Leonora's lead in curtseying.

'Thank you both for coming. Don't forget to give my regards to Lady Clementina. Was the Drummond who set up this library one of her relatives?'

'Part of the extended family, Your Majesty,' Aunt Leonora answered. 'The current patron is Arthur Hay Drummond, who assumed the name when he inherited Innerpeffray Estate.'

The Queen nodded. 'I believe I've heard of him.'

We followed Lady Georgina outside. Princess Louise fell in beside us. A Yorkshire terrier who'd been lying at her feet came along too.

'May I join you on your walk? I'd like to hear more about your library Miss...'

'Miss Iris Finlay, my niece, Your Highness. We would be delighted. It's a subject Iris can talk about all day,' Aunt Leonora added. Princess Louise was a very striking woman. She had lovely light blue eyes and wore her fair hair pinned in curls under a small blue hat. The Queen's words had been encouraging, but her demeanour had been as formal as I'd expected. This young lady was quite different. Aunt Leonora was fit and used to walking, but both she and Lady Georgina struggled to keep in step with Princess Louise, who strode with the ease of someone used to lots of exercise. Her dress of dark burgundy silk must have been less corseted than mine, which pinched my waist at every step. This young woman, who was only a few years older than I was, put me in awe. She seemed so very sure of herself.

Princess Louise turned and smiled, then waited until I reached her side.

'Tell me more about yourself.'

I told her that my father was a plant hunter, currently on an expedition in Ecuador.

'An intrepid plant hunter. How fascinating. How long has he been away?' Princess Louise asked.

'More than two years,' I answered. I was embarrassed by the wobble in my voice.

'And you've lost your mother?'

I nodded. 'When I was fourteen.'

Princess Louise gave me the kindest look. 'How terrible. I was a similar age when I lost my dear papa. I truly understand your loss. Does your papa encourage your love of botany? It was my father's interest in sculpture which led me into that path of study.'

'You are a sculptress?' I was surprised. I'd never heard of a lady sculptor before.

'A student of sculpture. Mr Boehm is combining my ongoing tuition with his commission to create a bronze sculpture of the Queen,' Princess Louise replied.

'Her Royal Highness is too modest,' Lady Georgina interjected. 'Princess Louise had pieces accepted by the Royal Academy both this year and last.'

Princess Louise acknowledged the compliment with a nod of her head. 'Of course, having access to royal subjects did help. I found Prince Arthur an easy and cooperative subject. I assure you I'm finding Mama's statue much more of a challenge. It's lucky I have Mr Boehm here to steady my nerve.'

Lady Georgina declared it too warm for a hill climb, so led us down a path beside the river. A flock of oystercatchers foraged amongst the stones on the far bank.

The Princess chatted to Aunt Leonora, asking her to describe Drummond Castle and how she came to be living there.

'I'm sorry to hear you lost your husband. My mama finds widowhood almost intolerable.'

'I hope it eases with more time. Archibald died over ten years ago. I'm very lucky to have such a good friend in Lady Georgina, and now I have Iris's company, too.'

'I've only lately come to appreciate the blessing of female friends,' the Princess replied. 'I missed my elder sisters terribly when they all married. Thank goodness Mama gave me permission to attend lessons at the National Art Training School, which improved my artistic technique, and also gave me like-minded friends.'

We turned back and followed a forest path back to the castle.

'Thank you for accompanying us, Your Highness,' said Aunt Leonora. She brushed her hand against mine, to make sure I didn't forget the final curtsey bob.

'On the contrary, the pleasure was all mine. You livened up what would otherwise have been a dull afternoon. I hope to meet you again.'

The Princess walked back to the door. Just then Mr Boehm came out. Her words were carried to us on the breeze. 'So how did your session go? Did that brute stand at her side the whole time?'

'He did,' Mr Boehm replied. 'I find myself in need of a cigarette.' He took a silver case from his pocket.

Princess Louise gave him a huge smile, took his elbow, and they both disappeared round the corner.

Chapter Twenty-One

July 1869 – Iris

The Queen's green leather-bound volume was embossed in gold: a central pattern of crossed leaves and a gold border. I opened it as soon as we were on the train. As promised, Her Majesty had inscribed it.

Presented
To the
Innerpeffray Library
By
Victoria Reg

Balmoral
June 1869

It was tricky to turn the pages wearing gloves, but I daren't risk touching the book with my bare hands. The next page revealed a very pretty black and white drawing of Balmoral. The title page was *Leaves from the Journal of Our Life in the Highlands from 1848 to 1861*. From the year after her marriage until the year of Prince Albert's death. The dedication page confirmed this.

TO

THE DEAR MEMORY OF HIM
WHO MADE THE LIFE OF THE WRITER BRIGHT AND HAPPY
THESE SIMPLE RECORDS
ARE LOVINGLY AND GRATEFULLY INSCRIBED.

The book was factual; a journal. Given the inscription, I'd hoped it would contain more about her relationship with Prince Albert. Instead, the intimacy had to be inferred by them being constantly together. Nevertheless, there were charming line drawings of the hills, and descriptions of long walks. The Queen was evidently a fan of the outdoors.

My mind wandered and I passed the book to Aunt Leonora and turned to completing my journal and letter to Papa. To be presented to the Queen was a huge honour. Princess Louise was unlike anyone I'd met before. Her spirit, her vigour and enthusiasm for life, and her evident ambition stirred me to want more for myself. I didn't have her wealth or position, but her determination was infectious. My skill was not with art, but I could hone my writing skills. The essay I'd prepared for the Queen was factual and free from errors, but I'd failed to consider how to fully engage my audience. A useful lesson. On our short journey towards Drummond Castle, I realised I hadn't thought of Rafael even once, all day. Perhaps my heart was mending.

A letter and a package were waiting for me in Drummond Castle. The letter from Professor Jameson was brief, but the content pleased me.

Jane Anderson

Hay Lodge, Trinity, Edinburgh

Dear Miss Finlay,
How delightful to hear from you. I am very fond of your father and
we spent many happy evenings together during the last two years. I
should tell you he mentioned you frequently and separation from you
was something he felt most keenly. I would love to meet you and I'm
sorry I missed you on your recent visit. If you find yourself in Edin-
burgh again, I do hope you will get in touch.

You mentioned that your father has delayed his return until next
year. Nevertheless, I anticipate I may still be here. In which case, it
would give me great pleasure to invite you both to visit me here at the
home of my friend Isaac Henry-Anderson in Edinburgh. He is a very
knowledgeable botanist, and I know he and your father will enjoy
each other's company.

Yours,
William Jameson

The package was from Elspeth Donaldson and contained
a book and a letter full of news of her life in Edinburgh,
including accounts of recitals and dances at the Assembly
Rooms, and witty anecdotes. I was glad I could reply with
news of my visit to Balmoral. She might find an account of
my sleepy Perthshire life dull. The book was a new edition of
Professor Hutton Balfour's book on botany, published by her
father's company.

Elspeth gave a very sincere invitation to stay with her and
Alexander in Edinburgh. Then finally, the most thrilling piece
of news.

*I told my father about meeting you, described your deep interest in
botany and gardening and also your publishing ambitions. He says
there is a gap in the market to meet the growing interest in gardening,
and that you might consider a pamphlet as a publishing trial?
However, I must warn you that he says illustrations add considerably
to the expense and hand colouring is most likely out of the question.
Very best wishes,
Elspeth Donaldson*

On Thursday, Aunt Leonora arranged for Mr Buchan to take
me to Innerpeffray Library. She was once again in bed with
stomach pains.

'I can delay until next week,' I offered.

'I'm sure Mr and Mrs Birnie are anxious to receive their
precious gift. I expect they have a waiting list of readers
hoping to view it.'

I asked Mr Buchan to take me via Muthill so I could take
Annie.

I clutched the precious present from Queen Victoria, now
wrapped up in brown paper to protect it from the elements.
Annie must have heard us arrive because she came to the
door. She was very pale. The business with Rafael must have
still been on her mind.

'I'm glad I found you at home. I'm going to Innerpeffray
to hand over a present from the Queen. She has dedicated
her book to the library. Will you come with me?'

'Fancy me having a friend who takes tea wi' the Queen.'
Her words were accompanied by a smile.

'I did and the Queen herself admired your work.'

'You are full ae flattery, Iris. Of course I'll come. I cannae
wait tae see the book and especially Mr and Mrs Birnie's
faces.'

At the library, I handed over the Queen's book. The Birnies were as thrilled as I'd hoped. Afterwards, Annie and I settled into the library to scour *Curtis's* for inspiration for the pamphlet.

'I think these flowers are too exotic for what I have in mind.'

'What were your favourite flowers in your parents' garden?' Annie asked.

'My mother was very fond of bright colours. Irises, of course, but she was also drawn to the colour pink. Roses, fuchsias, tulips, pelargoniums.'

'Pelar...?'

'Pelargoniums, it's the genus name for geraniums.'

'I'm sure Struan said they were working on breeding new colours ae geraniums and roses at Drummond Gardens.'

'Really? There are new colours of garden flowers arriving in nurseries all the time. I believe amateur gardeners would be very interested in such trends. It's such a shame that there will be no opportunity to produce colour in the pamphlet.'

'I'm sure you can use words tae describe the colour very well. The dark pink ae a ripe strawberry or the shade ae a bullfinch's chest.'

'You're right. It will be a challenge, but not impossible.'

'Maybe the printer might stretch tae hand colouring ae one shade only. The greens ae the stems and leaves are maybe no sae important, but you could have one streak ae pink in a flower, or even a petal. I could describe the mix of paint. One part vermillion tae ten parts cadmium white, for example. It would be child's play tae paint.'

'That's a brilliant idea, Annie. Let's make an example to send to Elspeth's father. I'll go down to the castle gardens tomorrow. Mr MacDonald might help me with some ideas.'

'If you send word ae your choice, I can ask Struan to pick

and prepare a flower for me tae draw. He assures me he knows how.'

The next morning I went in search of Mr MacDonald. Although he was a busy man, it was easy to get him talking about the new specimens he was so proud of. He showed me a variegated geranium and some pink fuchsias with a purple inner. As we walked, he shared his thoughts on how some plants were very fussy about certain soils or the balance of sunshine to shade, but said fuchsias and geraniums grew easily in Scotland.

I went straight back to the castle and started writing. *A Symphonie in Pink – Summer Ideas for a Scottish Garden* seemed a reasonable draft title. I wrapped the two flowers in some paper and sent them with a note to Annie. She'd obviously need freshly dissected ones to draw, but handing these to Struan would be the easiest way for her to explain what she wanted.

The next day I was in the garden walking with Aunt Leonora when Mr MacDonald came over holding a rosebud. 'This bonny rose is the same shade as thon pelargonium you liked.'

I took the bud delighted. 'Queen of Denmark. This rose grows beside the cottage on Mr Speir's estate. An excellent idea.'

I sent Annie a note.

Mr MacDonald has suggested the Queen of Denmark rose as a drawing subject. If you are able to come to Innerpeffray after church on Sunday, tell Struan I'll bring you home. We might call into Culdees Castle to look at the Queen of Denmark rose in the lodge garden. A view of the cottage will make a nice illustration for the front of the pamphlet.

. . .

On Sunday we spent a glorious afternoon in Innerpeffray schoolroom in excited discussion about our project. Annie had done a beautiful illustration of a sprig of fuchsia on the large paper Aunt Leonora had given her. She mixed a puddle of pink and one of purple. The drawing looked spectacular, with just two dashes of colour. She tasked me with adding the pink, to demonstrate that the little addition of colour took no skill.

'I believe we are onto something, Annie. Perhaps, though, we should not set our sights too high. Let's think about the Queen's book as a model. Put an image of a cottage garden on the front with a splash of colour and have some simple line drawings of the individual species set within the writing. This is so beautiful, but my guess is it's too big for pamphlet form.'

'Yes. And I'm nae sure we need tae show the dissected flower for this kind ae pamphlet aimed at amateurs.'

I nodded. 'That's it. Think about the intended reader. It's what I'm trying to do with my words. And of course, this is not for publication, we're just trying to capture Mr White's attention.'

'Let's go tae Culdees. I need tae remind myself the look ae the garden.'

I looked into her eyes to try to fathom her thoughts. 'Are you sure? It won't stir up painful memories?'

Annie sighed. 'I knew fae the minute I found Rafael gone that I'd been kidding myself. He wisnae really interested in me. Maybe it was just an amusement for him tae see me hanging on his every word.' She chewed on a ragged fingernail.

'I was taken in by him as much as you were,' I replied.

. . .

Mr Buchan dropped us at the stables and we walked round to the cottage front garden. I took a chair from inside and positioned it on the path. Annie sat down to work on her sketch.

'The roses are perfect. Could you change it to add some other flowers as well? Certainly a fuchsia and a geranium. We'll maybe need two or three more species.'

'Of course. Let me capture the dimensions ae the cottage and the rose. I'll leave the foreground blank until you decide what you want tae include. This is just a sketch, anyway. I'll polish it up later.'

The sound of horse's hooves alerted us to a visitor. Struan Cooper came marching around the corner. He didn't waste any time with polite preamble.

'Is he back? The village is full ae gossip about you and that bloody Spaniard, Annie.'

He glared at me. 'And this is your fault entirely.'

Annie stood up, ashen-faced. 'No. It's just me and Iris. She's been telling all about her visit tae the Queen and we're planning tae try and get a wee pamphlet published.'

Her words only enraged him even further. 'Visit tae the Queen? Can you hear yersel', Annie? She's playin' wi' you. Folks like us dinnae mix wi' the Queen's friends and we dinnae get published either.'

Struan marched over to me. He looked so furious, I took a step back.

'I telt you once already what will happen if you wear her oot. This week she's been up at five tae work, then using the time she should be resting tae draw stuff for you. Get back tae yer ain folk and leave us in peace.'

His last words were shouted in my face. Some of them were fair. I wanted the earth to swallow me.

Annie marched over and took my arm. 'Iris is my best and only friend. She's given me a hope ae life beyond the one I've got.'

Struan swallowed and I thought he might actually cry. 'Annie, I'm feard for you. We cannae be dreamers.'

Annie's crestfallen expression made me furious.

'Is it so wrong that we might strive for something better? Is getting up to do manual labour every day the right thing for Annie? I'm not pretending we can make enough money to live on, but I do believe we might succeed in raising enough to allow her to stop maid's work. Look at her ruined hands.'

Struan frowned. 'Since yer such best friends, you will surely hae telt her about yer tryst wi' the Spaniard in Drummond Castle glasshouses.'

I gasped. Annie looked bereft. She limped up the path and slammed the cottage door behind her.

'Go home,' I told Struan. 'Annie really is my best friend. I'll bring her back safely.'

He turned and left.

Inside the cottage, Annie was collapsed in a fit of tears on the couch.

'Annie—'

She put up her hand to silence me. 'Don't say a thing, Iris. He was playing wi' me and always set on you. I must be blind as well as lame no tae notice.'

I grabbed both her hands and sat beside her. 'Please, Annie. Don't let Rafael divide us. I don't deny I followed him into a compromising situation. He never kissed me and I confess I was jealous of you. I'm so sorry. I should have told you before.'

'Dae you think he was playing wi' us both?'

'Sadly, I think he was.'

'Then we are daft as each other. He was up tae nae good, Iris.'

I hugged Annie with all my strength. 'I fear he wasn't.'

I sat back and rubbed my face. 'But he's coming back,

Annie. We can't let him come between us again. We need to understand what he was up to. Tell me about that last evening you were together. What did you talk about?

Annie sighed. 'I cannae right remember. He gave me a wee glass ae wine, but it felt like I'd drunk a witch's potion. As if I'd flown beyond my broken body. Like I was strong and fearless. I felt beautiful, brave, capable ae anything.'

'Like you felt when you drank that tincture?'

'Aye, maybe, but much more powerful.'

'What did you talk about?'

'He was poring over my sketchbook. Praising me tae the heavens.' Annie's eyes widened. 'What have I done, Iris? He asked me about the huge orchid. I told him we copied it for your pa.'

I sighed. 'He asked me about what Papa was looking for, too.'

'Oh, Iris. You trusted me and I let you down.'

I gripped her hand. 'Don't blame yourself. If he'd been able to ply me with whatever was in that glass, I'd have told him too. He tricked us both, Annie.'

Annie's expression became determined. 'I wish he wasnae coming back, but I'll no be taken in again.'

'We will look after each other. Honestly, it's made me distrust my judgment when it comes to men. I'll be more wary in the future. I'd like to find a way to support myself so I'd not need to risk marriage.'

'I dinnae know about supporting myself' but I'd like to contribute better tae our housekeeping. My maid's wages are nae mair than a pittance.'

'So let's make a pact. We can make this work, but Struan is right, too. You mustn't make yourself ill by working too hard.'

Annie stood up. 'You're right and I need to find a way to

get Struan co-operating in this plan. I hate tae fight wi' him. I aywis long tae rush at things, but I need tae pace myself better.'

I stood and held out my elbow to let her take it. 'Let's get you home. We can talk about it later in the week.'

Chapter Twenty-Two

July 1869

Struan was embarrassed and knew he'd been too forceful in his confrontation with Iris outside the library. He could tell Iris cared that Annie should not make herself ill, and had been certain she'd stop Annie from working so hard, but the following days were just the same. Annie was still busy, evasive and feverish. After leaving Iris that day at Innerpeffray he found Annie taking off her bonnet at home, just as the girl had predicted. She wouldn't talk about her whereabouts except that she'd been painting. Struan already knew Annie hadn't always travelled with Buchan who was sometimes in the Drummond stables when Annie was out. Was Iris paying for the coach hire? But it made no sense to do so that Sunday, when Iris was in Innerpeffray so soon afterwards herself. Nevertheless, whoever was helping Annie work away from home, Miss Iris Finlay was the manager of the project and he was right to hold her responsible.

Later in the week, Annie told him excitedly that Iris had been summoned for an audience with the Queen herself.

He groaned. 'That proves what I've been telling you all

along, Annie. Gardener's bairns don't socialise wi' people who are summoned by Her Majesty.'

During the week the sight of Iris chatting to Mr MacDonald in Drummond Castle Gardens rattled him. He confined Iris to an angry place in his heart. He didn't want to think about her at work, but there she was, walking confidently through his parterre. Annie told him Iris was seeking out some pink hues for their first pamphlet. Mr MacDonald brought her a variegated geranium Struan had helped breed himself. The sight of her admiring it pleased him which was infuriating. Iris was making Annie ill, she was his sworn enemy in the battle to save his sister. Even thinking those thoughts sounded daft. She was just a lassie and he was losing his mind with rage.

Day after day there was no evidence that Annie was paying any attention to him. Then, one evening, everything changed. The worrying shine in Annie's eyes was extinguished but the normal happy light went out too. He arrived home to find her taken to bed and refusing to rouse. Over the following days she went to work but was listless. At nights Struan was kept awake by the terrible sound of Annie weeping. His sister wouldn't talk about it, forcing Struan to consult with gossips. On Sunday after church, when Annie went to Innerpeffray with the Birnies, he loitered on the road to Mrs Lamont's home.

'How is your dear sister, Mr Cooper? I thought she looked pale in church.'

He knew she was fishing for information.

'Thank you for asking, Mrs Lamont. You're sae kind tae be concerned for her health these weeks and I'll be honest, it's taken a turn for the worse.'

'I'm most sorry tae hear that. I'd blame that foreigner who's been swanning about in Mr Speir's gig. Annie wouldn't be so weary if he'd drive her all the way home. I thought they were maybe courting?'

Of course. Annie had talked about the botanist a great deal and then she'd stopped. The Spaniard's sliminess around Iris had made his blood boil. It had never occurred to him the man might have his eye on Annie too.

Mrs Lamont wasn't finished. 'I seen him at the train station with a heap of bags and boxes this week, so I'll guess Annie's got time on her hands now.'

Struan didn't respond, simply touched his cap and thanked her for her concern.

His rage climbed up a notch. Iris had been thick as thieves wi' the man. She'd introduced him to Annie. It was time to save Annie and blow this so-called friendship apart. He marched to Drummond Castle for the cart and onto Innerpeffray. Mrs Birnie told him he'd missed Annie and that she'd gone with Iris to Culdees. The cart journey all the way back to Muthill again gave him time to work himself up into a lather. He confronted Annie and Iris in the garden of the Spaniard's lair.

'Is he back? The village is full ae gossip about you and that bloody Spaniard, Annie.'

He directed his anger to Iris. 'And this is your fault entirely.'

Annie stood up, 'No. Iris has been telling me all about her visit tae the Queen.'

Struan thought he might explode. 'She's playing wi' you. Folks like us dinnae mix wi' the Queen's friends.'

'I telt you once already what will happen if you wear her oot,' he yelled at Iris. 'Get back tae yer ain folk and leave us in peace.'

Annie's pale face became flushed with anger. 'Iris is my best and only friend. She's given me a hope ae life beyond the one I've got.'

Struan feared he might weep with frustration. 'Annie I'm feard for you. We cannae be dreamers.'

Iris blethered some nonsense about them making money so Annie could give up maid's work. How dare she criticise their honest working lives. 'Since yer such best friends, you will surely hae telt her about yer tryst wi' the Spaniard in Drummond Castle glasshouses.'

They both reacted as if he'd struck them. Annie marched into the cottage and slammed the door.

'Go home,' Iris said. 'Annie really is my best friend. I'll bring her back safely.'

He turned and left.

Chapter Twenty-Three

July 1869

A week later, Aunt Leonora received a letter. Her expression suggested it must be good news.

'Is Papa coming home?' Even as I said it, I knew I was wrong. Papa would send such good news to me directly.

'It's from Georgina. Prior warning that we should expect a letter from the Queen's lady-in-waiting. A member of the royal household has taken leave of absence due to family illness in Germany. They want you to join the staff, Iris.'

'What?' I had to sit down to absorb the news. To live in Balmoral and be near to the Queen's family. Little Iris Finlay from sleepy Fowlis Wester. The expression on Aunt Leonora's face gave me an idea of how my mother would have reacted such an invitation. A huge honour, but as I considered the implications, my heart sank. 'I see,' was the best I could muster.

'Whatever is the matter?' Any other girl would jump at the chance. You do realise it's not the kind of summons you can turn down.'

'Of course not. But what will I be expected to do? I've no training in maid's work.'

'Nobody is going to ask you to clean out the fireplaces, Iris,' Aunt Leonora said with some sarcasm. 'This must be Georgina's good work on your behalf. I doubt Her Majesty formed a favourable opinion based on such a brief meeting.'

I remembered telling Lady Georgina about my frustration over dependence on Aunt Leonora. How thoughtless and self-centred not to realise Lady Bradley was helping me. 'Of course. I'm most terribly grateful.'

'Don't worry, Iris. Georgina will keep an eye on you and ensure you understand your duties. I must go and tell Lady de Eresby. This is such excellent news.'

How was I going to tell Annie?

The letter came the next day, making it clear this was a temporary appointment for the duration of this German lady's absence. My spirits were raised. I could please Aunt Leonora without being away from Annie for too long.

'It doesn't mention salary. I do hope the investment in new clothes will be worth the expense,' Aunt Leonora muttered under her breath.

'Do I really need new clothes? My blue dress was bought for Balmoral and I can manage with two.'

'Your green silk is too bright for the Queen's taste. I'll ask Mrs Graham to run up another dress using your measurements. What do you think about dark grey flannel? It seems that the ladies at Balmoral spend a lot of time outdoors and it won't be long until the weather turns cold.'

'Thank you, Aunt Leonora. I will repay you when I get paid. I will be proud to be able to do that for the first time.'

'I'm happy to see you well-dressed, Iris. Although the Queen leads a quiet life at Balmoral, you might meet some interesting people there.'

I knew she meant interesting and monied men, but

resisted the urge to argue that I had no interest in marriage. I was resolute in my intention to forge my own path in life and not to be taken in by any man. Being in genteel employment was at least a step in the right direction.

On Thursday afternoon I met Annie at Innerpeffray schoolroom. She was excited to show me the pen and ink sketches she had added to my descriptions of the geranium and fuchsia. She'd hatching to indicate the darker colour in the centre of the fuchsia flower and the shapely leaf of the geranium was perfectly formed.

'These are really good, Annie. We need perhaps one or two more species to create a balanced scene for the cottage on the cover.'

'What about a foxglove or a peony? The illustration will look better wi' a variety ae heights.'

'You have an artist's eye for imagining a composition, Annie. Foxgloves are a great choice, since they are easy to grow from seed. Cost will be an issue for many gardeners.'

'I'll sketch an idea for the whole scene wi' that in mind.'

I sighed, reluctant to tell Annie I was leaving. 'I have some news. I'm afraid I'm going away soon and I don't know how long I'll be gone.'

'Is your aunt travelling?'

'No, I've been offered a temporary post at Balmoral. To cover for a lady who has gone home to her family.'

Annie stood up to hug me. Moving too quickly and without her stick, she almost overbalanced. 'Congratulations. My pal Iris, working for the Queen. How exciting!'

'Do sit down, Annie. If you fall over in my company, Struan will have me hung, drawn and quartered.'

She giggled. 'He's not as fierce as you imagine. Just a wee

bit overprotective. It's ae been that way and he feels guilty too.'

'Why should Struan feel guilty?'

'Before he died, Pa telt him he had tae look out for me because it was him being the bigger twin that likely caused my limp.'

'That doesn't make sense.'

'No, it doesnae and Pa was wrong tae lay such a thing on Struan, but Pa was feard ae me being left alone when he took sick. Our house is too wee for secrets and I overheard their whispering. Pa told Struan that when we were born, they didnae expect two babies. Struan was born first, and as wi' maist births, it took time. The midwife was thinking ae putting her coat on tae go home when I turned up. I came out no breathing and blue in the face.'

'How terrifying, but I really don't see how that would leave you with a bad leg?'

'Me neither. I wish I wisnae such a burden.'

'Well, there's nothing wrong with my legs, but I feel I'm a burden, too. Let's keep on with our publishing plans and try to find a way to be independent of our families.'

Annie shook her head. 'You dinnae need tae feel responsible for me, too. That's just making the whole situation worse. You are setting off on your life, Iris, and I'm happy for you.'

'Annie, it was you who rescued me. I'd been so lonely. Our publishing possibility is dependent on your skill. It's the illustrations that make the brochure special.'

Annie smiled, but her expression said she didn't believe me. 'Iris, you've been chosen as special enough tae serve the Queen. You'll no be coming back tae live in this sleepy place. I know you plan tae keep house for your pa, but I'm no convinced such a life will be enough for you.'

I sighed. 'You know me too well, I've been thinking the same thing. I'm determined to look after Papa when he returns, but I do want more. That's why our plans are so important.'

Struan arrived in the cart. I hugged Annie. 'Wish me luck on my adventure. I gather the Queen leads a very quiet life. I might hate it.'

Tears threatened us both.

'I'll get the flowers to you before I go, but take your time with the drawings. I might be too busy to race through the pages like before.'

'I'll hae a shot at sketching the cover. Will I be able tae send it to you at Balmoral?'

I hugged her again. 'I think the only thing I can guarantee is the postie will know how to find Balmoral.'

Annie exchanged words with her brother in the cart. Struan looked at me intently. I caught something surprising in his expression. Almost as if he was sad at my going, too.

A few days later, I was packing my trunk when Aunt Leonora came in with a dress draped over her arms.

'It's here! I thought Mrs Graham had said she'd have to send it to Balmoral.'

'She's waiting for some fancy braid for the flannel dress, but I ordered this one too.'

Aunt Leonora laid a dress of moiré silk in silvery grey on my bed.

'My goodness, this is beautiful!' I ran my fingers across the shimmering fabric, which was light as a feather and cool to the touch.

'Your first evening dress. We can call it an early birthday present. I think you might have a need for it at the castle.'

Soaring excitement filled my chest. For the first time, I realised I was looking forward to this adventure.

'Thank you. I promise not to let you down.'

Chapter Twenty-Four

July 1869

Struan regretted his words about the Spaniard's duplicity with Iris as soon as he spoke. He was horrified by Annie's look of anguish before she marched off, and Iris's sad resignation. It had been his intention to destroy the friendship, but how would Annie survive if he'd got rid of her first and only friend? That utter bastard had played Annie and Iris and he'd been played as well. He was an idiot.

He waited anxiously for the sound of the gig. He never doubted Iris's promise to bring his sister home. When Annie came in and stretched up to hug him, he almost wept with relief.

'That terrible man came between the three ae us but we won't let him win,' she said.

They talked long into the night. 'You aren't mad that Iris had met wi' Rafael and didnae tell you?'

'No. Iris knew I was meeting wi' him and she warned me it was a terrible idea. Not that she knew he was bad, but that it might damage my reputation. I ignored her, Struan. Was it Mrs Lamont who telt you?'

Struan nodded.

'When I'd been in Culdees the road home is past her cottage. Aifter she saw us, I had Rafael drop me on the edge ae the village. So I had tae walk further.'

'He's such a terrible man. Rude tae me, rude tae the grooms at Culdees. How did you no see?'

'He's two-faced, Iris and I only saw the charming one. Also he spotted that beneath my broken body, my heart is just as longing as the next lassie. I'm shocked at myself. If he'd said he loved me and promised tae marry, who knows what kind ae bother I might ae got intae.'

This confession appalled Struan. He thought of his sister as a child but she was a woman now. He'd been completely wrong about Iris Finlay and with this revelation of her goodness, something new stirred. He loved his sister like life itself. He should have known that a place in her heart would have been well deserved.

'Does Iris hate me for telling you her secret?'

'I don't think Iris is the vengeful kind. She knows you're motivated by a wish tae protect me. I'm sure over time, she'll forgive you.'

His days in Drummond Castle Gardens were now as light as the sunny weather. All the flowers he'd tended with such care over the year were at their most beautiful. The de Eresby family brought visitors into the parterre and Struan basked in the glory of overheard praise. For the first time since the death of his father, he experienced a growing hope. Hope that Annie would continue to recover. She was healing, distracted by drawing up the Scottish flowers. He'd been sad when Annie explained they'd abandoned doing drawings of the dissected blooms. A short time dissecting for her had made him feel part of things. He didn't even drive much. They mostly met at Muthill and Iris picked up and dropped Annie without his help.

The stars aligned to put Iris in his path one Thursday. Annie asked to go to Innerpeffray and Mr MacDonald could spare the cart. Struan didn't see Iris when he dropped Annie off, but the leap in his chest when he saw them exit the library together in the evening, told him he was in deep trouble. Iris met his eye and he didn't see anything other than warmth. That was a step in the right direction. They drove home in silence, his thoughts were full of foolish hopes. He only saw Annie's stricken face when they reached home.

'Whatever's the matter, Annie?'

'Och, I shouldae guessed it. Iris is one in a million, so ae course Her Majesty was charmed by her too. She's been summoned tae go tae work for the Queen in Balmoral.'

'What? She's leaving? Leaving for good?'

'Iris says it's temporary until some German lady returns, but I can just imagine how well she'll get on. I bet they take Iris south wi' them when they leave Scotland.'

Struan had imagined working on Iris over the years. Some mingling through his sister, getting to know Mr Finlay when he returned Culdees. He needed time to be worthy of her. Many promotions to earn enough to support a wife and a lot of patience. Now she'd be mixing wi' royalty and lairds in Balmoral and some upper class type would see Iris's glory and be able to offer her the world she deserved.

'When does she leave?' he asked.

'Only three mair days.' Annie was so distraught he hoped she didn't see his crushed soul. He was embarrassed for being such a stupid dreamer.

Chapter Twenty-Five

August 1869 – Balmoral Castle, Aberdeenshire, Scotland

A boy with a cart was waiting for me at Ballater Station. I came into Balmoral from a different branch of the drive and arrived at the castle side door. Clearly, the servants didn't come past the front of the castle. I had no illusions about my status but was very nervous. I had no real idea of what would be expected of me, but was certain I wasn't qualified to work in a royal household.

The boy picked up my trunk and led me across the court-yard into the kitchen. Several kitchen maids and an older woman I took to be the cook, stopped what they were doing to turn and stare. A pot was boiling vigorously on the large range, filling the room with steam. The women wore grey and white uniforms and had their sleeves pushed up. It was unbearably hot, and it was no wonder that all were very red in the face. I felt horribly overdressed and a film of perspiration immediately formed on my forehead, a drop of sweat running down my cheek. I opened my mouth to introduce myself, but the boy called me through into what he called the steward's room.

'Lady Craigengar says yer tae wait for her in here.'

I stood in the middle of the room. I'd been given no invitation to sit, but in any case, the one stool in the corner was impossible for a girl with a hooped and bustled dress.

A woman entered dressed entirely in black, except for a white frill peeking out from her black cap. No hint of a welcome softened her severe expression. I curtsied, and she gave a curt nod. At least I'd got that right.

'You must be the new girl.'

'Yes, Your Ladyship.' I pulled back my shoulders, glad Drummond Castle had made me confident with modes of address.

The woman looked me up and down, as if I were an animal at market. She sniffed. 'It's beyond inconvenient to have someone new join us and I'd hoped for someone older. Do you work at Drummond Castle?'

'No, Your Ladyship. I live there with Lady Leonora Walker, who is a relative of Lady Willoughby de Eresby.'

'But you have no title?'

'No. My late mother was Lady Walker's sister.'

Lady Craigengar's evident disappointment was expressed with a deep sigh. 'Well, you'll have to do. Hopefully, it won't be for long.'

Just when I thought my welcome couldn't get any worse, Mr Brown appeared in the doorway. He glared at me and looked down at my trunk, frowning.

'Where's that laddie gone?'

'One of your staff, Mr Brown. I'll leave you to attend to it.' Lady Craigengar made towards the door, then turned around. 'You can report for work in one hour.'

'Of course, Lady Craigengar. But where will I find you and should I change into uniform?'

Lady Craigengar's scornful expression could have curdled milk. 'You've been honoured with a place in the royal household, young lady. Only the castle staff wear uniform. Lady Bradley agreed to brief you, but she is out with Her Majesty. If she hasn't returned, I suppose I'll have to deal with it. Meet me in Princess Louise's dressing room.' She narrowed her eyes to scrutinise me again. 'Your dress will do.'

I certainly wasn't going to ask how I would find the Princess's quarters. Nor was I going to give into the urge to cry.

'I'll tak up yer trunk,' John Brown said.

My grateful smile got no reaction. He pushed my small trunk with the toe. 'Is that all your luggage?'

I nodded.

'Your room's right at the top ae the tower, so I hope your legs are strong.' The man had a deep voice and spoke with a strong local accent I found difficult to follow. I hurried to match his long stride. When we reached the bottom of a flight of stairs, he nodded towards the long corridor stretching in the opposite direction. 'The royal quarters are all in the west wing ae the castle. Princess Louise's rooms are on the second floor. Her dressing room has the view over the rose garden.'

On the top floor, Mr Brown put down my trunk and opened a door. The small whitewashed room with a tiny window high on the wall contained a narrow bed and an armoire. 'This is it then, lassie. It's maybe no sae grand as yer Drummond Castle rooms.'

I hoped my smile looked confident. It in no way reflected what I really felt. 'Thank you, Mr Brown. I'm most grateful to have a room to myself.' In truth, the room was only slightly smaller than my Drummond Castle bedroom, but it was very spartan containing no ornament except a jug and basin on a washstand, set in front of a very small mirror. 'Does this room belong to the German lady?'

'No. Fräulein Bauer's room is opposite those of Princesses

Louise and Beatrice. When no on chaperone duties, she is German tutor tae the Queen's youngest daughter. I don't suppose you speak German?'

'I'm fluent in Latin and French, but no, not German.'

Mr Brown raised a bushy eyebrow. 'Which makes this appointment even mair ae a mystery.'

I gritted my teeth. I wouldn't demean myself by responding to his rudeness.

'You're tae report tae Princess Louise and while there's nae skill in chaperoning, it will be your maist important responsibility here.' He paused, then took a step towards me, and lowered his head to look me in the eye.

I resisted the urge to step backwards.

'Lady Craigengar leads the Queen's staff but I'm in charge ae Balmoral and moral conduct is of paramount importance tae Her Majesty. You're tae stick tae the Princess like glue and she's no tae be left alone with that man.'

Recalling the Princess laughing and on the arm of that handsome sculptor, I guessed which man he meant. But how could I possibly be held responsible for the conduct of a princess? My heart sank.

After Mr Brown left, I unpacked my small trunk, washed my hands and face, then fixed my hair before repining my hat. 'Don't be a baby, Iris,' I told my reflection. 'You're on your own now, so you will have to work it out.'

I exited my room into the silent castle and made my way back to the bottom of the stairs. I'd no confidence I could locate the Princess's dressing room, so wanted to explore before the appointed time. Sunlight spilled into the corridor from the other end. I walked in that direction until I found the open door was the sitting room where I'd met the Queen on my previous visit. I could see the castle grounds stretching up a grassy slope outside the bay window. I climbed the stairs opposite to the second floor, but found all the doors were closed. Should I knock on one? Hearing someone running up the stairs, I turned, expecting to see a child, and was astonished to discover it was Princess Louise, and in an extraordinary outfit. She wore a dirty paint smock, no hat, and her hair was dishevelled. A large brown streak was smeared across her left cheek.

'How marvellous, you're here.' Her cheerful welcoming smile came closer to dissolving my brave face than the previous bullying. Then her expression changed to alarm. 'Are they returned from Braemar?'

'No. Lady Craigengar said she hoped Lady Bradley would be back within the hour, but I haven't heard anyone else come in.'

'Goodness, has Craigengar been in the castle all this time? I thought she'd gone out with Mama and the others.' The Princess flung open one of the doors. 'You can help me change. I was modelling some clay, and I lost track of time. I'm meant to have prepared Mama's correspondence. There will be hell to pay if she finds I've been in the studio all afternoon.'

No sooner had I closed the door than the princess flung off the smock and the simple cotton dress she had on underneath. Her final layer was long cotton bloomers, a simple chemise and no corsetry at all. She hopped on one foot to pull off what looked like boys' hose. 'I stole them from Leopold's room. I couldn't find mine.'

Hardly a surprise. A chair, a dressing stool and even the floor were strewn with clothes. Her chest of drawers was open, and I spied hose peeping out of one drawer. Her open wardrobe was filled with dresses.

Princess Louise looked shame-faced. 'Sorry, it's such a mess. I didn't let my lady's maid enter this week. I overheard her whispering to Lady Craigengar and I will not be spied upon.'

My skin prickled as I remembered Mr Brown's instructions.

'Which dress would you like? Shall I find you some undergarments?'

'Thank you, you are a dear.' Princess Louise pulled a chocolate brown dress with black braiding out of the wardrobe and looked around the room for a space to put it down. I took it from her.

'Let me undo the fastenings for you. Your Highness, you might want to check...' I put my hand to my left cheek. Princess Louise looked in the mirror and laughed.

I located a set of hoops collapsed by the dressing table. Their weight surprised me. Constructed in some kind of featherlight, shiny metal instead of whalebone, this explained, at least in part, the Princess's easy movements when I met her last. Meanwhile, the Princess leaned over a basin of water to scrub off the clay, then ran her wet fingers through her unruly hair. I helped her into her hoops and dress while she tamed her hair with pins at lightning speed. I could easily imagine how such dexterity would lend itself to sculpture. The sound of carriage wheels on gravel in the courtyard below drifted up through the open window.

'Just in time,' she said with a conspiratorial smile. 'There's a matching bustle. I think it's on the floor of the wardrobe.'

I found this clever contraption. A complicated knot of stiffened ruffles. Princess Louise showed me where to attach it with buttons.

'This is ingenious, as are your hoops. Such clever innovations.'

'I've got my London seamstresses scouring the European market for anything that can achieve a respectable look, with least discomfort and fuss.' She pinned on her hat. 'How do I look?'

There was a tiny smudge of clay beside her left ear. 'Perfect, apart from just here.' I pointed to the place at my own ear, picked up her discarded washcloth, and handed it to her.

'I'd better go down before someone comes looking for me. Will you come?'

I looked around the chaotic room. 'I think I might stay and put some things away.'

'Thank you. Honestly, I hardly need a lady's maid usually, but I'm at such a crucial stage with my work this week, I can find time for nothing else.'

Princess Louise's cheeks were flushed, her eyes sparkled, and her whole body seemed taut with energy. A royal princess and perhaps the most extraordinary person I'd ever met. I was already a little besotted.

After the Princess left, I sorted through her discarded clothes. I found a large wicker laundry basket against one wall where I deposited all the worn undergarments. Most of the dresses could be rehung and once I'd tidied up the shoes on the floor of her wardrobe, I was able to put the others away. One long blue skirt was muddy along the hem and another had clay marks on both sides, as if she'd rubbed it with dirty hands. Those I laid over the top of the wicker basket. No doubt a laundry maid would decide how to deal with them. I couldn't find another painter's smock, so I hung the dirty one on the back of the door.

I ventured through the door to the adjoining room. This was clearly her bedroom. The bedding had been only hastily straightened. Once that was redone and all the drawers and doors had been closed, I awaited Lady Craigengar's arrival. I was certainly not going to seek out the royal party on my own. When the door opened after a rap of fingers, I was delighted to see Lady Georgina.

'I'm so sorry I wasn't here to greet you, Iris,' she said as she embraced me. 'The Queen felt well this morning and decided to make an overdue visit to her cobbler in Braemar. It can be hard to get her outside the castle grounds and we know to catch such a moment. How was your journey? Have you been shown your room?'

'Yes, and my journey was fine. Aunt Leonora insisted on accompanying me as far as Aberdeen, but I assured her I could manage the last leg alone.'

Lady Bradley's face fell. 'Did she? I wish I'd known. I might have come to spend a few minutes with her there.' She sighed. 'But I'd likely have had to cancel any such plan, since the Queen needed me today.'

'My aunt said if I didn't find it easy to get leave, that she'd perhaps come and stay in that nice Ballater guest house sometime next month.'

Lady Georgina beamed at me. 'That's an excellent plan. Although I can imagine we might find it a challenge to organise, given the capricious nature of our mistresses. Did Lady Craigengar explain the nature of your role with Princess Louise?'

'She didn't go into detail, but Mr Brown was very particular in emphasising my chaperoning duties.'

'Oh, goodness, did he meet you too? What a daunting combination. I'm so sorry.'

'I will be most attentive to my duties, but having spent just a few minutes in Princess Louise's company, I fear trying to contain her will be like trying to capture a whirlwind.'

'You will do your best and I've already seen your good influence. The Princess came into the sitting room singing your praises and admitted she'd left you up here tidying her room. That pleased the Queen enormously. Let's take a stroll outside. I think I need to talk you through some of the politics of living at Balmoral.'

We walked down the stairs together. 'There's a rather

lovely shortcut past the ballroom.' A short corridor led us onto a balcony above a large panelled room with a wooden floor and hung with enormous chandeliers. 'I do hope you will still be here when we have the Ghillies Ball at the end of the month. It is the one day when we shake off our gloom and the palace is filled with music, laughter and dancing. The royal party enters this way and everybody cheers for the Queen. Her Majesty sits in that alcove with her family, but the rest of us mix in with the dancers.' Lady Georgina gestured to the alcove on the right, lined with ornately carved wood.

'I'd love to see it. And are the guests really the ghillies? Is that why there are so many deer?' The top of the walls were decorated with dozens of stag heads.

'Prince Albert was an excellent shot. Most of these were his trophies. Her Majesty is extraordinarily proud of his prowess. As for the guests, all the staff come and we dance together. I expect the Prince of Wales will attend, and perhaps his married sisters too. Everyone but the Queen joins in and although she doesn't dance, she enjoys the spectacle. Last year, she even allowed Mr Brown to lead her onto the floor for a gentle few turns. He is a surprisingly good dancer.'

We went outside and walked over to the sunken rose garden. 'The key to doing well at Balmoral is to understand that everything revolves around our efforts to ease Her Majesty's grief.' Lady Georgina glanced back at the open windows of the castle and lowered her voice. 'Lady Craigengar can be tetchy and I'm afraid she and Princess Louise clash frequently, but Lady Craigengar and Mr Brown devote their entire lives to the Queen's happiness, and that, in the end, is the most important thing.'

Mr Boehm, the sculptor, came around the corner of the castle smoking a cigarette. He hastily ground it under his toe and approached us. 'Miss Finlay, welcome to Balmoral.' He stretched out his hand to shake mine. 'I hear you will join us for the sculpting lessons. I hope you won't find the experience too dull.'

'I'm certain I won't. I'm most interested to see you both work.'

'Princess Louise has prodigious talent and she will be delighted to have an appreciative audience. Poor Fräulein Bauer is not an art fan.' He made a small bow. 'I expect to see you both again at dinner.'

Lady Georgina gave a discreet cough. 'You might check your face before dinner, Mr Boehm. You still bear the evidence of your labours.'

The man put his hands to his cheeks and stopped when his fingers met a large patch of dried clay in his whiskers. He rubbed the spot rigorously. 'Well spotted, Lady Bradley.' He raised his exuberant eyebrows. 'I am most obliged.'

We watched him walk back towards the castle.

'It's good you are here, Iris,' Lady Georgina muttered under her breath.

Chapter Twenty-Six

August 1869

L ife in Balmoral Castle ran to a rigorous timetable. At first, I was overawed to be in such royal company, but I was amazed at how quickly the obvious boredom of the group infected me.

Lady Georgina explained. 'Her Majesty has become accustomed to being sad and positively discourages any levity in the conversation. I'm afraid any sign of happiness in others now offends her.'

Princess Louise generally spent her mornings working on her mother's correspondence. In dry weather, we joined a group for a walk after lunch. Then, the Princess sculpted most afternoons, accompanied by Edgar Boehm if the Queen wasn't sitting for him. Walking in the glorious grounds of Balmoral gave me the most pleasure. A favourite walk led up a steep gradient opposite the castle, but it was well worth the effort. The heather was in full bloom and the hills beyond the castle were wreathed in purple. Balmoral in the valley below with its walls of pale grey stone, topped with round turrets, was pretty as a picture in a fairy tale.

. . .

One morning, after two weeks in Balmoral, Princess Louise pushed all the letters aside with a groan. 'My goodness, this is deadly dull.'

I looked up from where I was mending a fabric tear in one of her dresses. The Princess had an extensive wardrobe, but she was both very active and rather careless.

'Iris, I remember you have beautiful handwriting?'

'So I've been told.'

'Come and sit here. There is a whole pile of non-confidential letters awaiting a reply. Mainly invitations to undertake civic duties, which Mama always declines. Let me dictate a standard reply to this one, then I'll take it to Her Majesty. She complains that I'm too slow and too keen to spend my time sculpting. If my mother approves of the idea, we might get through this dreadful chore at twice the speed.'

I took a deep breath before I put pen to paper. The letter was to the Provost of Laurencekirk and the creamy paper bore the Balmoral crest. Princess Louise dictated a letter excusing Her Majesty on ill health grounds and sending her best wishes. When I handed the paper to her, she blew on it to settle the ink.

'Your handwriting is much better than mine. Hopefully Mama will agree.'

In the afternoon, a package arrived from Annie. I took it up to the sculpture studio to read while the Princess reworked a section around the jawline.

'This is impossible to get right. Mama is sensitive about her jowls, but if I take them out, the likeness will be lost.'

Princess Louise stepped back to view the huge clay sculpture, placing her hands on her hips and glowering at her work. Luckily, the clay landed only on her smock. The laundry maid complained bitterly about trying to rid the Princess's clothes of stains.

'I need Edgar's advice. He always masters the fine line between flattery and reality.'

'I saw Mr Boehm head towards the river with Dr Jenner. Would you like me to fetch him?'

'Were they carrying fishing rods?'

I nodded.

'Then it can wait until tomorrow. Mr Boehm complains of backache caused by bending over his work, and casting a line seems to loosen his spine. Sculpture is one of those activities favouring those of us with shorter stature. Mr Boehm's height gives him problems.' The princess smiled at me, then her gaze settled on the papers I'd spread on the table.

'You have some more sketches from your friend?'

'Yes, and some back copies of *Curtis's* magazine borrowed from the library.'

Princess Louise wiped her hands on a rag and approached the table.

'Are these for your pamphlet project?'

'Yes. This is our front page. Annie has done a marvellous job of using the cottage as a backdrop to our imagined garden. In real life, this plot is overgrown and full of many more colours than the pink and white combination we are portraying.'

'Her talent is exceptional and what a beautiful cottage. Does Annie live there?'

'No. Annie lives in the nearby village of Muthill. This is the gardener's lodge in the grounds of Culdees Castle. I hope it might be my home one day, when my father comes back from Ecuador.'

The Princess's eyes were full of sympathy. 'You must miss him. Do you know when he will return?'

I shook my head. 'He is searching the high mountains for orchids.'

Just then, the door flew open and Mr Boehm swept in.

Princess Louise clapped her hands in delight. 'Edgar, what a lovely surprise! You must have sensed I needed you.'

He gave the Princess the kind of open grin only exchanged between firm friends. 'Jenner was called away and I feel foolish persevering with my terrible casting technique without his guidance.'

Princess Louise stepped towards him, and I thought for one horrifying moment that they were going to embrace. Thankfully, she held back, and Boehm merely squeezed the Princess's shoulder. Although I'd only been with them alone a handful of times, I was in no doubt about their closeness. I continued to be most uncomfortable about my chaperoning role, but I supposed my mere presence had the desired effect. I did my utmost to avoid Mr Brown and Lady Craigengar. I'd no idea how I would deflect any questions. What's more, if Princess Louise got any sense I was a spy, I was sure I'd face the same fate as her lady's maid, which would leave me with no role here at all. I was determined not to let Lady Georgina down.

Mr Boehm picked up the copy of Curtis's. 'I've seen this excellent magazine before. Mr Fitch is a talented man. Is it this month's edition?'

'No. I asked Mrs Birnie if I could borrow this old magazine to refresh my memory of South American orchids. I was just explaining to Her Royal Highness that my father is now concentrating his plant search on orchids.'

Mr Boehm opened the magazine and started to read. Suddenly, he laughed. 'Listen to this Loosey.'

I registered his use of the Princess's family nickname. Boehm had the magazine open at the description of Papa's large orchid.

'*Cattleya amethystoglossa*.' He held out the illustration for Princess Louise to see. 'Stems up to two to three feet high, strict, stout, erect, gradually thickened upwards, deeply grooved; upper joints sheathed.' He raised his eyebrows at the Princess and dropped his voice into a slow and deeply suggestive tone. 'Lip short; lateral lobes erect, with spreading apices; middle expanded, broader than long, very broadly obcordate or two-lobed, the lobes deep purple, with raised radiating corrugated papillose ridges.'

Princess Louise's full-throated laugh told me she was not at all offended. However, I could feel my face going red. I'd noticed no sensual interpretation when I'd copied the words for Papa. While I didn't honestly know why Boehm found them racy, the Princess certainly did.

'This certainly explains why English gentlemen are so keen on their orchids.' Princess Louise caught my horrified expression. 'Don't worry, Iris. Your papa was a man of the church. I'm sure he can resist the orchid's degenerative charms. Now, Edgar, please help me sort out Mama's jowls. She will throw a fit if she sees.'

Boehm took off his jacket and stood directly behind Princess Louise. She dipped her hands in a bucket of water, and when she placed them on the statue, he put his own on top.

He lowered his head close to hers. 'You need a gentle touch. Don't rush it,' he murmured into her ear, his tone as intimate as a caress. 'Close your eyes and imagine soft flesh. You need to smooth out the skin between her chin and ear. Keep the truth of the jawbone but stroke in some kindness.'

The Princess closed her eyes and leant back against him.

The sound of heavy footsteps in the corridor had me nearly jump out of my skin.

Boehm didn't panic but stepped backwards, slipped his jacket back on, then straddled a nearby Queen Anne chair, steepling his hands on the chair back. 'Well done, Your Royal Highness. Your technique improves by the day.' He spoke loudly at the same time as some person knocked, then barged straight in. Princess Louise's terrier, Jip, woke from his nap and began yapping around Mr Brown's feet.

'Good afternoon, Mr Brown. I wish you would warn me of your visits. I don't want Mama to see this before it's finished,' Princess Louise said.

I was impressed by the lack of tremor in her voice and her challenging stare.

'Aye, weel. I cannae see how her ain likeness could be a surprise, but Her Majesty sent me tae ask you tae join her in the study. She needs a letter rewriting.'

'You can tell Mama I'll be with her directly. Just give me a few minutes to clean up.' The Princess held up clay covered palms. Brown nodded his acknowledgement and turned to leave, unaware of the reality of the previous minutes.

Princess Louise and Mr Boehm looked at each other with sparkling eyes, containing their laughter only until the door was closed behind the Highlander.

Chapter Twenty-Seven

August 1869

S everal weeks later, Princess Louise had gone with the Queen to visit Braemar. The rain of the morning had cleared, so I grabbed the opportunity to resume my examination of the Balmoral rose garden. I walked down the few steps into the sunken garden, which acted like a bowl, intensifying the scent of roses. Compared to Drummond and even Culdees Castle, this garden was an undramatic affair, but something about its simplicity appealed to me. I bent my head towards a bloom, inhaling the heady scent, evoking memories of my mother's garden and of my aunt. I'd quizzed the old man in charge of Her Majesty's rose garden on my last visit, so I knew this to be a Tuscany rose. The contrast of the bright yellow stamens against the dark maroon petals was striking, and I loved the open shape. I wrote a description in my journal.

If only I had Annie beside me to capture its image. I was feeling homesick today and missing more than ever Annie's easy companionship. It seemed to be my lot in life to be isolated by my 'not one thing or another' status. At home, I was an ordinary girl temporarily living in a castle. Here, it was even worse. I was an employee but a very in-between kind of servant. I lacked the aristocratic birth shared by the ladies-in-waiting, but I spent my days too firmly in their midst to be welcomed by the castle servants.

My little room had turned out to be a good place to gather castle gossip. That was how I'd overheard the laundry maid complaining about Princess Louise's dirty dresses. Yesterday, I'd heard them talking about me below my window. Someone described me as a snob. That I was putting on airs when I was no better than them. The unfairness of that had me swallowing tears. I took a deep breath of rose scent; one day, when I had a garden of my own, I'd plant this Tuscany rose to remind me of my sojourn in Queen Victoria's castle.

I wandered over to a Queen of Denmark rose, a welcome reminder of Culdees. The next rose was pink too but with a much larger flower and was the chief constituent of Aunt Leonora's tonic. '*Rosa centifolia*,' I muttered.

'Is that the fancy name for it, then? My granny cries it a cabbitch rose.'

The unexpected voice made me jump. I spun around to find a kilted young man standing behind me. His smile implied his remark was meant kindly.

'It is indeed a cabbage rose,' I said. 'The Latin name means a hundred-leaved.'

'How come you ken so much about it? I heard you are a wee gowk like me. An ordinary bird hiding in a fancy bird's nest.'

Perhaps it was meant as an insult, but the comparison made me smile. 'The cuckoo isn't ordinary at all. A very clever bird with great ambitions for its young. I learned my flower knowledge from my father.'

'I thocht you were orphant?'

'No. Not orphaned. My mother died, but my father is travelling overseas.'

'Still on yer ain though. Maybe we could be friends?'

An offer of friendship? It was tempting, for I badly needed a friend. But my experience with Rafael made me suspicious of men's motives. I avoided the question by asking my own.

'So, how did you come to be a working here?'

'John Brown is my faither's brother. He fixed us both up wi' jobs here. What aboot you?'

'Lady Bradley is my aunt's best friend.'

'You win. A lady trumps a ghillie.'

'Mr Brown is no ordinary ghillie,' I replied.

'That he is not.' The man's lewd wink presumably referred to Mr Brown's relationship with the Queen. That they were lovers was surely the most ridiculous piece of gossip that had drifted in through my window.

Two carriages coming down the drive caused us both to turn.

'Back to work for us baith, then. Nice to meet you, Miss.' I shook his outstretched hand. 'I'm Lachlan Brown. Will you me tell me your name?'

'Iris. Iris Finlay.'

'A beautiful flower, of course.' He smiled, then turned and strode away.

At the end of my morning of leisure, I completed my parcel of documents to send to Elspeth Donaldson for her father, so I penned a note to Annie with the good news.

Dear Annie

I hope you are well. Our precious project has gone to Elspeth's father. I do hope he likes it. Princess Louise did me the honour of reading the pamphlet and she was astounded by your skilful artwork and declared it sure to impress any publisher. However, it occurs to me now that we gave ourselves a handicap by choosing summer flowers, which will be fading anytime now. If Mr White wants to publish, it won't happen until next year. Do you feel able to do more painting? Might we attempt autumn? Or perhaps go straight to winter? That's the most challenging time of year for flowers, and surely the season for white.

Send me your thoughts and I'll look for inspiration in the Balmoral gardens. Today I walked in the rose garden and the sight of a Queen of Denmark made me think of you. I miss you most dreadfully.

Your dear friend,
Iris

Annie's reply a few days later made me laugh. It contained no note, but simply a drawing of a dahlia. I accepted the challenge by return of post, reusing a sheet of paper that Princess Louise had spoiled and discarded. The royal crest would amuse Annie and hoped it wasn't a treasonable offence. Two words of suggestion in the middle of the page

Chrysanthemum morifolium

Mr MacDonald grew these vivid orange specimens in his greenhouse to supply Castle Drummond with colourful cut flowers.

Princess Louise was in a low mood the following week. I assumed Mr Boehm's absence was the cause, since he had recently gone to London. I was making draft replies to the

Queen's correspondence when she bounced into the room. Something had obviously restored her spirits.

'Leave that now. I need you to help me pack. Mama has given me leave to visit Edinburgh. My sister Beatrice has grown out of all her dresses. Mama cannot face the journey, so has agreed that I should accompany Beatrice, for Lady Craigengar has no clothes taste at all.'

'How marvellous! Edinburgh is a beautiful city. Do visit the Botanic Gardens if you have time,' I replied.

'Well, you might take me there, for I definitely need you with me.'

'Really? I would love to come.'

'Did your pamphlet arrive at your publisher? It's a shame this wasn't better planned. You could have given it to him directly.'

'I got a note from my friend Elspeth, his daughter. She confirmed that it arrived.'

Balmoral was in uproar. We were attempting to catch an early train from Ballater and the princesses' trunks were not yet in the carriages. The sound of their quarrelling could be heard from halfway down the corridor.

'Do hurry up, Beatrice. That you've become too fat for your dresses is the whole source of the problem. I'll ask Iris to let them out during the journey. Her needlework skills are much better than your maid's is.'

I hoped she hadn't offended Princess Beatrice's beleaguered lady's maid.

'It's all very well for you,' Princess Beatrice replied. 'Your wardrobe is full of colourful gowns. Mama has never let me choose anything gaily coloured.'

'If we ever actually get to Edinburgh, we can remedy that. Mama will allow a lighter colour for the Ghillies Ball.'

I walked into the younger Princess's bedroom to find her flushed and tearful, trying to cram herself into a too-small damask gown. Lady Georgina stood at the back of the room. She looked at me and rolled her eyes. I curtsied to the royal sisters.

'If you have thread in a suitable shade, I'm sure I can have the dress ready by the time we get to Edinburgh, Your Royal Highness,' I offered.

'That hardly solves the problem of what to wear,' Princess Beatrice muttered, wriggling out of the dress.

'Might you consider one of the gowns Princess Louise wore in Switzerland?' Lady Georgina suggested.

'Anything to get you dressed and ready to go,' Princess Louise replied.

'So much for me being fat,' Beatrice said scornfully towards her sister.

'Having curves is not a problem if they are in the right places,' Princess Louise retorted. 'I'll meet you downstairs in fifteen minutes. Don't be late.'

Princess Louise walked out wearing a triumphant smile. Young Princess Beatrice lacked her sister's way with words and inevitably came out worst in their verbal skirmishes.

'I'll go and fetch the dresses, Your Royal Highness,' Lady Georgina said.

Princess Beatrice's lady's maid handed me the damask dress with a grateful look. The girl often bore the brunt of the youngest Princess's petulant outbursts, so was perhaps happy to avoid being involved in any alterations.

'I had good news from home,' I told Lady Georgina on the way down the corridor. 'Aunt Leonora will meet us in Edinburgh.'

'I'm so glad,' Lady Georgina replied. 'I wrote to her and asked her to try. Balmoral life can be oppressive. We both need a change of scene and the company of a loved one.'

'The trip has certainly cheered up Princess Louise. She is at a loss without her sculpture lessons.'

'It is a problem for all Her Majesty's male staff. They are forced to be away from their wives for such long periods.'

'Mr Boehm has a wife?' I was so shocked I stopped walking.

'A wife and young daughter. I thought you knew.'

I shook my head. My naivety was revealed again. 'That explains Mr Brown's dismay at Mr Boehm's friendship with Princess Louise.'

'I'm afraid his married status is far from the only problem. Princess Louise is expected to marry royalty, as are all the royal children.'

'Imagine having to marry someone chosen for you. I don't think I could bear it.'

'It is the fate of most women. I am very lucky the Queen found me a refuge in her household. My single status is considered an asset here.'

'I am determined to never marry. I won't let my heart lead me into a poor choice.'

Lady Georgina sighed. 'You will find, young Iris, that the heart is not always obedient.'

She looked so sad, I realised she must have loved and lost someone. I would be very careful to guard against such a thing.

Lady Georgina pulled an embroidered green gown from the back of Princess Louise's closet. She examined it front and back. 'It could use a longer lace for Princess Beatrice.'

'I have some black lacing in my sewing basket.' I placed the damask dress on the bed. 'Let me go and fetch it.'

I hurried through the castle towards my room in the other wing. As I climbed up the spiral staircase, I met a pair of strong-looking, hairy knees coming down. Lachlan Brown carried my valise on his shoulder.

'Your loyal servant, milady,' he said in a joking tone.

'Thank you for taking it. I believe we will be off soon.'

'Then dinnae forget me on your jaunt to the capital.'

He was being flirtatious, but I had no notion how to deal with it. I smiled weakly and shuffled past him. A spiral staircase is designed to repel enemies, but it also brought those of the opposite sex too close for comfort.

Chapter Twenty-Eight

August 1869 – Holyroodhouse Palace, Edinburgh

We travelled the short distance from Canal Street Station in two coaches. Lady Georgina and I were in one, the princesses and Lady Craigengar in the other.

Lady Georgina laughed at my astonished face when we entered the gates of Edinburgh's Palace of Holyroodhouse. 'Did you imagine royal princesses would sleep in a hotel?'

The Palace of Holyroodhouse stood at the bottom end of Edinburgh's High Street in the old town. One aspect stretched up an ancient street of cobbled setts. The distance from here to Edinburgh Castle earned this road the grand title of the Royal Mile. The grandeur and history of this ancient and famous building left me speechless. I'd never actually seen it before, but I knew it from history books. I'd loved the dramatic stories about Mary Queen of Scots, and this palace had been a backdrop for both marriage and murder during her short years of freedom.

'Although I can't guarantee we wouldn't have been more comfortable in a hotel,' Lady Georgina said. 'Lady Craigengar, Mr Brown and I have a secondary mission here. Her Majesty has ordered the renovation of some of the rooms on the second floor. She wishes to be able to use her official residence in Scotland's capital and there was simply not enough liveable space. We are here to check progress and crack the whip.'

Mr Brown could be heard yelling orders in the courtyard. Several footmen came running towards the princesses' carriage.

'And so it begins,' Lady Georgina muttered.

Lady Georgina and I walked quickly to join Princesses Louise and Beatrice and Lady Craigengar, who were descending from the lead carriage. The royal sisters were bickering again.

'I get first choice of rooms, as I am the eldest,' said Princess Louise.

'You know perfectly well I shall need more space because the seamstress will visit tomorrow,' her sister replied.

In the end, Princess Louise chose the smaller room at the rear of the building for the superior view over where Salisbury Crags cliffs, which stood in front of the hill they called Arthur's Seat. I unpacked for the Princess, while she sketched the view from the window.

'I'm sorry you have to share a room with Beatrice's maid,' she said.

'I don't mind at all and the poor girl is convinced the palace is riddled with ghosts. She wouldn't be able to sleep alone.'

'I was very tempted to remind Princess Beatrice of the proximity of her grand room to Queen Mary's quarters and the bloody stairs where Rizzio died. Serves her right if it dawns on her in the middle of the night.' The Princess looked up from her drawing. 'I will be occupied with the seamstress's visit tomorrow. Why don't you drop your friend a note and see if she is free?'

. . .

The next morning I strode up the hill, having decided to walk to the Botanic Gardens. I chose the Royal Mile route to take in all the sights on the way. My journey took me past the old house which once belonged to John Knox. He and Mary Queen of Scots had been bitter enemies. He preached against female monarchs, calling Mary one of the 'monstrous regiment of women', and he abhorred her Catholic religion. Further up, I came to St Giles's Cathedral, from where Mr Knox launched his thunderous tirades. Up close, the church was dark and looming. It wasn't hard to conjure up his raging voice.

Turning north down the Mound and past the neo-classical styled Royal Scottish Academy, I stopped off at Alexander Hill's premises to buy Annie some new brushes and water-colour blocks in autumnal hues for our next project. It was a thrill to be able to buy things with my own money.

I arrived at the gates of the Botanic Gardens with my heart pumping, fired up by the vigorous walk and nervous about the future of our project. Elspeth's note had suggested meeting in the gardens again, since she was in the habit of accompanying her husband Alexander to his morning lecture with Professor Hutton Balfour. My pulse quickened even more when I saw her walking towards me in the company of an elderly man. The great publisher had come to meet me!

Elspeth and I embraced. 'Iris, I'm delighted to introduce you to Professor William Jameson.'

I hope I hid my disappointment. This was a man I'd longed to meet and now I was so puffed up with vain ambition I might have spoiled the moment. I curtsied. 'I am very glad to meet you, sir. My father sings your praises.'

'I'm delighted to meet you, Miss Finlay. I have great admiration for your father. Have you any news of his return?'

Professor Jameson was a great deal older than I had expected, perhaps even beyond his seventieth year. This thin man with a high forehead might once have been tall, but was rather stooped now and walked slowly, leaning on his stick.

'Sadly, I haven't heard from him for some time.'

Our chat was interrupted by Professor Jameson's interest in all the alpine-type plants in the Rock Garden, he explained such mountainous species were found in Ecuador too. We walked on downhill until the view of Edinburgh opened up.

'The route from Ecuador is tricky to plan,' Professor Jameson said. 'You might face bad weather going around the Cape or hit storms in the Atlantic coming north again. I experienced both this year.'

'I believe my father may risk the shortcut north, then across Panama.'

'Really?' The gentleman looked concerned. 'I understand the benefit of shortening the sea journey. Saltwater is an enemy to plant hunters, but he will face different challenges in Panama. The jungle there is dense.'

'Mr Speir, my father's employer, has taken on a Spanish gentleman. His plan was to investigate using the railway.'

Professor Jameson nodded thoughtfully. 'That might work, although I don't know anyone who has tried it. In my case, I also wanted to visit my sons in Argentina. The challenge will be all the man-handling of the valuable cargo between boats and train carriages. At least on a ship, it's easy to supervise once it's on board. What is the name of this Spanish botanist? I'm bound to know of him if he has worked in South America.'

'Señor Rafael de Rias,' I answered.

Jameson shook his head. 'Never heard of him.'

This pronouncement worried me, surely this South American expert must be well connected in the botanist community.

Elspeth changed the subject. 'Professor Jameson mentioned he might accompany us to the hothouses to point out specimens commonly found in South America.'

'If you ladies would find it interesting, I'd be delighted. And please don't be alarmed, Miss Finlay. I am too old for jungle treks these days, but I have to say the steam train north from Liverpool was a revelation, so taking a train through Panama may well be the best way.'

When the professor spoke about plants, we had a glimpse of his former youthful energy. Once he started talking, he was difficult to stop. He led us through the palm house, then out into the gardens, reminiscing about his years in Ecuador and all the rare specimens he had seen. After almost two hours, I had to leave to get back to Holyroodhouse.

'I wish I were able to spend all day here, Professor Jameson. Unfortunately, Princess Louise has some duties for me this afternoon.'

'You are working for a princess? I'm sure I'd remember if your father had mentioned that,' the professor exclaimed.

'It is a recent and temporary position, but yes, I have the honour of serving Her Majesty's daughter.'

'How thrilling that must be,' Elspeth said.

Professor Jameson put his hand to his forehead. 'I'm so sorry. I have used up all your time when you came here to talk to each other.'

'Not at all,' I assured him. 'It was a fascinating morning.'

'Definitely,' Elspeth said. 'Miss Finlay told me how much she wanted to meet you and I am so glad I was able to arrange it.'

I agreed to write to the professor with news of my father's plans and promised that Papa and I would try to travel to Edinburgh to meet him next year.

Elspeth took my arm, and we proceeded to the gate together. 'I hope that wasn't too boring for you?' I said.

'I confess I didn't even know what a liverwort was, and now I am very much better informed,' she replied with a laugh.

Elspeth had ordered a carriage to meet her mother in town and offered take me to Holyroodhouse first.

As we travelled south in the carriage, I described life at Balmoral to Elspeth, without being specific about my chaperoning duties. It seemed disloyal to the Princess to discuss it.

'I have some news of my own,' Elspeth said, placing her hand on her stomach. 'I expect to become a mother before the end of the year.'

'Oh, how marvellous!' I embraced her. 'Congratulations! You look very well and I look forward to meeting this baby.'

We were almost at Holyroodhouse before I summoned the nerve to ask what had been on my mind all day. 'How did your father react to receiving our pamphlet?'

'He said it was rather good. Did he not write to thank you?'

'No. But I realise he is a very busy man.'

'Incredibly busy. He has a new edition of the encyclopaedia coming out soon.'

We reached the palace gates. 'Let me out here, please. I'm not sure if we need permission to take a carriage inside.'

Elspeth laughed. 'Imagine Mama's reaction if I arrived late, and told her I'd been detained trying to gain admittance to Holyroodhouse Palace.'

I crossed the palace quadrangle in a low mood. 'Rather good,' seemed lukewarm. Why had I imagined that a man of business who published an encyclopaedia and scientific books would be interested in our amateur efforts? A horrifying thought struck me. I'd encouraged Annie to dream of a better life. The whole thing could leave her feeling worse off than before. Annie had changed during our friendship, growing in self-confidence. Had my friendship done more damage than good in her life? That responsibility weighed heavily on my conscience. It would take a lot of work to create an autumn pamphlet and it was most likely a waste of time. How could I tell her to forget it? It wasn't the kind of news to deliver by letter.

Chapter Twenty-Nine

August 1869 – Holyroodhouse Palace

I found Princess Louise pacing in her bedroom.

'Thank goodness you're here. I want to leave early. The whole party has gone for a drive around Holyrood Park and if we go now, we can avoid taking Lady Craigengar with us. I don't want her reporting back to Mama.'

I rushed down the stairs behind Princess Louise. Where in all earth were we going that she was so keen to keep a secret? Was it possible that Mr Boehm might be here and not in London at all? Would I be brave enough to challenge a princess if we were going into a compromising situation? I feared not.

The stairwell brought us out at the back of the palace and we headed to a gate. 'I've asked one of the footmen to get me a trustworthy driver.' The Princess flung the remark over her shoulder.

'Are we going alone?' I sounded feeble.

The footman opened the carriage door, and we clambered inside. 'Ask the driver to take us to fifteen Buccleuch Place,' she told him. 'And when we get there, he is to wait for us.' Princess Louise turned to me and smiled. 'Don't look so horrified, Iris. We are simply taking tea with a friend of a friend.' I looked dubious and she laughed. 'It is a lady.'

Princess Louise handed me a book. Its title was *Woman's Work and Woman's Culture: A Series of Essays.* 'My sister Vicky introduced me to a most wonderful woman called Josephine Butler. She is at the forefront of social reform. I really hope I can find some way to help her.'

I opened the book, and it contained a dedication to Princess Louise.

'Mrs Butler is the book's editor, and we are on our way to meet a Miss Sophia Jex-Blake, who is the author of one of the essays, *Medicine as a Profession for Women.* She has moved to Edinburgh to begin her studies to train to be a doctor. This was my chief reason for coming to the capital.'

I looked up from the book in surprise. 'A lady doctor?'

'Exactly. And whyever not?'

Buccleuch Place looked similar to most of those Edinburgh streets built in the previous century, a row of tall buildings constructed in sandstone, with the usual shiny black railings. Some had doorways framed by handsome arches and pillars, but not number fifteen. This was the simplest of black doors, devoid of any ornament, not even a proper doorstep. I prepared to get out of the carriage, but Princess Louise put her hand on my arm.

'Wait,' she said. The number fifteen door opened a crack, then swung open. 'Come now,' the Princess instructed. She got out of the carriage first and walked purposely with her head down, straight into the house.

I jumped down to follow her. The corridor inside this tenement building was dark. The Princess was already following a lady up some stone stairs and we were ushered into a flat at the back of the building. Why such a cloak and dagger arrival to meet a very respectable-looking woman? The south facing room with large windows was sparsely furnished, but clean. The lady had her dark hair pulled back and simply parted. Her complexion was fresh, with ruddy cheeks and dark eyes. She curtsied.

'I'm sorry about all the secrecy around my visit. I hate to create such drama,' Princess Louise said.

'Please take a seat, Your Highness. Miss...'

'This is Miss Iris Finlay, who has recently joined us to work at Balmoral. Iris has ambitions of her own, so, I am sure it will fascinate us both to hear your story. Iris, this is Miss Sophia Jex-Blake, surely set to become one of our first female doctors.'

Miss Jex-Blake poured us some tea. 'I would judge that is still far from certain,' she said. 'And to be honest, I'm grateful for your discretion, Your Royal Highness. I am attracting quite enough attention as it is.'

'Why are you uncertain? Josephine said you've found enough ladies to meet the university's requirements.'

Miss Jex-Blake passed round a plate of shortbread 'We have overcome one stumbling block, but we might face others. There are five of us now registered to sit the medical matriculation exams in October, and I believe we may attract a few more. I expect Isabel Thorne and Edith Pechey to move in here next week. We will cram for the exams together. Pool our knowledge to our mutual advantage, so to speak.'

'Women are so sensible. None of the competitiveness of men. I really admire you all. Doing something with your lives instead of merely settling for marriage and children.'

I sat straighter in my chair. This was a very interesting subject.

'I am sure my vocation lies in medicine not marriage, but Isabel is married with children.'

'An understanding husband, a rare thing indeed.'

'They are an unusual couple. Isabel has been living and

travelling in China and has recently studied midwifery. I expect she will have much to teach me.'

'And these five ladies responded to your newspaper advert?'

'They and others. Not everyone was free to come here to live and study with us.'

Princess Louise turned to me. 'Miss Jex-Blake is not a lady to take no for an answer, Iris. The university refused her permission to study because she was the only woman and it would be too much effort to accommodate her, so she advertised to find others with the same ambition.'

'You are lucky to be born in Scotland, Miss Finlay,' Miss Jex-Blake said. 'Your country has a long history of educating women. That's why I came north to pursue my ambitions. Edinburgh will be the first university to admit women to study medicine. Provided we pass the entry exams, of course.'

'Miss Finlay is a scholar too. She knows Latin and is well educated in botanical matters,' Princess Louise said.

'My father was an inspiring teacher,' I replied.

Princess Louise and Miss Jex-Blake talked at length about better opportunities for women. They shared news about Mrs Butler and the circle of radical friends they had in common. I recognised some names from newspaper articles, and I guessed the Queen would not have approved of their enthusiasm for reform, which explained the secrecy of our visit.

On the ride home, Princess Louise told me to keep and read the book. 'It's full of inspiring thoughts. However, it might be best if you read it when you are alone. Most definitely don't let Princess Beatrice or Lady Craigengar see. They would love to find some excuse to get me into trouble with Mama.'

We enjoyed an excellent dinner. Princess Louise had

briefed the chef to serve his tastiest dishes but no more than four courses. Tonight we had oysters, trout in a lightly flavoured butter and aniseed sauce, roast pheasant with prunes, followed by a French-style apple tart with cream.

Princess Louise put her linen napkin on the table with a deep sigh. 'Finally, a meal and no mutton. If I had to eat meat and potatoes even one more time, I would be led out screaming.'

I glanced sideways to see if Mr Brown reacted to the implied criticism of his royal mistress. His face remained impassive.

After supper, the whole party took a walk in the garden. As I was not being required, I sought a quiet spot to read Mrs Butler's essays. Surely the room everyone thought to be haunted was a place where I was unlikely to be disturbed. The bedroom at the top of the north-west tower was modestly-sized for a queen. It was laid out as if in readiness for Mary Queen of Scots return, because it was sometimes open for public viewing. How lucky to have it all to myself. The canopied four-postered bed was draped in sumptuous crimson curtains. Certainly, a bed fit for a queen. The ancient oak-panelled ceiling was carved into a honeycomb shape. It thrilled me to think that brave lady had looking up at it. She faced a lot of troubles in her years here, so no doubt she often lay awake. I sat down in the wing chair facing the fireplace to gain the benefit of light from the window and opened the book.

The following Essays have been collected with a grave and serious purpose, Mrs Butler's introduction began. The book contained ten essays in total, the authors proclaiming the necessity for social change. There were some shocking census statistics, highlighting the growing number of unmarried women supporting themselves when few professions or trades were open to them. Apparently, my experience was commonplace.

I was full of enthusiasm after my afternoon listening to Sophia Jex-Blake and Princess Louise converse. However, the prose was dry in style and I became annoyed by the lack of mention of Scotland. I'd gathered from this afternoon's conversation that these women considered our education of girls better, but I wasn't always certain that references to England excluded us deliberately or accidentally. Finally, I put the book aside.

The book was less invigorating than I'd hoped, but it got me thinking. I'd led such a sheltered existence. Were Annie's abilities in reading and writing exceptional? A lucky exposure to a husband and wife team at Innerpeffray who shared dedication and knowledge? Was my experience unusual too? Might things have been different if my brother had survived? Would Papa have had less time for me? Would my parents have sent my brother to university while I remained at home? The thought was uncomfortable. I must take responsibility for my future and not rely on any man.

My resolve was strengthened. Mr White's reaction was merely a setback. He hadn't even said anything negative. The Queen who had slept in this room had remained proud and strong in the face of overwhelming challenges. Josephine Butler's friends were determined to succeed in societal change. I would not give up my dreams so easily. Annie and I must persevere until we reached our goal.

Coming down from the tower, I could hear the royal party had returned from the garden. I scurried along the palace corridors to reach my room, but I stopped when I saw Mr Brown leaning on the wall beside my door, his arms crossed.

'Where the devil have you been hiding, lassie?'

I fought the urge to put my book behind my back, but discreetly turning its cover towards my skirts. 'My roommate is very talkative. I found a quiet place to read.'

'I hear you and your mistress have been oot gallivanting. Where did you go?' His tone was aggressive.

I felt a shiver of fear. 'To visit a lady acquaintance.'

He narrowed his eyes.

I judged it best to give him a half-truth. 'A Miss Blake.'

'It's no safe for the Princess to be oot on her ain in Edinburgh. Especially no in a public vehicle.'

I tried to look nonchalant despite my heart going ten to the dozen. 'Your party took all the carriages, and the Princess was not out in public at all. We went straight to her friend's house and back here directly. We met no one else.'

Mr Brown pushed himself away from the wall. 'Well, just you mind whit's expected ae you.'

I raised my chin. 'I fulfilled my chaperoning role, Mr Brown, and there is nothing untoward about taking tea with a friend in her home.'

He gave a curt nod and walked away. I'd told no lies, but he would likely be less pleased if he knew the acquaintance was a lady hell-bent on shocking the establishment.

Chapter Thirty

August 1869 – Holyroodhouse Palace

The next evening, Lady Georgina and I went to meet my aunt for supper her in usual Princes Street hotel. The meal was pleasant, but Aunt Leonora barely touched her food.

'Are you not hungry, Leo?' Lady Georgina asked.

'I'm a little nauseous after my train journey.'

'Should we order something else?'

'I'm fine. I ate a good breakfast before I left this morning.'

My aunt pushed her plate away and sat back in her chair. 'So, tell me all about your visit to yet another of Queen Victoria's palaces, Iris. I wish your mother had lived to witness your extraordinary life.'

'I wish my mother were still alive, too. Although my life would never have taken this surprising turn if I were not under your guardianship and assisted by Lady Bradley.'

'I'm not at all sure I've done you a favour, Iris. Serving the royal household comes with its challenges,' Lady Georgina replied.

'I'm happy. Princess Louise's company is stimulating and I

don't find her difficult. And to answer your question, Aunt Leonora, The Palace of Holyroodhouse is fascinating. To find myself walking the same corridors as Mary Queen of Scots is beyond my wildest dreams.'

'You are indeed a lucky girl. I should love to see the palace.'

'I anticipated you would be interested, Leo, so I sought permission to take you on a tour tomorrow. Come at two. Princess Beatrice's seamstress is returning for a fitting at that hour, and Iris and I are not required.'

The following day, as arranged, Lady Georgina and I showed Aunt Leonora around Holyroodhouse Palace. Climbing up to Mary Queen of Scots' rooms, my aunt had to pause on the stairs.

'Leo, you must eat more. You are getting too thin, and it's no wonder you feel tired,' Lady Georgina said.

Aunt Leonora sank into the Queen Mary's wing chair. The movement exposed her skeletally thin wrists and ankles. She winced and cradled her stomach.

'I know, but I find I've little appetite these days.' She looked up at the ceiling, then all around the tapestry-hung room. 'What a privilege to be here. That poor persecuted lady enjoyed some happiness inside these walls. Tell me, George, can we get access to the ballroom Sir Walter Scott described in *Waverley?*'

'The Great Gallery. Yes, of course. If you feel able for more walking?'

Fortunately, the Great Gallery was nearby, also on the north wing of the palace and on the top floor. A long room, it was apparently the biggest in the building. An excellent choice for hosting an eightsome reel. I could imagine the young Bonnie Prince Charlie coming into the room in his tartan regalia. It must have been quite a moment.

I walked down the length of this long room, hung with royal portraits, finding Robert the Bruce and Macbeth amongst the many Scottish kings.

'The King Georges didn't really use this as a royal palace,' Lady Georgina said. 'But Queen Victoria is keen to have people remember that she is descended from Mary Queen of Scots. We think it likely that Her Majesty will be able to stay overnight next year.'

Lady Georgina offered my aunt her arm. 'Now then, Leo. Let's find you a comfy seat and organise some tea before the royal ladies return from the dress fitting.'

There was tender concern in Lady Georgina's eyes as she escorted her friend to the morning room. They were both close to fifty, but recently Aunt Leonora had begun to look much older. I was about to go to the kitchens to organise a tea tray when a furious Princess Louise came storming into the room.

'Lady Craigengar has Mrs Butler's book. Did you leave it lying about?' Her tone was harsh.

Princess Louise was quick to anger, but it had never before been aimed at me. The humiliation was intensified by Aunt Leonora's presence.

'No. I put it in my bedside table drawer.'

'Well, you will find it is not there now. Did you tell anyone about our excursion?' Princess Louise had her hands on her hips. A pose I associated more with her sulky younger sister.

'Mr Brown quizzed me,' I admitted. 'I told him we visited a lady friend of yours and that it was entirely proper. I thought him satisfied.'

Lady Craigengar walked in with Princess Beatrice close behind her. She held up the green leather-bound book. 'Your Royal Highness, we should discuss this,' she said.

Princess Louise glared at her and noticed Princess Beatrice's self-satisfied smile.

'Is there some problem, Lady Craigengar? Might we deal with it later?' Lady Georgina said.

Lady Craigengar suddenly noticed the presence of my aunt.

'Lady Bradley, forgive me. I had entirely forgotten you had a guest.'

Princess Louise grimaced. 'Lady Walker, you are not seeing us at our best. Please accept my apologies.' My aunt, who had been standing since the Princess entered, curtsied.

'Not at all. I must thank you for allowing me to visit Iris and see the palace.'

'Please sit down. I am so sorry to have interrupted you.' Princess Louise held out her hand. 'Lady Craigengar, I am sure you have noticed that the book is inscribed to me. You can trust me to talk to Mama about it when we return to Balmoral.'

Lady Craigengar handed the book back, and the royal party took their leave.

My aunt sank wearily into her chair. 'Whatever was that all about, Iris? Have you been reading unsuitable books?'

'Not in my opinion. It is a book of essays arguing for better education and employment opportunities for women.'

'Oh, for goodness' sake,' Aunt Leonora exclaimed. 'I would have liked the chance to read it myself.'

Lady Georgina covered my aunt's hand. 'I'm sorry you witnessed that, Leo.'

'I worry about you, Iris,' Aunt Leonora said 'It seems your chaperoning duties extend to monitoring the princess's reading habits, which is ridiculous. But what did Princess Louise mean about an excursion?'

'Her Royal Highness wishes to keep it a secret. We went

to visit one of the essay authors. A lady who will sit entry exams to study medicine at Edinburgh University.'

Lady Georgina groaned. 'I'm afraid Her Majesty is deeply conservative by nature. Since Prince Albert's death she feels threatened by change of any kind. Lady Craigengar is probably right. The Queen will not approve of the book.'

Aunt Leonora's worried expression hurt me more than the Princess's rebuke. I hated to give her extra stress when her health seemed to be worsening.

'You really don't have to keep doing this, Iris. Would you prefer to come home?'

I was torn. My aunt didn't look well, but I felt loyalty to Princess Louise. 'You seem to have lost weight, dear aunt. They will find someone else if you need me?'

She shook her head vigorously. 'My health is up and down and this is a bad day after the delays in yesterday's journey. You must do what you prefer.'

'Apparently, Princess Louise will leave Scotland in September, at which point I shall be released.'

Aunt Leonora gave a decisive nod. 'Go and find your royal mistress, Iris. If she is happy to have you with her for the next few weeks, then I think you should stay.'

I organised tea, then excused myself to leave Aunt Leonora to catch up with her friend. Lady Georgina would go south with the royal party in the autumn and I knew that would be a sad day for them both. I found Princess Louise on her own in the evening drawing room, sitting on the end of one of the red sofas with her feet tucked under her skirts.

'I am very sorry, Your Royal Highness. I should have hidden the book under lock and key.'

Princess Louise sighed heavily and shook her head. 'It is I who should apologise. You did nothing wrong. I should have guessed my sister was behind this. I believe your roommate sneaked a look in the drawer and reported to her mistress, who entered your room uninvited and took the book. Anyway it has backfired. When I challenged Princess Beatrice, she confessed to her petty larceny and Lady Craigengar is appalled.'

'Still, I'm sorry to have been the cause of such a fuss,' I replied.

'Your aunt must think us all monsters. Is she taking you home?'

'No. She knows I enjoy working for you and is proud of my service.'

Princess Louise patted the couch, inviting me to sit down. She squeezed my hand. 'I'm very lucky to have you. I wish I could think of a way to take you with me when I leave, but we go to the Isle of Wight and I hear Fraulein Bauer will join us there.'

'I'm so glad you aren't angry with me. I thought I'd let you down.'

'There is no harm done. Lady Craigengar expected the book's content would be scandalous but is forced to agree it's a scholarly work. I reminded her that Papa encouraged us to read widely. Mama will accept that argument too.'

'That is a relief,' I agreed.

'The fuss is most likely not over. I am keen to actually do something for Mrs Butler's causes. Reading is one thing, radical activity will be quite another.'

I nodded, having no suitable answer.

What in all earth might radical activity be?

Chapter Thirty-One

August 1869 – Balmoral

Thankfully, Lady Georgina was granted permission to delay her return. She'd see my aunt home and come to Balmoral a day later. When I arrived back at the castle, there were two letters waiting for me. I opened the one in Annie's handwriting first. I'd sent the watercolour blocks to her from Edinburgh, and I was delighted to hear she had put them to use already.

August 20th 1869

Dearest Iris,

Your paints arrived, and the burnt umber is perfect for the dahlia. I'll keep the cadmium orange for the chrysanthemum. It's great to be started on a new pamphlet. I cannot believe you actually stayed in Holyroodhouse Palace. I confess I boast to the other maids about my friend who works for Princess Louise. I'm certain they thought of me only as a poor cripple before we met. Now I'm proud to call myself an artist and have you as a friend.

I've begun a plan for our autumn cover, taking into consideration the height and depth of plants that will make it come alive. Might we find a climbing plant to put on the cottage walls? Struan's friend Jock suggested a rusty-coloured ivy. Jock is Struan's co-worker at Drummond Castle and I met him this week. Struan tasked him with bringing me a chrysanthemum flower while it was still fresh. Mr MacDonald has Struan working all hours in the greenhouse on some new hybrid project they are doing together. My next confession is the sin of pride. Jock's interest in my painting projects made me sit up taller. And don't worry, dear Iris. I sense you worrying about a Rafael type of man. Jock is a simple Scottish laddie and very respectful. Like us, he is 'a wee bit obsessed wi' flewers', as he said himself.

I hope you had a good journey from Edinburgh and look forward to hearing from you.

Your dear friend,
Annie

The second letter, I saw it was also postmarked in Perth. The sender was a huge surprise.

August 20th 1869

Dear Miss Finlay,
Annie has asked me to post her letter. Since I have your address and no time to spend swithering, I've decided to write what's on my mind.

I owe you an apology, because I must admit I was wrong. First of all the business with the Spaniard was not your fault. His smooth talking has clearly fooled many people. While I don't know exactly what happened between him and Annie, I'm sure it was his behaviour that sent my sister into a spiral of despondency. I can tell she is getting over it now and the thing that has helped her recovery most is your publishing project.

Annie and I have talked about the project a great deal and it is very clear it brings her joy. The one thing I've always wanted for her. She tells me I'm over-protective and that I must stop treating her like a child. In fact, she said 'bairn', but Mrs Birnie always insisted letters must be written in English and I don't want you to think of me as an ill-educated man.

Finally, you might be interested in some news from the Drummond Castle Gardens. Mr MacDonald has tasked me to breed a new Scots rose, or Rosa spinosissima as I've discovered it's called, to create a hybrid of both the traditional white and more modern pink versions. It will be the bonniest thing you've ever seen. This year we produced a few flowers which were white with pink touches, but the bloom we are trying to create again has white petals on the outside and pink near the centre. I hope in May or June to show you a flower worthy of inclusion in your pamphlet.

I hope you don't mind me writing and that this letter finds you well.

Yours respectfully,
Struan Cooper

A letter from Struan Cooper. What a turn up for the books!

Annie's lovely letter pricked my conscience. I hadn't shared my anxiety about Mr White's lukewarm reaction to our pamphlet and was afraid her optimism might be based only on my foolish dreams. Struan's letter gave me some reassurance that I was doing the right thing in persevering. Whatever happened in the end, our project helped Annie recover from Rafael's terrible behaviour. Struan seeing the benefits would make Annie's life easier. Sharing of his work endeavours seemed like a gesture of friendship. When he'd been rude in the past, it was to protect Annie, an urge I definitely understood. I allowed myself to imagine how happy the three of us could be if Struan and I stopped treating each other as the enemy. I picked up a pen with an urge to reply to him, then realised he might not have told Annie he had written to me. A letter from me to Struan would seem very odd and it would ruin everything if I embarrassed him. I'd see them both in a matter of weeks. Penning my reply and thanks to Annie, I pondered her mention of this boy, Jock. If Struan allowed them to meet, I had to assume he was trustworthy.

A few days later, the party took out the Highland ponies. I grabbed the chance to stay behind and scour the grounds for an ivy that might turn to a suitable colour. Jip, Princess Louise's dog, trotted at my feet. Coming across a copper beech tree made me think we might include a sapling. Balmoral had some huge and beautiful specimens of beech. I mulled over how I might convey the burnished magnificence in words. Walking back to the castle with a branch in my hand, I spotted Lachlan. Jip gave a low growl and I had to stoop to reassure him. Jip was protective of Princess Louise and since I was often the one who walked him, he had obviously decided he was now responsible for me, too.

'There you are, bonny quine.' It occurred to me for the first time that the Aberdeenshire word for a girl might be derived from queen? 'What's wi' the branch?'

'It's for an art project. I like the reddish colour of the leaves. I was looking for some ivy in a similar shade.'

'There's an ivy kind ae plant that grows up at the venison store that turns a bright orange colour. Let me fetch some for you.'

Lachlan took off at a trot, his handsome kilt swinging in the rhythm of his steps. He came back with a huge swathe of ivy in his arms. 'Maybe this is nae good? It's still green but it does go a bonny orange-red colour later in autumn.'

'*Parthenocissus quinquefolia.* Of course. This is perfect.'

'You and your fancy names. What's it really called?

Virgin ivy came to my mind first, virgin being the literal translation of Parthenocissus, but I wasn't daft enough to say that out loud. 'It's a plant brought from North America. I've heard it called Virginia Creeper. This is perfect. I only need to describe the shape of the leaves.'

'Gie me the branch then. I'll cart it all back tae the house for you, so you dinnae snag your frock.'

'Thank you. I don't need so much of the ivy, though.'

He tossed most of the ivy into the undergrowth. 'Aye, right enough. Thon room's mair like a press than a bedroom.'

'I'm not complaining. A cupboard in a castle is still grand enough.'

Lachlan gave me a dazzling smile. He had the same strong jaw as his uncle, but without the perpetual glower. 'Aye. People think working at a castle is the maist glamorous thing. I dinnae tell them it's really just the same work as any big hoose.'

He handed over my specimens when we reached the castle. 'Will you be at the Ghillies Ball next week, Miss Finlay?'

'I will,' I replied, 'and please call me Iris.'

'Well, Iris, I will if you'll save me a dance.'

I nodded and returned his smile, and he went off looking pleased with himself. Was I breaking my resolve to avoid men? Surely there was no harm in a dance? Lady Georgina had told me that even the royal party were expected to dance. We anticipated the arrival of the Prince of Wales and his wife for the occasion any day now.

As I made my way to reunite Jip with his mistress, I heard a cry of anguish and met a tearful Princess Beatrice running down the corridor in a luridly-coloured tartan dress. I curtsied to the Queen on entering the room and quietly took a stool behind Princess Louise.

'You have upset your sister. You must apologise and make your peace,' Queen Victoria said in a censorial tone.

Princess Louise laughed. 'I merely warned her not to sit down, since she might be mistaken for a sofa cushion.' She laughed again.

'She is excited to wear an evening gown and attend the ball. You were the same at thirteen.'

'At thirteen I would certainly have taken my sisters' advice on my colour choice. Beatrice's stubbornness has got her dressed up in furnishing fabric.'

'It's lovely silk and not at all the same colours as the sofas. Besides, you know how much your papa loved tartan. Beatrice told me how she chose it to honour him.'

Fortunately, I was the only one who heard the princess mutter, 'nauseating little toad.'

A gentleman and lady entering the room distracted everyone else. I recognised the Prince of Wales from family paintings and stood to curtsey. The royal couple's presence lifted the atmosphere. Princess Louise chatted warmly with the Princess of Wales, a Danish lady whom the family called Alix. After dinner, Alix volunteered to join Princess Beatrice and read to the Queen, allowing Princess Louise to follow her brother to the billiards room.

'Shall I get some supper for Jip?' I asked. 'He hasn't eaten yet.'

'Would you? And let him outside one more time. He has become so fond of you, Iris. I believe he will miss you as much as I will.'

Twenty minutes later, I brought Jip to the billiard room.

The Princess asked me to hang onto the little dog. 'He likes to lurk under the billiards table and I'm afraid Bertie might stand on him.'

I sat in an easy chair and patted my lap. The little terrier didn't have to be invited twice. He jumped up, turned in a circle and settled down to sleep. I hadn't expected to find the Princess actually playing billiards. Clearly not for the first time either. My mistress was rather good. Between shots, she and her brother chatted about life in London and various aristocratic friends whose names I didn't recognise. My ears pricked up when Princess Louise's tone became accusatory. 'I hear there are problems at Walton Hall. Are you to blame for poor Harriet's situation, Bertie?'

The Prince of Wales looked alarmed. He glanced at me.

'You needn't worry about Iris. I trust her implicitly,' Princess Louise said.

He pointed his billiards cue at his sister. 'If we are to trade awkward questions, I might ask about your sculptor chap?'

'It's a complicated story, but you may judge for yourself. We expect him to return tomorrow. But seriously, you were always too fond of Harriet.'

The Prince of Wales looked wistful. 'God, she was a pretty girl. Do you remember the Ghillies Ball when I whirled her off her feet? She is wasted on dull old Mardaunt, but she has got herself in the most terrible pickle now.'

'Poor, poor Harriet. I hear her baby girl is very frail.'

He nodded. 'Born too early. I think the experience has unhinged Harriet. The story is that she's been howling and eating coal. In her madness, she has admitted that Lowry is the father.'

'So not you?' Princess Louise asked.

The Prince put down his cue and held up both hands. 'Not me. But I feel damned sorry for her. Harriet's own father has agreed to have her locked up.'

Princess Louise struck the cue ball with such vigour that it hit the table's edge and bounced off. 'It's outrageous. Men behave as they please and one indiscretion may cost a lady everything.'

'It is the way of the world.' The Prince looked up over his cue as he lined up his shot. 'You need to take care, Louise. You won't be forgiven twice.'

I didn't know what he meant, but pretended not to notice the Princess glance in my direction.

'I am being careful,' she replied quietly.

'Like me, you are too hot-blooded, sister. You need to marry soon.'

Princess Louise groaned. 'I've met no one I could even tolerate. In any case, I am too busy with my art. I'm glad you shall meet Mr Boehm. You'll like him and you must come to the studio. I don't pretend my work is anywhere near as excellent as Edgar's statues, but bit by bit, I'm improving.'

Once the billiards game was over the Princess hugged her brother and wished him goodnight. Their love was very evident. I envied their bond and wished I'd been blessed with siblings.

The Princess of Wales's presence diffused the tension between Princess Louise and her sister and it helped that Princess Alexandra declared Princess Beatrice's dress to be perfectly beautiful. We were in the younger sister's bedroom trying on the gown. Princess Beatrice had selected different shoes and the dress was now too long.

'What do you think, Alix? Might we need an inch taken up?' Princess Louise asked. 'There is nothing worse than worrying about standing on your hem when you are reeling.'

'One and a half inches, I think,' she replied.

Princess Beatrice looked alarmed. 'But the ball is tomorrow. We don't have time to send it back.'

'No need. Iris will sort it out,' Princess Louise said.

'It is a very wide skirt.' Princess Beatrice looked anxiously in my direction. There had been no further mention of her sneaking into my room.

'I would be delighted to help. Let me fetch my pin cushion.'

When I came back, Princesses Alexandra and Louise held Princess Beatrice's hands to keep her steady on a footstool, while I knelt at her feet to pin up the hem. It was going to be a long night of sewing to have the dress ready in time.

The next day was a happy whirl of preparations.

'Your dress fits you really well,' Princess Louise told her sister. I'd overheard Princess Alexandra encouraging Princess Louise to forget all point scoring. 'Your first ball where you walk in as a young woman, not a little girl.'

Princess Beatrice's eyes filled with tears on receipt of a compliment from her often critical sister. There was then a rush to help Princess Louise into her dress, so I arrived back at my room with barely time to change. I took my grey silk evening dress from my closet. It was like donning a second skin. 'Thank you, Aunt Leonora,' I whispered. My aunt's taste was perfect. A beautifully cut dress but in quiet colours. Not too revealing, but suitably fashionable, too. I couldn't see my full reflection in the small mirror, but could feel that the dress moved in the right way. I felt a flicker of excitement. My first ever ball and a handsome boy had asked me to dance.

I was about to go downstairs when the smell of smoke drifting in the open window alerted me to the presence of men outside. A murmur of voices.

'So,' said some stranger. 'Tonight's the night. Are we clear on the rules, Lachlan? Just a wee kiss willnae win the bet.'

'That'll be sae easy, I wouldnae even tak your thrupence, Willie Baxter. But I'll bring Iris Finlay right here and if you hide in thon trees, you'll be able tae judge my success by the way I mak her moan. That, bonny lad, will cost you next month's wages.'

The roar and the noise of raucous laughter suggested three or four men. Taking bets on my humiliation.

I sat down on my bed and let the cold shame wash over me. How could I have been so stupid? He'd said we could be friends when all along he only hoped to exploit my loneliness. I wondered when the next train to Perth would allow me to escape. But he underestimated my character and I was not going to let his scheming defeat me. Instead, I took a deep breath and shook myself. That dreadful man wouldn't send me scuttling home. The Princess would be looking for me. I splashed water on my face and looked in the mirror. The wretch deserved to lose one month's wages.

Chapter Thirty-Two

August 1869 – Balmoral

I returned to Princess Louise's room to help her finish dressing. Princess Beatrice was there and the girl's happy prattling grated on my nerves. It would normally have earned a rebuke from her cynical sister but Princess Louise's eyes also sparkled with excitement. No one seemed to notice my low mood but I wasn't sure how I would keep up a brave face through a whole evening. My first ever ball and now I was determined not to dance. This aching disappointment was my own fault. For a second time I'd mistaken wicked guile for genuine interest in me. Princess Louise was clearly certain she was adored but she was on a path likely to end in disaster. I resolved to never risk that.

Lady Georgina arrived to escort me to the ballroom. 'Your dress is gorgeous,' she said, as we descended the stairs.

I nodded but had to stare straight ahead and blink hard to keep the tears back.

We took our places in the reserved chairs beside the royal alcove in the ballroom. Lady Georgina whispered that Prince Albert had given careful thought to this room in the castle design. There was an entrance door from outside near the west wing and tonight everyone had come in that way. Now we all waited for the royal party to enter through the internal door which would bring them out onto a balcony. The ballroom buzzed with excited murmurs. Everyone was looking forward to the evening. Except me. I was sick to my stomach.

'You're pale, Iris. Are you all right?' Lady Georgina asked.

'Unfortunately, my monthly visitor is early and very heavy. I daren't risk dancing.' I crossed my fingers against the fib.

She screwed up her face in sympathy. 'That is such a shame.'

Just then, the piper's first note announced the imminent arrival of the Queen and, despite my dejected spirits, the eerie sound made my heart shift. The deep resonance followed by the piped high note. The sadness and the joy. Queen Victoria walked onto the balcony beside the Prince of Wales. She was tiny on the arm of her tall, handsome, bearded son. Yet her presence commanded the room to immediate silence. Her children and the Princess of Wales filed in behind her.

The Queen raised her hand.

'Thank you all for being here and welcome to the 1869 Ghillies Ball.' Her voice seemed high-pitched and so very English in present company. Yet, her genuine enthusiasm was clear. Everyone cheered. 'God Save the Queen.'

The Prince of Wales led his mother down the steps and a fiddler escorted his band onto the spot the royal party had vacated. The balcony became a stage. Once the royal family were seated, the lead fiddle player drew his bow across his strings.

The Prince of Wales led his wife onto the floor. The princesses followed, with Mr Boehm and Dr Jenner. Lady Craigengar and Mr Brown made up the eight required for a quadrille.

'Let the dancing begin,' Queen Victoria announced.

Once the royal party completed the first quadrille, the rest of the floor started to fill up. Princess Alexandra, who expected a baby before the end of the year, curtsied, signalling her exit. The Prince of Wales walked over and took Lady Georgina's hand, pulling her into the dance. Suddenly, I was alone. My anxious search of the crowd found Lachlan Brown in a rowdy group of ghillies at the far side of the room. They were taking turns to drink from a hip flask, being much less surreptitious than they probably intended. I looked desperately for some way to escape. There was a spare seat in the royal alcove beside the Queen's youngest son, a boy of around sixteen. Prince Leopold had returned from an educational trip with his tutor that afternoon, but I'd yet to meet him. I hesitated, unsure if the wooden alcove was reserved only for the royal family. Too late, Lachlan Brown was right beside me, he swayed slightly and when he spoke, his words were both slurred and very loud.

'Miss Finlay, you promised me a dance.' He grinned, then grabbed my hand, trying to pull me to my feet.

I snatched my hand away. 'You will have to excuse me, Mr Brown. Unfortunately, I'm not well enough to dance today.'

He actually laughed in my face.

'I've seen you striding aboot. You're the fittest lassie in the castle. Up you get.' He made to grab my hand again.

I put both hands behind my back. 'I am unwell. Please excuse me.'

The thunderous look he gave me reminded me of his uncle on a bad day. I had the impression that he was considering taking me onto the dancefloor by force.

Thankfully, my rescuer arrived. Lady Georgina put her hand on Lachlan's shoulder. 'I am sorry to disappoint you, young man. Sadly, Miss Finlay really is not well enough to dance tonight.'

Lachlan Brown turned on his heel and walked away. His group of friends dissolved into fits of loud laughter.

'I believe that boy has had too much whisky. Come and meet Prince Leopold. It is so very hard that the Queen will not allow him to dance due to his health. I'm sure your company will cheer him up.'

As we walked over, she said, 'I will explain your indisposition to the Queen. She likes the royal party to dance with the ghillies, but in this case, you will be excused.'

The quadrille was over and the fiddler announced the next dance was the Gay Gordons, a dance for pairs. Lady Georgina made the introductions during the lull in the music.

'Prince Leopold, may I introduce Miss Iris Finlay, who is stepping in to fulfil some of Fraulein Bauer's duties in her absence. Miss Finlay is unfortunately under the weather and needs a quiet spot while she cannot partake of tonight's dancing. She has already had to turn down one of the ghillies. Might she sit beside you to avoid any further awkwardness?'

The young man, who had got to his feet when we approached, bowed and gestured to the seat. 'I'm very sorry you are unwell, Miss Finlay, but I would be delighted to have your company.'

I curtsied and sat down beside him. Lady Georgina whispered in the Queen's ear. Her Majesty glanced over at me and gave a small nod.

'So are you a German teacher?' Price Leopold asked.

The music had begun again, so I had to lean in to make my reply heard. 'Unfortunately not. My duties are to chaperone Princess Louise.'

At that moment, Mr Boehm and Princess Louise danced past us. She was wearing an off-the-shoulder gown in shimmering dark green silk. It really suited her. Boehm twirled her

217

under his arm, then they set off into a vigorous polka. When the dance took them back to the side-by-side steps again, the Princess looked up into Edgar Boehm's eyes and gave him a doting smile.

'I can see you have your work cut out,' the young Prince said drily.

During the next lull between dances, I asked Prince Leopold about his European travels. He was very enthusiastic about the many cities he had visited. It occurred to me that being back under the protective gaze of his mother must be a difficult adjustment. Princess Louise had explained that her much-loved younger brother's haemophilia condition and delicate health made the Queen constantly fearful for his safety.

The noise level of a boisterous Eightsome Reel rendered talking impossible. All the dancers were smiling. The sharp stab of envy was strong as if inflicted by a Highland skene dhu. This was a once in a lifetime opportunity and I longed to forget my troubles and disappear into the happy throng. I glanced at the young prince and sensed he felt the same. Princess Louise came and sat beside us. Her face was flushed and her hair dishevelled. She hugged her brother.

'You look miserable. I'm so very sorry.' She turned towards her mother. 'Mama, could Leopold not do just a few turns on the floor?'

At that moment all eyes were drawn to a particular set of eight. Some ghillies were whooping while Lachlan spun Princess Beatrice's maid round and round. At the end of a final spin, he picked her up, then kissed her on the lips before he set her down. I guessed that whole charade had been planned for me. I didn't want his kiss but felt it as a deliberate slight. In the back-slapping that followed, Lachlan overbalanced and knocked over one of the other ghillies.

'I believe that answers your question as to why he cannot,' the Queen said.

Princess Louise frowned. She climbed the wooden stairs to talk to the bandleader.

'Miss Finlay, would you forgive me for deserting you? I'm very tired from the journey,' Prince Leopold said.

'Of course. I was thinking of retiring too.'

We both stood up, but Princess Louise came and took both our hands. 'You're not escaping just yet. You've just come back from Vienna, Leopold, and I don't believe for one minute that you didn't dance there. I want to see what you've learned, so I've requested a very gentle waltz tune. Edgar, Bertie, Beatrice and I will form a human barrier keeping the other dancers away. You and Iris will manage just a few minutes, then you will be allowed to go to bed.'

The young prince smiled indulgently at his sister. I sensed a deep warmth between them. A contrast to her constant bickering with her younger sister.

'Miss Finlay, I certainly won't insist, but do you think you could manage just a few steps?' Prince Leopold asked.

It was a royal invitation, so I was in no position to refuse. Prince Leopold took my hand and led me to the floor. The band struck up a lilted Scottish refrain. I was a novice dancer but as Princess Louise had predicted, her brother was very competent. Here I was dancing a waltz, in a beautiful dress in the arms of an actual prince. It would be every young girl's dream but my heart felt shrunken, like a hard walnut in my chest; humiliation had sucked away all joy. Prince Leopold led me around one circuit of the floor. In the very last turn, we danced past Lachlan Brown. His furious expression sent a shudder down my back. He said something to his friends that caused them to roar with laughter. When the dance ended, I curtsied and said a polite goodbye, before scuttling out the door and into the courtyard, with the noise of male jeering ringing in my ears.

Chapter Thirty-Three

August 1869 – Balmoral

T he day after the ceilidh was dreich. Incessant drizzle, leaving the trees and bushes outside the castle windows dripping, and keeping everyone inside. The mood was subdued. The Queen liked to keep the castle cold, but Prince Leopold persuaded her to have a fire in the sitting room, by complaining he was shivering. Her Majesty retired to the library. An hour later, Prince Leopold, who really didn't look well, said he would go back to bed. He stopped beside my chair on his way out.

'Thank you for the dance. Are you feeling any better, Miss Finlay?'

'Thank you, Your Royal Highness. I do feel a little stronger than yesterday.'

'I wish I could say the same.' The Prince inclined his head and took his leave.

Princess Louise was reading beside the fire. Jip was pawing at her skirts, so I offered to take him out.

The Princess looked up and smiled. 'Would you? This is so good I can't put it down.' She held up a slim, red, leather-bound book with a marbled cover. The spine had the title

Lorna Doone picked out in gold. Two identical books lay beside the chair leg. 'It's a trilogy and you must read it next. I'm sure to be on the next one by tomorrow.'

'I'd like that. Thank you,' I said. Jip, sensing he was in luck, was already beside me and looking up expectantly. 'Come on then, boy.'

I picked up the dog's ball before heading for my room. A game of fetch on the spiral staircase had the little terrier racing and up down to bring the ball back. By the time I donned my shawl and stepped outside, he was already panting but still wagging his tail.

'Just a quick walk, then. We both need some fresh air.'

We exited the castle and the dog ran ahead.

A deep voice rumbled just behind me. 'Stuck-up bitch.'

I stiffened, but kept walking.

'Flinging yersel' at thon Prince will dae you nae good.'

Incensed, I turned and faced him. Lachlan Brown stood with his back against the tower wall, sheltered from the rain by its turret. He was smoking, and I was quite sure the distinctive smell was the brand favoured by the Prince of Wales, who left half empty packets all over the castle. A man of Lachlan Brown's low character was surely capable of such petty theft.

'Don't be ridiculous.' I instantly regretted reacting, when his face contorted into a sneer.

'I ken exactly what you need, and you willnae get it fae that mummy's boy.'

I walked away quickly. There was threat in his voice and I could feel his stare drilling into my back. I kept my walk close to the castle, within steps of escape. For the first time, I was glad that my time at Balmoral was coming to an end. Princess Louise would go south before the end of September, and I would return to Drummond Castle. I'd never need to see that vile man again.

. . .

Lachlan Brown had unnerved me and I slept fitfully that night. The sound of rooks cawing announced dawn. Another day in Balmoral. Perhaps one of my last. I resolved not to let Lachlan intimidate me. After breakfast, Lady Craigengar tracked me down to give me my wages for August. I wasn't expecting her to exchange pleasantries, so was surprised when she lingered. It took her a few seconds to summon the right words.

'I must congratulate you, Miss Finlay. Princess Louise is delighted with your work and the Queen appreciates your calming presence too.'

I curtsied, astounded by the unexpected compliment. 'I'm happy to have been useful.'

'I'm afraid we won't need you now Fraulein Bauer is returning.' Lady Craigengar looked anxious.

'I'm glad to hear her family problems are resolved, and I always understood the temporary nature of my appointment.'

'What will you do?'

I was touched to hear the softening in her previously frosty tone. It seemed, I had finally won her over.

'I believe I'm needed at Drummond Castle. My aunt's health seems to have deteriorated. I hope my father will return in the new year.'

'Of course. There is a letter for you on the hall table. There were two letters in the same hand this morning. The other was for Lady Bradley, so I believe it's a note from your aunt.'

As soon as she left, I raced to the west wing to find my letter. Anticipation mounted because the bulk implied something extra inside.

Drummond Castle
August 28th

Dear Iris,

You'll be delighted with the enclosed letter from your father. Mr Speir says it's good news. I am sure you have mixed feelings about coming home to sleepy Perthshire. However, I am looking forward to your return. I confess it has been quite dull here without you. I saw both Mrs Birnie and your young friend Annie at church last Sunday, and I gather they have missed you too.

Please send me news of the exact date and time of your train and I will make sure that Mr Buchan is at the station to meet you.

Your loving Aunt Leonora

The first words in my father's letter confirmed my hopes.

Port of Guayaquil
Ecuador
12th August 1869

Dearest Iris,
I'm coming home. How I have longed to write those words to you.

The cargo is all packed, and the ship will sail north in the morning. Mr de Rias is a very persuasive man, and he assures me this quicker route gives my precious live specimens a better chance of survival. Certainly I know Professor Jameson lost many plants on his journey via Argentina and our route will save us several weeks. You will forgive me the sin of pride that this Spanish gentleman was so obvi-ously impressed by my assembled collection. I believe he had expected to do more expeditions on arrival, but he assures me we have more than enough plants and we shouldn't risk any further delay.

I must confess his given name makes me think of archangels. In ancient times, Raphael was the patron saint of travellers, sailors in particular. So surely I have the best possible companion for my journey home.

Rafael tested the train on his journey to Ecuador, and is convinced that the Panama Railroad can accommodate our precious Wardian cases. Amazingly the rail journey will only take six hours. If the winds are kind to us, I should be back well in time for Christmas. I so look forward to hearing all about your adventures at court. I hope you are not too much grown into a lady, and that I will still know you as my precious little Iris.

Your affectionate Papa

Six hours! Papa didn't say how long the South American leg of his sail would take, but I understood the Atlantic crossing could be done in a month. He might easily be in Scotland before November. The surge of elation was accompanied by an undercurrent of worry, Mr de Rias was definitely no angel, I hated that Papa seemed to trust him. One thing was certain, I must go home and make sure our tenancy of the Culdees lodge was assured. The girl who left Perthshire in July had been reluctant to broach the subject. The woman I now was would make sure Mr Speir was in no doubt of our expectations. As Papa said, Rafael was persuasive. The Culdees position and the gardener's lodge had been promised to Papa. I knew I could rely on Aunt Leonora to back up that argument. If Mr de Rias had ambitions to usurp us, he was in for a disappointment.

The long hall clock chimed the hours for ten o'clock. Princess Louise was expecting me in her studio. I bounded up the east stairs to collect the first volume of *Lorna Doone* from my room. It had been a useful distraction in my wakeful hours and I could return it to Princess Louise. I was a little out of breath when I reached the studio door in the west wing. Mr Boehm came into the corridor behind me.

'Good morning, Miss Finlay. Nice to see that the weather has dried up. Scotland seems to specialise in rain.'

'It is the reason the countryside is so green, sir.' My reply caused him to laugh.

I went in and curtsied. Mr Boehm kissed the Princess on the cheek.

'Good morning, Edgar. Good morning, Iris. What did you think of *Lorna Doone*?'

'I really enjoyed it, Your Highness.'

'I'll try to finish both the next volumes to pass them on before we go south.' Princess Louise glared at the huge clay model in front of her. 'I need to decide what to do with this, too.'

'You must persevere, of course,' Mr Boehm said.

Princess Louise looked despondent. 'It's simply not good enough. I've overstretched my abilities, attempting something full-size. I should stick to busts.'

'You mean to give up? I don't believe that for a minute.' Mr Boehm laughed and shook his head.

The Princess pouted. 'You can see it's not good enough.'

'Not yet, but some aspects of it are excellent. The drape of the skirt, for example.' Mr Boehm took the Princess's hand and pulled her onto the couch beside him. 'Loosey, are you fishing for compliments? It's not like you, and it's not at all what you've been training for.' The Princess looked embarrassed. Mr Boehm persevered. 'You have unparalleled access to the Queen and she is the subject most likely to find you a plinth. Your work is good, Excellence will take more time and practice.'

'I fear that could take years and Mama's weight gain causes her to like her appearance less and less.'

He shrugged. 'It doesn't have to be a contemporary image. Search the paintings in the royal collection for your inspiration.'

The Princess reached over to squeeze his arm. 'You're right. I'm being childish. I love how you always tell me the truth.'

'And the truth is, you have genuine talent. You should take this model to London. Continue to work on it to hone your skill. I'll need to transport my model too.'

'I'll ask Mr Brown to sort out crates and have them both taken south by train. You are right. I'll stick at it. I'm just downhearted about losing our daily contact so soon. It's unbearable.'

The intense look that passed between them confirmed that this was not only a conversation about sculpture.

'My statue is ready to scale up into the marble version. Come to my London studio to watch how it's done,' Boehm said. 'Please,' he added under his breath.

The Princess reached for his hand and he grasped it. 'Mama wants me in the Isle of Wight now, but I'll try to get away.' Her eyes were glassy with tears.

'We'll make it work,' he replied in the same quiet voice.

The room crackled with emotional tension. I coughed and stood up, then walked to the window. Jip jumped out of his basket and scampered hopefully to my side.

Princess Louise, perhaps taking the hint, moved away from Mr Boehm and picked up her sculpting scalpel. 'Would you walk Jip, please, Iris? I want to conquer the dress today.'

I scooped the dog up and put my cheek against his silky ears to buy me time to consider my answer and hide my discomfort. I daren't leave them alone.

Mr Boehm stood up. 'You don't need my advice on this part. I'll go and pack. I'll be back in an hour.'

'Could you go via the drawing room, Iris?' Princess Louise asked. 'You'll find Leopold languishing there. He was complaining about being bored. I promised him I'd pass on *Lorna Doone* once you'd finished with it.'

Jip followed me down the stairs, I found Prince Leopold. There was no need for a fire today, but the young man was in his usual chair, with a tartan blanket tucked over his legs.

'Miss Finlay,' he said, making to push himself out of his chair.

'Please don't disturb yourself, Your Highness. I'm on my way out with Jip, but Princess Louise asked me to bring you *Lorna Doone*.'

He took it from me with a smile. 'What is your opinion?'

'I enjoyed it. The author is excellent.'

'I've heard him compared to Walter Scott. Are you a fan of Sir Walter?'

'Yes. I've read them all. And I would say there are definite similarities.' When I curtsied and made to leave the room, a flash of disappointment crossed the Prince's face.

'Would it bore you if I walked with you? I'm afraid I'm rather slow.'

'Not at all. Jip always has a great deal of sniffing and scent-marking to attend to in the garden. Our progress is usually slow.'

The Prince put on his hat, of medium height and build, the youngest prince strongly resembled paintings of his father. We walked out into the courtyard, speaking again about his European tour in a very nostalgic tone.

When we drew level with the rose garden, I walked over to get closer look

'I observed you examining the roses yesterday. Have you an interest in flowers?' he asked.

'I do,' I confirmed. 'My father is a botanist. He is currently in South America collecting rare specimens.'

The ground was strewn with petals after yesterday's rain. Sunlight glistened on raindrops lingering inside the cup of a Tuscany rose bloom. I went closer to capture the memory and describe it to Annie. We might signal the changing seasons with such evidence of autumn weather. When I turned back to the path, the young Prince gave me his hand as I climbed back up the few steps.

'You must miss your father,' he said.

'I do, but today I had word that he has begun his journey home.' My smile froze when I spotted Lachlan Brown striding up the path from the river. He glared at me, then rushed off towards the castle kitchens.

The Prince and I walked onto the lawn, and I threw the ball to encourage Jip to run. Princess Louise was guilty of feeding him titbits and he was getting too fat. I tried to attend to the Prince's words, but Brown's angry expression had brought a sense of foreboding flooding back. After a few minutes, I called Jip back to my side. 'I should get back to the studio.'

Once inside, I said goodbye to Prince Leopold. I already had one foot on the stairs when there was a loud shriek.

Prince Leopold met my eyes. 'That was Mama,' he said.

I lifted my skirts, and we ran up the stairs. There were raised voices coming from the studio. Mr Boehm came into the corridor at such speed that he almost barged into us. He exchanged a glance with Prince Leopold and shook his head.

'I believe I'd best stay out of this,' the young Prince muttered, before following Mr Boehm back downstairs.

John Brown's loud voice rang out. 'You have gone too far! How could you expose Her Majesty tae such a disgusting and shameless apparition!'

'How dare you talk to me in that tone, sir! I will not tolerate it!' Princess Louise shouted back.

'For shame, keep your voices down. Have you learned nothing, Louise?' The Queen sounded dreadfully upset.

'You, of all people, may not lecture me on moral behaviour. I will not be bullied this time!' Princess Louise replied. Surely the entire castle must have heard them.

The Queen emerged. Her expression was furious and her face flushed deep red. John Brown hurried after her and I flattened myself against the wall to let them pass. I bowed my head and tried to enter the studio, but John Brown turned and caught my arm.

'Dinnae even think aboot it. You, miss, have failed in the simplest ae duties.' His tone dripped with scorn. 'You'd better go and pack, then find yer ain way tae the station. Summary dismissal wi' nae references is too good for you.'

I glanced at the studio door, hearing Princess Louise crying.

'Go and pack!' he shouted into my face.

I fled past him, blinded by tears and trying not to stumble on the stairs. As I ran through the castle and past the door to the servants' quarters, Lachlan Brown stood there smirking.

Chapter Thirty-Four

August 1869 – Balmoral

I slammed my bedroom door behind me and swept up the swathe of Virginia Creeper, determined to have it out of my sight. I had to stand on a stool to manage it and the tendrils clung to my fingers. I tore at them furiously, then pushed the whole thing out. An invasive climber. I was stupid for even considering it. Stupider still to find myself undermined by yet another treacherous man. Had I learned nothing? Lachlan's smug expression made me certain that he had told John Brown the Princess was unchaperoned.

I set about packing my trunk and shed self-pitying tears that Princess Louise had tricked me into leaving the room and I was to be punished. But then, how must the Princess be feeling? The Queen had never come to the studio unannounced before. Inadvertently, I'd triggered the lovers' discovery. Surely, I deserved the scorn of the Princess, as well as my dismissal for failing in my assigned task.

A scraping noise from the corridor alerted me and was I glad to welcome Jip into my arms. Losing this little fellow was going to be hard. I climbed onto my bed with him and considered my next move. I couldn't face going downstairs, and Brown's instructions were ridiculous. There was no way to get myself to the railway station without help. However, I loathed the notion of hanging around here feeling humiliated. A gentle rap on my door and Lady Georgina entered. Her sympathetic expression caused me to dissolve into tears. She put her arm around me and sat down, placing the second volume of *Lorna Doone* on the bed.

'Princess Louise sent me, and asked me to bring you this. I've heard about the whole alarming drama of today and she is very sorry to have involved you in it.'

I nodded and sniffed back my tears.

Lady Georgina glanced at the spaniel who was now curled up on my pillow. 'I'll let her know you've got naughty Jip. Everyone is scouring the castle for him.'

'I've been dismissed and told to leave.' I recounted the whole story about Lachlan Brown and why I believed he was behind the events.

She frowned. 'I've never liked that boy. His father isn't a kind man either. Mr Brown's brother is a bully and Prince Leopold hates him. I'll go to John Brown directly. This young scoundrel should be unmasked.'

'Please don't,' I said. 'It's only my word against his and, as his uncle, Mr Brown is much more likely to disbelieve me. Especially now he is so angry.'

Lady Georgina sighed. 'Let me ponder on it. In the meantime, it might be best to make plans to return to Drummond Castle. I want to accompany you, and I believe it might be easier to get leave from the Queen if we go soon. Then I can be back in time to accompany her to the Isle of Wight.'

'I hope you don't think me a coward, but I do think I'd prefer to go home.'

'I know how brave you are, but tempers are frayed downstairs. It's wise to stay out of the way, at least for now. Are you hungry?'

I shook my head.

'Then read your book and give me some time to work something out. I'll be back later.'

Reading on my bed in the middle of the day felt ridiculously indulgent, but it was good to escape into the next chapters of the book. The sound of footsteps some hours later pulled me out of the story. I expected Lady Georgina. Instead, Princess Louise came in. I jumped up.

'Lady Bradley says you are leaving. I'm so very sorry.' She took both my hands and squeezed my fingers. 'I expect you are shocked and angry with me?'

I shook my head. 'I feel like I've let you down.' The Princess frowned. 'Goodness, no. This has nothing to do with you.'

I considered explaining the connection to Lachlan, but decided it made no difference to the outcome.

'Edgar is packing his bags.' She glanced at my full trunk. 'It is really too much to have you sent away, too.'

'Only a few days early, and I suspect my aunt does need me now.'

'Still, there is no need to stay hiding up here. Join us downstairs. Mr Brown and most of the party have gone with my mother to Braemar. It's only Bertie, Leopold, and me. Edgar is clearing out his studio.' She pulled a rueful face.

I took a seat near the drawing room window and ruffled Jip's ears when he jumped into my lap. I stared out at the familiar view of the hills and surrounding woods. The leaves were turning colour to autumnal shades of gold, and the purple haze had gone from the heather on the moor beyond. Time to move on.

The smell of the Prince of Wales's large cigar filled the room. Princess Louise lit a cigarette. Prince Leopold took it from her for a single puff and she winked at him. Her elder brother leaned on his knees and moved a piece on the chessboard that sat between them. 'I remain convinced you will have more personal freedom if you marry, Louise,' he said. 'It will release you from Mama's constant vigilance. Since she is reconciled to you considering a non-royal, there must be someone you can tolerate.'

Princess Louise blew a stream of smoke into the air in an impatient gesture. 'Our situations are not comparable, Bertie. Your freedoms would not be mine.'

The Prince of Wales shrugged. 'I'll persuade Mama that you need to socialise more if she wishes a marriage. Come and stay with us in Kensington Palace. We'll throw some parties. It's just a case of being open-minded.'

Princess Louise wrinkled up her nose.

'We are only minutes away from Edgar's studio and you might attend your sculpture classes,' he said.

Princess Louise leaned over to cover her brother's hand. 'That means the world to me, Bertie. I've told Mama clearly that I mean to carry on. I'm grown up, so she cannot bully me anymore.'

The Prince of Wales looked sceptical. 'She is the Queen and she will have her own way. You must accept a suitable suitor.'

'If you can get me to London from of the Isle of Wight, I'll go to your parties, but please don't invite any sops,' Princess Louise replied.

Everyone adjourned to the billiards room but I stayed behind. The Princess was being kind, but there was nothing useful for me to do here. I met Lady Georgina at the door. 'I'm going back to my room before the others return.'

'The Queen plans to dine in town. Go past the kitchen. I've asked them to lay out bread and cheese for people to help themselves. Her Majesty has given me leave to go with you on the ten o'clock train tomorrow. I'll stay overnight at Drummond Castle and return the next day.'

I nodded. 'That's good news. Please tell the Princess I'm at her service if she needs me. If not, I'll aim to walk Jip in the morning before we leave for the station.'

The hours of the night dragged. I ventured downstairs at dawn. Jip came racing down the west wing stairs with his ball in his mouth. An early morning walk had become part of our routine. Who would walk him tomorrow?

I lingered in the rose garden, trying to memorise the species, for when I would create a rose garden of my own at Culdees Lodge, and plant a Balmoral rose as a reminder. I followed the dog onto the grassy area in front of the drawing room windows. Jip dropped his ball at my feet. Between throws, I turned to look up at the silvery-grey castle. I'd mostly been happy here. Princess Louise's encouragement had increased my daring. When I'd added my words to Annie's illustrations for the autumn pamphlet, I'd shared it with the Princess. She had penned me a personal note of recommendation to Mr White, promising to supply him with a foreword, if he decided to publish our work. Surely the association might help. Thoughts of Annie raised my spirits. We'd set to work on the winter pamphlet together as soon as I got back. My idea was to set the view of the small garden framed by the window from inside the cottage. I was sure there was holly amongst the hedge, which would hopefully be covered in berries. I imagined the red spots against the dark green holly. Perhaps I'd add a red-stemmed dogwood? One day soon, Papa and I could make that garden a reality.

The quiet of the morning was shattered by a loud bang. Instinctively, my hands went up to cover my ears. Someone nearby had let off a shotgun. Jip was no gundog and easily spooked by any loud noise. He cowered down in fear but when the gun went off even closer, he took off at speed in the opposite direction. I shouted to him to come back. He showed no sign of stopping, I picked up my skirts and ran after him. The dog had headed down the path towards the river. When I got to the water's edge, I stopped, my heart pounding. The recent rain had transformed the river from the usual benign and translucent few inches, into a raging progression of white seething water. Had Jip fallen in? I stared downstream but could see no sign of him. I called his name but he probably wouldn't hear me over the noise of the river. A deep and mirthless laugh caused me to whirl around. Lachlan Brown blocked the path. A shotgun lay open across one arm.

'I hear you've been sent packing, but I'm gonna tak what you owe me first.'

I returned the glare in his icy blue and vengeful eyes. 'Get out of my way.'

'Still nae manners,' he replied, coming closer.

I stepped backwards but my boot skidded away from me on the muddy bank. Lachlan reached out and grabbed my arm. Possession, not kindness. He pulled me back from the bank and spun me around until my wrist was up between my shoulder blades. Dropping the gun, he pushed me, stumbling towards a huge Scots pine. I put my free hand up to brace against the impact with its gnarly bark.

'Help me!' I screamed.

Lachlan made a noise under his breath, like an animal's growl, then flung me headfirst over a tree trunk lying in the ditch. All the air had already been pushed out of my lungs when he threw himself on top of me.

His low voice rumbled in my ear. 'Save yer breath. Naebdae can hear you.' His hands scrabbled at my skirts and petticoats.

Was this it? This man was going to do something that would leave me feeling ruined forever. Anger surged strength into my arms, and as his weight shifted to one side. I flung myself backwards. He fell off me and I staggered upright. For a spilt second, he looked astonished and ridiculous. The fabric of his kilt spread out, fan-like, across the browned pine needles on the ground. I started to run. As Lachlan's fingers seized my ankle, I saw Jip running towards us with John Brown behind him. The man's roar made Lachlan look up. His uncle charged at him like an angry bear. He tore Lachlan to his feet, then punched him to his knees again.

'You are a disgrace,' he yelled. 'I cannae believe one ae my ain kin would sink sae low.' He turned to me, shaking with anger. 'Did he harm you?'

I shook my head, putting my fingers to my cheek where it had been grazed by the tree trunk.

Mr Brown groaned. He lashed out to kick Lachlan, and the boy scrabbled away. 'Get hame and stay there!' he yelled. Lachlan took off at a run.

'I am so very sorry, Miss Finlay. Thank God I happened to be near a window. I heard the gunshot and saw Jip take off. When he reappeared without you, I feared for yer safety.' He shook his head, he looked near to tears. 'My ain flesh, I cannae believe it.'

All the fight left me, and I sunk to the ground. Jip crawled onto my skirts.

'Are you hurt?'

'Nothing serious,' I said, although I winced with pain when I took a deep breath. Perhaps I'd broken a rib?

Mr Brown stretched out his hand to raise me up. His expression and the tenderness of the gesture reminded me of the way he was around the Queen. This man was not to blame for the behaviour of his nephew. He held out an arm for me to lean on. 'Can you manage tae walk back tae the castle?'

'I think so.' Slowly, we walked back together. 'What will happen to him?'

'Dinnae even gie him another thocht. I'll involve the constabulary if ye wish it. But I think he'd like that mair than the beating his faither will gie him when I tell the tale.'

'He'll lose his job?'

'Oh, aye. My brother will be feart it'll cost him his too. The Queen is going tae be furious. I can assure you, Miss Finlay, Lachlan Brown will never set foot on this property again. He'll get nae other job around here either. We're proud folk and there's nae coming back once yer reputation is lost.'

I glanced up at him. His fury was clear in his clenched jaw and lowered eyebrows.

'There are boats going tae the Americas. I'm no payin' for his passage, but I'll tell my brother it would be for the best if he did so.'

As we neared the castle, Princess Louise and Lady Georgina were coming towards us. I glanced down when I saw their horrified expression. My grey flannel dress was torn and mud-streaked. I reached up and found pine needles in my hair.

'Let me deal wi' this,' Mr Brown said under his breath.

'Lady Bradley, might you attend tae Miss Finlay? She needs some ointment for her face. I'm hoping there are no other injuries.'

'What on all earth?' Princess Louise said.

'Let's go inside,' John Brown replied. 'I need tae assemble the right words before I report tae the Queen.' He turned to me again. 'I am sorry for all the injustice you've faced in this house, and most mortified for my connection tae it. I'll get leave fae the Queen tae drive you baith tae the station.'

Chapter Thirty-Five

September 1869 – Perthshire

We were quiet for most of the long train journey south. I was exhausted. The track took us close to the sea and the sky was blue, but I was barely aware of the view. As we edged nearer home, I fretted about my life prospects. Could I be happy simply keeping house for my father? My ambitions had grown and I wasn't Papa's little Iris anymore.

Lady Georgina's words broke my reverie. 'I wonder if Leonora would benefit from some sea air? I'm told Broughty Ferry is a nice spot.'

I ran my palms over the fabric of my silk skirt. My grey dress needed cleaning and mending, so Princess Louise had insisted on giving me one of hers. I took a deep breath, the pain in my ribs an instant reminder. Today, I'd surely earned the right to be honest.

'I am looking forward to spending time with Aunt Leonora, I've missed her. But surely early summer would be a better time for a seaside trip?'

A flicker of anxiety crossed Lady Georgina's face.

'What are you thinking?' I asked.

'Only that you are right. It's too late in the year for a windy seaside resort.'

I shook my head. 'Please, Lady Georgina. Is there something you are keeping from me?'

She looked panicked. 'You have had much too much trauma this week and Leo made me promise not to say,' she said.

'These last weeks have banished childish naivety. I mean like you to make my own way in this world, and I must do that with my eyes wide open. Did my aunt share her doctor's opinion with you?'

'Yes,' Lady Georgina replied simply and looked down at her gloved hands in her lap. She fidgeted with a button at one wrist, then met my eyes. 'You must know soon enough and I agree you've proven your maturity. I'm so sorry, Iris. The doctor could feel a tumour in her abdomen and advised that surgery would more likely kill her rather than do any good.' Tears ran down her face. 'My darling Leo is leaving us. I'm travelling not only for your benefit, but because I'm afraid she might not be here when I return with the Queen next year.'

I gasped. 'That is what I was afraid of. I should have been at her side this summer.'

Lady Georgina shook her head vigorously and dabbed her eyes with her handkerchief. 'I offered to get you released after Edinburgh but she didn't wish it. However, she tells me she now finds breathing more difficult every day. I'm so sorry, but I believe you will be able to see the poor state of her health when you meet her. She is very relieved that your papa is on his way back.'

The pain in my bruised ribs radiated out to engulf my chest. Aunt Leonora had been a strong and capable presence throughout my childhood. My gentle mother was always over-shadowed by her confident older sister. Mama was never strong, but I had expected Aunt Leonora to live deep into old age. Losing someone else was impossibly unfair. A sob escaped me. Luckily, the dress's single pocket held a handkerchief, a fine cotton square, embroidered with tiny blue flowers. I shook it out and a piece of paper fluttered to the carriage floor. I picked up the handwritten note.

My Princess, I will love you until the end of time

All my love Walter

Lady Georgina must have seen my expression. She snatched the note from me.

'Who in all earth is Walter?' I blurted out.

Lady Georgina gave a sigh of exasperation. 'Louise, really!' Shock stopped both our tears. She coughed and rubbed her face. 'It is fortunate this particular dress wasn't chosen by Princess Beatrice.'

'Is this the Scottish soldier who was sent away? The castle servants talk about him.' I hesitated, but here in this private carriage was surely my only chance of getting straight answers. 'They also gossip that Princess Louise bore him a child. Is that true?'

Lady Georgina sighed. 'I'm most sorry to hear that servants talk about that, and honestly, I don't know.'

'The cook didn't see me come into the kitchen. She said that Princess Louise was most open in her infatuation and often unwell in the autumn after this man left.'

'That's a huge leap of logic, but I would agree those two things are accurately described,' Lady Georgina replied. 'Walter Stirling was banished back to his regiment, then Princess Louise was absent from our party at the end of 1866. When she came back to the Queen's side in 1867, her spirit seemed quite crushed. I've been pleased to see her back to her old self this year. Although this recent fuss with Mr Boehm shows she hasn't learned to curtail her passions.'

'It explains some of the things she said back to the Queen,' I said quietly. 'Poor Princess Louise. If she had a baby and was made to give it away, that must have been unbearable.'

'It's a common enough occurrence I'm afraid.'

My head snapped up. 'Did that happen to anyone else I know?' I had always suspected Aunt Leonora harboured a sad secret. This was as direct a question as I dared.

She smiled and shook her head. 'No. Neither Leonora nor I have ever had children. But I think it's one of the reasons she will be so pleased to see you again. She loves you like a daughter.'

'I will devote myself to making her as comfortable as I can. Maybe with careful nursing, I can prove the doctor wrong.'

'I hope so.' She squeezed my hand.

Chapter Thirty-Six

September 1869 - Drummond Castle

S truan sunk the spade into the muddy bank, and put his weight into levering the clod of earth and leaves free. The water immediately flooded beyond the blockage, allowing the burn to run clear again. It was a job that needed doing. However, it was certainly not the most urgent task on his list, and could easily have been done by one of Mr MacDonald's younger lads. Struan would have come up with some excuse if challenged, but knew full well he was standing there because it was the only spot on the estate with a proper view of the castle approach road. Mr Buchan had told him he was going to the station, and he'd set off over an hour ago. Just at that moment, the familiar carriage turned into the long line of beech trees. Struan hoisted the spade onto his shoulder and strode towards the castle. He forced himself not to run.

The formal gardens were all laid lower than the level of the castle. He had to walk the entire length of the terrace below the esplanade to emerge on the path beside the old keep. He propped his spade against the balustrade, then took out his pruning knife, giving a passing impression of being busy with another task that didn't need doing. He felt like an utter idiot, but was powerless to be anywhere other than here. The gravel crunched below the carriage wheels as it came under the arch and pulled up at the entrance to Lady Walker's quarters in the castle. Mr Buchan opened the door and held out his hand. Struan knew instantly that the emerging buttoned black boot and stout ankle were not hers. His heart sank.

'Thank you so much, Buchan.' Lady Bradley turned back towards the carriage.

'Welcome home, Miss Finlay,' Mr Buchan said. Words that made Struan want to hug the man.

Iris took his hand and climbed down from the carriage. Struan's daft heart stuttered at the sight of her. The last three months had dragged. He'd told himself to expect no reply to his letter, but the truth was being so ignored left him feeling crushed and foolish. Iris seemed different. He'd expected her to return a lady. Her expensive looking brown silk dress and jaunty bonnet would likely fit right into Queen Victoria's Balmoral and her beauty left him breathless. But Iris's face was pale, her expression strained, and she looked awfy thin. Mr Buchan exchanged a concerned look with Lady Bradley. Something was wrong. Both ladies lifted their skirts and Buchan followed them into the castle with the luggage.

That was it. Just a glimpse, but enough to create a new sort of turmoil. He had to find out what ailed Iris. She'd surely confide in Annie. But then what? If someone had hurt her, he'd want to kill them. His grip stiffened on the knife in his hand. Looking down, he saw his fingernails were rimmed with mud. She'd always been beyond him, and now the gulf was even larger. What would she think if he went charging off to avenge her? She'd be embarrassed, that's what.

'Eedjit,' he muttered to himself. 'Stroo-an dinnae make a fuss.' He borrowed Annie's phrase, saying it out loud. Annie had been telling him the same thing since they were bairns. Now Iris inspired the same protective urge, except this was worse. He longed to protect her, and also to put his arms around her, to inhale her scent, to kiss her lips. The whole situation was a mess, and he had no hope of a satisfactory end to it. Struan picked up his spade and stomped off towards the glasshouse where Mr MacDonald indulged in his passion for hybrid roses and Struan was now completely obsessed, too. It was a good place to be alone. He needed to dwell in the joy of having Iris home, and talk himself out of overstepping his place.

This glasshouse was unheated but protected from the elements, keeping the temperature several degrees higher. Here the specially selected roses flourished under his tender care. The fertilisation season was almost over, but one white rose, a perfect *Rosa spinosissima*, had hung onto its petals until now. The draught caused when he slid the door closed created a stir in the air and the last but one petal fell on top of the pile surrounding the rose stem. He took his paintbrush out of its protective leather case and knelt between the rose beds. It was an oddly quiet spot in the garden without the presence of bees. They kept insects out of here, to avoid the introduction of pollen from an unknown rose. A critical moment had come. This was now his realm, and he felt the weight of the responsibility given to him by the older gardener. 'It's a job for a young lad wi' a steady hand. I think you'll bring us the luck that's evaded me,' MacDonald had said.

Struan used tweezers to pick the pollen from the open face of the bright pink specimen across the path, then dropped it into a jam jar he'd boiled sterile for this very purpose. The brush made of sable was a gift from Annie, one of those Iris had brought her from Edinburgh. This combination made it extra precious and perfect for the task. Grains of pollen clung to the tip of the brush, which he tapped over the white rose's stamen. Out of the corner of his eye, he saw the pink rose lose some of its petals, too. The two final blooms. The last chance this year to create the hybrid. Now came the waiting. Some parent plants had already grown the orange hips, showing his previous pollinations had worked. Each stem had a tag bearing the date and details of the pollen donor plant. Struan took a fresh label, a pencil stub, and a piece of string from his pocket. Below the date, in the same tiny writing, he wrote

Iris's return.

Chapter Thirty-Seven

September 1869 – Drummond Castle

L ady Bradley and I reached my aunt's sitting room; her appearance was better than I'd feared. In fact, much better than the last time I'd seen her in Edinburgh. Aunt Leonora got to her feet, and looked alert. However, when I walked into her embrace, I could feel she was much thinner.

'How are you, dear Aunt? I've missed you so much.'

'I'm perfectly well.' She cast a questioning glance in Lady Bradley's direction. When Lady Bradley shrugged, her expression became more accusatory.

'I made Lady Georgina tell me what your doctor said, and I'm here to look after you. I think you've lost more weight.'

My aunt sighed. 'I cannot bear it if you are all going to make a fuss the whole time, I hate being treated like an invalid. I'm having a good day and as to being thinner, I would say the same about you, young lady.'

We all sat and Lady Georgina patted my aunt's hand. 'I'm sorry for breaking your confidence, Leo. Iris is too perceptive these days and I couldn't lie to her. And I agree Iris has lost weight. We've had a particularly exhausting and trying time in Balmoral. I have lots to tell you.'

'Really? Well, I hope some of the stories are exciting. I swear I'd do better if I were not so bored.'

'I think you will agree our stories are exciting enough,' Lady Georgina replied. She gave me a wry look. 'To be honest, I think Iris and I both wish we'd had rather less excitement this week.'

My aunt clapped her hands together. 'I can't wait to hear about it, but save the details for the supper table. The de Eresby family are away for a few days, and the Baroness told me we might use their dining room to have a celebratory meal on your return. I for one am hungry.' She gave me a challenging look.

I laughed. 'What a splendid idea. I'm very hungry too.'

The story about Princess Louise and the subsequent discussion lasted right through supper. Lady Georgina led the way by talking openly, and it was clear the subject of the Princess's previous love affair and possible pregnancy was a topic they'd discussed before.

Aunt Leonora initially looked startled at her friend's frankness, but then followed her lead. 'I feel a great deal of sympathy for Princess Louise. She gives away her heart too easily.' She turned towards me. 'I know you admire her, Iris, and I do see how her audacity and determination are attractive, but the Princess's lack of caution has brought her a huge amount of pain. I don't think she is a good role model for you.'

'I do admire her, particularly her ambition and determination when it comes to her artistic principles. But I can assure you, dear Aunt, I shall never be compromised by infatuation with any man.'

Aunt Leonora looked at me curiously. 'Whatever are you talking about?'

'Iris, your declared intent to give up on all men is perhaps a little hasty,' Lady Georgina interjected and shot a look at my aunt. 'And could be misconstrued without the whole story of the Balmoral events.'

I sighed. 'Can we talk about that tomorrow? It's been a very long day.'

The maid came in to clear the plates, giving me a reprieve from any more awkward questions.

Lady Georgina rose from the table. 'Now, Leo. You're going to let me help you to get ready for bed,' she said. 'I'm delighted to see you looking a little better, so let's try to keep it that way.'

When we parted on the staircase, Lady Georgina hugged me goodnight, and whispered in my ear, 'You might give me some time alone with Leonora tomorrow. I shall tell her about your horrible experience and it might take me some time to calm her down.'

I nodded. 'Goodnight, and thank you.'

I was awake early the next morning. Thankfully the weather was dry. I left a note for my aunt saying that I'd gone for a walk but that I would be back before Lady Georgina left to catch her train. I strode out across the formal gardens, then into the woods beyond. When I got to the top of the hill, I could see the roofs of Muthill in the distance. I calculated that I could walk there and back with half an hour to spare. I'd go to Annie's, and if she wasn't at home, I'd leave her a note.

Annie's front door was open and I called out her name. She came to the front step with a dishtowel in her hands. Her expression was so full of joy to see me, and the surge in my own spirits confirmed what I'd missed most while in Balmoral.

'Iris! Struan told me they were expecting you back this week. You have no idea how pleased I am tae see you.'

I hugged her tight. 'You cannot be as pleased as I am to see you.'

'Can I get you tea? I'm longing tae hear all about your adventures in Balmoral.'

'And I've lots to tell you, but I can't stop for long right now. I must be back to say goodbye to Lady Bradley. She accompanied me on the train here, but she's going back to Balmoral this afternoon. When can we meet for longer? I'd like to visit Culdees to plan our winter article.'

'Aye, I've been thinking on it, too. In fact Struan said he might be able tae get a cart later this afternoon. He went in extra early tae be free tae take me.'

'I'm delighted your brother is more amenable to our publishing plans.' I hesitated, but wanted to get everything out in the open before I saw Struan next. 'Did he tell you he wrote to me?'

'He did. It took some courage tae dae it. He isnae much ae a letter writer and men arenae good at admitting when they are wrong.' Annie laughed, which set her off into a coughing fit. It took some time before she could stop.

I rubbed her back. 'Your cough sounds terrible.'

'Dinnae worry. I aywis get this in the winter. It's a constant battle tae keep the hall tiles clean up at the big house. People keep trailing their muddy boots through, and bicarbonate ae soda makes me cough.'

'I might be able to meet you at Culdees later, if I go with Buchan to the station. I could get him to detour there on the way back? Maybe around four?'

'A good plan. See you at Culdees Lodge later, then.'

Struan

. . .

Struan was chopping up wood for the glasshouse stove. Wielding the axe allowed him to channel his bad temper. The sight of Iris striding up the hill beyond the gardens before eight in the morning, had made his spirits leap. She had that effect on him every time. He'd climbed the hill too, just to prolong the sight of her. However, when she kept going towards Muthill, he experienced swooping disappointment. Iris was going to visit Annie this morning. His ruse to be near her in the afternoon wasn't going to work. The vicious repetitive movement caused even his calloused fingers to blister. The axe was at the top of an arc, when Iris came hurrying back up through the gardens. He could tell she was happy from her gait, her jaunty movements a barely contained skip. He stood there with the axe still above his head, grinning stupidly. He prayed he'd get to hear her voice later.

Struan worked on through the afternoon without stopping to eat the scran in his pocket. An apple and a pie, homemade by Annie, so it would be a grand one, but excitement scared off his appetite. He wanted to be certain no last minute task would detain him.

'I'll be off tae the blacksmith wi' that wheelrim, Mr MacDonald.' He must have somehow kept the elation out of his voice, because the man didn't even look up.

'That's fine, Struan,' Mr MacDonald replied.

'And it's still okay tae bring the cart back the morn? Annie's hoping I'll take her on an errand.'

'That's fine, lad.'

The carthorse rattled down the Muthill road, like she sensed his impatience. Struan jumped down and ran into the blacksmith, rolling the large and currently wobbly wheel in front of him. 'Thon's the wheel that needs straightening, Jimmy.'

'Nae bother, Struan. I can have it done while you wait, if you wantae hang on a minute.'

Struan had already turned. 'Annie's expecting me, Jimmy. I'll pick it up first thing. You can just leave it beside the door for me.'

Annie was already standing outside the house when Struan turned the corner into their lane.

'What are you sae happy about?' she teased him.

'It's a bonny aifternoon and I'm taking my best girl oot for a hurl when I should be at work. Who widnae be smiling?'

She grinned up at him. Annie was as pleased as he was to have Iris home.

Chapter Thirty-Eight

September 1869 – Drummond Castle

After taking Lady Georgina to the station, I asked Mr Buchan to stop at Culdees Castle, pleased to see lights on in the parlour. Mr Speir appeared at the window and raised his hand in greeting. He was already opening the front door when I reached it.

'You are back from your royal adventure! How nice to see you, Iris.'

'I'm pleased to be home. I was hoping to borrow the key to the lodge? Father should be home within weeks. I'd like to think about the furniture we will need from storage.'

I scanned his face. Was he offended by me getting straight to the point? I saw no sign of that.

'Good idea, I'll fetch it for you.' Mr Speir disappeared for a minute, returning with the key. 'I hope everything is in order. I admit I've not even been inside since Señor de Rias left.'

Even the sound of the man's name made me want to shudder. How was I going to cope with him coming back? What if he and Papa had become friends?

'Thank you,' I said, taking the key. 'I'm meeting Miss

Cooper at the lodge. We are looking for inspiration for a new painting project.'

'How is your young friend? She didn't borrow the key while you were away. Perhaps she was too shy?'

'Perhaps. She enjoys visiting Innerpeffray and does most of her painting there. I'll return the key in an hour.'

'No need,' he replied. 'I'm planning to ride before dusk. Once I've finished the stained glass I'm working on, I'll walk down to the stables and pick up the key.'

'Is it for another church? The colourful windows in Muthill kirk are marvellous.'

Mr Speir smiled broadly. My experience with Princess Louise had taught me that even wealthy artists like their work to be admired.

'I'm renovating the chapel here and the glass is for the new windows. I hope you and Lady Walker will visit once it's complete in the spring.'

'We'd be delighted.' Having seen my aunt, I hoped that the doctor was wrong and that she'd live to see many more springs.

When the gig pulled up beside Culdees lodge, I found Annie and Struan waiting for us. 'Welcome back, Miss Finlay,' he said.

I heard sadness in his tone. Not replying to his letter could have been misconstrued as rudeness. Struan was such a prickly sort, it had made me over cautious. 'Thank you, Mr Cooper. I'm very glad to be home.'

Annie laughed. 'Och, listen to you two. I wouldae thocht by now you might use each other's given names. All this Mr This and Miss That makes me feel awkward.'

I smiled. 'You are quite right, Annie. I'd be happy if you might call me Iris if you don't object to me using Struan?'

'I'd be honoured, Iris.'

Was the man actually blushing? He glanced over in Mr

Buchan's direction, perhaps thinking he'd be criticised for the informality. But Buchan was distracted by a rider cantering down the drive. I recognised a stable boy from Drummond Castle. Was there some emergency? Had my aunt been taken ill? An icy sensation flooded through me.

Buchan spoke to the boy and then walked towards us. 'I'm most sorry, Miss Finlay. We'll need to head back in a few minutes. Apparently, the Baroness is coming home a day early and I must be at the station again by five.'

The ice receded, replaced by relief. 'We'll just have a quick look at the window view, Annie. Then I'll come back another time.'

Struan cleared his throat. 'I could take you hame, if you dinnae mind travelling in a cart. I've a wheel tae pick up fae the blacksmith. We could swing past, then I'd take you hame.' Struan seemed nervous about his offer. He flushed with embarrassment again. 'Annie'd come wi' us, of course.'

'Thank you,' I said. 'That's an excellent solution. There is nothing wrong with travelling in a cart, and I'm sure Mr Buchan would be grateful not to risk being late for the Baroness.'

'I admit that I'd prefer to get going straight there now,' Mr Buchan replied. 'I can vouch for the safety of Struan's driving.'

'Well then, that's settled.'

Annie and I headed for the cottage. Struan said he'd wait for us in the stable block. The sofa, desk and chair were exactly as we'd left them on that fateful day when Annie had thrown her stick aside in fury following Rafael's deception. She was bound to be reminded.

I glanced at her and she pulled a face. 'Let's not think about him now.'

'I agree. He is a problem we will deal with together if he comes back.'

'You're not afraid ae him taking the lodge?'

'I was, but talking to Mr Speir today, I think our tenancy is safe.'

'That's grand news.' Annie smiled and laid her sketchbook on the table. 'I've got some ideas for the winter pamphlet.' She propped her stick against the desk and sat to open her sketchbook. 'There are fewer options in winter. The snowdrop of course.' She opened her book to a page with a delicate drawing of a single, tiny, white flower. The life-sized flower was vibrantly white on the yellowish watercolour paper.

'That is a marvellous drawing, but snowdrops are too small to work within the cover image.' I went to the window. 'All our other covers have the view of the front of the cottage. I think our winter one should be from in here, to give the reader the sense of being cosy inside, looking out on a garden.'

Annie nodded and flipped to a blank page. She began sketching the hedge and trees at the end of the garden. 'The beech hedge is turning a bonny colour,' she murmured.

'The dark green yew tree is a good colour for contrasting with holly berries. I've an idea of keeping to a theme of green, white and red.'

'So let's imagine a wee holly bush in the corner.' With just a few strokes of her pencil, she conjured the impression of spiky leaves and peppered it with berries. 'The foreground could be covered in snow,' she added.

'We need more red, but it's too late for roses and too early for tulips.'

Annie smiled. 'I've an idea already. Struan told me about cyclamen. There are some amongst the trees at Drummond Castle, and they have such pretty leaves. I've drawn it in pink but I believe I believe it comes in a red colour.' She flipped open to a drawing of a pink cyclamen.

'Gorgeous, Annie. I love the patterned leaves. But how did you draw the flowers? It's too early. Did you find it in *Curtis's*?'

Annie beamed at me. 'It was Mrs Birnie's doing. She knew I was down with you being away, so she ordered in a new magazine. *The Floral Magazine*. You'll love that the writer is a minister, Reverend Henry Honeywood Dombrain. The magazine is a good model for our work. It's not so academic as *Curtis's*.'

'What an excellent name, very poetic. I'll try to come to Innerpeffray soon to look at the magazine.'

Annie chuckled. 'Miss Iris Finlay is a grand name for a botanist, too. I don't think the snowdrops are too wee. Cyclamen and snowdrops can grow densely. I can create an drawing wi' a carpet ae both flowers at the base ae the hedge. Let me give it a try.'

'Excellent. We have a plan. Maybe we should get going? We shouldn't keep Struan waiting.'

Annie shrugged. 'Och, Struan willnae mind, I'm longing to hear mair about Balmoral. You said you'd write and tell me about the Ghillie's Ball but never did.'

I grimaced. 'It didn't turn out to be a happy evening at all. Come and sit with me on the sofa and I'll bring you up to date with the next chapter in the sins of men.'

When I told Annie the story about Lachlan and his behaviour at the ball, she looked horrified.

'I cannae believe anyone would be sae cruel.' Annie stretched to clasp my hands.

'It gets worse, and the next story involves Princess Louise as well. Will Struan wait another ten minutes?'

Annie's eyes widened. 'He will have tae because you cannae leave me hanging without the full story now.'

When I got to the end of the tale, including the events of the final day, there were tears in Annie's eyes. 'You poor thing. What a terrible man. And honestly, I'm shocked at the Princess's behaviour.'

I didn't share the story about the Princess's earlier liaison. Even Lady Georgina couldn't be sure if it was true. 'I was shocked too, and annoyed that she involved me. But the Princess never intended me any harm. I feel sorry for her. Despite her wealth and position, she isn't free to do as she pleases. It seems she must accept a suitor. I know loving a married man is wrong, but she will have to give him up and that must be very hard.'

Annie reached for her stick, and I helped her to her feet. 'We'd better be getting going before it gets dark,' she said.

We met Mr Speir coming out of the adjacent stable block. 'Excellent timing. I've just been looking at the rooms we're converting as accommodation for Señor de Rias. I am most fortunate to have the services of two excellent botanists.'

I smiled but said nothing. The thought of the Spaniard being within a stone's throw of my home made me feel sick.

'I've asked my factor to have all the chimneys swept in the lodge and I'll build you a larger coal bunker. With your father's ill health, you'll need a fire in his bedroom.'

I stared at him in astonishment. Annie was leaning on my arm and I felt her stiffen. 'My father is perfectly well, Mr Speir. He doesn't believe in an overheating a bedroom.'

Mr Speir appeared confused and mortified. Struan, who had just turned up, looked from face to face. The awkwardness of the moment must have been very clear.

'I hope I haven't broken a confidence. Perhaps your father didn't want to worry you? Rafael said he thought it important that I should know.'

I bristled, furious about Rafael's involvement, but fearful it might be true. 'What exactly did he say?'

'He said your father had contracted a fever and he'd been persuaded that an early return to Scotland would be wise.'

I shook my head. 'That doesn't at all match with the details Papa sent in his last letter.'

Mr Speir took the lodge key I proffered. 'No harm in getting the chimneys swept. An empty property always attracts nesting birds.' He turned and hurried up the path.

Chapter Thirty-Nine

November 1869 – Drummond Castle

I settled back into my previous life more easily than I'd expected. Mrs Birnie's happy reaction to my return made me realise how my circle of people had expanded. Papa's withdrawal from life after my mother's death had narrowed my world to only two people. Now I could count Aunt Leonora, Annie and Mrs Birnie as true friends. I also corresponded with Princess Louise and Lady Georgina, their stories from court keeping me connected to that life, too. The Princess had managed to escape to Kensington Palace and her recounting of her social life was very witty, especially her cruel dissection of the men who tried to woo her. The most surprising addition to my friendship group was Struan Cooper. Now, when he came to pick Annie up, he always came into the schoolroom. He was a knowledgeable extra contributor to our discussions and my previous antipathy had evaporated. Our past misunderstandings could be attributed to his devotion to Annie.

Sadly, Aunt Leonora's health dipped again, and I cancelled several visits to Innerpeffray Library. She had been bedbound all week. I had to coax her to eat. Today, she agreed to have some chicken broth. After she managed to eat some of the soup, she fell back against her pillows.

'I feel terrible for you having to cancel your arrangements again, Iris. What was it you had planned to do?'

'Please don't worry about it. Annie and I have almost finished the winter pamphlet. We are only searching for one more flower to feature. We're concentrating our search on the new magazine I told you about.'

She managed a weak smile. 'I love it when you talk about your work so passionately. Your father is going to be so proud.'

Mention of my papa made my heart sink. I'd had no news in weeks. I only knew he was heading for Southampton, rather than Liverpool, because Mr Speir reported being updated by Rafael.

'I have an idea,' Aunt Leonora said. 'Why don't you ask Annie to come here? I'm sure the Baroness wouldn't mind, and in any case, they will leave for Lincolnshire soon.' She looked wistfully towards the windows. 'I wonder if I will ever visit Grimsthorpe again?'

My aunt never alluded to the progression of her illness. The thought of how much time she might have left made me as sad as she sounded.

'I should love to sit quietly and listen to the pair of you talk and work. Being an invalid is so dejecting. I'd like to see these magazines too. Surely Mrs Birnie would let you bring them here?'

'I know she would. I'll go to Innerpeffray on Thursday, pick up the magazines and bring Annie back with me.'

I sent Annie a note about the plan. When I arrived at her house, I could tell she was a little reluctant. She was nervous about coming inside Drummond Castle, but agreed the plan made sense.

'I love Innerpeffray Library, but the journey there and back takes time,' I reasoned. 'Drummond Castle is much nearer to your house. Also, it doesn't depend on Struan getting use of the cart and time off work. Now the days are dark earlier, working in the evening isn't practical.'

'You're right, but I dinnae think Struan sees it as a chore. He's become as enthusiastic about our pamphlets as we are. There will be a long face when I tell him he isnae included.'

'There's only the last flower to think about. We'll go back to Innerpeffray when we come to start the spring pamphlet. Ask Struan to think about which plants we might feature.'

In fact, Annie's presence made Aunt Leonora determined to be out of bed. I helped her through the sitting room and made her comfortable under a blanket, sitting in her wing chair.

'Might I see what you have done so far?' she asked.

Annie showed her the sketchbook and I read what I'd written. I explained our dilemma over the cover sketch. 'We need another splash of colour to balance up the picture, but there are so few flowers in bloom.'

Mrs Birnie had ordered some back copies of *Floral Magazine* for us. Aunt Leonora joined in, searching the magazines for ideas. We spent an hour leafing through the pages and showing each other the pretty illustrations. Aunt Leonora was the happiest I'd seen her in days.

'What about a rhododendron bush?' Annie said, holding up a picture.

'That's an great suggestion and they do bloom early, but I'm not sure you could really call them a winter plant. I might write to Mr Donaldson and ask if there is a variety that blooms in January. Elspeth's husband is a rhododendron expert. I forgot to tell you I had a letter from her just this week, Aunt Leonora. She wrote to tell me she had safely delivered a baby boy.'

'Excellent news,' she said, laying down her magazine. 'We must try to get you down to Edinburgh in the new year, so you can meet him.'

'I would like to go at some stage. I promised Professor Jameson that Papa and I would try to visit before he returns to Ecuador.'

I stared unseeing at the page, trying to calm my thoughts. Every day with no news made me more anxious. Papa originally planned to avoid travelling across the stormy Atlantic this late in the year. I feared Rafael's eagerness to deliver the specimens to Mr Speir might have caused a rash decision.

'Are you determined your colour needs to come from a flower?' Aunt Leonora asked. 'The most charming sight in a snowy garden is the bright red plumage of a robin. You could place one in a tree.'

Annie and I looked at each other. Was this the answer?

'I do love a wee robin,' Annie said.

'It's a wonderful idea, Aunt Leonora. And look at this illustration, Annie. We could have the rhododendron buds in the garden scene just showing a hint of colour, but sketch the plant in bloom on its individual page.'

Annie returned the following week to execute the final drawings, whilst I wrote the pages associated with the rhododendron suggested by Alexander Donaldson. Aunt Leonora felt well enough to be out of bed again. There was no escaping that her illness was progressing, but she still had some better days.

I set about writing the letter to Mr White.

'I'll get on wi' thinking about spring,' Annie said.

I smiled, hoping I hid my fears. I'd heard nothing since I'd sent the autumn pamphlet. Was it a waste of time to finish the seasons? Should we look for a different publisher?

Just then, a Drummond Castle maid came in with Aunt Leonora's post. 'There is something here for you, Iris,' my aunt said.

Seeing the publishing company's name on the envelope made my heart quicken. 'We have a response from Mr White.'

Annie grabbed her stick and came to look over my shoulder. I started to smile as I read it.

'I can tell from your faces that it's good news. Well done, girls!' Aunt Leonora said.

'The best news. Not only does he want to print them quarterly, he plans to publish all four seasons in book form. He is delighted with the notion of Princess Louise's endorsement in the introduction.' I glanced at Annie as I related the next bit. 'He needs some minor changes to some sketches. His engraver wants to advise us on how we can make the illustrations easier to reproduce. He'd like us both to come to Edinburgh.'

Annie shook her head. She limped back to the desk. The rounding of her shoulders spoke of her dejection.

'I cannae go,' she said sadly. 'The mistress up at the big house wouldnae gie me the time off.'

My heart broke at her expression, and disappointment swept through me, too. I tried to summon a brave face. 'Going in person is out of the question for us both right now. I'll ask Elspeth to intercede on our behalf. I'm sure we can find a way to make this happen from here.'

'I hope you don't mean you cannot go to Edinburgh because of me!' Aunt Leonora sat straight-backed in her chair, looking her previous formidable self. 'It would be much better if you travel together. Mrs Milton, your mistress, has been an acquaintance for over twenty years. I'm sure I can convince her to give you a few days off, Annie. I will offer to hire a stand-in maid for you. Although she can most certainly afford to do that herself.'

Annie and I exchanged glances. The idea of going to Edinburgh and taking her to the Botanics was thrilling. I could tell she longed for it too.

'You are too generous, Lady Walker,' Annie said. 'Let me talk tae Struan about it.'

* * *

Struan had been working in the Drummond Castle nursery beds very close to Muthill when he got drenched in a downpour. He ran home to get dry trousers. He was well used to getting wet, but it was that kind of dreich weather that chilled you to the bone and he'd a busy afternoon planned. Fear gripped him when he heard Annie coughing before he reached the door. She got ill most winters, and it scared him senseless. He entered and found her in tears. When he rushed to put his arm around her shoulders, he discovered she was also wet through, and shivering.

'Whatever is the matter? You need tae get oot ae those wet clothes, you'll catch yer death. The rain drove me hame tae change too.'

He placed a blanket around her shoulders and knelt in front of her. 'Tell me what's wrang?'

Annie opened up her mouth to reply, but another coughing fit silenced her.

'Had they on yer knees scrubbing floors when it's pouring outside? What's the point on a day like this?'

She heaved to get her breath. 'It's only me that takes sae badly wi' the smell and it's no why I'm crying.' She gave him a pitiful look that pierced his heart. 'I'm sad tae let Iris down. Mr White plans tae publish our work, but he'd wants us both tae go tae Edinburgh.' Another gasping breath. 'He'd like me tae meet the engraver. I said I had tae work, and Lady Walker wants tae talk tae the mistress tae get me time off, but, Struan I cannae let her dae that. Everyone will hate me if I get special treatment. The housekeeper is already moaning about my coughing and for doing the floors sae slow.'

He stood up and took her hands to raise her. 'Dinnae cry, Annie. They people you work for are heartless. Change your frock. I'll make tea before I go back.'

When Annie came from behind the curtain that hid her wee bed, he handed her the tea and waited for her to sit down. 'Tomorrow morning, you tell them yer giving in yer notice.'

'Oh, no, Struan. I cannae. I need tae bring something in tae help pay our bills.'

'Mr MacDonald is right pleased wi' me. I've had another wee raise. We can manage wi'oot the pittance they pay you. Anyway, surely the Edinburgh man will pay you for this thing?'

Annie frowned. 'Yes, but we dinnae know how much. He said he'd discuss it face to face wi' us.'

'Does Iris want tae go?'

'Aye, although she is nervous to leave her aunt. Lady Walker is insistent she can manage for a couple of days.'

'Then I'm sure it's better Iris has your company. It's safer if there's two ae you. Have you a plan of where tae stay? It's a big city for two lassies on their ain.'

'Elspeth Donaldson, Mr White's daughter, has said she'll put us both up.'

'Then, if Iris is able to go, you must go wi' her.'

The determination in his voice was not at all how he felt. His heart was already hurting at having no glimpse of Iris in weeks. Also, the idea of both girls in the city on their own scared him. But Annie was a grown woman. His life was getting better. She deserved betterment, too.

'I'm proud ae you, Annie. People should see your drawings, yer talent is special. That it's brought you a friend is a blessing, and I ken fine it makes you happy. The money's no important, but make sure the fella pays you what it's worth.'

The light of hope came back into Annie's eyes. Struan knew he was doing the right thing. His promised raise wouldn't come through until next year, but he'd put in overtime until then. Luckily, some of his glasshouse work could be done in lamplight. Overtime was scarcer in the short days of winter.

'I've got tae get up the road now. Write Iris a note telling her you'll come, and I'll drop it off at the castle.'

Chapter Forty

November 1869 – Edinburgh

Annie had never been further than Perth in her whole life. I worried she'd be frightened, but I underestimated her. My brave friend was on the edge of her seat in the train, exclaiming at every new sight. I held my breath when we transferred to the ferry. Surely, the waves would scare her. On the contrary, she squealed with delight and tilted her face as if to catch the sea spray. 'How clever is this? A boat journey in amongst the train.' She had to reach for her hat to prevent the wind taking it.

I laughed and tugged at her hand. 'Come inside, Annie. Struan will kill me if I let you get soaked.'

In Granton, we caught another train, this time getting out at Scotland Street Station to find Mr White's carriage waiting for us. When I explained Annie walked with a stick, thoughtful Elspeth had arranged it.

The carriage took us directly to Elspeth and Alexander's home, just behind the Botanic Gardens. She must have been watching for us, because she appeared on the front step, her new baby in a blanket in her arms. I rushed to hug her and pulled the blanket away from the wee boy's face to get a glimpse. 'He's gorgeous, Elspeth. I hope you'll let me hold him later?'

'John often cries for hours in the early evening and only walking him makes him happy. I assure you another pair of arms will be most welcome!'

'Elspeth, this is my excellent friend Annie.'

Elspeth reached out to shake Annie's hand. Annie swopped her stick to her left hand to shake it.

'The amazing artist. You have a legion of admirers in Edinburgh, Miss Cooper. Not just my father, but my husband, too. Alexander even showed your pamphlet to Professor Hutton Balfour.'

I gasped. 'That's a tremendous honour, Annie. Professor Hutton Balfour is the Keeper, the most senior botanist in the Botanic Gardens.'

Elspeth smiled. 'Alexander said he will try to introduce you both. Professor Hutton Balfour is very encouraging to young enthusiasts.'

The next morning, we had an early breakfast.

'How far is your father's office?' I asked Elspeth. 'We promised to be there by nine.'

'North Bridge,' she replied. 'But my brother, Adam, has agreed to take you. He lives in the house next door, and he's going in that direction, anyway.'

Elspeth walked us down her path, running parallel to the front garden of the large house next door. 'Our building was originally the servants' quarters, but Papa had it converted for me on my marriage,' Elspeth explained. 'Alexander won't earn much until he's fully qualified, and he wanted me to have a comfortable home.'

Our carriage from yesterday pulled up.

'Perfect timing. You hop in and I'll let Adam know,' Elspeth said.

The shiny black front door swung open, a tall man exited, and the brass letter box clattered as he closed it.

Elspeth bade her brother 'good morning,' and kissed his cheek.

Adam White was a man of few words. He didn't speak until the carriage swept past the Theatre Royal, onto the North Bridge. 'My father has arranged for you both to meet young Mr Bartholomew, our engraver. I'll have someone take you up.'

Young Mr Bartholomew turned out to be a middle-aged man with a greying beard, receding hairline and spectacles. My expression must have betrayed my surprise. He smiled and extended his hand. 'I have been young Mr Bartholomew since I joined my father's engraving business nearly thirty years ago. I expect I shall keep the title until my dying day. Which of you is Miss Cooper?'

'I am,' Annie said, bobbing a curtsey.

'Then you must be Miss Finlay, the writer?' I took his extended his hand. 'Mr White is delighted with your words, Miss Finlay. While my focus is on the illustrations.' He turned back to Annie. 'I'm most glad to meet you, Miss Cooper. I believe we might have a long working relationship. Your illustrations are first class.'

Annie flushed with pride. 'Thank you, sir. I hope to learn how I can improve and make your engraving simpler.'

'That's the point entirely. Sit beside me. Let's go through your sketches together.'

Mr Bartholomew described the engraving process and explained why some of Annie's sketches were tricky to copy. Challenged to create a simpler version of her dahlia, Annie took out her sketchbook and set about the task immediately.

'Excellent, Miss Cooper. Your speed and steadiness of

hand is exceptional. Mr White is right to be excited about this project.'

'I'm sorry tae have given you difficulties. Let me know which drawings need redoing and I'll set to it straight away.'

Mr Bartholomew took out his pocket watch and flipped it open. 'I believe Mr White said he would see you at ten thirty. Perhaps you might come to our offices this afternoon? We used to be almost next door to here, but we moved to larger premises this year. The map printing side of our business requires a lot of space.' He handed Annie a card. 'The new office is near George IV Bridge, just the other side of St Giles.'

Just then, a clerk came to say Mr White was expecting us. 'Miss Cooper isn't familiar with Edinburgh, but I know my way,' I replied. 'We will come together, if that is acceptable?'

'Of course. Just tell the receptionist I'm expecting you.'

The clerk guided us to a boardroom on the top floor of the building. Our pamphlets were spread out over the large table. I squeezed Annie's hand, and she grinned. The stupendous view over the Edinburgh rooftops, to the Walter Scott Monument and the castle beyond, drew us towards the large window. After a few minutes, the door flew open and a tall gentleman entered. 'I'm sorry to keep you waiting, ladies. I am James White.'

'Miss Iris Finlay,' I said. 'And my friend, Miss Annie Cooper, the artist.'

He turned to Annie. 'I met John Bartholomew on the stairs and he informs me I've found an artist who is as quick as she is talented. Now, ladies, please sit. I am a man of business and you will excuse me if I get straight to the point. I intend to publish your work as quarterly pamphlets. The idea and the quality are both good and there is a growing interest in gardening, particularly amongst lady amateurs.'

'Thank you, sir. We are delighted,' I said.

Mr White held up his hand. 'You might not be so pleased when I tell you what I'd like from you now.' He turned to me. 'Although I believe I can sell your work on its merit alone, I'll be honest, it's the involvement of the Princess Louise that makes me believe we should risk combining the seasons into a book. Are you certain you can obtain her words as an introduction?'

'I'm certain. We became close over this summer and Her Highness is a woman of her word.'

He leaned over the desk, his gaze determined and penetrating. 'Could you get it quickly? I'd like to have the book ready to print before the end of the year.'

'I believe I can.' In my heart, I wasn't sure. Princess Louise was loyal, but also busy. How do you give a deadline to a princess?

'So you will need the spring pamphlet included, sir?' Annie asked.

Mr White pursed his lips and sat back in his chair. 'Yes. Can it be accomplished quickly?'

Annie nodded and glanced at me. Her eyes sparkled with excitement.

'We have already begun,' I replied. 'We chose yellow as the colour theme. Annie has already done drawings of the primrose and crocus, and I've written those pages. I believe we could complete the daffodil and tulip within one week?'

Annie nodded.

Mr White beamed with delight. 'Excellent. Elspeth said you were a very determined young lady. My plan is to begin the quarterly pamphlet series with winter, then aim to print the book in time for the Christmas market. It gives you less than two weeks to complete everything. Too much?'

'No, sir,' I replied.

'Bravo!' Mr White pushed an envelope across the table. 'We must agree terms, of course. My lawyer has prepared contracts for you to sign. I realise you will want to consider the details carefully before signing. I assure you, this is the going rate.'

In the carriage on the way to the engraver's office, I opened the envelope. I'd little idea what kind of amount I was expecting, but the sums for the book and each individual pamphlet exceeded my wildest dreams.

Annie, reading beside me, gasped. 'Iris, is he serious? The fee for the book alone is three times what Struan gets paid in a year. One pamphlet is more than my whole year's maid work.'

'And that's just for the first print run. If they sell well, we will earn even more!' We laughed and hugged. 'This will change both our lives, Annie. But can we manage the deadlines? It's a lot of hard work in a short time.'

'No, Iris. Hard work is polishing tiles on your knees. This is being paid for something I'd dae for free.'

I put my arm around her shoulder and hugged her. 'We're going into business, Annie.'

Chapter Forty-One

November 1869 – Edinburgh

The next morning, we were up at dawn. Elspeth had kindly set aside her dining room for us to work in. Annie sat on one side of the table, where the light suited her best, and I opposite. I finished the words for the crocus, while Annie redid the cyclamen drawing for the winter pamphlet. Mr Bartholomew had asked for simplification of the leaves.

'Annie, there will be no crocus in this garden in the spring if the owner doesn't plant bulbs. We must add the instructions in the winter pamphlet. Or should it be in autumn months?'

'I'm nae sure. Shall I write and ask Struan? I need tae write anyways tae tell him we're staying on a wee bit longer.'

'Good idea. If you add my bulb query, I can take your letter. I'll walk to the post box with my letters to Princess Louise and Aunt Leonora.'

'Did you tell your aunt about the money?' Annie asked.

'I decided to keep the details on the fee until I get home.'

'I'll dae the same,' she replied.

'Do you fear he won't think it a fair amount?' I asked.

'Would you prefer to hold off on the contract signing until you can speak to Struan?'

Annie shook her head. 'I'm sure Elspeth's father wouldnae cheat us, and it's so much higher than I could have imagined. I'm embarrassed, tae be honest. Struan is proud ae his job, and he works long hard hours, yet my half ae the money will be more than his wages. It doesnae seem right.'

'I'm sure he'll be so pleased for you, Annie. And just because we have one publishing deal doesn't mean we will get others. Struan has a steady job with a good employer. It's different.'

When I returned from the post box, I met Elspeth in the hall. 'Where have you been so early?'

'I had some urgent letters to post and we have a great deal of work to do this week. In any case, Annie and I are so excited we hardly slept.'

'I believe Alexander and I are almost as excited.'

I hugged her. 'The day we met, changed my life,' I said.

'I've just taken in tea and toast for you both. Your labours need fuel,' she replied. 'Oh, and Alexander came back from the Botanics with those magazines you need. He said Professor Hutton Balfour was delighted to lend them from their collection. He's asked Professors Hutton Balfour and Jameson to join us for supper the day after tomorrow.'

'Excellent,' I replied. 'I want to see the professor, but we are going to need every daylight hour this week to finish the project.'

'You are welcome to stay as long as you need,' Elspeth said.

'You're so kind. I'd prefer not to leave Aunt Leonora any longer than is necessary. We've achieved so much since yesterday. I believe we will meet the deadline.'

Baby John's loud crying summoned Elspeth up the stairs. 'Someone else who needs fuel,' she called back.

. . .

The next day, I dropped off the signed contract with Mr White. I showed him Annie's revised illustrations, which he approved, and asked me to deliver to Mr Bartholomew. 'Did Bartholomew advise you we aim to do the winter pamphlet illustration, using Annie's idea of highlight colour inside the front cover of the book?'

'Annie told me. She is at Elspeth's, working on it as we speak.'

'Splendid. If the book goes to a second print run, we may replace it with the spring or summer image. Your cheques will be ready tomorrow. Are you happy for Adam to bring them to you?'

I'd been thinking about this problem. 'Neither of us has bank accounts. I'm hoping Aunt Leonora can organise something for us with her banker in Perth.'

'Of course. Then would it be useful if I gave you both five guineas in cash? In case you meet any unexpected expenses in Edinburgh?'

'Thank you. We would both be grateful.'

By the end of the following day, I'd finished all my written passages and Annie was working on her last drawing of a yellow and red tulip. We'd found an illustration of a variety named La Plaisante in *The Floral Magazine* from 1867. Annie was using it as an inspiration for her own version. This tulip was mainly yellow with some pink streaks. A perfect promise of summer.

We rushed to change for dinner and only had time to make an attempt at fixing each other's hair before we heard the front doorbell announcing the arrival of the guests.

'Never in my wildest dreams would I have thocht I'd one

day eat dinner in such a fancy house in a dress once worn by a princess. It just isnae believable.'

'Before we leave Edinburgh, we should go shopping. We only have two passable evening gowns between us. Something we should remedy.'

'I can think ae a thousand things more important tae buy than new frocks,' Annie answered, whilst turning this way and that, admiring herself in the mirror.

'I'm not planning on buying many dresses, either. But Mr White wants us to come south for the launch and that dress is too long for you. Take great care not to trip going down the stairs. If the talented artist falls to her death, then both our publishing careers will be over.'

Annie laughed and we carefully made our way down the staircase.

In the dining room, Annie was seated beside Professor Hutton Balfour, and I beside Professor Jameson. Alexander asked Annie's permission to show both gentlemen her sketchbook. I fetched it from the cupboard where we'd stowed our work earlier, to let the maid set the table for dinner. Soon, the murmurs of praise were overtaken by the academics entering a discussion about some new varieties of tulips and the mistake of prioritising colour over robustness.

When dessert was served, Professor Jameson turned to me. 'Any update on your father's progress?'

I grimaced. 'Not one word from him. To be honest, I'm worried. Señor de Rias told Mr Speir they'd chosen Southampton as their destination, but they should have been here by now.'

Professor Jameson scowled into his apple pudding. 'It makes no sense that I don't know this man. I've been in South America for over forty years. I know every single botanist with any reputation. Tell me. Was there anything distinctive about him? Perhaps I've just forgotten the name.'

I shrugged, unwilling to say, 'Handsome, eloquent. Untrustworthy.'

Annie answered for me. 'Professor Jameson, Iris and I have some strong reservations about this man. He has a way of getting information out ae you for his own ends. And the missing smallest finger on his right hand is most certainly distinctive.'

'Oh yes. I'd forgotten. Also, he carries an ebony cane,' I added.

Professor Jameson had been about to sink his spoon into the apple charlotte. He looked at Annie with a startled expression, sighed and laid down his spoon.

My anxiety rose. 'You recognise the description! Please share your thoughts. I fear my father is in dangerous company.'

'I might be wrong and I never actually met this man.' The professor rubbed his chin. 'I hope it's a coincidence. When I passed through Argentina on my journey home, the horticultural community was still talking about a scandal from the year before. A terrible tale, in fact. A wealthy young heiress had been found dead. Her maid described the poor girl's final days of violent stomach disorder, then paralysis the day before her death. The maid accused the woman's husband of not allowing her to send for a physician. On her family's insistence, the authorities did an examination of the deceased.'

My heart was galloping. I could hardly bear it, but I had to hear his words. The professor stopped talking. He glanced at me.

'Please tell the whole story,' I whispered.

He bowed his head. 'They found poison in her stomach. Several newly planted *Brugmansia*, or angel's trumpet as it's commonly known, found in the couple's garden was considered a likely source. They issued an arrest warrant for husband, but he had disappeared with all her money. That man was a botanist known as Eduardo Ximenez, although the authorities concluded this name was bogus. My sons both knew the man, and they were horrified to admit they'd trusted him to the extent he had been in their homes.'

The professor looked at me with anguished eyes. 'They showed me the wanted poster. It described Eduardo as around thirty years old. Handsome, dark-haired and eyed, and with a very smart and upright appearance.' The professor looked so dismayed, it was as if the next words were dragged out of him. 'The poster also said that he was missing the smallest digit on his right hand.'

Annie's hands flew to her face. I closed my eyes.

'That's him,' Annie said. 'Rafael is that poisoner.' I opened my eyes to see Annie's anguished expression across the table.

A shocked silence hung in the air. Everyone looked aghast. Poor Professor Jameson appeared close to tears. 'Do remember that this man never stood trial. I am only reporting hearsay,' he said quietly.

'Was this Eduardo a Spaniard?' I asked.

'He claimed to be Colombian and I doubt he's Spanish. Any South American would know the difference.'

I pushed my plate way. 'I must go home and speak to Mr Speir. I've long feared him to be a viper in our nest, but a murderer?! This is worse than I could have imagined and the man is intent on inserting himself into our lives. I must put a stop to it.'

'I promised to see Mr Bartholomew tomorrow. You must leave without me,' Annie said.

I shook my head. 'Of course, I'll not leave you. I hope I may get a reply from Princess Louise tomorrow. Then everything for the publication will be in place. If we are right about Rafael, then he's a dangerous man, but he will simply deny it and accuse me of being a hysterical woman. I think I'll write to Aunt Leonora and share this terrible story before our return on Friday. I'm furious but must keep calm. My aunt is wise and will advise me.'

Professor Hutton Balfour coughed. Everyone turned to look at him. 'I'm most sorry that you face such a dilemma without your father here to guide you. But surely he will be home very soon? Do you need to rush in? Sadly, this is not the first instance of a man of science killing a relative. There was a famous case in England with a Mr William Palmer. That man's motive was also financial gain. Without such a motive, I doubt this man is a danger to your father.'

Annie's face was drained of all colour. 'I believe I may have already been a victim of his scheming. He courted me with pretty words and flattery, then gave me some draught that made me feel carefree and happy.' Annie looked down at her hands. 'I live with constant pain, but after drinking what he gave me, it was as if I could abandon my stick and fly around the room.'

'Cocaine,' muttered Professor Jameson. 'Useful as an anaesthetic, but dangerous in the wrong hands.'

Elspeth gasped. 'Did the bounder harm you, Miss Cooper?'

'Physically, no. But he led me to lie to my brother and undermined my relationship with my greatest friend.' Annie glanced at me. 'I showed him the illustration of a giant orchid we had copied to send to Iris's father. Finding a similar plant was Mr Finlay's secret ambition, and I betrayed it. Mr de Rias left for Ecuador immediately after.'

'*Cattleya amethystoglossa,*' Professor Jameson said. 'I've heard the rumours of a huge orchid in the Ecuadorian mountains, but I've never seen it. Did your father say which orchids were in his cargo?'

I shook my head. 'No. But he said that the specimens he gathered impressed de Rias. I will write to my aunt tonight, and then retire. I'm quite exhausted.'

Annie and I both stood up.

'I'll commit my story to paper and send a copy here tomorrow,' said Professor Jameson. 'If you fear not being believed, my confirmation might help.'

'I shall confirm this infamous story reached my ears, too,' added Professor Hutton Balfour.

'We wish you the best of luck. Please let me know if I can do anything else,' Professor Jameson said. A ripple of agreement went around the others.

Dread was like a huge knot in my stomach. I professed bravery, but truthfully, I was afraid.

Chapter Forty-Two

December 1869 – Drummond Castle

S truan was working on the beds near the castle's sundial. The letter in his pocket made him so over-joyed he imagined it felt warm. Annie had written about the good news and said she was happier than she could ever remember. He was so delighted for her, and for Iris. Then, the few sparse lines to him from Iris about bulb planting caused him to experience similar elation. She wanted advice, and she'd come to him.

A movement near the castle caught his eye. It was Mr MacDonald, who came down the steps, walking purposefully towards him. The man's serious expression surely meant some bad news.

'Has something happened tae Annie?' he asked, hardly able to breathe.

'Don't worry, lad, your sister is fine. I'll no lie though, there is some bad news. Lady Walker has summoned me to ask permission to talk tae you. She needs yer help.'

'Of course, sir.'

Why on all earth would a titled lady want his help? He followed MacDonald back towards the castle. His thoughts raced ahead. If it wasn't Annie, then surely the problem lay with Iris. If something had happened to her, he thought he might die. Mr MacDonald climbed the stone stairs quickly. Struan kept right behind him. 'Please, can you tell me what's wrang?'

MacDonald laid his hand on Struan's sleeve, then knocked on the door. 'Don't worry, but it's best you let Lady Walker tell you.'

Struan's heart was pounding. He told himself if something had happened to Iris MacDonald would have been distraught, he had a soft spot for her. A premonition seized him. This was something to do with that Spanish bastard. Iris was unhappy that he travelled with her father and his own personal dislike amounted to hatred. The man had hurt both Annie and Iris; he was the worst of men.

'Come in,' said a female voice.

MacDonald led Struan into a small sitting room.

Lady Walker was propped in her wing chair but in her dressing gown. 'That will be all, Effie,' she said to the maid. The unlikeliness of being sent for in these circumstances increased his anxiety. Lady Walker had a letter and a handkerchief in her hands, and she had been crying. Please God no.

'Young man, I will get to straight to the point. We have never met, but I've heard good things about you and I need your help.'

'Anything at all,' he replied.

'This morning I have had the most dreadful news. Mr Speir came in person and he had thought he would find Iris here. He came to tell us he'd had word that Mr Finlay perished on the voyage from Panama.'

'What! No! Poor Iris.' Struan knew the feeling of losing a second parent all too well. The thought touched a nerve that he'd imagined healed. 'My sister wrote tae say they'd be hame day aifter tomorrow.'

'That was the plan. But this might change things. Can you read?'

It was a fair question. His father could not. Still, he was embarrassed that she assumed him illiterate. 'My sister and I both benefitted from Mrs Birnie's teaching.'

'Then I think you should read this letter. It came addressed to Iris this morning. In the circumstances, I thought I should open it.' She hesitated. 'It's highly confidential. Mr MacDonald says you are utterly trustworthy.'

He nodded and took the letter from her outstretched fingers.

'Read it aloud. I want to make sure I've understood it properly.'

29th November 1869

'Dear Iris,
Excuse my informality, but I don't even know your second name. Mine is Ellen McKinnon, and I am a nurse in the London Hospital. We have a very ill patient in our ward, and I believe he might be your father.'

He looked up at Lady Walker. 'Mr Finlay is alive?'
'It seems he might be, but read on.'

'He was brought to us by a ship's captain from a vessel which has recently docked in Southampton. This man told us he sent his sailors to attend to a corpse, but they found the man was still breathing. He had him rushed him here, but this patient cannot move and hasn't spoken. The captain thought his name was Bernardo da Silva, but he has no papers on him. This gentleman had been ill in his cabin for almost the entire journey. All the captain could tell us about this man is that he believed he was a plantsman. He and his companion travelled with many specimens.'

285

'His companion. What happened tae that Spanish rogue?' Struan asked.

'My thoughts exactly. I'm afraid the answer is that Mr de Rias is presently at Culdees Castle.'

'What! He should be flogged,' Struan said.

Lady Walker briefly closed her eyes. 'I share your sentiments, but it is possible that Mr de Rias genuinely thought Andrew was dead. For the time being, I think it best we keep this new information to ourselves.'

'He left him for dead in his cabin?' Struan clenched his fists.

She shook her head sadly. 'Read on.'

'This patient seems to have some kind of creeping paralysis and we feared he would die without regaining consciousness. However, this morning he came round. He seemed distressed, and I realised he was looking towards his jacket on the back of the chair. I searched the pockets and told him they were empty. He still seemed to plead with his eyes. So I searched again and found a letter in a hidden breast pocket. I hope you can forgive that I opened it, for I had no other way of helping this man, who I believe is your father. I'm most confused to find this man's daughter resides in a Scottish castle. Sincere apologies if I've misconstrued the letter.

If he is your father, Iris, I cannot tell you how sorry I am to send you such bad news, and I do not want to raise your hopes. The doctors believe he has not long. If you wish to see him alive, please come quickly.'

He handed the letter back to Lady Walker. 'What will you do?'

'I want to run to Iris. To comfort her. To warn her, this sliver of hope will likely to come to nothing.' She turned her palms upward on her blanket. 'But look at me. I'm not even well enough to rise from my chair.'

Struan was struggling with his emotions. The enormity of what was coming to Iris took him to the verge of tears.

Lady Walker took a deep breath. 'I have an unreasonable request, Mr Cooper. I want you to go to Edinburgh and break the news.'

'Me?' To be such a messenger might make her hate him.

'I know it's too much to ask,' Lady Walker continued. 'If I could be sure Iris will come back here, I wouldn't ask it. But my niece is determined and brave. She needs to read this note from her father.' She held up a second letter. 'I fear she will then go straight to London. It seems speed is of the essence, but she must not go alone. Would you go with her?'

He instantly decided. If Iris needed help he would do anything. Even if it cost him her friendship forever. 'I would be honoured tae be given such trust,' he said quietly. 'If Mr MacDonald can spare me, that is.'

Mr MacDonald nodded. 'Any service to help you in this sad time, milady.'

'I fear you must leave today, Mr Cooper. If this man is Andrew, he may not last long. Also, day after tomorrow they will be on their way back. Yet another day will be lost.'

He gritted his teeth and nodded. 'I'll go hame tae wash and change intae my Sunday best. I'd hate tae embarrass Iris and my sister. Annie telt me they're staying wi' gentlefolk in Edinburgh.'

Struan's train arrived in Edinburgh's Canal Street Station just after ten o'clock at night. Lady Walker had advised him to go to her Princes Street hotel, since it was too late to disturb Iris's hosts. He walked up to the hotel entrance, but found it intimidatingly grand. Also, he wanted to be certain he could find this family's address. Struan consulted the street map he'd been given, noting Mr White's own company had published it. He replaced it in his pocket, turned up his collar against the cold, and began the walk north. After thirty minutes, his route took him past the entrance to Edinburgh's Botanic Garden. He knew he must be close, for Annie had described it as almost next door. He turned into a row of huge stone villas, counting down the numbers until he came to the correct address. As described by Annie, this house had a second entrance. He observed from the pavement opposite that the house lamps were blazing and at that moment, the front door opened. Three gentlemen came out. Struan stepped out of the streetlight illumination and into the shadows.

'Goodnight Alexander. Thank you for your hospitality,' said a man with a long grey beard.

'Goodnight, Professor Hutton Balfour. I shall see you tomorrow,' the other replied.

Struan knew the girls were staying with an Alexander Donaldson, the son-in-law of their publisher. He was a medical man and a student of the Royal Botanic's famous Keeper. Iris and Annie were clearly mixing in the most exalted botanical society.

'I am mortified to have so upset Miss Finlay,' the other man said. In the light from the open door, Struan could see real distress on his face. A shiver of fear ran through him. Had Iris somehow already heard of her father's misfortune?

'It's a terrible business, but I think it better that she knows, Professor Jameson. This fellow sounds like a very bad sort.'

Struan recognised the professor's name as someone Iris had described. The Scots botanist who lived in Ecuador. A candidate for the title 'bad sort' immediately sprung to mind. Had the botanist somehow heard of de Rias leaving Iris's father for dead?

The two botanists said their goodbyes and set off in a

westerly direction. A female figure appeared at the top window and stretched up to draw the drapes. Iris's face, illuminated by the brass chandelier behind her, betrayed her as overwhelmed by troubles. Now he was bringing her more bad news. Surely she didn't know about her father being in hospital, or she wouldn't be heading for bed, but Lady Walker had instructed him not to disturb the household tonight.

'Sleep in peace one night more, sweet Iris,' he whispered.

Chapter Forty-Three

December 1869 – Edinburgh

My bones felt heavy as I dressed to face my day. The only remedy to avoid collapse was to be busy. My first task was to post my letter to Aunt Leonora. Surely my next priority was to confront Mr Speir with the terrible truth about this man he had trusted. Thoughts of the poor Argentinian woman's agonising death gave me nightmares. Rafael had drugged poor Annie, and she was so slight he might easily have caused her permanent harm. I trembled at the thought, not simply with fear, but also fury. I clung to Professor Hutton Balfour's words. Rafael was clearly a monster, but my father had no money. Surely, my deep sense of foreboding was misguided. I pulled on my boots to take my letter to the post box, and prayed the morning delivery would bring the confirmation from Princess Louise. Now I was a woman of business, I was not about to let this vile Spaniard, or Colombian, or whatever he was, make me react hysterically. I needed to keep a cool head to secure this future for myself and Annie. With my aunt's help, I would unmask Rafael de Rias too.

I kissed Annie, who was already seated in front of her

sketchbook. A maid in the room was clearing the last of the table settings from last night. 'I'll be back in ten minutes,' I told her.

The astonishing sight of Struan at the front gate stopped me in my tracks. 'It's you,' I said stupidly.

'I've come wi' a message fae your aunt.'

'Oh, Struan, is she worse?' My voice cracked. I hoped for help from my aunt, forgetting how ill she had become.

'Can I come in?' he asked.

I hadn't thought my spirits could be lower. Fear tightened my chest, so I could hardly breathe. I took Struan inside.

Annie looked from him to me, and said, 'Oh no! Whatever is the matter?'

Struan smiled sadly at his sister. 'There's a message for Iris.' He turned to me and held out a letter. 'I've been fretting aboot how tae handle this. I think it's best if you start wi' this letter.'

The envelope had an odd address, simply to *Iris, care of Drummond Castle, Perthshire*. The look of distress that passed from Struan to his sister increased my fear to panic.

I read the letter, a voice in my head was repeating no, no, no. 'There must be some mistake?' I whispered, glancing up. Struan's expression offered no reassurance. The sensation was as if all the connections down my spine were uncoupling. I clamped my hand on the table to keep myself in the chair.

Annie rushed to my side and put her arms around me. 'Is it your pa?' she asked.

'That monster has poisoned him!' Voicing it out loud tipped me over the edge. I struggled to breathe.

'What? Were you expecting this terrible thing?' Struan shouted. He looked outraged. I couldn't reply.

'We learned just yesterday that Rafael de Rias is not who he claimed,' Annie said. 'The professor telt the story ae a botanist who is wanted in Argentina for killing his wife wi' poison. We think it's surely the same man.'

'The man's own wife? Has his evil no limits?' Struan said.

I twisted my handkerchief into a tight knot. 'I must go to London. Perhaps there is something I can do to save him. Maybe there's an antidote for this poison?'

Struan passed me another envelope. 'You should read this too, Iris. It's what the nurse found tae know how tae write to you. You should also know that Mr Speir visited your aunt before the nurse's letter arrived. De Rias reported to Speir that your father perished on the voyage.'

'That's what that devil intended,' Annie said.

I took the flimsy letter from its tiny envelope. 'Oh, Papa,' I whispered. The handwriting was shaky, but most definitely my father's.

The middle of the Atlantic
November 1869

Dearest Iris,
My darling girl, I love you so much, and I fear that first in grief, and then in this latest obsession, I have voiced it too rarely. If you are reading this, then I have failed you. My selfish ambition took me into harm's way, just as you feared. I am so very sorry. If I could turn back time, I would never have indulged in this self-centred pursuit. My pride at finding not one but two rare orchids had me puffed up with vanity. I also confess to having had the time of my life on my Ecuador adventure, and thankfully, it led me back to our Lord. I fear I will not survive to see you again. I will die having made my peace with God, but I do not know how you can forgive me for leaving you alone.

This strange malady began the day we came off the train. Rafael says he recognises it as a South American disease which can afflict those who work in high altitudes. He carried medicine with him which he hoped would help, but his best efforts have been in vain. I deteriorate with every passing day. We are still at least one week from port, and I feel my strength ebbing away. It's like sinking into a bog. This affliction is engulfing me from the feet upwards. I haven't been able to leave my cabin since one day out of Panama. Now I struggle even to use my chamber pot. I pray for strength to survive long enough to avoid a sea burial. Rafael promises to get me back to rest beside your mother. He has been so solicitous. You will know where to find this letter, beside my heart and your mother's lock of hair.

Darling Iris, please don't imagine my last days have been miserable. Your letters describing your time in Balmoral and, even more importantly, your botanical pamphlets, make me hope you can manage without me. My marvellous sister-in-law will be the best person to guide you through your life. I confess I found her stridency annoying when she disturbed the peace of your gentle mama. But her determined independence is a feature I see in you, too. Your alliance would have pleased your mother. She adored her outspoken sister. Please don't think your mama chose domesticity because she lacked spirit. If she hadn't found herself in the straight-laced life of a cleric's wife, she might have loved dancing a waltz amongst the royals, and her painting skills may have been acknowledged. I'm very proud of you for bringing that glory to your friend

I might be wrong. Perhaps the longed for recovery will materialise. If not, I need you to be certain of my love. Look out for the little plant I'm sending home just for you.

I trust you will profit from my discoveries too. I am sure Rafael understands the significance of both orchids. The new Ecuadorian variety of the huge orchid is what I promised Mr Speir, but the little inky orchid might prove more valuable. Its startling colour is bound to create a stir. Mr Speir is a good man. The accolades belong with him, but in my absence, I'm sure he will pass on my financial reward to you. I've told Rafael to request the small orchid bear your name. Orchidaceae masdevallia irisii, perhaps? In truth, the name fits the form. Rafael believes we should describe it as a black orchid to satisfy the collectors. It appears black when viewed from a distance. In fact, the colour is a deep, dark purple. With its bright yellow striped centre, the flower reminds me of our lovely Scottish growing iris. My darling girl, you are as extraordinary as both flowers.

Forgive my handwriting. The malady is spreading to my fingers and I feel my breathing is now affected too. I am so very sorry. Never doubt my love, my darling Iris.

Your loving
Papa

I passed the letter to Annie and Struan to read. I imagined his paralysis gripping me. Icy fear crept through my body. My poor papa. I had to go to him.

'I'm so very sorry, Iris. What will you do?' Annie said.

I stood up. 'I must go to London. He might still be alive. His doctors need to know he's been poisoned.'

Struan reached out and laid a kind hand on my arm. 'Let me come with you,' he said. His eyes were full of compassion.

'Thank you for the offer, but Annie will need you for the journey back.'

'No, Struan. Go and help Iris. I most certainly can manage on my own.' Annie banged the table with such a thud that she knocked her stick onto the floor.

Struan retrieved her stick. 'Let's make a plan. Iris, are you sure you want tae do this? It sounds like he won't be able tae talk tae you and we might get there too late.'

'I need to be at my father's side if it's still possible. Poor Papa didn't suspect that rogue, so it falls to me to make sure he reaches his proper resting place.'

'Lady Walker read the nurse's letter and guessed your

response. She asked me tae go wi' you. But if you prefer it, maybe Mr Donaldson would go? He likely knows London when I dinnae.'

'I think I'd prefer to keep this a between us. But what about my aunt? Is she fit to be left alone for even longer?'

'I'll be honest, she isnae great. Annie, I hope you dinnae mind, but I suggested you might go tae Lady Walker. There's no reason to go hame and I think she's taken a shine tae you.'

'Of course. I'd be a burden in London but I'd be honoured to assist her. After nursing Ma and Pa, I'm good at it.'

'Then it's decided. If we send a note, Mr Buchan will meet you off the train.'

A thought struck me. 'Struan, what about Rafael? Is he at Culdees?'

'I'm so sorry, Iris, but I believe he is.'

'If he gets word that my father is alive, he might try to harm him. And what about Annie? Will she be safe?'

'Another reason to keep this quiet. Mr MacDonald and Mr Buchan are the only others in on the story. I believe they can be trusted.'

'I'll add a note to my letter for my aunt, warning how dangerous de Rias is. Drummond Castle is a safe place for Annie to hide. This man must face justice for what he has done.'

I went to my room to pack. When I tried to replace the letter in its envelope, I found a small packet inside, labelled it *Iris's orchid*. Inside, nestled in one corner, were a dozen tiny black seeds, no bigger than grains of sand.

Chapter Forty-Four

December 1869 – Edinburgh

After Iris left the room, Annie fell to crying. 'This is all my fault. It was me who let Rafael know Mr Finlay was searching for a valuable orchid.'

Struan took her hand. 'There's nae need tae blame yersel' I never liked that man but he surely must have the gift ae the gab, since he's fooled everyone. Even Mr Speir, who is a man ae the world. It seems Iris's pa still didnae suspect him after weeks in his company. The best thing you can do for Iris now is help her aunt. That poor woman looks worn out, and Iris surely cannae cope wi any more tragedy.'

Annie sniffed. 'I'm sure I can at least make her mair comfortable.'

Iris was packed and ready to leave by the time the three critical letters arrived. She placed he damning notes from the two botanists safely in her pocket, and read the letter from Princess Louise aloud to us.

Kensington Palace
December 1st 1869

Dear Iris,
How lovely to hear from you and how thrilling that you are going to be published! I'm sure your publisher understands I cannot bestow any official royal approval, but if he thinks your association with me may get you attention, then I'm delighted. My glowing praise in the enclosed note is honest, and I wish you all the luck in the world.

Excuse me for making this letter very short. The Queen has summoned me to the Isle of Wight. I am hoping I don't have to stay there for too long.

Please keep me up-to-date with progress.

Best wishes,
Princess Louise

'I'll take the Princess's note to Mr White this afternoon, before I visit Bartholomew's,' Annie said.

Struan exchanged a concerned look with Iris.

'Stop it, both ae you,' Annie chided. 'I am perfectly capable. I was trapped most of my girlhood because there was nae money tae help me get fae one place tae the other. Some coins in my purse for a carriage puts me on a level footing wi' everybody else. When I'm at the engraver I work wi' grown men and I see them regard me seriously because they admire my work. A cripple makes a slow maid but my bad leg is nae handicap tae my drawing. I've finally found my place in the world.'

. . .

Iris had an awkward conversation with the Donaldsons about a London appointment. They'd heard the truth about Rafael, but it was too soon to be making accusations. It meant she had to hide her desperate state of mind. She was so pale, but also so outwardly composed. Struan's heart was full to bursting with admiration.

'Don't worry, Iris,' Elspeth said. 'I'll travel with Annie on the steamer across to Burntisland and settle her on the onward train. I hope your London business gets resolved quickly.'

Struan picked up Iris's bag and saw Elspeth Donaldson give him a sideways glance. No doubt they thought him a rough chap to be accompanying her. Iris told Elspeth that Struan had been sent by Lady Walker. An unlikely sounding story, despite it being true. Struan planned to do some investigations about de Rias in London. He was just the right kind of rough chap for that.

They sat in silence as the train travelled south through the Scottish countryside. It turned out the north of England looked much the same. Struan could tell from Iris's expression that her mind was in turmoil. Perhaps it would help to talk things through.

'I'll accompany you tae the hospital then see if I can find out any mair aboot this scoundrel. Dae we know how he came to visit Culdees? I guess he's no a Spaniard and his name isnae Rafael?'

'Professor Jameson is certain he wouldn't pass as a Spaniard in South America. His sons thought he might have been Colombian. I suppose he claimed Spain in this country to distance himself from any rumours. I remember being told that Señor de Rias came to Culdees from a company owned by William Bull. They supplied Mr Speir with plants.'

'Mr MacDonald bought specimens fae this nursery, too. They're based in King's Road. I'll start there. Then I'll maybe do some poking aboot amongst the pubs in the King's Road neighbourhood. I've heard that's where maist ae the plant nurseries are. We should be thankful to whoever whacked off his wee finger. That, plus his foreign accent will stick in folks' memories. How far is this hospital fae King's Road?'

Iris sighed. 'I've no more idea than you, I've never been to London before. Elspeth insisted I took her map.'

Iris came and sat on the bench seat beside Struan and spread the map across their knees. He inwardly cursed himself for finding a flicker of joy in her proximity in such terrible circumstances. It turned out the hospital was deep in east London. Whilst King's Road was in the west.

'My God, London's a big place. Where will you stay?' Struan said.

'I've no idea. Alexander Donaldson revealed that Whitechapel isn't a very nice area. My questions were necessarily vague. I didn't want them to know I was heading to a hospital. I pray my father is still alive. If he is, I want nothing more than to be by his side.'

Struan was glad when Iris slept through the last hours of the journey, she might get no sleep when they reached their destination. He hoped the motion of the train would keep her asleep.

Struan's love for Iris had hit him like a lightning bolt. The months of emotional confusion was love cracking open his heart like a hard seed, sending up a fresh green shoot. Tender, vulnerable but also vigorous, there was no stopping it now. Sitting here opposite her, listening to her breathe, he had no choice but let it grow. There was no turning back, and surely she needed his help in this terrible venture.

Chapter Forty-Five

December 1869 – London

The train didn't get into Kings Cross Station until ten thirty at night. We picked up a Brougham carriage outside. There were many people on the streets as our we left the station, but as the minutes crept on, there were fewer and fewer pedestrians. As we progressed towards the Whitechapel area, dire descriptions from Mr Dickens' novels raced through my imagination. We halted in a narrow street, I thought we must be getting close to our destination. I pulled down the carriage window to see what was going on. Thoughts of Fagin and his band of pickpockets sprung to mind, and I hastily drew my head inside.

Struan nodded in approval. 'Best no stick your head oot in case something comes past. You might lose your bonnet or worse.'

We set off again and soon pulled up outside the hospital. I paid the driver, then we walked through the arches. At the entrance I explained to a porter that I'd been summoned by a nurse named Ellen McKinnon.

'No visitors at night. Come back in the morning,' he said, making to close the door.

I grabbed his sleeve. 'Please,' I implored. 'She wrote that my father is dying and I've travelled all the way from Scotland.'

He sighed. 'Come inside. I'll see what I can find out.'

We waited at the porter's desk. Struan stood tensely beside me, screwing his cap between his hands. After ten minutes, the porter returned, accompanied by a young nurse with a rosy complexion and dark hair.

The nurse smiled sympathetically. 'You must be Iris. My name is Vera. I'm Ellen's sister and we've been expecting you since we received the note from Lady Walker today.

'My aunt wrote to the hospital?'

'Saying you were on your way, and she sent a banker's draft to cover this patient's care. We moved him to a private room.'

My heart was thudding. 'My father is alive? Is he recovering?'

The nurse's expression changed to one of dismay and acute discomfort. 'Oh. Ellen said she'd made it clear. He is alive, but we didn't expect it. The poor man was already much too ill when he got to us.' She shook her head. 'Let's waste no more time. Follow me.'

I turned towards Struan. He held up his hand. 'I'll no intrude.'

The nurse took me up a flight of stairs to the floor above. She paused at the nurses' station. 'We keep the ward lights off at night.' She picked up a lamp, lighting the way to open the door to a small room.

After the brightly lit corridor, I could only make out the shape of a body in the bed. Vera McKinnon walked past me to set the lamp on the bedside table. When the light fell on Papa's face, I gasped in shock. He was barely recognisable. His cheeks and eye sockets were so sunken and his skin so yellow-tinged that it looked more like a parchment-covered skull than my dear father. I dropped my valise, rushed to the bedside and took his hand, which lay lifeless on the starched sheet.

'I'm sorry he won't know you're here. We gave him something to help him sleep.'

Papa's noisy breathing was distressing. There was a hesitation after each out breath that made me fear the next breath wouldn't come. 'Has he got worse since he was admitted?'

Vera pulled a chair over, allowing me to both sit and still hold Papa's hand. 'He has.' She sighed. 'I'm so sorry, but the doctors consider him on the brink of leaving this life. He has stayed hovering there, much longer than we'd have expected.' She left the room and came back with a woollen blanket, which she draped over my shoulders. 'I'll leave you. If you need me, I'll be on the main ward next door, or at my desk.'

When she left, I took my father's cold fingers to my lips. 'I'm right here, Papa,' I whispered.

Through the long hours of the night I prayed, just as I'd heard him do with my mama on her deathbed. Light crept in gradually and half-heartedly. I stood and walked to the window to stretch my legs. There was no view except the wall across an internal courtyard. I heard some nearby church chime out the hour of seven. When I went to sit again, Papa's eyelids fluttered. Perhaps showing some drifting towards consciousness? If he could hear me, I must reassure him.

'Good morning, Papa. I've waited too many long months to be able to say that to you again.' I got no reaction, but that didn't mean he couldn't hear me. 'I travelled down from Scotland yesterday. A shorter journey than it might have been, since I was already in Edinburgh. You will be pleased and proud to hear my news.' I described our publication plans, keeping my voice light and happy, hoping it might reach him. I thought I heard a stutter in his in breath, then a long smooth out breath. Was it a sigh?

When his eyes flew open, it took every ounce of self-control not to shriek with joy. 'Can you hear me, Papa? Do you know where you are?' I realised his gaze wasn't settled on my face, but somewhere behind me. He seemed not to see me. I squeezed his hand. 'Papa, it's me, Iris.' His eyes slid towards me. I caught a flicker of confusion. Then suddenly, he became agitated, blinking and thrashing his head from side to side.

I leapt up. Put my hands on his cheeks and brought my face right up close to his. 'Papa, don't worry. It's all right. You are safe. I'm here.' He became still, but his breathing was much more laboured. The effort had drained him and he looked desperately sad. I stroked his face.

'Shoosh, shoosh,' I whispered. Just as he would say to me when I was a little girl. 'It's all right. I got your letter. You mustn't worry. Everything is going to be fine.'

I had thought that I might ask him questions. Perhaps gather more information to incriminate Rafael. But now, I realised the most important thing was to make his last moments peaceful and happy. His eyes flickered and closed. Was that the last time? Had I committed their colour to memory? I appealed to my mother in my head. A prayer for help. I felt as if the resolve in my next words came from her.

'I'm so proud of you, Papa. Your plants reached Mr Speir safely, and he is delighted. Your reputation as a great plant hunter is secure, and I am going to be fine. Aunt Leonora sends her love and promises to be at my side. Your lessons have given me the skill to be published, and with the income from that I'll be well provided for.'

My father's lovely clear blue eyes opened again. He looked tired and sad, but somehow also peaceful. 'I know how hard you fought to wait for me,' I whispered. 'Thank you. But don't fight it anymore. Mama needs you. She has waited too long.'

His gaze went back into the distance and slowly he closed his eyes.

'I love you, Papa,' I whispered.

Papa's shallow, noisy breathing slowed, then the breaths came no more. I allowed my tears to soak his pillow, but quietly, in case his soul remained.

Chapter Forty-Six

December 1869 – London

I don't know how long I sat with my head on the pillow beside his. I raised my head when Vera came in.

'Ah, he's gone. He was waiting for you, Miss Iris.'

I looked more closely, because the voice sounded different. This nurse wore the same starched, white cap and long white apron over her dress, but although there was a strong resemblance, she was much taller. 'I'm Ellen. I'm the one who wrote to you.'

'Thank you. I'm so grateful I was able to be with him.'

Vera came in too. She walked over to the bed and lowered her cheek near Papa's face, perhaps to check for his breath. 'The Lord has taken him,' she said.

Too choked up with emotion, I could only nod. She tucked his long, pale hands by his side and took the sheet as if to cover his face.

'Please, one more minute,' I asked. I leant over and kissed his cheek. It had cooled. His soul had gone. 'Goodbye, Papa.'

Nurse Vera raised the sheet over his head.

Ellen gestured to my valise on the floor. 'You came straight from the station? Then please come back to our family home, which is very nearby. Have some tea and perhaps something to eat? You must be exhausted.'

'Thank you, that's very kind.'

'Will you stay here for a bit longer, Vera? I won't be long,' Ellen asked. Her sister nodded.

I glanced back at the bed. 'What will happen...?'

'We will keep him here at the hospital until you give us instructions,' Ellen replied.

She picked up my valise, and I followed her towards the stairs. 'I spoke to a young man on the way in this morning. He said he was waiting for you.'

'Oh gosh, yes. That's Struan. He must have been here all night. How awful. I never even thought.'

'Is he a relative?'

I shook my head. 'My elderly aunt who wrote to you is my only living relative. Struan is a trusted family friend. Aunt Leonora asked him to accompany me, so I didn't travel alone.'

'A very loyal friend. To travel all day and sit here all night'

'Yes. I believe he is.'

I could see Struan from the top of the stairs, sitting on the floor with his back against the wall. His arms were around his hunched up knees. I'd been here for over nine hours. Had he really sat there on the floor all night? His kindness struck into my heart with such force, I stopped walking. Nurse Ellen perhaps feared I might faint precariously near the head of the stairs. She dropped my bag and put both arms around me.

'Young man, we need some help here,' she called.

Struan sprang up to his feet and raced up the stairs. 'Oh, Iris. Is he—?' He looked straight into my eyes with concern.

I nodded. 'He was so very poorly, Struan. I told him I would be fine, that Aunt Lenora would look after me and he should go.' Bravery deserted me. 'But God forgive me, I lied. What if Aunt Leonora dies too?' I fell against Struan's shoulder and cried. His hands tentatively rested against my back.

'Let it go, lass. It's no good tae hold it in. You will hae Annie and me at your side, I promise.'

I drew in a shuddering breath.

'You need tea and a hot breakfast. Will you come with us, Mr...?' Nurse Ellen said.

'Cooper, but call me Struan,' he replied. 'Thank you, tea would be grand. Let me carry Iris's bag.'

'We're just around the corner,' Ellen explained. 'My mother runs a boarding house for nurses.'

Ellen led us round nearby a corner and down an alley, where close-packed houses with wooden shutters were overflowing with grubby children. We stopped at a well-scrubbed stone doorstep and Ellen pushed open the door. She sat us down at a large kitchen table which almost filled the room. Molly, Ellen's mother, left her washing up in the huge sink and set about around cracking eggs into a bowl while Ellen served us large cups of sweet tea from an enormous teapot.

'Have you somewhere to stay, miss?' Molly's mother asked. 'I've a vacant room with the bed all made up. You look done in, if you don't mind me saying.' Her accent reminded me of an Irish lady who lived in Crieff.

'Oh, Mammy,' Ellen said. 'This lady will likely want to go to a hotel.'

'Not at all,' I replied. 'If you have a room, I'd be very grateful to stay. I expect there are arrangements to be made with the hospital, which might take a few days.'

'Are you sure?' Ellen looked uncertain. 'We had no idea your father was a gentleman when we admitted him.'

'Oh no, our family isn't titled. His name is...' I hesitated,

'...was Andrew Finlay. He was a Church of Scotland minister before he became a plant hunter.'

'But you live in Drummond Castle?'

'For the last two and half years, whilst my father was away, with my maternal aunt, Lady Walker. My background is not at all grand.'

Mrs McKinnon looked towards Struan. 'I'm afraid we only take lady lodgers.'

'Of course,' Struan replied. 'Since Miss Finlay is staying longer, I've a mind tae dae some digging into what this Spanish devil has been up tae in London. I'm sure he changed the arrival port fae Liverpool tae Southampton for a reason.'

'I might know of this man,' Ellen said. 'The ship's captain was furious that your father had been literally left for dead by his foreign companion.'

'That's him,' I said. 'We knew him as Rafael de Rias, who told us he was Spanish. But it seems he has often claimed to be other nationalities. Did the captain describe the man?' I asked.

'No,' Ellen replied. 'But apparently this foreigner took his luggage too. The captain said he found your father's cabin completely empty. He registered your father here under the name Bernardo da Silva, since it was that on the ship's passenger manifest. But the captain suspected this was false. A man who called himself Alfredo da Silva entered both names on the passenger list and he spoke Spanish, but some of the crew swore they'd heard the two men conversing in English when your father came out of his cabin, early in the journey.'

Anger coursed through me. I clenched my hands at the thought of what the man I knew as Rafael had done. 'Do you have an address for the captain? I'd like to talk to him.'

'I'll check the admission records. I believe he left a name

and address. He wanted us to let him know how your father fared.'

'Can the doctors dae anything to prove your pa was poisoned?' Struan asked. 'I'd like tae help get this vile creature hung.'

'Poisoned?!' Ellen gasped. 'Dear God, are you sure?'

'I think so. Papa was perfectly well when he left Ecuador, and I've discovered that this man poisoned his own wife in Argentina.'

Ellen leaned out to cover my hands, and I felt her mother's fingers on my shoulder. I'd been touched by so many kind people in the last hour, I fell to crying again.

'Surely the doctors will be able to tell if this poor man was poisoned?' Ellen's mother said.

'Perhaps?' Ellen replied. 'But after five days on the ward, any poison traces might be gone.'

'No need to dwell on such things now,' Ellen's mother added. She placed a plate of eggs in front of me. 'You must eat and then you must sleep. Everything else can wait.'

I smiled gratefully at her. Exhaustion left me unable to think. I hadn't slept properly in so many days, my body ached.

Struan scooped up his eggs in a series of swift forkfuls and stood up. 'I'll bid you all good day,' he said.

'I'm sorry we cannot offer you a bed here,' Ellen said. 'But we might recommend somewhere nearby?'

'Thank you, but I'm heading to the King's Road and I've a mind tae try out these omnibuses. A two-storey carriage for ordinary folks is a kind of miracle. Billy the porter told me which one I should catch and where I should change.'

He came to place his hand on my arm. 'Please wait for me before you go searching for this captain. Rafael, or whatever his name is, will have been sly. I want tae talk tae people before the trail goes cold.'

'Thank you,' I said. 'Right now, I have more important priorities than that wretch. I must go back to the hospital and talk to Papa's doctors.'

'I might stay over near the King's Road,' Struan said. 'I'll be back tomorrow morning.'

I stood to hug him. A spontaneous action which somehow seemed right. 'Good luck with your efforts, but be careful.'

'Will you send a note tae Scotland so Annie knows we're here?'

'I'll write a note to Aunt Leonora before I sleep. Tell her Papa's gone but I got here in time.'

Struan nodded, then he was gone. Was his quest dangerous? This boy who I once thought my enemy was suddenly more precious than any other.

'Be careful,' I called after him.

Chapter Forty-Seven

December 1869 – London

Billy the porter's description of Piccadilly Circus with its winged boy was so accurate, Struan had no hesitation in jumping off the bus. He found himself in mayhem. So many horse-drawn vehicles. However would he find the particular omnibus he needed? That there were so many horses in London was a huge surprise. Dinnae panic, he told himself. Just sit tight for a bit. He set his bottom on the edge of the fountain and watched. Eventually, he spotted the omnibus he wanted. It stopped near him to let some ladies in huge hats alight.

'King's Road?' he shouted to the conductor and the man stuck up his thumb.

Struan climbed up the spiral staircase. Billy had told him it was cheaper on the top deck. In any case, he was keen to watch London go by. The conductor took his fare, and he settled down for the ride. His thoughts flew back to Iris. He would never forget the pain of his own father's death, but Iris's father had been murdered. How does a person deal with that mixture of grief and anger? Iris's face on his shoulder, her body shaking with sobs. Being so close and yet unable to ease

Iris's pain was unbearable. At least he could make sure de Rias didn't get away with murder.

Struan read the street names as they went along, eventually they arrived at Sloane Square. Billy had said that this grand square sat at the entry to King's Road. Struan didn't know where on this street he'd find William Bull's premises, so stayed onboard. It was an extremely long road and his perch gave a perfect view of all the nurseries. Urban London had given way to a kind of countryside. There were houses and shops, but also acre after acre of plant stalls and glasshouses. In the nursery beds at the back of the plots, he could even see exotic trees. He spotted a sign. William Bull was one of the largest, with an enormous expanse of glasshouses. Struan got off further on in front of the Cadogan Arms Inn and walked back. He browsed through several nurseries to gain confidence before risking Bull's. Iris would have been interested to see how many of the shoppers were women. Well-dressed salesmen operated in some establishments, and most of them were very handsome. Watching salesmen fawn over the well-to-do ladies made Struan think it wasn't coincidental. Rafael de Rias would have fitted in perfectly. Struan had decided to create a story based on truth, so he told these men that he was a Scots plantsman from the Drummond Castle Estate and was scouting for new specimens.

When Struan entered William Bull's premises, he found a dazzling array of plants of every kind. The most expensive species were in the greenhouses. People flocked to gaze at the exotic and peculiar-looking pineapple plants. He heard one man demand the largest they could supply, as a centrepiece for his mistress's Christmas table. Next door were the hothouses full of orchids. Pride of place was given to a huge and bright pink Brazilian *Cattleya amethystoglossa*, the very orchid that had inspired Iris's father. A gentleman asked the price and was told ten whole guineas. Struan could hardly believe his ears. More than four months of his own salary for a single plant. Surely this was what gave de Rias the idea of making his fortune in orchids. And how like that rascal to do it on the hard labour of another. Struan needed to get some insider information about the Spaniard's connection to this company, but he'd no way of knowing which of these men to approach. He took one more turn around the premises, then retired to the alehouse opposite to wait.

Several of the top-hatted salesmen came in, but Struan waited until he recognised the worker he'd observed supervising the restocking of the primula stand. He guessed from the man's clothes that he was a nurseryman. Luckily, the place had become busy, so Struan slid up his bench and offered the man a seat.

'I'm going tae the bar. Can I get you a drink?' he said, tipping his empty glass at the man, who nodded in reply. He set the drinks down. 'My name is Struan Cooper. I noticed you were working over the road. I'm a plantsman fae Scotland and I'm thinking aboot seeking work down here. Any advice about the best employers would be welcome.'

'Well, you've come to the right chap. I'm Ernest Gillingham and I've worked here for over twenty years.' It turned out that Ernest loved the sound of his own voice and he was soon rattling on. The way he decried some of the rival companies gave Struan the feeling the man was a gossip. Just the right kind of person who would have something to say about de Rias. He had already revealed his scorn for the dandy salesmen.

'I met a foreign chap in Scotland, a botanist who boasted he worked in the King's Road. I wonder if you might know him?'

'We have plenty of foreign types here, Dutch, French, German, you name it. What's his name?'

'He used the name of Rafael de Rias, but I've heard he's inclined tae change his name more often than his fancy tailcoat. He had the same look as your salesmen.' Struan nodded towards the various dandies sitting in a padded booth. 'He carried an ebony cane and was missing the smallest finger on his right hand.'

Ernest practically spat his ale across the table. 'Oh, I know him all right. I hope he's not a friend of yours?'

'Definitely not. The opposite, in fact.'

The man drained his glass and sat back in his seat. 'It's a long story and one I shouldn't really repeat, for William Bull is so embarrassed he doesn't tell it.'

'I'm the canny sort. I promise I willnae repeat it around, and if it's a long tale, I better get you another drink.'

Once Ernest had slurped his beer, he brought his head in close and talked in a whisper. 'The first thing I'm sure of is that you won't find this bloke hanging around here. If that cheeky beggar shows his face, William Bull will have him in the jail before you can say Michaelmas daisy.'

'What did he do?'

'The braggart brought references from a company in Paris and said he was a Portuguese called José Dias. The rogue was silver-tongued. He flattered Mr Bull and even conned his way into the man's own home. It seems the boss foolishly shared his idea for a new kind of Wardian case. Too much wine, I'd wager. Apparently, Dias stole the draft plans from his desk. Next thing William Bull knew about it was when gossip came from Liverpool docks of this new design being boarded on a boat to Panama. The boss had arranged for José to deliver some glasshouse specimens to a new customer, but it turns out he had the nerve to take along some orchids in cases he'd had made to the new design. When Dias's references were checked, they were false. You can be sure that William Bull has that design patented now.'

'That's exactly how he came to our area this year.'

'Tell me, what did this fella gain from the deception? I wouldn't get on the wrong side of William Bull for the sake of a few orchids.'

Struan hesitated, trying to decide how much to tell this man. 'I think he arranged tae be invited tae join a plant hunting trip in Ecuador. The expedition returned this month.'

Ernest shook his head, looking confused. 'It can't be the same man. It can have been no earlier than May when he crossed the Atlantic. No time to mount a plant hunting expedition.'

'No time to hunt, but time tae steal another man's plants.'

Ernest puffed the air out of his cheeks. 'Well, I'm not surprised. William Bull knows him to be a thief.'

This was it. Struan's chance to destroy de Rais's reputation and put an end to him working out of London. Why not drive it home?

'A thief and a poisoner. Two different botanists have recounted the tale of a man of his description poisoning his wealthy wife.'

Ernest slammed down his drink. 'Are you serious? Wait until I tell Mr Bull. He might count himself lucky to lose so little if he shared his table with such a man.'

Struan drained his glass. 'Thank you for your company, Mr Gillingham. I'd be grateful if you'd listen out for any sign of jobs and also any word of this foreign rascal. The plant hunter who was the victim in this latest scheme was the father of my friend.'

Ernest shook Struan's hand with enthusiastic vigour. 'I'd like to help you and I wager Mr Bull would do too, but I really doubt José Dias would risk coming back to King's Road.'

'Perhaps you're right. Any unusual activity in the trade of

valuable orchids might be a clue. I'm assuming the thief plans tae sell some of his ill-gotten gains.'

'I'll ask around. But how will I find you, Mr Cooper?'

'Please call me Struan. I've not found any lodgings yet. Where would you recommend?'

'You might ask the landlord in the Colvill Tavern? His wife rents rooms. It is just after Lincoln Street if you walk east.'

'Thank you. I'll try there. Do you mind if I seek you here again, Mr Gillingham? I've enjoyed your company.'

'Oh, call me Ernest, lad. Thank you for the ale. I'll ask around for you on both counts.'

Struan found the Colvill Tavern and ate a supper there. Afterwards, he paid for his room and flung the knapsack he'd been shouldering all day onto the bed. This full-sized bed with a deep mattress was fancier than any he'd ever slept in. His own, inherited from his pa, was stuffed with straw, on a bed constructed from wood offcuts.

Struan wondered if Iris was still awake. His heart urged him to rush back to Whitechapel to see her. Reluctantly, he rejected the idea. He planned to snoop about the orchid glasshouses first thing in the morning. De Rias might not risk coming here, but if he'd sold some plants, this area was surely the most likely destination.

Chapter Forty-Eight

December 1869 – London

I woke to a brief moment of contentment, rested after so many days of no sleep. Then I remembered. Papa was dead. A chasm opened inside me. Complete desolation. Was this loss of faith?

Papa's unnatural death was too hard to bear. He made a career out of helping people accept that every death was part of God's plan. An acceptance that failed him on my mother's death. Was I similarly flung out of grace? I detested that Rafael de Rias consumed my thoughts. He didn't deserve it.

Although it wasn't fully light, I could hear many female voices. When I heard the chiming of a clock, I realised the sleeping draught Vera had brought from the hospital had kept me asleep for an unbelievable eighteen hours. From the sound of happy chattering and laughter, I guessed the day shift nurses were readying to leave for work. I'd chosen a good haven. Being amongst so many hard-working and worthy women gave me a modicum of comfort. I dressed, but only when the front door had slammed several times and quiet reigned again did I go downstairs to sit at the kitchen table. Vera came in from her nightshift and wordlessly squeezed my shoulder. She'd brought in a bag of warm crumpets from the baker. She buttered one and pushed the plate across to me.

'I have no appetite,' I told her.

'I'm sure you don't, but Ellen told me she's making arrangements for you to meet the doctor. If you gad about without eating, you will faint. Nurse's orders,' she added.

There was a rap at the door and Vera went to open it. I ignored the skip in my heartbeat at the sight of Struan. You would have thought that grief would have curtailed my unreliable and untrustworthy heart. He devoured the crumpet Vera put in front of him.

'Did you learn anything?' I asked.

'A poisoner and a thief, just as we thocht.' He went onto describe how Rafael had stolen Mr Bull's design. 'It isnae likely that the rogue would risk running intae William Bull, but you never know. The expanse ae nurseries is like a village.'

'Why do you think he would come to London at all?'

'I have a theory. I need tae do mair checking.'

I glanced at the clock above the range. 'I promised I would meet the doctor at nine-thirty. We'll seek out this ship's captain afterwards.'

Struan smiled when Molly gave him a second crumpet. He held it between his teeth while he slipped on his jacket.

Struan offered me his arm as we walked towards the hospital, and I was glad of it. I was determined to control my emotions but not so stupid as to imagine I could get through this ordeal alone. The throng of pedestrians was intimidating, even busier than Edinburgh. What energy I had wasted detesting this kind and thoughtful man beside me. I should have guessed from the beginning that Annie would never adore a brother who wasn't worthy.

'I've asked my contact at William Bull tae listen out for any sign ae something new or valuable turning up on King's Road. Surely, de Rias changed the port for some good reason.

Southampton isnae the usual destination for plant hunters coming fae the Americas and Liverpool would certainly have been mair convenient tae reach Scotland,' Struan said. 'I wager he found a way tae sell off some plants before he travelled north.'

'But could a few plant sales be a motive for killing my father? He killed his wife to inherit a fortune.'

'I've been snooping around the orchid houses. A large amethyst orchid sells for ten guineas a plant.'

'Incredible. Papa confirmed he found the large orchid he sought, but that is promised to Mr Speir. If Rafael was going to steal all the cargo, he could have taken off without going back to Perthshire.'

'Maybe this ship captain could tell us what was on the cargo list. Rafael might have kept some plants tae dispose ae himsel'.'

'Good idea,' I replied.

All too, soon we arrived at the hospital.

'Shall I wait here?' Struan asked.

'Would you come up? I expect I have to decide whether to involve the police and I value your opinion.'

The doctor shook his head grimly when I described Rafael's history as a poisoner and my conviction that he'd killed my father.

'Nurse McKinnon told me she already advised we might not be able to prove it, and I'm sorry to say I agree. Firstly, the poison would have cleared your father's system and secondly, although there are tests for a substance such as arsenic, I doubt we'd be able to identify a plant-based poison.'

'What would happen if I went to the police?'

'They would ask us to test your father's stomach contents.'

I shuddered and shook my head. 'Papa reserved a place for himself beside my mother in Fowlis Wester churchyard. Tests would add a pointless delay. I'd like to take him home.'

'I have details of an undertaker who can organise the transport of a coffin by train. Would you like me to arrange for him to visit you on Monday?' he said.

'I think it's best,' I answered.

Struan chaperoned me back to Mrs McKinnon's home very late in the afternoon and decided to delay our visit to the captain until Sunday, when we'd more likely find him at home.

I could tell that Struan felt as dispirited as I did. Our journey through the poverty-stricken streets of Whitechapel, then onto the captain's home in Limehouse, was thoroughly depressing. The captain lived in a reasonably nice terrace overlooking the Thames, but along the way there and back, we passed people living in conditions that made rural poverty look comparatively pleasant. Poor families living in filthy, overcrowded rooms that would be considered unfit for animals. However, I was glad we'd found the captain. Without his actions, I'd not have had the chance to say goodbye to Papa. I was glad to thank and repay him for those costs he'd covered at the hospital. Unfortunately, he'd explained that although the cargo manifest numbered the plants, it only gave them generic descriptions. Not enough detail to identify particular specimens.

I was glad to be back in the welcome warmth of Mrs McKinnon's kitchen.

'I'll head back to King's Road again. Perhaps Ernest Gillingham will have left a message with better news.'

'Wait a minute,' I replied. I held up the letters Mrs McKinnon had just given me. 'One of these is from Annie.' Struan came to stand beside me

3rd December

Dear Iris,
I am so very sorry to hear of your father's death. Although it wasn't a surprise, it is a terrible thing to have endured. I wish I was there to comfort you. Your aunt is distraught, but she is also a formidable lady. When I told her I wanted to visit the Culdees glasshouses, she approved my spying plan. I am sure this tale will infuriate my brother, but I hope Lady Walker's support might excuse my behaviour. I believe coming out of hiding was worth it for the things I learned.

'Oh, Annie,' Struan muttered. 'You were telt tae stay put.'
Jock learned from his brother that Rafael de Rias is not presently at Culdees Castle. When Lady Walker double-checked with Mr Speir, he told your aunt that Rafael suggested taking the new orchids as gifts to the Botanic Gardens in Edinburgh. No doubt, he is absent from Culdees Castle for reasons related to his own reputation or profit, but it emboldened me to visit Culdees Castle hothouses.
I'm afraid to confess I told Mr Speir a lie. I said that you were too bereft to talk to anyone, but that you had requested a painting of these new orchids. Mr Speir showed me other specimens of the two enormous orchids he'd sent with Rafael to the Botanical Society. He reported one would bear his own name, but the other would carry the name of your father. I've included both sketches. But, Iris, there is something more. I counted over forty orchids. Your father will certainly be famous because Mr Speir believes several of them to be new species. But there is nothing matching the description of the plant your father wanted to name after you. The black orchid isn't here.

I laid down the letter and stared at Struan.
'That's it,' he said emphatically. 'We're looking for a black orchid.'

Chapter Forty-Nine

December 1869 – London

On Monday, Struan found Ernest Gillingham in the same public house. They sat facing each other and spoke the same words in unison.

'A black orchid.'

'How did you know?' Struan asked.

'The whole of King's Road is talking about it today. Mr Bull is furious that this foreign beggar will make a mint out of a new plant and he wasn't even been given a look in.'

'So he came tae King's Road tae sell it?'

'Not that coward. He used a fellow called Chalmers. Another rogue, but a minor one. Archie Chalmers was told which nursery establishment to approach and made them pay a fortune to secure the rights to auction it.'

'Auction? Like at a horse market?'

'Just like it, if the horses are priceless Arab stallions.'

'How dae you know this?'

'I told William Bull your tale and your hunch the foreigner might have something to sell. My boss had Chalmers dragged into his office. If Chalmers had known your man was an enemy of Mr Bull, I wager he'd have turned down this task at any price.'

'Have you seen the plant?'

'I have not, but Mr Bull has. He says its colour is unlike anything he's seen before. Every orchid collector in England is going to want one. He's green with envy and now determined to end José Dias's career. He wants to meet you.' Gillingham looked up. 'In fact, here he is.'

Struan followed his gaze. The man coming towards them had side-whiskers and a receding hairline, but he'd expected such a successful businessman to be older. This man striding purposefully across the bar was surely only in his forties. Struan stood and shook the gentleman's hand. He had a strong and vigorous grip.

'So, lad. I hear you are looking for work. If you can help me bring down José Dias, I'll give you a job tomorrow.'

Struan could feel that his face and earlobes turning red. William Bull was an influential man in the horticultural world and he was about to be caught lying to him. He looked down at his hands.

'Mr Bull, I'm honoured tae meet you. I am indeed a nurseryman and maybe one day I'd love tae work for you.' Struan took a deep breath. 'But not right now.'

He looked up and into the gentleman's eyes. William Bull had a straightforward look about him. Struan decided to trust him.

'My whole reason for being here is the man you knew as José Dias. We believe he was guilty ae poisoning his wife in Argentina. I'm sorry tae report that it seems he has struck again. Rias or Dias, or whatever his name is, used your Wardian Case design to get himself trusted by my friend's father, who was a plant hunter in Ecuador. We believe this honest botanist found the black orchid there and that the foreign scoundrel killed him tae gain the wealth for himsel'.'

Mr Bull thumped his clenched fist on the table. 'Then we must go to the police. What's his name, this friend?'

'My friend is a young lady. Her name is Iris Finlay. She is only eighteen, and this wicked man has left her an orphan.'

'The absolute rogue,' Bull said with a scowl.

'Unfortunately, we have nae proof and we cannae yet prove that Dias stole the black orchid, either. Iris's father died in hospital in London and we will travel north for her father's burial soon. We hope we can find the evidence there. Keeping all this information secret is vital. Dias abandoned Andrew Finlay for dead and has nae idea we are on tae him. It's important tae keep the element ae surprise.'

William Bull nodded. 'Gillingham here is one of my most trusted employees and we'd like to do whatever we can to help you. What do you advise?'

'We'd be most grateful if you would keep a lookout for Dias. He is such an arrogant bugger. I believe he willnae be able tae resist attending this auction. Perhaps by then we will be able tae ask the peelers tae arrest him.'

'I've already booked my seat at the auction. It's scheduled a week hence. No intention of bidding, of course, but to see who will pay upwards of one hundred pounds for an orchid.'

'A hundred pounds? Are you sure?'

'That's the estimate, since they only have two for sale, it might go higher.'

Struan shook his head in disbelief. 'Andrew Finlay was an honest man who would have passed all his finds tae his wealthy patron, but he would have received a handsome reward. As it stands, Iris is left wi' nothing. That is maist unfair.'

'That poor girl. How will she support herself? Did her father leave her no inheritance?'

'He had none tae give her. However, she has an elderly aunt and also some skills. In fact, you might soon hear her name. Mr White of Edinburgh will publish baith her book and her first quarterly pamphlet this month. My sister is the illustrator.'

'How very fascinating. I know White, of course. I shall ask to be added to the subscriber list. It seems you know some modern women, Mr Cooper. The rise of the horticultural female may overwhelm us all.'

'I'm maist proud tae be associated wi' them, Mr Bull.'

'A botanist who is a botanist's daughter. That makes me even more determined to help in this endeavour. Leave me an address and I'll keep you abreast of any developments.'

Bull gave Struan his card. Since Struan had nothing to write on, Bull gave him another on which he wrote Iris's address. Mr Bull looked up in surprise. 'Drummond Castle?'

'The prestigious address doesnae reflect Miss Finlay's full circumstances. She presently lives wi' an ailing aunt who resides there. She isnae connected wi' the de Eresby family.'

'Nevertheless, this is a prestigious association. I have a good relationship with this family. We have supplied many items to Drummond and Grimsthorpe Castles. Now, I'd better be off because I'm expected at home.' He gave Struan a calculating look. 'Would you care to accompany me on my journey down King's Road? I fancy I need to take a second look at this black orchid.'

Struan thanked Ernest Gillingham for his help. The man was still beaming from his boss's high praise, and clearly enjoying being part of this secret assignment. Struan fell in step with William Bull's brisk stride. They were close to the Colvill Arms Inn when Bull dived up a side alley. He wove his way confidently through the plant stalls. Several men tipped their hats at him. He circumvented the main orchid house, then stopped beside another glasshouse, much like the others, except there was a heavily built guard on the door.

'Evening, Jeremiah.'

'Good evening to you, Mr Bull.'

'I need to take another look at that orchid.' Bull's wide smile looked very assured.

'I'm so sorry, Mr Bull. My instructions are no one is to enter.'

'No stranger, of course. However, you are well aware that they already admitted me today.' Bull took advantage of the man's confused look and strode straight past him, Struan close behind. 'We will be in and in out in two minutes, Jeremiah.'

The glasshouse hummed with the sound of the heating pipes. The warm, humid atmosphere was a stark contrast to the cold London air.

'Stupid man needs to bleed his pipes. I supplied this system but I cannot help it when my customers don't follow my instructions.'

Shadowy greenery lined the walls. In the centre stood a single bench. 'Hard to see in this poor light, but this extraordinary specimen has a colour and form I've never seen before in a plant.'

There were two plants on the bench. At first Struan could only make out that this medium-sized orchid had very dark flowers with a bright yellow centre. He leant closer to peer at an individual flower. About the size of the palm of his hand, this flower had three sepals, forming a shape like a triangle, and each sepal had a very long spike protruding from it. These sepals and spikes appeared to be black. Purple and white stripes radiated from the bright yellow flower centre. Its eerie appearance sent a shiver through Struan. It was like something not of this world. Nothing like a friendly iris. Struan stepped back. At that moment, a single flower fell silently onto the bench.

'That's not good,' Bull said. 'Let's go.'

Chapter Fifty

December 1869 – London

After Struan left, I replied to Annie's letter, congratulating her on her sleuthing and asking her to advise my aunt that I would stay on to make arrangements to bring my father's body back to Fowlis Wester. I wrote also to the Donaldsons, telling them my father had died, but gave no details, unable to face the questions that would follow. Also, if there were to be any chance of outwitting Rafael de Rias, it might be better to keep my knowledge of his crimes a secret. After a great deal of thought, I also enclosed a note which I asked them to pass onto Professor Jameson.

6th December, 1869
Whitechapel,
London

Dear Professor Jameson
I know this is going to distress you. The fear on your face was a
premonition, and so I'm very sorry to tell you that my wonderful
father has died.

I managed to find him in London and be at his bedside for his final
hours. It is in utmost confidence I must share that I'm certain that the
man I know as de Rias and your sons knew as Eduardo Ximenez
poisoned him, but it seems this will be impossible to prove. It appears
the motive for this senseless act was nothing more than greed and
perhaps fame.

I hope you can remember Papa as he was when you saw him last.
You were a good friend to him during his adventures in Ecuador, and
his time there brought him a happiness that had eluded him for years.
He achieved his dreams and also found the Lord again in the moun-
tains of the land you call home. It is a comfort I can salvage from the
cruelty of his death that he died happy and at peace with God.

I hesitated before sending you news because I know it will upset
you. However, apparently Rafael is currently in Edinburgh and may
well present himself at the Royal Botanical Society. It would be such a
shock for you to come across him without warning. I decided it would
be better if you are pre-warned. Unfortunately, since we have no
proof of any crime being committed by this rogue, he may remain free
to live his life. De Rias does not know that I've learned of his treach-
ery, nor that you alerted me to his previous crime. At present, he
perhaps still believes my father died onboard their ship, and this is the
story he has told everyone at home. It is my intention to unmask him
when I return to Perthshire. I am certain that with your testimony I
can at least have him ousted from his place of trust at Culdees Castle.

There is one more piece in the puzzle you might help me with. In my father's final letter to me, he described his pride in discovering a new Ecuadorian variety of Cattleya amethystoglossa. I believe the registration of this huge orchid is the purpose of de Rias's Edinburgh visit. However, Papa also described finding another orchid he believed would thrill all orchid collectors. Apparently, this plant's outstanding feature is its colour. The orchid is of deepest purple when closely examined, but from a distance people will perceive it as black. This demon has spirited away the plant before he reached Culdees. Annie's brother, Struan, is currently looking for it in London. Perhaps it might turn up in the collections of wealthy collectors north of the border too. If we can find the orchid and prove Rafael stole it, we can at least have him exposed as a thief.

I plan to travel home soon, and you will be able to reach me at Drummond Castle. My father's funeral will be in Fowlis Wester church. I will send you more details, in case you wish to attend.

Yours in deep sadness,
Iris Finlay

The undertaker visited me in the McKinnon home and was confident that he had all that was required to send my father home. He explained there was some paperwork required by the railway company, which would take a couple of days. I signed all the necessary forms. We agreed I'd brief the station master in Crieff and appoint a Scottish undertaker.

Back in Drummond Castle, although it was less than two weeks since I'd left Scotland, I felt like a different person after the triumph of Edinburgh, followed by the horror of losing my father. When we got back, Struan came in to visit Annie and report his progress to Aunt Leonora. He encouraged Annie to stay one more night, reasoning that their empty cottage would be very cold.

After he left, Annie showed me how to make the herbal tea she'd been giving my aunt every day. Aunt Leonora said it helped her digestion, and she certainly looked better than she had in weeks. I was glad to be back but dreaded visiting Mr Speir. The revelations about Rafael would be difficult to explain, and it was vital to choose the right words. The very notion of that man returning to live amongst us was too nauseating to even contemplate.

The next day, Annie and I emerged into the castle court-yard and Struan put down his hoe and walked up from the garden to meet us.

'Was Mr MacDonald in agreement about giving you even more time to help me?'

'Nae question aboot it. I've never known Mr MacDonald tae be emotional, but telling him ae yer father's last days reduced him tae tears. Like me, he never warmed tae the Spaniard. But having heard how he has made you and yer father suffer, I believe he might react violently if de Rias ever came here again.'

'Did you tell him about the black orchid?'

'I did. I hope that was all right? He agreed he would keep the story tae himsel until it's public knowledge and immediately suggested I should come wi' you tae describe it tae Mr Speir.'

We dropped Annie at the house, then proceeded to Culdees Castle. The housekeeper told us we would find Mr Speir in the chapel, supervising the last stages of installing his stained glass into one of the windows. A kaleidoscope of colours flung light through the glass onto the floor. When he turned and saw me, Mr Speir's happy expression disappeared.

'Oh, Iris. I am so terribly sorry. I blame myself for this tragedy.' His eyes flickered towards Struan.

'Mr Speir, you are certainly not the one at fault. This is Mr Cooper. He is the brother of my painter friend, Annie. He has come to help me explain.'

Struan snatched off his cap and shook Mr Speir's outstretched hand

'Is there somewhere we can speak in private?' I asked him.

'Of course.' He turned to address the workmen, 'Carry on, gentlemen. If you come back next week, I should have the next window soldered and ready to fit.'

We followed Mr Speir to his drawing room, where he rang the bell and asked his housekeeper for tea. I noticed her glance curiously at Struan in his gardening clothes. Mr Speir, to his credit, hadn't batted an eyelid.

When the woman left the room, I took a deep breath. 'Mr Speir, I've come to relate a terrible story about the death of my father, and I promise you it is not the one you've been told.' I continued to tell him the whole tale and then handed him my father's last letter to me.

He'd looked horrified throughout my speech. His hand shook while he read the letter. 'I invited a viper into our midst. What kind of man would lie about the death of a gentleman who trusted him and deny his daughter the right to be by his side? I am appalled.'

'The kind of man who is wicked beyond measure. He thought or hoped my father was dead when he left him on that ship. I believe he was trying to conceal the fact that he poisoned Papa.'

Mr Speir sat forward on his chair and grabbed the arms. 'What? Surely not!'

'You know I met Professor Jameson in Edinburgh?'

'This man who so helped Andrew in his work and whose office received my correspondence?'

331

'Exactly. When I described Señor de Rias's appearance, he said he had heard of him before.' I passed him Professor Jameson's statement, and also Professor Hutton Balfour's note. 'The esteemed Keeper of the Botanic Gardens had also heard the story. A botanist turned murderer is a sufficiently scandalous tale to spread around the world.'

Mr Speir read the letters. 'Iris, this is horrendous. We must find justice for your father.'

'I'm sorry to have to tell you. He has done you harm, too. Have you received a specimen of this black orchid?'

He shook his head. 'No, but de Rias told me many plants died on the voyage. Perhaps it didn't survive?'

'It certainly survived. Some specimens are to be auctioned in London. Mr Cooper has seen them.'

Mr Speir put his head in his hands. 'Are you telling me this man killed your father for an orchid?' He looked anguished.

'It seems that these plants will fetch hundreds of pounds at the auction. I believe my father's life was indeed extinguished for an orchid. The same orchid my father hoped might be named after me.'

I stifled a sob and Struan moved to the couch and put a comforting arm around me.

'Tell me what you've seen. How can we stop this rogue?' Speir asked Struan. His face was flushed with anger.

'That Wardian case design de Rias brought you was stolen fae a man called William Bull. Bull will aid us in our plan tae put that rogue in jail. But I think we must caw canny. If he knows we are on tae him, he will run. Mr Bull will advise us ae the orchid auction date. I believe this man's failing is arrogance and I dinnae think he'll be able tae stay away.'

I pulled myself together. 'While I want to see de Rias brought to justice, my first duty is to bury my father. This afternoon I'm meeting the Fowlis Wester minister to prepare for the arrival of Papa's coffin. He has agreed the funeral will be on Saturday. When word of that gets out, de Rias will know that my father survived his abandonment and his identity was established. When do you expect him back here?'

Mr Speir rubbed his eyes wearily. 'I'm not sure, and I feel a fool to admit that I have no way of reaching him. He might be back tomorrow for all I know.'

'Then I will continue to stay in seclusion at Drummond Castle.'

'That seems wise,' said Mr Speir.

'We visited the ship's captain to find out more about the shipment of plants. Unfortunately, the cargo manifest simply listed the number of plants without details of the species. Do you happen to know how many plants arrived in Culdees?'

'I do,' Mr Speir replied. 'Three hundred and fifty-one.'

'Then he is a brazen thief. Over four hundred plants were unloaded in Southampton. Might we inspect the plants you received?'

Mr Speir looked close to tears himself. 'You can, but I find I barely care. All my pleasure and excitement about these specimens has evaporated. It was a vain endeavour that resulted in your father's death.'

Struan groaned 'The scoundrel deserves tae be unmasked. I hope, sir, that you will help us catch him. After what he did tae Iris, he shouldnae walk free,' Struan added.

With a deep sigh, Mr Speir said. 'You are right, young man. I will help you if I can.' He took a small key from a hook near the door. 'You'll find the most valuable orchids are in a padlocked glasshouse.'

Chapter Fifty-One

December 1869 – Perthshire

Struan had no notion how he ended up with his arm around Iris. It was not a thing he could have dared to imagine doing, especially not in the presence of Mr Speir. But hearing her voice break, and watching her brave face falter, he couldn't prevent himself. It was simply an instinct. Iris didn't shake his arm off. When she turned her face into his arm, his heart contorted. However, he was acutely aware the gesture was inappropriate. He had to meet Mr Speir's eyes while he described his alliance with William Bull, all the time conscious of where his fingers rested on her flannel sleeve and where Iris's cheek leaned against his elbow. When she recovered herself, he discreetly removed his hand.

Iris asked Mr Buchan to wait here for them, tucked in behind Culdees Castle. Taking her trap towards the stables and glasshouses was too public. Instead, they walked down the track together.

'Are you all right?' Struan asked.

'I fear I might break down every single time I have to describe what happened to Papa. A life taken for an orchid is beyond vile. I feel sick at the thought of even looking at orchids.'

'We dinnae have tae do this now. I could come back later on my own.'

'We should see what arrived at Culdees while de Rias is still away.'

'Do you want tae look for this plant yer pa sent you?' Struan asked nervously. 'I dinnae want tae upset you, but it makes my blood boil tae think that rogue has maybe taken that too.'

'I'm embarrassed to dread it might be the huge orchid I helped him look for, or maybe the black orchid, since it reminded him of an iris?'

'Perhaps he labelled the plant for you? But if it's a valuable orchid I'm sure we willnae find it here.'

Nearing the end of the track, they cut through in front of the lodge to reach the hothouses. The extra structures Mr Speir had built over the summer were filled with new plants. The outer glasshouse contained a wide variety of species, including some strange-looking shrubs Struan couldn't name. One spikey-leaved specimen had an enormous but now fading bright orange flower, with yellow tips. He doubted it could live outside in Scotland, so would be imprisoned under glass forever. He was more interested to see a salvia that might be suitable for a colder climate. The shrivelled and dry blue and white flowers on a hairy stalk were almost as tall as him. Finally, they reached orchids, which were suspended at head height, allowing the blooms to cascade down. At the end of that row was a glass door, through which they could see some enormous orchids.

Iris reached out for his hand, squeezed it, then slipped the small key into his palm. They had crossed some threshold where such physical contact seemed natural. Struan hoped he hid the extent to which it made his heart leap.

'Would you go in? I don't think I can,' Iris whispered.

Inside, the temperature was higher and the air more humid, reminding Struan of the glasshouse where William Bull had shown him the black orchid. There were a dozen orchids, two with eight-inch blooms. One variety was frilly, white with yellow centres, another cream with lilac-coloured spots. However, there was nothing like the dark orchid he had seen in London. He was bending in to examine the roots of one of the flowers when he heard the door open and a cold draught swept past him. Iris's scent and the sound of her breathing into the silence, sent the hairs up on the back of his neck. He daren't turn in case he gave his feelings away.

Her fingers reached past his arm to touch the orchid's aerial roots. 'Imagine, Papa took this down from the high branches of some tree in faraway Ecuador,' she whispered.

'I wonder which one is being named in his honour?' Struan said.

'I hope the white one,' Iris replied. 'Pure like his soul.'

She sighed. 'I must go. Mr Cowan is expecting me in Fowlis Wester.'

The next day, Struan was tending to the rose hybrids when he saw Mr MacDonald coming across the garden with Mr Speir. He walked onto the path to meet them.

'Mr MacDonald has just been singing your praises, Mr Cooper. Which makes it all the more remarkable that he is happy to lend you to me for an urgent piece of work.'

'Mr MacDonald knows the truth of Miss Cooper's bereavement,' Struan added.

Mr MacDonald nodded. 'That poor Miss Finlay has been so cruelly bereaved makes me furious. If you think Struan can help catch that man, I'd be delighted,' MacDonald said.

'What do you have in mind?' Struan asked.

'I want to find out what the man is up to,' Mr Speir said. 'He sent a note saying he is going to the Botanic Gardens tomorrow, and requesting time to visit more breeders in the area.'

'No doubt selling the plants he robbed fae you,' Struan said. 'Should I tell the police?'

Mr Speir shook his head. 'The man belongs in jail, but we lack proof. I need someone to track his movements. Am I right that this rogue doesn't know you?'

'He has seen me here in the garden, but I'm sure he won't remember.'

'Well, go and get ready, lad. It's off to the big city for you again,' said Mr MacDonald.

'I've already appraised Lady Walker of the plan,' Mr Speir added.

Struan did up the buckles on his knapsack. Luckily, the guesthouse he'd found in Edinburgh would process laundry, for he hadn't nearly enough suitable clothes for city living. He heard a trap outside. Expecting Mr Buchan bringing letters from Iris to take to Professor Jameson and Professor Hutton Balfour, he opened the door. Instead, there was the glorious sight of Iris herself heading across the yard.

'I brought you the letters in person because we had an exciting delivery this morning and I wanted to bring Annie her copy.' Iris held up two copies of a pamphlet with Annie's winter drawing on the front.

Struan leaned against the range and offered his seat to Iris. They only had two proper chairs.

Annie's delight when she looked at the little magazine made him even happier.

'Iris! It's simply beautiful,' she said.

'I'm glad tae see you before I go, Iris,' he risked adding.

'I wanted to thank you in person for undertaking this on my behalf. Mr Speir called in to describe his plan. I must admit I'd like to know what de Rias is up to. I wonder if he will see the announcement about Papa's funeral? It's going in *The Scotsman* today.

'Och, Iris. Here's me prattling on about our publication and you're planning a funeral. It's just too sad. What day will it be held?' Annie asked.

'On Saturday,' Iris said.

'I'd like tae come. I'm sure I can find someone making the journey from Muthill if Struan isn't back.'

'Have you a plan for how long you'll stay in Edinburgh?' Iris asked him.

'As long as that rascal stays there,' Struan replied. 'Mr Speir has given me a generous allowance in case it takes some time. But I'm thinking the news of the funeral might send him running. I cannae imagine what excuse he could give you for leaving yer ailing faither behind.'

'I hope it's a terrible shock to him that I've come home with a body to bury, but he won't know how I came to hear, or that I've heard the stories from Argentina.' Iris placed her hand on Struan's arm. 'Do be careful, Struan. If he guesses things are closing in on him, it could make him dangerous.'

'Poisoners and thieves are sleekit and wicked but no brave. De Rias doesnae frighten me.'

'He is a rat, and that type can turn when they are frightened.' Iris slid her hand down his forearm and squeezed his wrist. Struan's heart did an actual jump. Iris turned towards Annie. 'I've come to ask you to come back with me to Drummond Castle. My aunt is insistent that you shouldn't remain here alone. I would appreciate it too. I need to make plans for the funeral. I'll get strength from your support.'

'I'm most sorry that I'll likely miss the funeral,' Struan

said, 'and it's terrible cold weather to be standing in a graveyard.'

'It is and of course neither Annie nor Aunt Leonora are robust enough for that.'

Annie turned towards Iris with a determined look. 'I'll be at your side when you need me. I havenae had breathing problems much this winter.'

'Because, thank God, you've no been on yer knees scrubbing tiles and blackening doorsteps,' Struan said.

Annie held up the magazine and smiled shyly. 'I'm a fancy published artist nowadays.'

Iris smiled at Annie. 'Our book comes out next week, too. The formal invitations to the launch in Edinburgh came for us both when I was in London. But I also got a condolence note from Mr White yesterday, and he said he would understand if I didn't feel able to come.'

'I certainly shan't go without you,' Annie said.

'I can barely think past Saturday, but I would also love to hold the book in my hands,' Iris replied.

'It's vile that he could be allowed to take that from you too,' Struan muttered. He glanced up at the clock. 'I'd better go. I need tae reach Edinburgh before it's too late tae disturb Mr and Mrs Donaldson.'

'I've written to them.' Iris handed him the three envelopes.

Annie stood to hug him. There was an awkward second where he considered hugging Iris, too. Instead, he raised his hand, feeling foolish.

Iris rushed to embrace him. 'Be careful,' she whispered in his ear. Those words and her warm breath on his neck almost had him on the floor.

Chapter Fifty-Two

December 1869 – Perthshire

Mr Cowan had volunteered to have my father's coffin in his house for the two days before the funeral. This was a relief. I was loathe to ask to take it to Drummond Castle, and most people who would want to pay their respects would be from his old congregation. Also, and most importantly, I had little idea what had to be done. I'd coped with all the terrible things I'd faced in recent days, but this task dumbfounded me. Aunt Leonora was having a bad week so I didn't want to bother her with questions.

On the afternoon of the coffin's arrival by train, Aunt Leonora woke up in pain. Annie volunteered to stay with her and I proceeded to Crieff Station alone and from there to Fowlis Wester. I arrived to find the room assigned for the coffin, filled with flowers. Mrs Munro came in and rushed to enfold me in her arms.

'Och, Iris. I'm so very sorry. And don't you worry, I'll sort everything out.

The hall's clock was silent and covered by a sheet. The mirror in this room was covered too. Mrs Munro opened all the windows. Every action reminded me of the days after my mother's death. My mind had locked these memories away but not lost them. I could hear my breathing fast and shallow. The undertakers came in bearing the coffin, and Mrs Munro instructed them.

'When did you father pass?' she asked me.

'Last week,' I said. My voice sounded strangely far away.

Mrs Munro made a 'tsk' noise and gathered up some hot-housed lilies from amongst the flower gifts. The smell hit me with horrible familiarity. The floor rushed up towards me.

When I came round, I was sitting in an armchair in the sitting room and Mr Cowan was beside me, looking anxious. They fussed around me like a child.

'She is just a lassie, this is too much tae ask ae her,' Mrs Munro said, her face tear-streaked.

'Miss Finlay, let us help. We will deal with people calling to pay their respects. Then, I'll keep the service short and Mr Bruce will organise the men to assist me with the burial. Having the service on a Saturday is fitting for a minister of the parish and many will attend,' Mr Cowan said.

'I am most grateful, but I must see my father to the end of this journey. I was not allowed to go to my mother's burial but I as his only living relative, I insist on it.'

After I sufficiently recovered, they sent me back to Drummond Castle and instructed Mr Buchan to ensure that I didn't climb stairs unaccompanied. I felt like a stupid baby and also very relieved. I couldn't imagine how I would face people's questions about my father's death. How could I could dissemble in a Church of Scotland manse?

I woke on the morning of the funeral to find the world covered in snow. Baroness de Willoughby had sent her condolences from Grimsthorpe Castle and told us to use her large carriage. We would be glad of it today. It would protect us from the weather and was large enough for four people. Lady Bradley had arrived the day before. This lovely surprise had caused Aunt Leonora to cry.

'I will sleep in Leo's bed,' Lady Georgina had said. 'We shared as girls, and it seems fitting to come full circle. When I said goodbye last time, I feared we might not meet again. Having been blessed with more time together, I want to be with her for every minute.'

In the morning, I went up to find Annie up from her couch and already dressed.

Lady Georgina emerged from Aunt Leonora's bedroom. 'I told Leo to rest a little longer. I'll take a breakfast tray in to her. Also, I forgot to say yesterday. Princess Louise sent a mourning dress up for you, Iris. It's one she wore when her father died and is too small for her.' She nodded towards a black dress that was draped on the end of the couch. Wide-sleeved, buttoned down the front, it was a little old-fashioned, but stroking the silk upper I could tell it was very much finer than the one I'd bought in a last minute dash to a London store.

'You must tell her how thankful I am. Her kindness is a light on a very dark day.'

'Her intervention ensured I was able to be here. She wanted to come to the funeral, but the Queen wants her on the Isle of Wight next week and was worried that snow might trap her up north. Christmas was important to Prince Albert, and the Queen is superstitious about having all her children around her.'

When we reached the manse, the undertaker's carriage pulled by black horses was already there with the coffin inside. Many of Papa's congregation lined the streets and filed behind us, as we slowly made our way up to the church. It took an immense effort to keep my composure. I saw Mr Speir's carriage outside and found he and his wife in the second pew. The church was bitterly cold and I felt everyone's eyes on my back. After raising my eyes above the coffin to the stained glass windows, I squeezed them closed in prayer. I was determined not to break down and barely heard the minister's words. Aunt Leonora's hand on my knee told me it was over.

Once outside, Lady Georgina was adamant that walking through the snow to the grave was too much for Annie and Aunt Leonora.

'I'm sure I can manage,' Annie argued.

At that moment, an old man in front of us nearly fell when his stick skidded in the snow.

'Please stay safe in the carriage, I'll go to the graveside with Iris, Annie,' said a voice at my elbow.

I turned to see Mrs Birnie.

We took a few steps down the treacherous path, then Mr Bruce, my father's elder, appeared at our side. He bowed his head, 'I am so very sorry, Miss Finlay. This is a terrible day.' He inclined his head to Mrs Birnie, too. 'I didn't know you were acquainted with Mr Finlay.' Mr Bruce offered us his elbows as steadying arms down the path.

'With every single ecclesiastical man in this corner of Perthshire, I should think. I have been lucky enough to know Iris since she was a little girl. Her father used to bring her with him to the library. I think he would be so proud to know she will become a published author of an illustrated gardener's companion next week.'

'I've always seen God's glory in nature's flowers. You will be pleased to hear that my father found his way back to God in the high mountains of Ecuador.'

'Miss Finlay, I cannot tell you how pleased I am to hear that,' Mr Bruce said.

The snow was now coming down at a forty-five degree angle. The sight of the gash of open black earth amongst the snow-covered graves gripped my chest like a vice. I'd insisted on being here and breathed deeply to fight an urge to faint. Mr Cowan began his graveside words as soon as I was beside him. There were some anxious moments when the pall bearers tried to find steady footing in the frozen mud, whilst bringing the coffin over the grave. The anxiety of that kept my tears at bay. They lowered father's coffin into the spot beside my mother's. I crouched to take a handful of earth and fling it on top. 'She's waiting for you now, Papa. I love you.'

Mrs Birnie's arm slipped through mine. The wet hankie I was screwing between my fingers was now useless. She quietly slipped me a dry one.

Mr Buchan stood waiting beside the carriage. Annie's anxious face was at the window.

'Mrs Munro has organised tea at the manse. I've agreed to their insistence that I need not be there.'

'I'll go home to Mr Birnie, now. It's good you have your friend by your side. I hope you can rest tomorrow but you would both be welcome at the library on Monday, if you feel up to it,' Mrs Birnie said.

'Thank you. I think Aunt Leonora would appreciate some time alone with her friend. Lady Bradley will go back to Her Majesty soon.'

'They are an inspirational example of the endurance of female friendship.'

On Monday, Annie and I went to Innerpeffray Library. Being back in such a happy place after these terrible weeks pricked my eyes with threatened tears. I shook my head, breathed deeply, then hugged Mrs Birnie.

'My spirits are so raw. It has been the strangest month.

Annie and I had just signed contracts with our Edinburgh publisher, when I got word that my father was in hospital in London.'

Mrs Birnie had bent over the desk to admire our winter pamphlet. Her head snapped up in surprise. 'I thought your father died on the ship.'

I shook my head and told her about finding him in hospital and spending the night beside his bed.

'I don't understand. How was he left in London? I saw the Spanish gentleman in Muthill two weeks ago.'

I glanced at Annie. 'I can't prove it but I believe he thought Papa so close to death that he'd get away with it. We are convinced the man we know as Rafael de Rias poisoned my father.'

Christian Birnie gasped. Her hands flew to her face. 'You must go to the police, Iris.'

'I have no proof. We believe he is a thief, too. Some plants that came here from Ecuador didn't make it to Culdees Castle.' I brought her up-to-date with Professor Jameson's tale and how Struan was presently in Edinburgh, trying to work out what de Rias was up to.

'Well, I'm glad young Struan is helping you. He's a good lad.'

I smiled at Annie. 'So I have learned.'

Mrs Birnie went off to get the 1868 back copy of *The Floral Magazine* we'd asked her to order for us. Annie wanted to do some draft sketches for Mr White and required some ideas for fresh pictures. It was good to have a task to concentrate on and by the end of the afternoon, Annie had sketches of a couple of pelargoniums, a pansy and a camelia and I'd drafted some words.

'I think this year I'll start sketching my own ideas from gardens,' Annie said.

'Good plan,' I said. 'We might take a walk around Drummond Castle to search for things that will work in a small garden. We should start winter 1870 now.'

Before we left, I spoke quietly to Mrs Birne. 'I need your advice. Annie and I are invited to Edinburgh at the end of this week. Mr White has printed all four seasonal pamphlets as a book. There is to be a reception. I must let him know if we will come, but we really shouldn't in the circumstances.'

'What would your father say?'

'I'm certain he would tell us to go. A published book is a dream come true for Annie and me and this may never happen again.'

'Then you have your answer. In any case, people in Edinburgh won't know your mourning attire is recent.'

'I must go to find some proof to prevent de Rias from coming back to Culdees.'

'I hope you find evidence,' Mrs Birnie replied. 'It's impossible to contemplate him strolling around as a free man.'

'I'm dreading meeting him, to be honest. I don't trust myself not to strike him.'

'I'll whack him wi' my stick,' Annie added with feeling. 'Teach him to walk about wi' a cane when he disnae need one.'

Chapter Fifty-Three

December 1869 – Edinburgh

S truan was furious before the man even opened his mouth. Just the look of de Rias, preening himself in a tight-fitting navy coat and trews and wearing a wholly false smile under his shiny silk topper, had him balling his fists in rage. This man had ruined Iris's life, yet there he stood, looking completely guilt free. If anything, de Rias's arrogance had grown. His strutting demeanour reminded Struan of Mr Speir's prize peacocks. He'd like to take that shiny ebony cane and break it over his head. The cane enraged Annie. She was furious about being taken in by a man who used a cane as a mere stylish accessory.

Botany students gathered to witness Mr Speir's orchids being named and inducted, which must mean that de Rias surely had no clue that Iris had the measure of him. Struan's task today was to lurk at the back. To watch and wait for the right moment. It took a huge effort.

Alexander Donaldson was in the group, but Professor Jameson wasn't present. Struan met with him and Professor Hutton Balfour that morning and they decided the professor's presence in Edinburgh would spook de Rias and the

Ecuador connection might cause students to ask awkward questions. The subject came up anyway.

A tall student spoke. 'Professor Jameson's talks on Ecuadorian regions helped us to understand the complexity of this great country. What is your view on this country as a botanical source?'

De Rias's confident demeanour wobbled. 'Many South American countries share the mighty Andes mountains and that lends an extra dimension to the climate.' He was waffling, and Struan could tell he was rattled. 'Is this man one of your professors? I don't think I know him?'

A lie. Rafael would have heard the name from Andrew Finlay.

'Oh no,' the hapless, student continued. 'Professor Jameson from Quito University is a Scotsman who is fully settled in Ecuador. We are most lucky to have him visiting us in Edinburgh this year.'

De Rias's colour faded. His jaw twitched. 'Ah yes, of course, but he was not in Ecuador when I visited.'

Struan grimaced. Was the game up? Although he knew this stage was imminent. The announcement about Iris's father's funeral today had been in the press. De Rias might immediately change his plans. The recent development was that Professor Hutton Balfour had been contacted by a laird on the edge of Edinburgh, who told him de Rias had volunteered to assist him in some South American plant hunting. But, even if he was out of their lives, they must surely prevent the wretch from inveigling others into his web. At the end of the lecture, Struan followed de Rias out onto Inverleith Row. There was a carriage waiting for him and it sped de Rias away. Struan cursed himself for not anticipating this likelihood.

Struan returned to Professor Hutton Balfour's room to discover the botanists in heated debate. Professor Jameson wanted the police called in immediately, whilst Professor

Hutton Balfour preferred to give de Rias further time to further hang himself.

'What are your thoughts, Mr Cooper?' Professor Jameson asked. 'This scoundrel clearly has no idea about Ecuador.'

'I agree, Professor, but I fear it's an argument too subtle for the average Edinburgh policeman. I'd liked tae have caught him selling something that belonged to another. That was our hope wi' the London auction.'

'And there is no news on that?' Professor Hutton Balfour asked.

'Not yet. Mr Bull sent me a note tae say the auction had been delayed until next week.'

'Well, I have a present problem. Mr Crawford, is recruiting a plant hunter. He has asked me for a reference for this gentleman and I clearly cannot give one. I referred the man to Mr Speir.'

'I think that is the wisest option. Mr Speir is aware of the missing plants, as well as de Rias's violent history. I'm sure he wouldn't give a good reference.'

'Then it's time to advise the police to be ready to pounce. I've invited Mr Crawford to Mr White's book launch for Annie and Iris on Friday, and suggested he bring Señor de Rias along. If the bounder has the nerve to turn up, the bobbies will have him.'

'I'll drop a note tae the girls.'

Struan posted his note to Annie and Iris. He missed them both so much, and love for Iris was a source of near constant and worsening pain. He feared he might soon give himself away and embarrass Annie. Was he brave enough to put an end to pointless agony? Surely getting out of their lives was the only sensible answer. He reread the last paragraph in Mr Bull's last letter.

I'm most sorry that you're not now hurrying back to London as we expected. You should know I have prepared an official offer of employment for you. The more I think on it, the more I'm convinced it is the right thing to do. I have ambitions to expand my business and need a young man like you in my close team. I will, of course, offer a handsome salary to entice you to London.

Struan's time in Edinburgh had opened his eyes to the extent of Iris and Annie's triumph. Professor Hutton Balfour assured him they could expect a lucrative career ahead. It was the best news for them both. Jock confided that he planned to ask Annie for her hand, when his January pay rise came through, Struan's sister would be well looked after. Capturing de Rias would be his last act of devotion to Iris. Time to stop moping around like a devoted puppy.

Two days before the book launch, Struan was in a meeting Professor Hutton Balfour had called with James White. They'd decided that the publisher should be briefed about the planned police presence. The Donaldsons were at the meeting too.

Professor Hutton Balfour placed his clasped hands on the table. 'I need your permission for this, James. It might spoil the atmosphere of the party.'

Elspeth Donaldson's tears spilled over. 'Papa, please. I cannot imagine how poor Iris has coped with keeping this secret, along with all her other trials. Surely we should help?'

James White rubbed his hands together. 'Of course, we'll help. I've already asked *The Scotsman* to send a reporter. Don't worry about the atmosphere. If they get a scoop on the snagging a South American felon, it will be the talk of Edinburgh. Nothing sells books like a sniff of scandal.'

'I never considered our book to be scandalous, Mr White. Please enlighten us.'

Struan's heart did a backwards somersault at the sound of Iris's voice. He reached out his arm as she and Annie walked further into the room. Iris squeezed his hand before Elspeth Donaldson wrapped herself around her. Iris looked stunning. All in black, of course, but the coat and veiled hat contrasted beautifully with her shining blonde hair. He had to content himself with a hug from Annie, who also looked extremely smart in a new black coat and hat. 'You look like a sophisticated city lady,' he whispered to his sister.

'Iris had an outfit from Princess Louise and I raided Lady Walker's wardrobe,' she whispered back.

Professor Hutton Balfour welcomed both women. 'We have a plan to flush the South American out at the book launch, Iris. Do you mind?'

'Mind? Of course not. I placed my darling father in a snowy grave on Saturday because of that bounder.'

'I can't promise the plan will work. Sit down and you can tell us your opinion,' Professor Hutton Balfour said.

Annie slipped Struan an envelope. 'An update from Mr Bull.' he said, recognising the handwriting.

While Professor Hutton Balfour sought Iris's agreement to go with him and Professor Jameson to brief the constabulary, Struan pushed his thumb in to break the envelope seal. He was relieved it didn't contain an employment contract for he still hadn't decided, and when he read the contents, he couldn't prevent a laugh.

'They cancelled the auction,' he said. The orchids lost all their blooms one-by-one and are clearly dying.'

Professor Jameson gasped. 'Tell me, Mr Cooper. What were the conditions in that London greenhouse?'

'Much like the large palm house here. Warm and humid.'

Jameson shook his head. His expression was scornful. 'That's what happens when the plantsman lacks the advice of the real plant hunter. Mr Finlay was searching in the highest cloud forest in Ecuador. It is a very rainy, and relatively cool environment. If Andrew found a black orchid there, it would die in humid warmth.'

Iris pushed her veil off her forehead. The slow smile that spread over her face felt to Struan like a warm balm. 'A fitting outcome. But surely these buyers in London will be furious?'

'They are. Bull says that Archie Chalmers, the rascal who brokered the orchids, told the police all about the chap he knew of as Alfredo da Silva. The police have posted a search warrant with a reward.'

'Miss Finlay, if you have the energy, I believe we should visit the police station today,' Professor Hutton Balfour suggested.

Struan pocketed the final sheet of the letter.

I sent the employment offer to your home address. I suggest a start date of 1st January.

Chapter Fifty-Four

December 1869 – Edinburgh

I should be quietly mourning my father at home, but quiet prayer doesn't sit well when one's soul is tormented with anger. It was my Christian duty to forgive de Rias, but the news that he was so lacking in remorse that he was trying to join another plant hunting expedition, had me raging. Surely I must protect others from my sad fate? When I entered Professor Hutton Balfour's lecture theatre, I thought there was a stranger present. The realisation that the handsome gentleman at the front was actually Struan in a new suit was a jolt. I'd caught myself creating an excuse to see him before he travelled south last week. My devastation and utter grief were very real. How could I entertain other feelings, too? It was a mystery, but I was very glad to have someone I trusted completely at my side. In fact, this gathering had brought together so many friends. My world had expanded beyond recognition. That we were united in working against de Rias made me hope for the very first time, that we might prevail.

. . .

Annie and I went to visit Bartholomew's printers with Mr White the next day.

'I must confess to changing the title,' Mr White said.

Annie and I both cradled a book in our hands. *A Ladies' Gardening Companion* was emblazoned in red on the front. I frowned. 'There is nothing in the content that it is specifically for ladies.'

'I know, and I apologise for not consulting you both. However, it has been a huge rush to get it printed this month and the feedback we got from early readers was conclusive. There is a growing market for books aimed at female gardening enthusiasts and we expect a lot of our purchasers will be gentlemen delighted to have a suitable Christmas gift for their wives.'

Annie looked towards Mr White, her eyes full of emotion. 'Thank you, Mr White. It is simply beautiful,' she murmured.

I felt chastised. The book was indeed beautiful and what did I know about marketing books? Annie's drawing of the wintry garden was in directly after the title page. The flashes of red berries and on Aunt Leonora's robin were particularly effective.

'Mr White, you have done such an amazing job in such a short time. I'm so glad I got the chance to describe the venture to my papa. I only wish he were here to see it.' At that, my eyes filled. Annie squeezed my hand and I managed to compose myself. 'Tell me, Mr White. How do you really feel about a police presence at the event? I think de Rias is unlikely to come, but if he does, there will be a scene.'

'Delighted to help. I'm disgusted by what happened to you and your father. If there is anything else I can do to bring this rogue to justice, please just tell me.'

. . .

Mr White had hired a hall in the Assembly Rooms in Edinburgh's George Street. In the afternoon, he announced that a rush for ticket sales had moved the event to a larger room. I was so caught up in thoughts about de Rias, that nerves hit me only then.

'What if people expect me to be an expert gardener? I can tell you the Latin name for almost every flower, but don't ask me for advice on soil or garden pests. I'm not a proper gardener at all.'

'Couldn't Struan back us up for such questions?' Annie asked.

'I'll likely no be beside you, Annie. My task is watching oot for de Rias.'

'Surely he won't come? My name is on the book. He is bound to make the connection.'

'I've seen Mr White's guest list. Every horticultural family in Scotland is on it. Remember, White Publishers has all the contacts through publishing Professor Hutton Balfour. It is the type of gathering which might just tempt de Rias. His contract wi' that Mr Crawford isnae signed yet,' Struan said.

'Good,' I said. 'Mr Speir told me he's coming down. He has delayed responding to Mr Crawford. It gives us the chance to entice de Rias into the trap.'

Struan left the Donaldsons early to scout the room out before guests arrived. Mr White picked Annie and me up, and Elspeth was most excited to be part of the authorial party. Alexander Donaldson had opted to go with Struan, keen to be involved in de Rias's capture. When the carriage turned off Hanover Street into George Street, we found it blocked by dozens of vehicles.

Mr White leaned across the carriage to Annie and me. 'Congratulations on this crowd. Yours is the publication of the year, ladies. I have already ordered a second and larger print run.'

When we eventually reached the Assembly Rooms entrance, Mr White was a well enough known figure in Edinburgh to attract attention and a murmur of recognition scurried through the throng of ladies near the door.

Mr White whispered, 'Your audience awaits you.'

We entered the foyer, then went up a flight of stairs. Inside a very busy room, we were led towards the stage. My heart thudded at the thought of being the centre of attention. Professor Hutton Balfour was already sitting on the stage. Mr White had apparently persuaded him to say a few words. I took Annie's hand as we ascended the stairs and sat side-by-side. She was very pale, and I guessed was as terrified as me.

Mr White stood up first and said a lot of kind words about Annie and me. How taken he had been with our excellent idea, and how surprised to find out our relative youth.

Then Professor Hutton Balfour stood. 'I have a letter of recommendation to read from Her Majesty's daughter, Her Royal Highness Princess Louise.'

There was a murmur of appreciation in the crowd, and I exchanged a look with Annie. I'd had a letter of condolence from the Princess, but hadn't read the glowing contents of her letter to Mr White. Movement at the back of the hall caught my attention. Two policemen entered and stood on either side of the door. We had set the net, but was de Rias even here? I spotted Struan walking around the perimeter. Alexander Donaldson was circling the other side of the room, his expression was tense. I assumed they hadn't found de Rias. Professor Hutton Balfour quoted Princess Louise as calling me a special friend. An exaggeration, of course, but I could see the effect on the upturned faces of the dozens of ladies near the front. When the speeches were over, Annie and I were asked to stand for the applause, and I thanked everyone for coming. Mr White urged everyone to come up to meet us at the signing table.

For the next half hour, I was completely busy exchanging pleasantries with people and signing copies of the book. The introduction of a gentleman grabbed my attention.

'Iris, this is Mr Crawford. He is very eager to meet you,' said Mr White.

I looked up at the tall red-haired man in front of me.

'I believe we have an acquaintance in common, Miss Finlay. At least he told me he accompanied your father to Ecuador.'

My cheeks were burning. I took a deep breath and reminded myself that this hapless man was innocent. 'My late father spent several years searching for plants in Ecuador. What is the name of your acquaintance?'

'Your father has passed?' The red-haired man looked confused. 'Mr de Rias didn't mention that.'

'Did Señor de Rias accompany you today?' I asked, a tremor in my voice.

'He did. He has been staying on my estate. We've been discussing how to populate the new glasshouses I'm planning.'

Professor Hutton Balfour came to stand at my elbow. Mr Crawford smiled broadly. 'John, there you are. You owe me a letter.'

'Apologies, Graham. It's been a busy month. I hear you have acquired a new orchid.'

Mr Crawford leaned towards the botanist. 'Señor de Rias has sold me a specimen that you must come and see. He promised there is no other in the country.'

Professor Hutton Balfour raised his eyebrows. 'What colour is this plant, Graham?'

Mr Crawford looked very excited. 'You will not believe this, John. But this orchid is black.'

I heard Annie gasp.

A shout came from the back of the room. Alexander Donaldson was running towards the door. 'He's there, Struan. Stop him!'

A tall man in a hat and cloak sped for the exit, shouldering a policeman out of his path. Struan ran towards him. The man stood suddenly still and tall. His arm arced as he unsheathed his cane above his head. There was a glint of steel. A woman screamed. The blade came down and Struan clutched at his shoulder, a blossom of red on his shirt. He disappeared from view.

Annie shouted 'Struan!'

'No!' I pushed my chair over and leapt down from the stage, then broke into a run towards the back of the room.

Chapter Fifty-Five

December 1869 – Edinburgh & Perthshire

De Rias sliced the second policeman's arm to make his escape. Another charge to the long list against this felon. Kneeling beside Struan, I feared I would lose him. My skirts were soaked with blood, it was clear Struan's life was in danger.

The room was in chaos.

Someone shouted, 'Chase him.'

Another, 'Get a doctor!'

Panic rose in my chest. I grasped Struan's hand. 'Don't you dare die on me, Struan Cooper. I cannot lose you too.' He smiled at me but I thought his face was getting paler by the second. His brown eyes flickered, please God, not flickering out. 'Keep your eyes open.'

Alexander Donaldson knelt beside me. 'Press your shawl over the wound,' Then he used his tie around Struan's shoulder to stem the bleeding.

'Should we take him to the Royal Infirmary?' Elspeth said.

'My good friend Joseph Lister is back in Edinburgh,' said Mr White. 'I'll send word for him to meet us at your home and he will advise us,' Mr White said.

. . .

The Donaldsons had Struan installed in their spare room. Mr Lister thought Struan stable enough to keep him there and to let Alexander keep an eye on him. He emphasised his advice to wash the wound with carbolic soap and keep it clean. Elspeth promised to feed him broths and stews to get over the loss of blood.

'He's not out of the woods yet, but I'm hopeful,' was Alexander's opinion the next morning.

The scandal made the front page of *The Scotsman*. The illustration on the front showed a lady author on her knees in front of the wounded young hero. Their enraptured expressions informed the nation and made me face the evident truth of my love.

Later, Annie turned up white-faced with a sheet of paper in her hand. 'I wanted to wash Struan's clothes and I found this in his trouser pocket.'

I sent the employment offer to your home address. I suggest a start date of 1st January.

'That's Mr Bull's handwriting. Did Struan plan to go to London?' I said.

'He's not fit to go anywhere, but, Iris, does he think I'd go with him? I don't want to live in London.' Annie was distraught.

I hugged her. 'We must make sure he gets better and knows we need him here.'

. . .

A few days later, Alexander Donaldson declared Struan fit to travel. He and Annie were installed in Culdees Castle, where Mr Speir had Struan under doctor's supervision. In Drummond Castle, I explained the whole story to Aunt Leonora and Lady Bradley, who'd sought leave to cover my absence.

'What drama and poor Mr Cooper. They didn't find de Rias yet?' Aunt Leonora asked.

I shook my head. 'Not yet. The police are searching.'

There was something in my aunt's expression which made me look again. After a heartbeat of silence, my aunt began. 'George and I have been reflecting on my life and considering whether we made a mistake,' she said.

'I've decided I am doing you a disservice in being less than honest. I want you to go on in your life knowing who I really am.'

Lady Georgina raised my aunt's fingers to her lips and kissed them.

'I don't think anyone imagined I was in love when I married Lord Archibald. Perhaps his friends might have used the term lavender marriage. Archibald found himself in need of a wife when he was threatened with exposure in a London scandal. What nobody realised was the dissembling was as true for me as it was for Archie.' Aunt Leonora stretched out to take both of Lady Georgina's hands. 'I never loved Archie, but I have loved George nearly all my life.'

Lady Georgina kissed my aunt's cheek. A gesture full of tenderness.

'You are old enough to be asked to understand, and I don't want to die a stranger to you,' Aunt Leonora said.

I nodded, too stunned to find the words to reply.

'We had hoped that we might live together when I retired from the Queen's service,' Lady Georgina said. 'I am heartbroken to realise that we'll never fulfil our dream.'

Aunt Leonora leaned over and placed her hands on my knees. I covered them with mine. 'I'm so sorry,' I said.

'Don't make my mistake in your life, Iris. You needn't make a bad marriage to provide a safe home. I've asked my lawyer to draw up a new will, and I want you to know about it now. My early death means I will never get to the end of poor softie Archie's inheritance. I am passing it all onto you, with the instructions that you must use it to buy your own property. Something that remains in your ownership if you choose to marry.'

I knelt in front of the couch to hug them both in turn. 'I hope you will live for a great deal longer.'

'Oh, I've no plan for an imminent exit. But I might not make it to your wedding.'

'Did you guess that I have someone in mind?' I whispered. 'I thought you'd consider me too young.'

'My advice as an old woman is to follow your heart, Iris.'

Next morning I received a note from Struan.

Meet me in the Culdees glasshouses in an hour. Come alone.

I didn't delay and finding Mr Buchan wasn't in the stables, I attached Daisy to the gig, her leg having fully healed. 'Come on, old girl. We have an important meeting.'

I found Struan inside the first glasshouse, a white bandage, keeping his left hand strapped up to prevent him moving his shoulder. He grinned when I entered, then reached out to take my hand.

'I'm surprised Annie let you out of your sick room.'

'I asked her tae cover for my absconding and promised

362

she would be the very next person tae hear, if my guess is right.'

Struan stepped sideways to reveal a bright lilac lupin plant on the bench behind him. I clapped my hand over my mouth. 'How did you guess?'

'I had a thocht. Four hundred and one plants on the ship's manifest was a strange number. All the other specimens are pairs. Three hundred and fifty-one reached Mr Speir, so I yesterday I asked about any odd plants arriving in the Culdees glasshouses.'

My chest ached at the realisation. 'Oh, Papa. I forgot about the lupin.'

'In one of his first letters, he described them...' I couldn't continue, as the bitter poignancy of the lupin with the non-poisonous seeds hit me.

Struan encircled me with his good arm. 'Don't cry, Iris,' he whispered into my hair.

'He said they looked just like the lupins in Scotland.'

I cradled the pot in my hands. A wooden label was pushed into the soil. *To replant in our Culdees garden,* was written in my father's handwriting. 'A final gift,' I murmured.

'A common lupin, de Rias wouldnae be interested than that,' Struan said.

'It's more precious to me than the most valuable orchid.' As I leaned over to replace the lupin on the bench, the clay pot fell off and shattered on the ground. 'Oh, no!'

'Dinnae worry, Iris. I'll get it a new pot, till you want tae plant it.'

'Look at this, Struan.' I'd cupped the root ball with my hand as the pot fell. There nestled amongst the white roots was a nugget of gold.

'Truly a precious gift fae yer father, that's lovely, Iris.'

'Enough gold for a wedding ring,' I whispered, staring into

his heavenly brown eyes. 'My aunt advised me to follow my heart.' Then I kissed him.

'Your aunt would surely advise you tae choose a gentleman.' Struan pulled away, looking hurt and confused.

'I think we all underestimated my aunt. Do you think she sent you to help me without knowing she thrust us together?'

He frowned. 'Don't toy wi' me, Iris. You must know how I love you.'

'And I love you. I've my father's money from Mr Speir and my aunt will give me funds to buy a house. What I have in mind is a house with a garden and grounds to build a nursery business. Marry me, Struan, and we will do this together.'

Struan shook his head. 'I had dreamed of asking you. Now you are even further out ae my league. People will tell you it's foolish tae marry a poor gardener.'

'I might answer you were foolish to fling yourself in front of a Spanish rapier without asking such an important question first.'

Struan smiled. 'I doubt I'd have summoned the nerve. I'd thought ae moving tae London tae escape the pain ae living wi'out you.'

'Annie found the letter. I hope you didn't think we would allow that. Mr Bull can find another assistant.'

Struan beamed. 'I've the best news. The police have de Rias. William Bull wrote tae say he'd men in every port and his people in Dover recognised de Rias trying tae board a boat tae France. He might have ditched his lethal cane, but he cannae grow a new finger.'

'Will they charge him with Papa's murder?'

'I'm no sure, but even if they cannae, there's the thefts and wounding a policeman is a serious charge.'

I hugged Struan with joy. 'Are you going make this day perfect by answering my question?'

'Can I answer it wi' another? Iris Finlay, will you marry me?'

'I will,' I replied.

Chapter Fifty-Six

June 1870 – Perthshire

S truan swept Lady Leonora up in his arms and carried
her to the top of the Culdees Castle stairs. There, he
deposited her in her wheeled chair. Lady Georgina
kissed her papery cheek and pushed her to her place in
Culdees Castle chapel. Struan walked to the front to await
Iris's arrival. Today was the second weekend in June, almost
exactly six months since Andrew Finlay died. It had become
very obvious that Iris's aunt wouldn't be with them for much
longer, and she so wanted to attend the wedding. It was
Robert Speir who had suggested the castle chapel as a venue
for a small and private event. He had also volunteered to walk
Iris down the aisle. Looking around him, Struan realised it
couldn't have been more perfect. Annie had worked tirelessly
beside the castle housekeeper to fill the chapel with flowers.
The assembled few were too small a group to be called a
congregation, but every single person was someone who loved
them and supported their decision. Reverend Cowan had
travelled from Fowlis Wester to marry them. A Church of
Scotland minister in a private chapel of a staunchly Episcopalian family was unconventional, but then everything about

this wedding was out of the ordinary. Mr Speir's young wife, Emily, sat proudly beside her husband's empty seat. She was very obviously pregnant. Their first baby was due later that summer. The minister met his eye and smiled when they heard the gig arriving on the gravel outside. They'd been blessed with a sunny day. Iris had been determined that Daisy should deliver her to her wedding. Struan had gone up to help Mr Buchan groom her this morning. Annie had sent him with flowers to plait into her mane. Struan, in turn, had brought three of Mr MacDonald's hybrid pink and white roses for Annie to place in Iris's bouquet. The tiny plants which had grown from the fertilised seeds he'd called Iris's rose wouldn't bear blooms for another year or more. MacDonald had promised Struan could take it to his own glasshouse when it was ready.

The sound of Iris and Annie's happy voices drifted up the stairs. It was the most wonderful noise he had ever heard.

* * *

Annie and I had a glorious morning dressing for my wedding day.

She had cried when I asked her to be my bridesmaid. Now she grinned as she admired her dress in the mirror. 'Throughout my childhood this is one of the many roles I thocht people would consider me no use for,' she admitted.

I clasped Annie's hands. 'I need you at my side always. Our publishing adventure is as important as ever.'

Mr Speir met us in the Drummond Castle courtyard and led me to where Mr Buchan held Daisy's harness in front of the gig. Annie walked behind me, managing my short train with one hand.

Daisy's coat gleamed like a shiny conker and her dark mane was woven through with flowers.

'I gave them to Struan, and he tells me he did that himself,' Annie said.

'Somehow, I cannot imagine him plaiting flowers.'

'My mother taught him to plait my hair when I was very young and not strong. He wanted to do something helpful for me.'

'I continue to learn about my fiancé. Is there some other secret you are keeping from me?'

'Only that he is the best man in the entire world and that making you my sister is a sign ae his genius.'

Mr Spier helped us both into the gig, then climbed in beside us. Struan and I would spend our wedding night in the Culdees gardener's lodge. Our new house near Muthill wouldn't be ready until the end of the year. Mr MacDonald had given his blessing to Struan's appointment by Mr Speir to lead the team in Culdees. He raised his eyebrows when Jock told him he would move over too, becoming Struan's deputy. Annie would stay on in Drummond Castle for the rest of my aunt's life, which sadly might not be many more weeks. The plan after that, was that she'd move into the lodge. Struan told me in confidence that Jock would ask Annie to marry him after our wedding, so she'd be mistress of the lodge herself, when Struan and I moved to our own home. I thought she'd already guessed Jock's plans. Her happy glow was fuelled by more than just the overflow of our happiness.

Mr Buchan kept Daisy's pace to a trot. When we passed through Muthill, I discovered our wedding was not much of a secret. Of course, the banns had been read out in St James's and someone must have revealed the time of the service. It seemed like every woman and child in the village had gathered to watch us pass through. Mr Speir threw coins. Not at all the correct order of things, but we would not return through the village and nothing about my little wedding was being done by the traditional order.

When we pulled up outside Culdees Castle, I gazed up at the red stone façade, to the first-floor windows of the little chapel. I knew all my closest people were gathered inside. The huge entrance door swung open and Robert Speir led us into the castle. We paused at the bottom of the grand staircase.

'I dinnae mind stepping aside for this bit,' Annie said.

'Absolutely not. We shall come up the edge and take our time, so you may use the banister.'

'Let me carry your stick up for you,' Robert Speir said. 'Is this a new one?'

'Aye. Jock made it especially fae a piece ae white ash. The ribbon wound around it is the same as in Iris's hair. I think I've enjoyed all the dressing up for this wedding even more than Iris. The whole thing is like a dream.'

'I rather think you look more stunning than me. Pale pink suits your dark colouring,' I told her.

We stopped again at the top of the stairs. Annie raised my

long veil to reach up and adjust the posy of flowers I'd pinned to my lace bodice. She smiled and kissed my cheek. 'That's no true at all. You are the bonniest bride in the whole world and my lovely brother is the luckiest man.' She squeezed my hand and went behind me to lift my train and veil. The tiny chapel lacked a church organ, so when my aunt revealed that Lady Georgina had a fine singing voice, it wasn't hard to persuade her to sing me in. The opening note of 'Ave Maria' was my cue to start walking. 'I am channelling him. He is here,' Robert Speir whispered.

I nodded and was glad of the veil to hide the single tear I allowed myself.

The chapel was no bigger than the Culdees Castle drawing room, but its simple whitewashed beauty was completely perfect. Morning light threw diamonds of coloured light onto the floor through Robert Speir's hand-made stained-glass side windows. The triple arched windows that made me think of Innerpeffray Library, bathed the altar in sunlight and there beneath the chancel arch stood my Struan. His head was bowed. Perhaps praying or caught up in the soaring beauty of Georgina's voice. Then, as we approached, he turned and smiled. The sense of peace and surety surrounding me, had me grinning back like an idiot. We were both young idiots, but we were perfectly aligned in our love.

Everyone stayed to toast our health in the Culdees Castle drawing room. My last act when leaving Culdees was to place my wedding flowers into Annie's arms. I kissed her. 'I know you could likely catch them, but I don't want you throwing your new stick about.'

'Thank you,' she said quietly and sneaked a smile at Jock.

Her happiness perfected my own.

Then, in the afternoon, Mr Buchan and Daisy drove us down to the lodge before returning to see the Drummond Castle party home.

'It was the best day,' Struan said, after he had carried me over the lodge threshold. He set me down gently and kissed me again. 'And you are the maist beautiful bride there ever was.'

'Annie predicted you would think that.'

'My sister has been second guessing me my whole life. She even managed tae fall in love wi' you first.'

We sat together on the new couch, which was a wedding present from Princess Louise, modelled on her dressing room one, which I'd admired at Balmoral Castle. Through the window, the garden looked magnificent. All the efforts we'd put into planting here, I was happy that Annie and Jock would enjoy this view next. I unpinned the now wilting posy of sweet peas from my neckline and set them in a glass of water. Then, I unbuttoned the top two covered buttons and fetched the packet of seeds from its hiding place in my petticoat.

Struan laughed. 'Will you plant them? Mr Crawford's specimen died too, but I believe I could get the black orchid tae grow in Speir's coolest glasshouse.'

I shook my head. 'I cannot face growing orchids and this particular one has done nothing but make people angry. Mr Speir agreed with my suggestion that we don't tempt fate.'

'Well, keep them safe. They seeds were sent tae you, no Mr Speir. If our business fails, or Speir disnae like my work, or if yer publishing wave of success crashes, then we might need them one day.'

'Are you worried attempting a nursery business is too much, when you've got Culdees garden to worry about?'

Struan smiled and kissed my fingertips. 'I believe I can manage this garden quite easily. Cooper Finlay Plants is something we can grow together slowly.' Struan reached up and took down my headdress of flowers. He loosened my hair, then kissed me slowly. 'We have all the time in the world, Mrs Cooper.'

'We do, my darling husband.' Then I put my forefinger on his lips. 'But I confess I prefer the name Finlay Cooper Plants.'

He laughed and lifted me up in his arms. 'Finlay Cooper is even better of course.'

We walked past my mother's piano and perhaps it was Struan's tread that persuaded out a sound. Not a discordant jangle but a single high E note. I heard it as a loving message from my mother. I'd have it tuned and fill this cottage with joyous music.

Scots Glossary

ae - of

ailed- made unwell

awfy - terrible

aye - yes

aywis - always

blether - talk nonsense

bonny - pretty

dreich - drizzly, overcast

dour - sour-faced

drooth - thirst

eedjit - idiot

fae - from

feard - afraid

gey - very

gie - give

gowk - cuckoo

hae - have

hurl - ride in a vehicle

ken - know

Keep - Block shaped ancient stone castle

kirk - church

mind - remember

skene dhu - ceremonial dagger

telt - told

thocht - thought

thon - those

wee - small

weel - well

Author Note

The Orchid Hunter's Daughter is a work of fiction.

This novel was inspired by a visit to the magical Innerpeffray Library near Crieff in Perthshire, Scotland. The UK's first lending library was founded in 1680. It has been a museum since 1969 and is now under the guidance of the current female Keeper, the endlessly helpful and patient Lara Haggerty. It is open to visitors between March and October and I thoroughly recommend a visit.

I love to include real characters from history in my fiction and this time that includes several real botanist. I am lucky to live within walking distance of Edinburgh's Royal Botanic Garden and their excellent library was a great source of information on botanical publications and famous botanists, including Professors Jameson and Hutton Balfour.

Finally, I read several books to build the world of Balmoral in the 1860s. My version of Princess Louise's story was highly influenced by Lucinda Hawksley's excellent *The Mystery of Princess Louise*. I am indebted to her for research into this amazing woman.

Afterword

If you enjoyed this book I would be hugely grateful if you could write a review.

Acknowledgments

The support of my family has been absolutely crucial. Thank you for your patience and love, Mark, Louise, Calum and Helen.

Writing is tough. If you are thinking of taking it up, I would encourage you to join a writing group. You need writer friends who will tell you the truth but also have your back when things go wrong. My writing group of Alison Belsham, Hannah Thresher and Kristin Pedroja are like my family and I love them.

I helped found the Edinburgh Writers' Forum in 2019 as a source of writerly networking and support, also the Edinburgh Women's Fiction Festival in 2023. Thank you to all the amazing writers who come along and have become part of my bookish family.

Thank you to The Romantic Novelist Association, particularly the RNA Facebook Indie Chapter.

Huge thanks to Lara Haggerty at Innerpeffray Library. Leonie Paterson and all the staff at Edinburgh's Royal Botanic Garden. Also, Lucinda Hawksley for her amazing insight into Princess Louise.

Finally, thanks to Debi Alper and Helen Baggott for their expert editing and Maggie Sokolowska for her beautiful cover.

About the Author

Jane Anderson is an Edinburgh based writer of historical fiction. Born in Fife, Jane originally studied English Literature at Edinburgh University. She spent most of her working life living in countries as far-flung as Vietnam, Azerbaijan and most recently, Egypt. Now she is firmly entrenched in her bookish Edinburgh life. Retelling history from the point of view of women is where the fun begins.

Jane also published *The Girl Who Fled the Picture* in 2023 and *The Paintress* in 2024. You can read more about this author's writing life on Jane's website:

https://jane-anderson.co.uk/

.

www.ingramcontent.com/pod-product-compliance
Ingram Content Group UK Ltd.
Pitfield, Milton Keynes, MK11 3LW, UK
UKHW042239191025
464145UK00002B/36

9 781739 459048